THE BRIGHT
SIDE OF
DARKNESS

The Bright Side of Darkness

J. E. Pinto

DEDICATION

for Kate
who helped me get the story started

and for Jim
who made sure I kept writing
until I found the end

Endorsements

J. E. Pinto is a skillful and creative author who has a powerful ability to create characters and plots which draw her readers into the stories she weaves. The characters, context, and story lines of *The Bright Side of Darkness* is a stellar example of this fact. In addition to finely crafted contexts and story lines, the thoughtful writing causes readers to more deeply think about facets and issues of everyday life. I very much look forward to reading more in the future. – Dr. Al Adams, pastor and author

There are many heroes and heroines in this story. It touches on the deepest truths of human nature. This story is full of human compassion, lessons of love, and inspiring moments that will keep the reader hooked. – William Greenleaf, Greenleaf Literary Services, Rio Rancho, NM

J. E. Pinto has a way of writing that makes you feel the characters are as alive as if they live just down the street. *The Bright Side of Darkness* shows not only how a blind person copes in a sighted world, but also how one person can impact another in a positive way. If only we could learn to care about each other in the same way. – Debbie Hardy, speaker and author of *Free to Be Fabulous.*

Table of Contents

ACKNOWLEDGMENTS

Writing a book is a very private, introspective process at first. The elusive magic of creation and the relentless pains of soul-bearing must be undertaken alone as the story grows, matures, and pours out in its first raw burst of potential.

But there's where the privacy ends. No book worth reading is written in a vacuum. I would like to thank the many people who have read my manuscript and given me suggestions, advice, and editing over the years. Special thanks to Becky Mandez, Cindy Furubotten, and Angie Kingston, who read the manuscript aloud to me at different stages during its evolution so my words would come to life.

I am very grateful to Debbie Hardy, a fellow writer and friend of mine, who has given generously of her time, effort, and expertise to help me publish this book.

William Greenleaf, owner of Greenleaf Literary Services in Rio Rancho, New Mexico; Dr. Alaina Adams, pastor of First Christian Church of Osceola, Iowa, and author of several devotional books; and Debbie Hardy, author and speaker, have all endorsed my novel. I would like to express my appreciation for their kind words.

I am grateful to Marie Stone van Vuuren, of SV2 Studios, LLC, who created the original cover art for this book.

PROLOGUE

There's nothing a damn bit bright about sunshine when you're seventeen and you see it from the wrong side of a jail cell window.

It isn't that I'm moping for my lost freedom or anything. I wouldn't give a half a crap for my life anymore now that the crew is scattered to the four winds, and all I have left of Daisy is her parting note in the waistband of my jeans and a wilted dandelion dangling between my fingers. But it seems to me that the Man Upstairs could have marked my downfall with a terrific thunderstorm or at least a few nasty black clouds out of the west.

When there's a war or a funeral or some other sad thing going on in the movies, the sky usually turns dark and ugly, and the rain pours down in buckets. The longer I stare at the square of sunlight streaming through the tiny window of my cell and stealing across the floor, the lonelier I feel. August 27, 1986, is slipping by the same as every other hot, heavy day, and I'm the only one in the world who knows that nothing will ever be all right again.

It hasn't always been this way. I ought to have known better than to believe I could reach out and snag a piece of paradise, but for a little while I had it on my fingertips. Breaks are hard to come by for kids from the projects, though, and sure enough, all I ended up with at the last second was empty hands.

I'm doing my level best to hold off a flood of memories, but my mind keeps drifting back to the sweltering summer evening when the chain of events began that shattered my world into a zillion pieces.

First thing tomorrow morning, some juvenile court judge will decide if my life is worth rebuilding. Maybe he'll have better luck with my future than I did with my past.

PART ONE

Chapter 1

The sun was low in the west when me and Stacy and Bryan got to the baseball diamond behind the high school. The heat had backed off to that sort of sticky mugginess that makes July evenings in Texas feel like they drag on forever.

The field was crowded. Usually the students at the public high school in Bertha City blew off that team pride stuff parents and teachers were always screaming about. But lots of us showed up when we took on the rich kids from the classy private academy across town because we wanted to see them get stomped.

You might think there was a lot of bitterness between us—the cops obviously thought so because they were swarming all over the place during the game—but for the most part, it was like we lived on two separate planets. We stayed downtown, and the rich kids stuck to their own turf on the other side of the highway. They looked at us like we were dirt, and we didn't look at them at all unless it was to kick the crap out of their baseball team.

Anyway, the only place left on the bleachers was at the bottom near the popcorn stand. We chased off a couple of junior high kids and spread our jackets on the splintery benches to claim spots for Tim and Mark, the other two guys who always hung out with us.

"Want a Coke, Rick?" Stace asked me. I flipped him some change from my jeans pocket, and he and Bryan headed for the soda machine. They went everywhere together.

Stace and Bryan Thomas were twins, and you could barely tell them apart with their light skin and jet black hair, but they were as different as two guys could be.

Stace banged his gums together way too much. I mean, there was no shutting that kid up. He was always clowning around and making funny remarks and mouthing off to teachers and cops. It landed him in a heap of trouble, but he really couldn't help it.

Bryan was a quiet, bookish type who made good grades in school and played tennis. Not even the crew could get him to talk much. He mostly kept to himself, thinking his own thoughts and hardly ever voicing them, till you got him on a court with a racket in his hand, and then he was all action.

He and Stace were usually dressed sharper than me because they had a real family with two working parents. You can't judge guys by their clothes, though. The twins were all right for being two years younger than the rest of us, and we'd always accepted them as part of the crew. The crew had grown up as tight as brothers.

There was this blond chick sitting by herself on the bench below mine with a black and tan German shepherd lying at her feet. I nodded and smiled at her, but she didn't glance around, so I turned away.

I'm not like some guys, always having to be noticed by chicks, and it was awful hot to knock myself out being social. I wasn't real taken with girls yet anyway, not like Tim, who could have taught old Romeo a whole pack of slick tricks. All that dating stuff seemed like a lot of hassle to me. I mean, a guy chugged along just fine doing pretty much whatever he wanted. Then he got hooked up with a girl, and the next thing you knew, he was falling all over himself trying to be respectable. Give me a break!

The twins came back with the drinks, and after a while Tim and Mark joined us.

"Anyone need a cancer stick?" Tim pulled a pack of smokes out of his pocket and passed it around. We all lit up, all but Bryan, who was too serious about tennis to blacken his precious lungs. He'd had his eye on a sports scholarship to some big eastern college or other practically since he started kindergarten.

Tim Bennett was a redhead with sort of shifty-looking eyes and a good build. He was tall, but he slouched all the time. He looked like a pretty tough customer because he had this set to his face that let you know he'd back up anything he said. He would, too. The crew joked that his rap sheet took up its own private file cabinet down at the police station—fighting, mostly, and drinking. Tim wouldn't go out of his way to be nice to anybody he didn't like, but he'd offer a stranger his last dime in a heartbeat if he thought no one was watching.

Mark Romero was small and wiry. He was a kick to be around, always laughing. He didn't cut up like Stace, he was just real happy, except when something touched off his blazing hot temper. He cussed too much maybe, but most of it was in Spanish, so it

15

didn't count. He never needed booze to have fun. He could get a thrill out of a scrap or a baseball game or anything else that happened to be going on.

"Hey, babe," Tim called to the little blond. "Your boyfriend's kind of hairy, ain't he?" He wasn't always the nicest to girls at first, but he was a charmer once he picked them up, and for some reason most of them would have followed him right into a burning building.

She turned toward us. "For your information, Captain is a guide dog."

She was a cute girl. She had on a yellow dress that was snug around the middle, with straps that went over her bare shoulders. Her awesome figure caught my attention first thing. But when I gave her a closer look, I noticed something funny about her eyes. They were sort of blank in her face. It wasn't every day you saw a chick with a dog at a baseball game, so we were all interested.

"What's a guide dog?" Stace asked. Tim fired him a nasty scowl, and Stace decided to give up the floor.

"I can't see, so he's trained to help me get around. It's really great because I can go anywhere by myself since I got him." She smiled, and she had the most knockout smile I'd ever seen. It lit up her whole face. "He behaves himself so well, just waiting quietly for me, that sometimes people don't even notice him till we get ready to leave a restaurant or something."

A sly look came into Tim's eyes, and I figured he was about to start in with his usual crap. I wished he'd let the girl be. He could get real mean lots of times without trying to when he lost interest in

16

picking up a chick. Those kind of kicks leave me cold, especially if the girl is blind or something.

"That's a good one. You're not really blind. You just couldn't get a two-legged date for the game." Tim wiggled his fingers under her nose. "How many fingers am I holding up?"

Her smile faded. She spoke tiredly, like she'd said the same thing a zillion times before. "I'm really blind. I can't see your fingers."

God, she was a fox. Most girls would kill for those golden curls and that fair skin. I'm blond and light-colored myself, but it's not such a big deal for a guy. Anyway, if you weren't looking right at her eyes, you'd hardly know she was blind. She was dressed too nice to be from the bad part of town but not like a rich kid, either, so I guessed she must live in one of the middle-class subdivisions out east. I wondered what she was doing alone in our neighborhood with night coming on.

Tim moved close to her on the bench and laid a hand on her knee. "Try to guess what I look like."

I knew she was getting mad and scared by the way she clenched her bubble gum between her teeth. "I don't know what you look like, and I don't care, either. I know what you act like—a show-off." That girl had nerve.

Tim began to chant, tapping his finger on her knee. "Three blind mice. Three blind mice."

"Oh, that's original," she snapped.

"Too cool, a babe with an attitude." He laughed and put an arm around her. "That's the way I like 'em."

The fear was plain in her face by then, but she held her head high. I heard her quick, shallow breathing as she tried to pull away. "Take your hands off me!"

His grip on her tightened. "Hey, boys, meet my main squeeze. Love is blind, you know." He snickered at his own joke.

"Aw, lay off, Tim," I said.

"What?" He let go of her and stared at me, surprised.

"You heard me. I said lay off."

A year before, he would have knocked me flat and not thought twice about it. I'd gotten to be a fairly good size, though, and no slouch of a fighter, and lately he hadn't been too sure he was ready to take me on. It put some strain between us because Tim had always been used to giving the orders, but we didn't fight much among ourselves.

He hesitated, then stood up, hitched his thumbs in his belt loops, and swaggered off toward a group of chicks without saying another word. He didn't come back.

I turned to the girl. "Don't take Tim too serious. He's a jerk sometimes, but he don't mean nothin' by it."

She shifted uneasily on the bench, seeming to decide whether or not she could trust me. "Are you going to start in on me now?"

"Naw, I don't get off on that. What's your name?"

"It's Desiree, but everybody calls me Daisy."

"I'm Rick. That's Mark, and those two morons are Bryan and Stace."

She put out her hand, and we each shook it awkwardly. "I don't bite or anything, I promise," she said.

The five of us sat there watching the game, and Captain just stayed stretched out on the ground with his head resting on Daisy's foot, as quietly as she had said he would. Those rich kids thought they looked cool as hell in their spiffy white uniforms, but they were covered with dirt and sweat the same as our guys pretty soon. We all got a laugh out of that. I went out for baseball once, but me and the coach couldn't stand each other. I hated him ordering me around like he thought he owned me or something.

Me and Daisy hit it off right away. I'm usually not much of a talker, but she loosened me up somehow. Before I really noticed what I was doing, I moved down to sit on the bench next to her and started telling her stuff I didn't even like to think about, much less say out loud.

"My dad took my mom to some fancy restaurant in Amarillo last Valentine's Day," I said. "He'd been saving up for months so they could go." My voice hardened. "I guess he should've put new brakes on the car instead. They skidded off the road on their way home in the pouring rain. They were both dead in a ditch before they knew what hit 'em."

"My God, that's awful." Daisy touched my arm for a second, then pulled her hand away and bit her lip. "My dad's in jail. He drank a little more than usual one night last fall. I can't even remember what I said that set him off, but it was probably nothing, like always. I ended up in the hospital and then in foster care."

"Oh." I thought that sounded dumb the second I said it, and then I made it worse by adding, "Your foster parents aren't from around here then. I haven't seen you before."

"Nope. They live in Amarillo." Daisy made a sour face. "My foster mother freaked out whenever I did anything by myself. She cut my meat for me, she laid out matching clothes every morning, she probably would have dressed me if I hadn't drawn the line. She kept calling me a poor little dear. Pity makes me sick, so me and Captain skipped town as soon as she went to bed last night."

"Weren't you scared?" I asked.

"Sure, but anything is better than being smothered to death, and I found out years ago that I won't get anywhere if I stay home every time something scares me." Daisy chewed on her lip again and started fiddling with the silver cross that hung on a chain around her neck. "Besides, my dad had a parole hearing yesterday, and I wasn't about to stick around and see if he managed to slither out onto the streets."

"But the social workers will hunt for you, don't you think?"

"They've probably called out the bloodhounds by now. They'll want to track down their helpless little blind girl before her disappearance hits the newspapers and trashes their public image or something. But my dad's the only one who really worries me."

20

"What does the sucker look like? I'll kick his butt if I catch him alone in an alley some dark night."

"How would I know? I've never seen him except in my nightmares."

I laughed. "I guess that was a stupid question."

Daisy shrugged. "Forget him anyway. He has a court order to stay away from me, and if the parole board had a lick of sense, they kept him locked up tight."

"Well, you're a gutsy chick, I'll give you that." I tried to picture what it would be like to walk around everywhere with my eyes closed, and I didn't think much of the idea. It didn't seem to slow Daisy down, though.

"Hey, Rick, check out that old fatso over there." Stace pointed toward the far end of the bleachers. "A guy who packs a beer gut like that shouldn't be seen in public without a shirt."

"He must think he's a stud," Mark scoffed. "He's got to be at least forty, and there he is in the middle of a flock of chicks all young enough to be his daughter."

Whenever I glanced up from the game after that, the fat man looked like he was eyeballing Daisy. At first I blew him off, thinking he'd never seen a girl with a guide dog before and couldn't get a grip on his curiosity, but the way he kept staring at her really started to bug me after a while.

Scoping out a chick like she's a slab of meat is pretty low-class, but homing in on a blind girl who doesn't know she's being drooled over is downright scummy. If the sick puppy had figured out that Daisy couldn't see and pegged her as an easy target, I wished he'd make a move on her so I'd have a reason to blacken his wandering eyes. He just studied her from a safe distance, though, and the field was too thick with cops for me to pick a fight with him.

I did my best to ignore him and keep my mind on the game so I wouldn't lose my temper. But if I could have known at the time how that man was going to plunge all our lives into the pits of hell, I swear to God, I would have found a way to kill him on the spot.

We clobbered those rich kids good. The whole public-school crowd started yelling and cussing at them, all in innocent fun, of course, and they gave it right back till their coaches herded them onto their bus.

Some of our people hurled rocks and bottles after them as the bus pulled away, and the cops booted them off the field. The cops were there to stop trouble on the school grounds. If we wanted to beat the crap out of each other in the streets, well, that wasn't their business. I don't have much respect for cops, but I try not to be rude to them if I can help it.

"Where'll you go now, Daisy?" I asked as we got ready to leave. I'd lost sight of the pervert in the mob of sports fans, but I still didn't want to let her go drifting around by herself in the dark.

"I'm not really sure. I hung out last night in a doughnut shop drinking oceans of rotgut coffee, but my flight plan is kind of vague from here."

"Come with us." I reached for the bulging satchel on the bench beside her. "It wouldn't be the first time

I put someone up at my place, even when Mom and Dad were alive."

"You just want a girl to keep your bones warm tonight," Stace snickered.

"You just want your head busted," I snapped. "Shut up before you get your wish." He shut up.

Daisy held back a little at first, but it wasn't like she could go with a better offer, so she tagged along and didn't make a big thing of it. I thanked my lucky stars for her good sense as we picked our way through the crowd toward the street.

Tim had taken off in his stepdad's car, which he hot-wired whenever his stepdad was too plastered to stop him. So we started walking the long way home, trying to hitch a ride. I guess we looked pretty shady because we hardly ever got picked up, especially when more than two or three of us were together.

That dog Daisy had was real smart. He wore a leather harness, and she held onto the end of a U-shaped handle that was hooked to it. He walked on her left side, staying a half a step in front of her all the time.

He guided her around potholes in the sidewalk and paused at curbs and even kept her from hitting a tree branch that was hanging over her path. He wouldn't let her stray into traffic, and he understood when she told him to go right, left, and forward. She said a school out in California had trained him and given him to her for free.

"Can you take him everywhere?" Bryan asked.

"Yep." She gave the dog a scratch under the chin. "Wherever the public can go, Captain can go. It's the law."

We stopped at a convenience store to get Cokes when we were about halfway home, and good old Tim was there, pumping gas into the wreck he called a car. There was no chick with him, which surprised me.

"Hey, I think I've seen your ugly faces somewhere before," he greeted us, all hard feelings dried up for the moment. "Want a lift?"

"Where were you eight blocks back?" Mark asked, and we all climbed in.

I wasn't sure if Tim was soused or not. It was sort of hard to tell with him. He'd been drinking like a fish ever since I could remember, and since his stepdad was a professional boozer, he got stuff for the rest of us whenever we wanted it. I wasn't worried about him falling asleep at the wheel or anything because he knew what he was doing. He'd hot-wired cars for years, too.

~~~

He drove home with no problem and parked beside the apartment building where the five of us guys had bunked forever. Tim and his stepdad and Mark and his grandma lived in the two upstairs units, and me and the twins' family had the ground level ones. They were each just a single room with a kitchen built into one corner.

Tim staggered a little as he got out of the car. "Well, I see the Barn's still standing. I keep hoping a friendly tornado will haul it off while we're out and about."

Mark put out a hand to steady him. "Where would you stash your worthless bag of bones then?"

"No-count slobs like me always find somewhere to roost. But I suppose the Barn keeps the rain off as good as any place else."

"Why do you call it the Barn?" Daisy asked as we climbed the front steps.

Stace grinned. "I started it. The building used to be part of an old mission, fifteen or twenty years ago. There's this butt-ugly neon star on the roof that flashes, 'CANDLE IN THE WINDOW LOW INCOME HOUSING', like we really need that fact advertised to God and everybody. One day I said I knew how the three kings must have felt being led to the stable in Bethlehem by a gleaming star."

"I bet that star didn't stand out as bad as ours, though. That blazing beauty would scorch the eyeballs of a blind man." Mark clapped a hand over his mouth and shot a guilty look at Daisy, but she was laughing along with the rest of us, so he sailed smoothly on after a second. "Anybody hungry? Grandma promised me raisin cookies today."

"How does it feel to be spoiled?" Stace led the mad dash up the stairs.

Mark had lived with his grandma since he was three because his mom walked off and left him in a grocery store one day. We all called her Grandma, and she was a mother to me and Tim as well as Mark. She didn't know about half the wild stuff we did, but she didn't know what all Mark did, either. It was

25

better that way, her having a heart condition and everything.

Tim stepped in front of me and Daisy before we made it to the stairs. He eyed her yellow sundress and matching sandals, and a bitter edge came suddenly into his voice. "In case you need a reality check, Daisy, this ain't a castle Rick has swept you off to. The joint looks like a cell block with concrete walls and linoleum floors and bare light bulbs, and we all have to share one pay phone and one public bathroom. So you better make up your mind to get along with the neighbors."

"I gave up on fairy tales a long time ago, Tim," Daisy answered coolly. "My foster mother bought me a whole new wardrobe so she could show me off to her friends like a pretty china doll, but I'm no stranger to hard times."

Tim shrugged. "We'll see. Old Man Garner is the only one who lives like a king around here."

"Who's he?" Daisy asked.

"Our landlord, unfortunately," I said. "He struts around in a business suit and flashes his gold watch every chance he gets to remind us that he's got money and we don't. His 'penthouse suite' has its own john and phone, so naturally he thinks he's royalty."

"He collects antiques and expensive art and crap, and he has to be sure to open his door wide when we go to pay the rent so we don't miss the view." Tim smiled with grim satisfaction. "I usually remind him that Uncle Sam springs for his water and lights because he runs this housing project. That puts him in a grand old huff every time."

"It sounds like he lives here just so he can have folks to look down on," Daisy said. "I hate him already."

"Join the club." Tim turned to walk away. "We best get upstairs before those porkers leave us nothing but crumbs."

Grandma was in her housecoat and slippers, and she had coffee for us along with the raisin cookies. The old lady used to dish out as much joshing as she took from us before her health started going down the drain. Her smile was as sunny as always that night, but her collarbones jutted out sharply above the ruffles at the top of her nightgown, and I was shocked to see how deep the little creases around her eyes were. She gave me and Tim each a hard squeeze and a pinch on the cheek, and we exchanged worried glances over the knot of white hair that didn't quite come up to our shoulders.

"Grandma, this is Daisy," I said.

"*Mucho gusto*." Grandma took the girl by the hand and showed her to a chair. She didn't miss a beat over Daisy's being blind, and I was proud of her for that.

"She's glad to meet you." I translated because Grandma got English and Spanish mixed up a lot. Mark did, too, when he was mad.

Mark told us to keep the music low because Grandma wasn't looking so hot. It didn't matter anyhow because she wouldn't have put up a fuss if it was loud enough to blow the roof off, but we humored him just the same. After a while he convinced her to go lay down, and they disappeared behind the sheet that curtained off her bed from the rest of the room. She liked him to pray with her a little each night. He even went to church with her sometimes if he wasn't working. Stace ribbed him about it once and wound up with a fat lip, so nobody made a big deal of it.

I hadn't set foot in church since Mom and Dad died. The preacher at their funeral blathered on and on about how Almighty God needed two more angels to sing forever in the choirs of heaven.

I asked him afterward why Almighty God couldn't have been satisfied with the zillions of people who were already dead and left my folks alone. I figured I needed them more than God did, and neither one of them could carry a tune in a bucket anyway. The preacher came up with some lame excuse, and I told him to shove it.

I would have said a lot more, too, but the twins' mom, Sharon, sidetracked the preacher while their old man herded me out the door. Ed and Sharon had promised the social worker who came poking around after my folks died that they'd look out for me, and they obviously meant to keep their word. It was a good thing they weren't big on religion because they couldn't have dragged me back to church on a bet.

Mark's cat popped out of an open dresser drawer while he was still behind the sheet with Grandma. She skirted Daisy and Captain, bristling, and then leaped to a safe place on the window sill above Stace's head.

Stace coaxed the cat down and settled her in his lap. He ran a hand gently along her spine till she

28

closed her eyes and started to purr. "Scrappy's got to be the ugliest critter that ever walked on four legs."

"Is her name really Scrappy?" Daisy asked.

Stace nodded. "Mark yanked her out of a tug-of-war between two stray dogs when she was a kitten. She lost part of an ear in the tussle, but Mark said she put up a hell of a scrap, so he named her Scrappy."

I topped off Daisy's coffee cup and snagged another cookie for myself. "If Mark was starving to death in a ditch somewhere, he'd give that fleabag his last crust of bread and never bat an eye."

Stace had almost lulled the cat to sleep when he suddenly snatched her up by the scruff of the neck and dangled her in front of Captain's nose. The dog, who'd been lying by Daisy's chair like a statue since she sat down, bounced up and lunged for the cat.

"Captain, knock it off!" Daisy gave his choke collar a quick snap. "Stace, would you please—"

That was all the further she got because the cat hissed and then yowled, clawing the air, and in the same second Mark stepped from behind the curtain. He jerked Stace up by the armpits and pinned him against the wall. Scrappy shot across the room and bounded onto the top of the refrigerator like she had rocket boosters strapped to all four paws.

"Next time I catch you messing with my cat, I'll feed you to her!" Mark wasn't joking.

"Okay, okay, give it up already," Stace squawked.

Mark let him go, and he lost his balance and hit the floor with a thud.

"I think Captain was hungry," I laughed.

"He's been taught to blow off cats and other animals, but ignoring one shoved in his face like that would be asking too much of a saint." Daisy patted the dog on the head, and he reached up and licked her hand.

"We ought to clear out of here so Grandma can have some peace and quiet," Tim said. "Come to my place for something with a little more kick than coffee."

"Bryan and Stacy, you go home now," Grandma called from behind the sheet. "Your parents are worried I think."

"They're always worried. It's a law of nature," Stace grumbled.

I felt a familiar stab of jealousy. No one cared anymore if I stayed out all night or not. It was stupid for me to think that way because I knew the twins would trade their right arms for the freedom I had. But somehow freedom isn't much fun when nobody gives a damn what you do with it.

I was glad Daisy couldn't see my apartment. It looked like a war zone, with dirty dishes piled high in the sink, garbage overflowing from the trash can, and undone laundry spilling out of the basket onto the couch and the bare floor. My place always looked like that because I didn't clean up more than I absolutely had to. The furniture had seen better days, too, a long time ago.

"You take the bed and I'll camp on the couch," I said when I'd showed her around the room wall by wall like she asked.

"I don't want to take your bed or anything. I can handle the couch just fine. I could be on the streets."

"Look, I may have been raised in the projects, but I know how to treat a girl." I tossed her satchel onto my bed. "I even put clean sheets on this morning."

"It sure is nice to be in a place where I can feel safe for a change. Me and Captain have been expecting a devil around every corner since last night." Daisy kicked off her shoes and sank onto the bed, and all at once I saw how worn out she looked.

"You'll be safe enough here. Don't count on me to keep an ear out for night prowlers, though. I'd likely snooze through the end of the world."

Chapter 2

Daisy was still asleep when I left for work early the next morning.

I had to hold down two jobs since Mom and Dad were gone, so I bussed tables in a greasy little diner and ran the cash register at a neighborhood sweet shop. I liked the diner job all right because the manager left me alone. She was a chubby, middle-aged woman with a booming laugh and a bit of a mustache she was always trying to get rid of with one home remedy or another. She gave me meals along with my pay and let me snag leftovers for the crew whenever I felt like it.

But the candy store owner was a stooped old geezer who walked around all the time with his face pinched up like he smelled garbage, and he'd been a pain in my butt since the day he hired me. He never took his eyes off me when I was in his shop, like he thought I'd want to filch his fancy chocolates and crap. I didn't eat sweet stuff much except Cokes and Grandma's cookies.

It was late afternoon when I finally started home. It was roasting hot out, and I was tired and in a bad mood from being under the eagle eye at the candy store for hours. Some people think anyone who lives in the projects will steal anything that isn't nailed down. A lot of guys do, but I bet most of them take up the habit because they know nobody trusts them to begin with.

So anyway, I was trudging along, kicking a bottle down our street. It was a crummy street with run-down buildings and junked cars and graffiti all over the place. I gave the bottle an extra hard kick in front of the Barn, and it hit Mr. Garner's shiny new van with a thud. I stopped to check out the dent in the passenger door. It was pretty noticeable, and I knew the landlord would pitch a hissy fit. But it served him right for driving a car like his in a rust-bucket neighborhood. Besides, it had been an accident, and he couldn't know I did it.

As I opened the door to my apartment, a whiff of frying meat floated out into the hallway. The homey smell stopped me in my tracks for a second. It took me back to a time when I might have drifted in on a hot summer evening and found my mom standing in the kitchen, smiling when she saw me. In the dreary months since my folks had died, I guess I'd gotten kind of used to the stink of stale cigarettes and dirty laundry.

I stepped into the apartment and got another shock. I barely recognized the place. It was actually neat for the first time in ages. The piles of clothes were picked up off the floor, the bed was made, the ashtrays and the trash can were empty, and Daisy was flipping hamburgers.

"Rick?" She turned away from the stove. "Is that you?"

"Yeah, I just got off work." I tossed my tennis shoes on the floor, then thought better of it and kicked them under the bed where they would be out of the way. Losing my shoes is always the first thing I do when I walk in the door. "Sorry I disappeared on you this morning, but you were sound asleep. I didn't want to bother you."

"I must have been really tired. The midday soaps were on when I woke up."

"You've been busy since then. You didn't have to clean up the place, you know."

"I'm no freeloader, it was the least I could do. Anyway, I was bored."

I laughed. "I'd have to be awful bored to bust my butt like that."

"I could tell. Want a burger?"

"Yeah, but where'd you get the meat? Not out of my freezer, I know that much. It's as good as empty." I sat down at the table, which wasn't littered with magazines and beer cans as usual. Daisy's dog came over to greet me, tail waving, and I gave him a quick scratch behind the ears before I started fixing a hamburger bun.

"Captain was out of dog food, so I walked down to the corner a while ago and asked some guy at the bus stop how to get to the supermarket. He gave lousy directions, like most people at bus stops do. When I finally found the store, I decided to bring back some extra things in my satchel."

I put down the ketchup bottle. "You went cruising around by yourself?"

"Sure. I'm a big girl."

"Daisy, listen. This is a rough neighborhood. I'm not trying to baby you like your foster mother did or anything, but there's lots of dirt bags around here who'd pick you out as an easy target even before they knew you were blind."

"Captain has to eat."

"You should have told the twins to run to the store for you. I only work till two tomorrow, so we can go somewhere after that if you want."

"Sounds good to me."

"Promise you won't take off on your own again, though." When she balked, I reached out and clamped my hand down on her shoulder, hard. "I'm dead serious. It ain't safe. What if your dad turns up? He could have you in his car and gone before you ever knew what happened."

Daisy flinched. "Okay. I hate to be a prisoner anywhere, but I get your point. Ease up, you're hurting me."

"Sorry." I let go of her shoulder and reached for my burger instead. "It'll be great having a cook around. How do you manage? I mean, I can see, but I swear I'd burn the water if I was making ice cubes."

She smiled, and I couldn't get over how awesome that smile was. "I know when a burger is done by the way it smells and the way it stays firm if I touch it. I check everything out with my fingers, so get used to my germs. I'm always tasting stuff, and I try to set utensils down in the same spot every time so I don't have to spend all day searching for them."

"That seems like a lot to remember. Do you ever goof up?"

"Yeah, believe me, I've pulled some real doozies." Daisy chuckled. "I switched salt for cornmeal in a batch of muffins once, but the evidence went straight down the garbage disposal, so it's our secret."

"My lips are sealed."

"While we're on the subject of true confessions, Rick, has that bed ever been made in its life?"

"Nope. Making beds is against my religion."

We ate without much more chatter, and then I gathered up the table scraps. "Rouse your lazy butt, Captain, you'll love this."

"No! Don't give him stuff off the table."

"It's just a bite of bread and a few pieces of lettuce. What's the matter?"

"He never gets anything but dog food. That way I can take him into stores and restaurants and not worry about him making a pest of himself."

"I can see that. He didn't even look up from his snooze while we were eating." I tossed the scraps in the trash can. "Too bad, old boy, this ain't your lucky day."

"The two things I have to tell people most about Captain are not to pet him when the harness is on and not to feed him from the table."

"The crew won't have a problem remembering about the snacks. We can't give Scrappy anything, either."

"Mark's cat? Why not?"

"Me and Tim tanked her up on beer one time so we could watch her stumble around and bump into furniture. It was funny as hell. Only then Mark walked in and had a stroke."

"He's so laid back. I can't imagine him getting that upset."

"Oh, he blew a fuse all right. Most of what he said was in Spanish, and it came out faster than rounds from a machine gun. But we got his drift real plain when he grabbed one of those notched sticks we prop the windows up with. He swung it around above his head and let it fly like a boomerang, and it zipped through the space between Tim's left ear and my right one and sailed on out the window behind the couch and into orbit."

"Wow!" Daisy giggled. "He really went over the top, it sounds like."

"Well, we cut a piece of cardboard for the window, and we had plenty of time to be reminded of the scene because it was weeks before we got up the money to help Mark pay for new glass. He said we could've killed his cat, and then he wouldn't have rested till a bone from each of our bodies was planted in every county in Texas."

"It's amazing how close you can get to an animal. I've only had Captain a few months, but when I go someplace without him, it feels like my arm is missing."

"Mom never let me have any pets after my gerbil got loose and died in her clothes hamper, but Mark loves that cat of his like it's his kid or something."

Me and Daisy did the dishes. I'm not much on washing dishes, but when you bus tables for a living, there's nothing worse than looking at a heap of dirty dishes in your own sink. Besides, it would have been the pits to blow all Daisy's hard work by leaving the kitchen a mess.

When we were done, Daisy showed me a braille magazine she had in her satchel. I'd never seen anything like it. Instead of regular writing, there were just a bunch of bumps on the pages for her to run her fingers over, but she said the magazine was the same as the print copy you could get in any drugstore.

She wrote me out a braille alphabet with this metal board she called a slate. She used this little pin she called a stylus.

I had to look at the bumps with my eyes because my fingers weren't sensitive enough to tell any difference between them. The pages in the magazine just felt like pieces of sandpaper to me, but I got to thinking that braille would have made a cool secret code for the crew when we were kids.

The others came over later. Tim had a nasty bruise above one eye, which we all pretended not to notice. He could have landed himself in a fight almost anywhere, but most likely his old man had missed the car last night. We sat around playing poker for thumbtacks – there wasn't enough cash between us to make actual betting worthwhile – and trying to decide where to go. We were never invited to each other's places. We just walked in and sat down. The apartments were always unlocked in the daytime if we were home.

There was a hammering on the door, and Mr. Garner hollered for me to open up.

"Take a hike!" I yelled over the blaring radio.

He opened the door himself and stepped in anyway. "Turn off that insufferable noise you call music."

"Blow it out your nose," Mark said. No one touched the box. Old Man Garner was too dense to know good tunes when he heard them.

"Do it now or I'll call the police and press disturbing the peace charges." The landlord drew his mouth down into a scowl that was supposed to scare us, I guess.

"You mean disturbing the butthead," I muttered, but I killed the radio.

"The television, too."

"Man, you ask a lot busting into a guy's place like this." I shut off the TV, though. I knew the real reason Mr. Garner had dropped by and figured I might as well get it over with. The landlord didn't bother us much without a reason because he thought he was too good to be seen with us, which was fine since we didn't want him around anyway.

"Rick, now that I have your undivided attention, maybe you would be kind enough to tell me how my van got dented today."

"How should I know? You're not paying me to keep track of your car."

"I saw you kick the bottle that hit the passenger door. That's how you should know."

"So shoot me."

"It would be my pleasure." His cheeks started getting red. "I want forty-two dollars and seventy-one cents to fix it by tomorrow afternoon."

"You must be high or something! It's hardly even dented. Have you seen Tim's car lately? He's still driving it."

"I'm not interested in the disgraceful condition of Tim's car." The red was creeping steadily toward his receding hairline. "It's about time you start taking responsibility for your actions. I expect to be paid by three o'clock tomorrow."

"You shouldn't park snazzy wheels like those on this street. You're just asking for trouble."

"No, I'm asking for cash. By three o'clock sharp." The landlord tapped his shiny gold watch to drive his point home.

I glanced around at the others, and they all nodded. We always kicked in for each other when things got tight.

"Okay, okay. You'll get your damn money. Don't split that fancy suit of yours worrying about it."

He started out the door. "I won't worry. If I don't have every dime by three on the dot, the police will worry about it."

"If the cops get in on this, you'll wish you were never born," Tim snarled at his disappearing back. Calling the cops was a deadly sin in our neighborhood, and even threatening to do it wasn't a real bright idea.

Mr. Garner stopped and faced us again. "You losers would get a lot further in life if you learned some respect."

"Speaking of getting a lot further, why don't you get a lot further from here?" Daisy suggested, and we all snickered.

"Another smart mouth. Just what we need around here." He turned away in disgust. "Three o'clock, Rick, don't forget."

"How could I?" I cranked up the radio again as the landlord slammed the door.

The guys scattered to their rooms, and in a while they came back with what they had. Daisy made me take the last five bucks she had tucked in the bottom of her satchel. Between that and her trip to the supermarket, she was tapped out. Mark handed over the four wrinkled dollar bills he'd kept stashed under his mattress for ages to start saving for a hymnal Grandma wanted. That was the best he could do because the old lady had doctor bills that were adding up to more than his gas station job paid lately, even with help from Uncle Sam.

I had seven dollars that I'd put aside for cigarettes, and the twins brought six between them from their folks, who weren't stingy with money when there was any. After a long time, Tim surfaced with a twenty. He might have stolen it somewhere, or maybe he got it from his stepdad, who played serious poker. He didn't say, and I didn't ask.

But none of us could come up with the seventy-one cents, even by shaking out all our couch cushions to look for coins that might have fallen down between them. The cushions had already been robbed, and Garner would hold out for every last penny, as if the creep really needed to suck us dry.

"It'll turn up somewhere," Mark said. He was like that. He never worried about anything.

And the funny thing is, it did turn up. A woman left two quarters and two dimes and a penny on the counter at the candy store the next morning.

"Hey, lady, you forgot your change," I called, but she hurried on out the door without glancing around. The boss wasn't looking, for once, so I slipped the coins in my pocket. It wasn't like they were his anyway. I'm so lucky it spooks me sometimes. I didn't have to worry about paying the others back, either. Sooner or later, one of them would get in a jam and take whatever I could give him. There were no debts. That's just the way we did things.

~~~

I looked forward to going for a walk with Daisy all morning. We left her dog home and strolled up and down the streets, holding hands and talking.

"What's it like to be blind?" I asked.

She thought for a second. "I was born this way, so I don't know any different. I don't stew about it much except when someone judges me to be stupid or helpless because my eyes don't work. That drives me up the wall."

"Well, everybody gets judged. You wouldn't believe the way the average chick looks at me—like I'm about to mug her or something. If you could see, you probably wouldn't have given me the time of day because of my long hair and raggedy clothes."

"Think what I would have missed, and for retarded reasons like those." She smiled and squeezed my hand.

"When I know from the first that folks expect me to steal and fight and get boozed up, I mostly just go ahead and do it instead of trying to change their minds." I kicked at an empty beer can and watched it roll away in the gutter. "I know I'll never amount to anything, but I hate getting it thrown in my face all the time."

"Who says you'll never amount to anything? There's no telling where you'll be in a few years if you put your mind to it."

"You talk like my folks. They were always carrying on about how the future was full of promise for me. But I reckon I'll be bussing tables till I die, so I might as well get used to it."

"I hope you never get used to it. People who judge you can't keep you down if you don't buy into their crap." Daisy stopped walking and turned to face me. "I get sick of feeling like I have to prove I'm as good as anybody else, even without my eyes, but it's better than believing there's something wrong with me."

"There's nothin' wrong with you. I guess the world blows off a lot of cool people, though. Mark gets judged right from the start because he's Mexican."

"That's so dumb. I'm lucky in a way because people are all the same to me, no matter what color they are."

"I wasn't being nosy bringing up your blindness, was I?"

She shrugged. "You were curious, and talking about it doesn't bug me. It's a part of who I am, like my curly hair and my sweet tooth, and that's all there is to it."

We rested on a park bench in the shade of a spindly little bush. I had paid Garner off before we left so I wouldn't be tempted to buy cigarettes, which meant we couldn't get Cokes, either.

The park took up a whole city block. It was just an open grassy space with a lot of broken bottles and trash strewn around. There weren't enough trees to make it a good hangout spot, so it was empty in the blistering sun.

"You know what I want to do?" Daisy asked. "There's nothing in my way, is there? I want to run across the grass, right now, as fast as I can."

"It's awful hot."

"I know, but I love to run for the free feeling I get from it. I'm usually so tied down, having to hang onto a person or a dog all the time."

So I jogged beside Daisy as she raced across the park, laughing, with the breeze blowing her golden curls every which way. When she was out of breath and I was sweating up a storm, we flopped down next to each other on the patchy grass.

She picked a dandelion and handed it to me. "What does it look like?"

"It's yellow. But you don't know what yellow is, do you?"

"No. My mom used to try telling me about colors sometimes, but I couldn't picture them in my mind."

I studied the flower for a minute. "Well, it's sort of soft and fluffy-looking, like it feels, I guess. It's pretty. I never really checked one out before."

"That gets me about sighted people. They don't take time to enjoy what they look at. There are so many things I'd love to see that everyone else walks right past every day—the flag waving in the wind, the way clouds change in the summer sky, Christmas lights shining in store windows, all sorts of things."

"Maybe we're too used to it." I put an arm around her. I was starting to like her a lot. I'd never felt that way about a girl. "You know what? You're pretty, too, like the flower."

She giggled. "I guess I don't think about my appearance a whole bunch because I feel like the real me is something more than blond curls and blue eyes."

"The real you is a sweetheart." All that wasn't half bad for me. I wasn't a pro with chicks like Tim.

She slipped the dandelion through a buttonhole on her blouse and picked one for me to stick in the pocket of my T-shirt.

But I brushed it aside. "The guys would never let me live down a sissy thing like that. Listen, the Midsummer Madness Dance is going on at the school tomorrow night, and I was kind of wondering if you wanted to go with me." I hadn't planned to ask her. I tried not to seem too hopeful.

"Okay, but I don't dance real well."

"Shoot. Nobody else does, either. They play mostly slow songs toward the end."

"Is it a dressy dance or what kind?"

"Anything you've been wearing would be fine. It's only in the gym, and they let you in if you're decent. I'll just have on jeans."

"Sure, why not then? Sounds like fun." Daisy grinned and wiped her forehead with her shirt sleeve. "We better get out of the sun before we roast to death."

We stood up and brushed the dust off our clothes. I could hardly believe my luck, and as I glanced around, I was floored at how a dumpy little city park could turn into paradise just because Daisy was there. My feet barely touched the ground all the way across the grass.

I saw as we reached the curb that there was a fat man sitting on the fender of a dented green Jeep a little way down the block. He looked familiar, and after a second I placed him as the slob who'd been scoping Daisy out the night before at the baseball game.

It wasn't all that odd to run into the same guy two days in a row in a fairly small city, but the way he was eyeballing us gave me a real uneasy feeling about him. I'd had my fill of snooping social workers in the hellish days after my folks died, so if one of their investigators was following Daisy, I knew she had good reason to steer clear of him.

It didn't sit well with me, either, that I didn't know what had happened at her dad's parole hearing. I would have liked to ask the stranger what the hell he was gawking at. There was too much street noise for him to hear me, though, and he got in his Jeep and drove away as soon as we turned in his direction. Besides, I was afraid it would freak Daisy out if I let her know somebody was watching us. I decided to keep my eyes open and my mouth shut till I could figure out what was stirring in the weeds.

~~~

The guys were smoking on the front steps of the Barn when we got home.

"So when's the wedding?" Stace asked.

"You're not invited," I said. "They don't let idiots in church."

"We were looking for you to go goofing around with, Rick." Tim made a fair show of sounding casual, but the muscles in his face were tense, and I knew he had a chip on his shoulder because I'd been hanging out with Daisy instead of with the crew. He was tough, but I'd known him all my life, and I could read him like a book.

Daisy went inside to get her dog, and I sat down and lit a cigarette from Mark's pack. In a few minutes, she came out with Captain.

"Does Rick protect you as good as that mutt of yours?" Tim asked.

Daisy laughed. "I bet Captain wouldn't let anybody mess with me."

"I wouldn't, either. Tim's just jealous because this is the first time I've had a girl and he hasn't." I gave the redhead a grin and a thump on the shoulder. "Move over, pal, you finally met one who doesn't think you're hot stuff."

He glared at me, then turned back to Daisy. "What would that dog do if I hurt you?"

"There's one way to find out." She did me proud with her backbone.

He grabbed her roughly, jerking her off balance on the steps. I reached out to steady her, but she'd already caught herself with one hand on the splintery wooden railing. The low growl and the curl of Captain's lip backed Tim down. He let her go, his eyes smoldering like hot coals.

"Chill out, bud." Mark offered him the smokes.

47

Tim took one and tossed the pack back without a word.

"Captain's trained not to growl or bark at people," Daisy said. "But I suppose any dog would stick up for his owner."

"That better be the last experiment, too," I warned. "Anybody the hound don't tear up, I will."

Tim was really steamed by then. I was sure he would have liked to ram my burning cigarette right down my throat. He tried to stare me down, but it didn't work, and after a minute he got up and stalked off. He fired up his stepdad's car and roared away in a cloud of smoke. I felt sorry for him. It isn't easy for someone who's always called the shots to come down in the world. He and Daisy obviously weren't going to be friends, which put me in a great fix, but I reckon there's no law that says everybody has to like each other.

"I guess you won't be going stag with us to the dance," Bryan said to me.

"You guess right. I got me a date."

The twins and Mark started asking Daisy questions about her blindness, and pretty soon they all drifted inside to check out her braille stuff. It was an oven in the Barn, so I was still lounging on the steps when Tim came back.

"How's about going to the pool for a while, just us two," he suggested. "The car's out of gas, so we'll have to hoof it."

"Why not? It's hot enough out here to make the devil sweat."

The pool was too crowded to do any real swimming, but at least it was wet. Nothing else was said about Daisy, but on the way home, Tim brought up Mr. Garner's van.

"You know, if he wasn't so full of crap, I would have offered to pull out that dent for him. My stepdad still has some tools left from when he worked in the body shop." Before Tim quit school, he'd been an artist in the welding and auto body classes.

"That slime would never have been happy with the job you did anyway."

"I guess not. But me and Mark were thinking just today what a trip it would be if the two of us went into business together. He learned all about engines and stuff in that job training program last summer, and I get off on turning bombs back into beauties."

"Too bad you can't use the school garage anymore. Your old man's bucket of bolts would be good to practice on."

"Yeah, right. It'd take an act of God to get that rolling rust factory looking decent."

We were walking past the playground that sits beside the pool. There was some kind of a ruckus going on. When we glanced over we saw half a dozen junior high kids throwing rocks at a little girl, hooting and laughing. She looked to be about three or four, and she was all curled up under the slide, trying to hide from them.

"The next jackass who chucks a rock gets his arm busted!" Tim called.

The kids dropped their game and scrambled for a way to escape with some of their pride. We strode

49

toward them. I guess we were more than they'd bargained for, even with numbers in their favor, because they took off in a hurry.

"Don't trip all over yourselves running away," Tim growled. "It wouldn't be worth the sweat for us to rip your heads off."

"I hope you feel tough as hell picking on a baby," I added. "Your mamas would sure be proud."

Tim bent down and scooped up the little girl. Her eyes got real big, and then she started wailing.

"Aw, stop it already," he said gruffly. "Those boneheads are gone, and I won't eat you or anything."

He walked around with her in his arms and stroked her dark hair till she calmed down. I stood watching, dumbstruck. It wasn't often that Tim's kinder side showed through, and it always threw me for a loop when it did. When the kid was quiet, he carried her over to a group of women gossiping at a picnic table.

"She's mine," one of them said, not looking too concerned.

He stuffed the kid into her lap. "You ought to try watching her or something."

The cow told him to mind his own business, and he cut loose with a lewd crack or two about her looks and her origins as he turned away. We went on home, and the set of his shoulders let me know I best not breathe a word about what had happened. Tim worked hard to keep up his bad reputation.

Chapter 3

Grandma chased us all out of her apartment the next evening, and she and the twins' mom made a big fuss dressing Daisy up for the dance. I got the feeling the two ladies were as excited about the whole show as Daisy was. The twins and Mark hung out at my place while I got ready.

"What is there to eat around here?"

Mark took a swig from the Coke bottle and let out a burp he must have dragged clear up from his ankles. "Can't you hear my guts grumbling?"

"Grandma probably heard that belch upstairs, and she's half deaf." Stace tipped his chair back and propped his feet up on the table. "I wouldn't give him any grub, Rick. Once you start feeding strays, they never leave, you know."

"There's some cake in the fridge unless one of you chow hounds already stole it." I rummaged in the closet for something decent to wear. "For God's sake, guys, were you all born in a gutter? Stace, get your big feet off my table. You're gonna kick that Coke bottle over."

"Shut up, I am not." He kicked over the bottle, of course. The Coke bubbled out and ran off the edge of the table and onto the floor. He cussed enthusiastically and let his chair legs hit the linoleum with a thud. "Who died and made you Mr. Manners all of a sudden?" he griped at me as he tried to mop up the puddle with a paper towel. "Must be from having a woman around. I've never seen this place so neat. And she bakes cake even."

"I made the cake." I threw a pillow at him. "If you'd help out at your place once in a while instead of bumming around running your mouth, you might learn to bake, too."

"Me? Bake? I got a rep to protect."

"Watch it. I bake sometimes," Mark said as he got busy tearing apart my refrigerator. His cat started rubbing up against his leg and yakking away at him in her own tongue.

Stace chucked the pillow back at me and lobbed another one at Mark, and in the next second, pillows were flying thick and fast. I found a clean black T-shirt and a pair of jeans with only a few small holes in the knees and stripped down to my boxers and socks. Tim came in as I hurled a couch cushion at Bryan. I slipped in the wet spot where the Coke had spilled and landed flat on the floor.

"What's up?" Tim laughed. "Or should I say what's down?"

I grinned up at him. "Hey, Tim, you got taller."

"Hate to break it to you, buddy, but they won't let you in the dance like that." He poked me in the ribs with his foot. "Even a stud like you has to wear clothes."

"Too bad." I got up and pulled on the jeans, then admired my chest in the mirror. "I was gonna impress 'em all tonight."

"You wish." Mark had managed to find the cake and was making a mess trying to cut it.

"You should be a chef, Mark. Give me that knife." Bryan elbowed Mark aside and hacked the cake into half a dozen gigantic slices.

Mark broke his piece in two and gave the bigger part to Scrappy. I don't know if most cats like chocolate cake, but Scrappy thought Mark was God, so anything that came from his hand had to be okay.

"You all eat like a bunch of pigs," I grumbled between bites. "Keep your mitts off that last piece. Me and Daisy are going to split it for breakfast."

"Rick, quit fooling with your hair," Tim ordered. "I came to tell you that you can take my stepdad's car since the twins' old man had a flash of insanity and decided to let me drive his truck. The tank's full again, but you'll have to get by without keys."

"Cool. Who needs keys anyway?"

"There's a couple six-packs in the trunk. I made sure the old buzzard won't wake up tonight. Get in a wreck, though, and we both die."

"I'm a good driver." I covered my face with shaving cream.

"Who got that speeding ticket last month then?" Stace just had to ask.

"The only reason it wasn't you, little maggot, is that you aren't old enough to drive."

"Scrape that face," Stace chanted with his mouth full. "Buzz the fuzz. Slit your throat. Draw some blood."

I pitched a blob of shaving cream at him. It splattered on the wall behind his head. "What, are you jealous because you haven't started shaving yet? Why don't you grow a mustache for the dance?"

"Why don't you grow a brain?" Stace scrawled a smutty word in the smear of shaving cream with his finger.

53

Bryan got a wet dishrag and scrubbed the swearword off the wall. He didn't always have a sense of humor. "I don't know why you're getting all decked out for a girl who won't see how you look anyway," he said.

"Just for the record, it's none of your business," I snapped. "When I need fashion advice, though, I'll be sure to ask you for it."

I left the guys in my apartment and went upstairs to find Daisy. I stopped and stared for a second when I saw her. She had on a pretty blue skirt and a white blouse, and her blond curls were pulled back from her face with a silver hair clip that matched her cross necklace. As I stepped close to her, I recognized the faint scent of Sharon's favorite perfume.

"You look great," I told her, giving Grandma and Sharon a quick thumbs-up sign to thank them for everything.

"Way too good to be slumming around with a guy like Rick," Mark called from the doorway, laughing. I flipped him the bird and then flashed him a grin as he hurried off to catch up with Tim, who was yelling for him to get a move on.

Me and Daisy drove around for a while instead of going straight to the school. I like to show up at dances a little late when there's some action. If you get there before things start popping, you have to stand around looking dumb and watching everybody else stand around looking dumb.

I was waiting at a stoplight a mile or so from the Barn when I spotted a faded green Jeep in my rear view mirror. I recognized it right away as the one I'd seen the day before at the park. As soon as the light changed, I took off on a winding course, zigzagging up and down residential streets and ducking in and out of alleys and parking lots. The Jeep held its distance, keeping two or three cars between us most of the time, but I never lost sight of it for long. I'm no private detective—I didn't have to be. We were being followed, no two ways about it.

"Daisy, what kind of car does your dad drive?" I asked, doing my best to sound casual.

"He was always trading one junker for another, when his license wasn't suspended, that is. Why?"

"I like to keep my eyes open, and it would help if I knew what to watch for. That's all."

"Aren't you being a little paranoid? We don't even know if the jailbird has made his great escape yet. There's no sense thinking about him before we have to."

She was right. It would be a shame to derail our first date by telling her some clown seemed to be bent on making it a threesome. After all, I tried to convince myself, the spy in the Jeep might be just a moron with nothing better to do than tail people who were minding their own business. In any case, I figured it was time to make tracks for the dance where we could lose ourselves in the crowd.

The Jeep passed us and disappeared up the street when we turned into the dirt parking lot behind the school, but I had a nasty feeling I hadn't seen the last of it. I tried to put it out of my mind for the moment, but it kept nagging at me, sort of like a dull headache that wouldn't go away.

We could hear the band before we got out of the car. It was just some local garage gang willing to play for free, and the music was third-rate at best, but at least it was loud enough to make the ground shake. I felt the bass thumping in my chest as I led Daisy into the building.

The gym was packed. A lot of the girls were wearing skirts or summer dresses, but most of the guys had on T-shirts and jeans. No one paid much attention to the fact that Daisy was blind, which surprised me. She was real cute, and everybody wondered who she was and how I, a loner who was still half scared of chicks, got her for the dance. I liked the way we were stared at. She was a pretty good dancer, too, even if she didn't think so. We did the fast songs, and when the music slowed down, I held her tight and rocked her under the globe of spinning colored lights that hung from the ceiling. My heart beat a million miles a minute, and I felt tingly all over. I thought about stealing a kiss, but I didn't have enough guts to try it on the crowded dance floor.

"Let's sit down, okay?" Daisy suggested when the band knocked off for a break.

"Aren't you having fun?"

"Sure, it's great. But I get dizzy sometimes when the music is really loud. I can't see what's going on or hear, either, and I feel sort of cut off from the world around me."

I found her a seat at a table in the cafeteria and went to the car for some beer. There wasn't supposed to be drinking at the dances, but the teachers and cops who were there were ignoring it. A lot of them were afraid of us. The rest just didn't care. When I got back to the table, some guy was sitting next to Daisy, pretending he couldn't tell she was blowing him off. He split when I shot him a few murderous looks. I was kind of proud of my evil eye, which I'd started perfecting in the mirror when I was twelve.

The guy staggered back a while later, though, plainly sloshed. "How's my little blind bat?"

"Beat it, jack," I warned.

"Dump this bum and come with me, baby." He draped an arm across the back of Daisy's chair. "You got a cute smile. Did anybody ever tell you that?"

"I suppose you think you're cool." Daisy scooted her chair away from him so suddenly he almost fell over. "Go find yourself a cave to crawl in and die."

"You heard her. Scram!" I was on my feet. Like I said, I can look as mean as the devil when I want to, and I wanted to just then.

He glanced over at me and snickered. "You were so hard up for a date you had to settle for a blind girl, huh? Does she kiss with her eyes open or closed?"

"Let's take it outside, pal. Wait here, Daisy."

She grabbed my arm. "Rick, you don't have to do this."

I didn't answer, but I was in too much of a hurry to pry her off my arm, so she jogged along with me out to the parking lot. She let me loosen her grip at the curb, and I stepped onto the dirt lot by myself. The punk with the big mouth was right behind me. He snatched up a beer bottle and busted off the end.

"Hey man, keep it fair." I knocked the bottle out of his hand, and the fight was on.

He was stronger than I took him for and fairly sure on his feet, even as drunk as he was. But I belted him in the mouth as hard as I could and aimed a few quick jabs at his nose before he got through spitting curses between his mangled lips.

Then an evil blow to my jaw sent me reeling, and the lowlife stuck out his foot and put me down while I was off balance. His boot heel slammed into my left side once, and then again, as I gulped for air. I heard myself let out a tortured gasp, and I wondered, as a haze of pain swept over me, if some of my ribs were cracked. I felt a piece of the busted bottle brush against the side of my head as I dodged another vicious kick and scrambled to my feet.

I was still in the action, though, and I proved it to my enemy with a fist that smashed into his already swollen nose and let loose a satisfying river of blood. It was torment for me to breathe, but I'd die before I let anybody know it. I've lost fights often enough, but I've never lost my pride in one.

A couple of exasperated cops broke us up after a few minutes, and three or four others chased off the noisy crowd of rubberneckers that had sprung up. I hate people who stand around gawking at a fight, especially when they don't know the guys who are going at it. The pros get paid big bucks to beat each other up for show. I don't.

The principal came out of the school, looking more disgusted than mad. He started in right away, scowling and shaking his finger, but I tuned out most of what he said. I figured I'd probably heard it all a thousand times before anyway. When he got done preaching, the cops threw in a warning or two of their own and ordered us off the property.

"Sorry our date turned out like this," I said as me and Daisy drove away. "I guess that's the price you pay for taking a pretty girl to the dance."

"No, it's the price you pay for being macho," she snapped. "I didn't ask you to be my bodyguard."

"Then I was supposed to sit there and let that jackass run his mouth?"

"I can take care of myself."

"Fine. Next time the fun is all yours." I honked angrily at a driver who was dawdling at a stoplight and cranked the radio up loud enough to rattle the car windows.

Daisy turned down the music after a minute and laid a hand on my knee. "Rick, I didn't mean to yell at you. But I'm not used to somebody sticking up for me, and I was afraid you'd get jailed. Are you okay?"

I shrugged, then winced as a hundred fiery arrows raced up and down the left side of my body. "Yeah, cracked ribs maybe. They never haul guys in for skin fighting. Shoot, they'd have to lock up everybody around here if they did."

"I couldn't get close enough to hear the principal. What did he say?"

"Just fed us a line about how nice it would be if we acted like gentlemen instead of apes. I'm suspended for the first two days of the fall semester, and I can't go to their stupid dance next month. No sweat. I wasn't going back to school anyway."

"Why not?"

"I failed last year, so I'd still be a junior. I was always a big flop in school, and I never got along with teachers. Besides, I have to work for a living."

I can't stand the way teachers only care about the smart kids and the ones who kiss up in class, so I make it a point to mouth off to them every chance I get. That's probably why none of them ever gave a damn about me.

The others followed us to our favorite little drugstore on Palmer Avenue. The place stayed open late in the summer, and we liked to hang out there sometimes in the evenings when we didn't feel like going home.

"The dance wasn't exactly sizzling with action anyways." Stace jumped down from the back of his dad's truck. "And where one of us ain't wanted, the rest won't be seen either."

"I bet they're not grieving much because we split," I said.

"We're too good for those buttheads anyhow," Mark scoffed. "We've got kicked out of better places than that before."

"Hey, buddy, you're bleeding all over my car." Tim leaned in the open driver's window. "Did that guy cut you up? If he did, I'll look him up and teach him how to fight."

"Hate to blow your fun, Tim, but I rolled over on a piece of busted glass." I put my hand to the side of my head where it itched and was surprised to find it damp with blood. "I didn't know I opened a vein. Sorry about the car."

"This heap's been through worse." Tim took a bandana from his pocket, spit on it to keep it from sticking, and pressed it against the cut for me. "I saw the other guy before he took off. I think you broke his nose."

"I hope so." I got out of the car, wincing a little and cursing under my breath. "I need my ribs taped. They hurt like hell. Daisy, don't get all keyed up just because you hear the word blood. It's no big deal."

She'd been fiddling nervously with the silver cross on her necklace, but she only shrugged and scowled. "I guess I'll have to get used to your battle wounds, won't I? I can't see how maimed you are, so if I don't hear anything about exposed organs or severed limbs, I won't worry."

"We best not tell her he sawed off your left ear then," Tim said to me, purposely ignoring Daisy's sarcastic tone.

But Stace must have lost his last shred of tact somewhere on the way to the drugstore. "Ooo, it looks like there's trouble in paradise. I'll lay money on Daisy if there's gonna be another fight."

I glared at him. "There's about to be one between you and me. Shut your fat trap while you still got teeth in it."

"Aw, cool off, Rick," Bryan said as he got out the first aid kit his dad always kept in the back of the truck.

He rummaged in it till he found some strips of cotton cloth and a roll of medical tape. Then he bound up my throbbing ribs, and Mark taped the bandages tightly in place. Knowing how to patch each other up came in handy lots of times, not just after fights.

Mark handed me my dirty T-shirt. "I ought to be a sawbones. I'm dropping my bill in the mail, so get ready to be screwed."

We went into the store to goof around and flip through the weekly tabloids. There was a big wooden barrel of peanuts the clerk kept by the cash register for his shoppers to munch on. It wasn't long before we had empty shells scattered all over the floor.

"Check this out." Bryan tried to break the tension between me and Daisy by passing around a magazine. "A four-hundred-pound Texas housewife gave birth to an alien's baby. Get a load of the hams on that chick."

Then Tim and Mark took straws from the dispenser and blew the paper wrappers at each other, and Stace reached up into the soda machine to snag a Coke and got his arm stuck. We all stood there laughing while he twisted helplessly around on the floor, grinning sheepishly and cussing his head off.

"Smooth move, space case." Mark finally wrenched Stace's arm free. "You know, we should auction you off to the zoo or something. You could pass for a baboon without half trying."

"Look who's talking." Stace leaned back against the soda machine and rubbed his elbow. "You'd have to take a nice long bath, though, before they'd let you in the monkey house."

The old man who ran the store just sat behind the cash register, stroking the stubbly beard on his chin and giving us dirty looks over his granny glasses. He was scared spitless of us, for some reason. We didn't cause him much trouble except maybe to drive off his paying customers, but he'd never said two words in a row to any of us.

"Anyone got a cancer stick?" I asked.

When Tim tossed me one, I couldn't get the damn thing lit because my hands wouldn't quit shaking. He lit it for me and stuck it in my mouth. The cigarette started to calm me down, but we had to pass it back and forth because it was our last one. The clerk had taken to keeping the smokes he sold behind the counter. I couldn't blame him for trying to cut his losses, but I would have given just about anything right then for a fresh pack.

An older guy lurched in. His dark hair was tied in a greasy ponytail at the back of his neck, and he stunk to high heaven of beer and cheap tobacco. I was sitting on a stool near the coffeepot, feeling kind of lousy, to tell the truth, and the others stood around by the door. The stranger must have taken a shine to Daisy, judging by the way he stared.

"Why don't you peel your eyes off her and stuff them back in their sockets already," Mark suggested, firing me a questioning look, which I ignored. Standing up for Daisy was a dangerous job, and I hadn't won any points with her the last time I tried it. I sat back and waited for her to show me what she could do.

"Hey, cutey, let's go for a spin." The drunk latched onto her hand. "I'll take you to the stars and have you back on the ground before morning."

"No thanks, wino. I only date within my own species." She snatched her hand away.

"I ain't drunk hardly. How could you tell anyway? You can't see, right?"

"You reek enough to make my eyes water, and you can barely talk. Go slobber on someone else."

"You need to learn a few manners, missy, and I got all night to teach you." The drunk grabbed Daisy by one shoulder and jerked her roughly toward the door.

I sprang up, but before I made it off my stool, Tim spun around and belted the guy so hard it sent him flying backwards into a rack of sunglasses. Glasses rained down all over the place, and the rack and the drunk crashed to the floor.

"All of you, out! Now!" The old man behind the counter was suddenly on his feet with fire in his eyes and a baseball bat gripped in both hands. "And don't come back, ever! You hooligans have finally worn out your welcome!"

I stood there staring, goggle-eyed and dumbstruck. You'd never expect a mild-looking grandpa to turn into a wildcat like that. One guy with a baseball bat, if he was crazy enough, could flatten all of us, so everybody made tracks for the door. Bryan grabbed Daisy's arm, and Mark dragged me along by the sleeve of my T-shirt, which ripped, and shoved me into the back seat of Tim's car.

"Now look what you did, you reject," I groused. "That was my favorite shirt."

He was too busy driving to pay attention. We weren't in danger anymore, but Mark never needed a reason to drive like a speed demon, and we all cheered him on. I bet both cars topped eighty-five easy on the way home. I might have enjoyed the ride a little more if I didn't feel like I'd been hit by a city bus.

I was halfway hacked off at Tim for slugging that drunk since Daisy was my girl and not his, but I was proud of him, too. He and Daisy weren't wild about each other, but she was with me, so he'd stick up for her. I guess that was sort of her initiation because after that she was one of the crew.

I had a word with her, though, when we touched down alive in front of the Barn. "You know, Daisy, you better watch who you mouth off to. It works while there's people backing you, but you could catch all kinds of hell if you rile up the wrong guy when you're on your own."

"What was I supposed to do, stand there prim and proper and let that scum paw all over me?"

"I ain't in a mood to argue. Don't say you weren't warned." I stormed into the building and slammed the door. But I got to missing her before I made it down the hall to my apartment, so I walked back outside and took her hand. "Don't mind me. I feel like I tangled with King Kong and got the worst of it tonight. I guess that made me a little cranky."

"You have a point anyway." Daisy smiled, and my ribs didn't seem to ache quite so bad when I saw her face light up.

Grandma sure was a great lady, and I loved her almost like a mother. She didn't get in a sweat about my fighting or how jacked up I was. She just swabbed out the cut on my head and made me choke down a mug of the nastiest infection-fighting tea that was ever brewed. She knew all about herbs and roots and things and always had some potion or other ready when one of us got sick or hurt.

I forced down the last gulp of the foul concoction. "My God, Grandma, your witchcraft is gonna kill me one of these times. That rotgut numbed everything from my lips on in."

She pinched my cheek playfully. "You stay out of trouble then, *mijo*, and no more tea for you."

Grandma had called me her son in Spanish. She said all of us were her kids, not just Mark.

~~~

When I got home from work the next day, Grandma had made me up a big pot of beans and a batch of tortillas. She and the twins' mom cooked stuff for me every so often to make sure I ate decent meals. They fixed food for Tim sometimes, too.

Me and the twins went to Mark's place to help him and Grandma clip coupons, which we did every month when the grocery store circulars came out. Grandma always bribed us by putting on a mammoth taco feed afterward.

"Where's Tim?" Stace asked. "If he thinks he's getting tacos without manning the scissors, he's insane."

"You better not stand between him and the grub while you tell him that," Mark warned. "The old porker puts the rest of us to shame every time."

The old porker burst in just then. He marched right up to Grandma, grinning from ear to ear, and pulled the hymnal Mark had been saving for from his jacket pocket.

Her eyes lit up as she took the book from him. "Oh, look! These are the old songs from Mexico!"

"Sing your heart out, Grandma." Tim flopped down on the couch, beaming like a little kid at a birthday party. "Hand over those scissors, Bryan."

Grandma thumbed through the hymnal for a minute. Then she closed the book suddenly and turned to Tim, frowning. "*Mijo*, where did you get this?"

"From the Easter Bunny. Hey, you can save thirty-five cents on toilet paper."

She took hold of his arm and fixed her eyes on his face. "You didn't steal it, did you?"

"So what if I did? What'd you have to go and ask that for?" Tim glared down at the circular Bryan had tossed him.

"Tim, you can't steal a book from somewhere because you think I should have it." Grandma dropped the hymnal into his lap. "Take it back where you got it."

Tim's joy went out like a light bulb. "Aw, come off it. You should get something you want for once. That ain't asking too much out of life."

"I don't want anything bad enough that you need to steal it for me."

"Well, Mark was going to buy it, but that damn Garner had to bleed us all dry so he could fix his stupid van."

"I know. We'll have the money again pretty soon." Grandma patted his hand, trying to reassure him.

"Yeah, right. Something always comes up." Tim yanked his hand away. "Besides, those chicks at the Christian store would think this is a good cause, bringing godly music to the great unwashed. They gaped at me like I was a real live nun-eating demon when I walked in there."

He held the hymnal out to Grandma one more time, flashing her a doubtful smile. But she just shook her head and picked up a pile of coupons to sort through. So he stuffed the book back in his pocket and stomped out of the room, cussing for all he was worth. He slammed the door behind him.

He didn't show up for tacos, either. But he and Grandma must have worked out a truce because I saw them drinking coffee on the front steps later on. The old lady was needling him about how you could spot his hair a mile off. Tim wasn't thrilled about being a redhead. He griped that it made him too visible so people tagged him all the time for things he didn't do, as if he was a saint or something. None of the rest of us would badger him about his hair unless we had a death wish.

Bryan had gotten real hot to learn braille, and Daisy went to the twins' place after the taco feed to coach him. I was still feeling pretty rotten from the fight at the dance, so I dozed for a while before I joined them.

As I walked into the twins' apartment, I heard Daisy saying, "I just don't know where I might have put Captain's harness."

I glanced around the room to see if I could spot it. Stace was holding it and snickering to himself as Daisy felt for it on the couch and the floor. I was about to offer to break his scrawny little neck. But his dad, who had come up behind me, got his mouth open first. Ed roofed houses for a living and was built like an Army tank, so it was always an awesome sight when he blew his stack.

"Hey!" he yelled, making me and Daisy jump. "Where the hell do you get off, messing with a blind girl? Give that to her, now!"

The self-satisfied smirk died instantly on Stace's lips. He stared down at the floor and held the harness out to Daisy, mumbling, "Sorry."

Daisy was a little shaken up herself. "Forget it."

"No, don't forget it." Ed slammed his lunch pail onto the table. "I wish you'd shape up and act more like your brother. You'd never catch Bryan pulling a stupid trick on a blind girl."

"So Bryan's the angel and I'm the idiot again." Stace fired a furious look at his twin, who was lost in his own world, tapping away with Daisy's slate and stylus. "Can't you lay off that crap for once?"

"If the shoe fits, wear it," Ed snapped. "It takes an idiot to pick on somebody who can't fight back, don't it?"

"Who says she can't fight back? You don't need to feel sorry for her because she can't see, if that's what you mean."

"And you don't need to give her a hard time, either, do you?" Beads of sweat popped out on Ed's forehead, and his cheeks started to turn a dangerous shade of red.

Stace had to keep on pushing, too, as usual. "Aw, lighten up, for God's sake, nobody died."

"You all don't have to fight about it. It's nothing, really." Daisy came to stand beside me in the doorway with Captain. "Maybe we better go, Rick. I'll come get my braille stuff later."

Mark pushed past us into the twins' apartment. "Has any of you seen Scrappy? I've been looking everywhere."

Stace shrugged, and even Bryan glanced up from the braille he was making and shook his head.

"I haven't laid eyes on her all day, now that I think of it." I frowned, puzzled. When Mark was home, that cat hardly ever let him out of her sight.

We all mounted a search, but after three hours of walking the streets around the Barn, peering into garages and garbage cans, everybody gave up except Mark. He was out calling for Scrappy most of the night.

The cat never turned up. Mark didn't say another word about her, but I lost count of the mornings he stumbled in looking like he'd marched halfway across hell with his shoes off just in time to grab a bite and head for his job at the filling station.

Chapter 4

I had a bad dream a few nights after the dance. I'd been tormented by nightmares ever since Mom and Dad died, but there had been nobody around to hear me shout in my sleep till I jerked awake in the darkness, and Daisy was calling my name and shaking me urgently.

"Come on, Rick, wake up. It was just a dream." She kept her hand on my shoulder as my mind slowly cleared. "Should I turn on the lamp?"

I sat up, breathing hard. I was glad she couldn't see the tears on my face. "Naw, I'll be okay now. Sorry I woke you up."

Daisy settled down next to me on the couch. "Do you want to tell me about it?"

I shrugged and shook my head, but even as I did, I moved closer to her and reached for her hand. I was humiliated by my weakness, but I needed her company. I'm not big on bleeding all over everybody. There's something about those quiet hours before daylight that shreds a guy's defenses, though, and I'd nursed my own pain way too long.

"Mom and Dad took me to a traveling carnival in Amarillo for my tenth birthday. I got on the Ferris wheel, and my folks snagged another seat, and we waved and yelled to each other as we spun around and around. I see it like it was yesterday in my dreams." My voice cracked. "Only then their seat flies off the wheel and shoots up into the clouds, and I start screaming at them, begging them to come back. But they just get smaller and smaller till they're gone."

I was bawling for real by then. Daisy clasped my hand silently as I fought for control. After a while she offered me a tissue from the box on the coffee table.

"I know how you miss them," she said softly. "My dad's a drunk and a menace, but I loved my mom. She finally died of breast cancer last summer, after it ate every ounce of meat off her bones."

My pride kicked in. "Aw hell, I'm blubbering like a baby."

"So you're human. What's wrong with that? I cry for my mom a lot."

"Damn it, you're a girl! It's fine for you to cry! Just leave me alone, will you?"

Tears sprang into her eyes, and she jerked back from me like I'd taken a swing at her. "I'm sorry! I was trying to … I mean …"

I couldn't believe I'd made Daisy cry. She wasn't sobbing out loud, but her breath came in shaking gulps, and her eyes were wide with fear. Worse than that, her face had gone as white as the nightgown she was wearing. I was dying to say something that would calm her down and turn her fantastic smile back on, but I couldn't think of anything. So I just put my arms around her, and we sat together like that for a long time.

"Are you scared of me, Daisy?" I finally got up the nerve to ask. "You looked like you were about to faint when I snapped at you. I'd hate it if you didn't trust me."

Daisy scrubbed at her eyes with the back of her hand. "I do trust you, really, but it freaks me out when somebody blows up in my face. My dad made me that way, I guess. He gave me a nasty shiner the last time he went off on me, and broke my leg in two places."

"I could kill the son of a bitch with my own bare hands," I said, trying to keep the fury out of my voice. "I swear to God, I'll never let anybody hurt you again, not ever."

Some promises are a whole lot easier to make than they are to keep, and I had no idea at that moment how many times those words would come back to haunt me.

"Okay, Rick, I'll let you be my bodyguard, since you want the job so bad." Daisy giggled and cuddled up next to me on the couch, resting her head comfortably against my chest.

My heart started beating so fast I wondered if she could feel it pounding away under her ear. I ran my hands over her golden curls, then traced a finger around the curve of her chin and down along her throat. I kissed her lightly on her forehead and eyebrows and cheeks, and finally my mouth found hers and landed hungrily.

She let out a satisfied sigh as her lips parted for me, and I held her tight, breathing in the scent of her soft blond hair. I drew her down under the old patchwork quilt my mom had made for me, and she seemed to melt into my arms as if she'd always belonged there. For a little while, snuggled up in the darkness, we had nothing to be sad about and nothing to fear. There was no room in the world for nightmares.

But my bad dreams didn't go away. I spent a lot of dreary nights in front of the TV, wide awake, with the volume turned down low so I wouldn't bother Daisy again. Sometimes I would sit by the bed and watch her as she slept, but then I would ache with loneliness and wish I could wake her up and hold her. Finally, in the early hours of a Saturday morning, my sorrows drove me to the john with a bottle. Me and Jack Daniels chewed the fat till I blacked out.

When I came around, the twins' mom was kneeling beside me on the bathroom floor. She had just gotten off the late shift at Jerry's Bar and Grill. She was still wearing her work smock, with her pen and pad sticking out of one pocket and her tip money jingling in the other, and she smelled like cheap cigarettes and greasy French fries.

She wiped my face tenderly with a wet paper towel. "Was it your folks again?"

I opened my mouth to answer, but all that came out was a little whimper. The room was spinning violently, and I felt sick enough to die.

"Oh God, Sharon," I finally groaned. "What'd you have to turn the light on for?"

"Richard, honey, this won't do you a lick of good. You know that." Sharon sighed. "When you sober up, you'll miss your mom and dad as much as you ever did."

Sharon and Grandma were the only people on the planet besides my mom who could get away with calling me by my full name, which I hate with a royal passion. Anybody else who tried it would end up on the floor hunting for missing teeth.

74

I moaned, and everything I'd eaten in recent history made a second appearance. Sharon washed off my face and then cleaned up the mess on the linoleum while I lay there wishing I would pass out again.

"Let's get you to bed now." She tossed the empty bottle into the trash can, then rinsed her hands at the sink and dried them on her apron. "You ought to go see one of those counselors at the public health clinic. The county offered to foot the bill, you know, after your folks died."

"Spare me." I sat up, cradling my throbbing head in my hands. "I could talk till my tongue fell out. It wouldn't bring Mom and Dad back."

"The whiskey isn't doing it, either, is it?" Sharon hauled me to my feet with her arms around my middle. She was no lightweight, so it wasn't much of a job for her.

My ribs were still sore from my fight at the dance, and the pain cleared my head a little as I stumbled out of the john and across the hall to my apartment.

I dug for my keys in the pocket of my ratty old bathrobe. "Don't say anything to Daisy, okay? She'd just worry."

"We all worry. But maybe now that you got yourself a girl, you'll get your act together."

"Daisy's the best thing that's happened to me in a long time." I steadied myself with one hand on the doorknob and fumbled to get the key into the lock. "I think I love her, Sharon. Ain't that a trip?"

"She's a pretty one, that's for sure. She reminds me of your mom, the way her hair shines when the sunlight hits it." Sharon took the key out of my clumsy fingers and unlocked the door for me. "Can you make it from here?"

"Yeah, thanks. This stays between us, remember."

"Then I don't want to scoop you up off the floor again, you hear? Your dad would have strung you up for this." Sharon shooed me into my apartment with a wave of her hand. "Take some aspirin, and drink a glass of cold tomato juice first thing in the morning. It'll keep you from getting queasy."

I don't think an ocean of tomato juice would have kept me from getting queasy, no matter what Sharon said. I didn't have to work that Saturday, which was a good thing. But I didn't get to sleep off my hangover because my guts had declared war on me by sunup, and I had to go charging back across the hall to the john.

Daisy had to pick that morning to fix me her famous raspberry pancakes, too. Her blindness was a stroke of luck for me. I ate every bite, and she didn't have a clue that I was green around the gills. I wasn't tough enough for seconds, though.

~~~

The Barn was quiet that afternoon. The twins went somewhere on foot with their dad, and me and Mark loafed in his place, watching a stupid kung-fu movie on TV while Grandma and Daisy mended clothes. The crew needed stuff mended pretty bad, and when Grandma opened up her sewing basket,

76

Daisy offered to help out right away. I caught Grandma sneaking a peek now and then to see how Daisy managed to sew without looking. I was getting used to the fact that Daisy could do just about anything she set her mind to, in spite of her blindness, so it didn't surprise me that her stitches were tight and straight. She did a lot better than I would have, even looking right at the needle and thread.

The kung-fu movie was about to end when all hell broke loose across the hall. Tim and his stepdad started yelling and swearing and throwing things at each other. They got into some incredible battles when the old coot wasn't passed out drunk someplace or off dealing cards to buy his next high. I hated to be around when they started in because I had to dodge flying objects as best I could, and the way they cussed made me want to crawl under the couch or something. But they were buddies—two of a kind. Maybe they even loved each other. Anyway, Tim seemed to like it that he was free to run his own life without his stepdad acting like he gave a damn about parenting.

"I wish they'd shut up," Mark said. "Turn down the TV a little. Grandma, go put your feet up, okay? I'll bring you some hot tea."

I turned down the tube, and Grandma went to rest, grumbling about the mountain of dirty dishes in the sink.

"Rick, you've just been drafted." Mark tossed me a dishrag. "Come on, give me a hand."

"Lincoln freed the slaves." The floor was still heaving under my feet.

"Lincoln ain't here or I'd put him to work." Mark snapped me with his towel. "Hop to it, you lazy waste of skin."

But the fighters didn't shut up. The Barn was never quiet for long, and when Tim and his stepdad got themselves fired up, the best thing you could do was stay out of their way. Pretty soon there was a huge crash, and they boiled out into the hall, going to town with their fists. We all used to get madder than blazes to see the way Tim got clobbered around, but lately he was giving it right back to his stepdad. They fought their way down the stairs, and the front door slammed behind them.

"It's bad this time," Mark said. "Maybe we should go after 'em."

"Naw." I shrugged. "Enjoy the silence. They'll give out before long and come back as tight as ever. They always do."

They didn't come back, though, so in a few minutes we left the dishes and went to look in their apartment. The place was a wreck—furniture tipped upside down, broken glass all over the floor, a hole punched in the closet door. Worse than that, there was a big smear of blood on the linoleum by the stove. Me and Mark glanced quickly at each other when we saw the blood. We sprinted down the stairs and out the front door.

Tim lay on the sidewalk at the foot of the porch steps, face down and motionless. Mark rolled him over gently, and my guts tied themselves in knots.

His face was bruised and bloodied so bad I might not have recognized him if it hadn't been for his red hair. A deep gash ran clear across his forehead, splitting it wide open above his eyebrows. One eye was swollen all the way shut, and the other one looked wild. His left arm was twisted at a funny angle on the sidewalk. I could see the broken bones through the skin, which was already turning a wicked purplish black color.

"Hey, Rick, you got taller," he rasped, grinning weakly up at me.

I couldn't answer because his face looked even more gruesome when he smiled. He left off joking and fell silent, breathing heavily.

"Just stay still." Mark took a bandana from his pocket and started to wipe the blood off Tim's mouth and nose. "Did your old man do this?"

"Who else? God Almighty, I think he jacked me up real bad this time."

"Buddy, that's the truth." I dropped down next to Mark and brushed the tangled hair back from the cut on Tim's forehead. It was plainly the work of a knife. I couldn't keep myself from shuddering. "Would you quit bleeding, for Christ's sake?"

"You two are the best, always been great to me." Tim's words were sort of slurred. His good eye drifted closed.

"Shut up talking that way!" Mark gave his body a rough shake. "You're gonna be okay, so just shut up!"

"Watch it. You can't jostle him like that." I glared at Mark. "His ribs might be broke or somethin'."

"Naw, my face is busted," Tim mumbled. "My arm ain't working right, and my face is busted."

Old Man Garner came out onto the steps just then, carrying his leather briefcase. He stopped and stared. "Don't you hoodlums ever do anything but beat each other up?"

Mark muttered something cute in Spanish and then turned his back on the landlord, still dabbing at Tim's face with the bloody bandana.

"Make yourself useful for once in your miserable life, Garner, and go get the twins' mom," I ordered. "Tell her we need a cardboard box and a roll of duct tape."

"What on earth for?"

"So we can rig up a splint for his arm, stupid. Would you move it?" The only way to get anything out of the landlord was to bully him. He went.

Sharon didn't even flinch when she saw the way Tim looked. That woman had amazing nerves. She needed them, I guess, living in the Barn. She handed Mark a dish towel and told him to hold it tight against the wound on Tim's forehead. Then she ripped apart a big fruit box and lifted his broken arm carefully in both of her hands so I could roll a flat slab of cardboard around it.

"Damn you, Rick, get your paws off me!" Tim growled. "That hurts like hell!"

"No kidding. I've almost got it now. One more second—there. Tape, Sharon?"

"They'll have to sew him up. Stick a cast on him, too." Sharon fastened the homemade splint in place with a long strip of duct tape. "The charity clinic on Harding Street is open every weekend now. The brakes are out on our truck, so we'll have to go in his car."

"Good thing his stepdad didn't take off in it," I said as I pushed to my feet.

"He better never show up around here again, damn his sorry ass." Mark went on grimly calling down curses on him in Spanish.

After a lot of struggling and swearing, we got Tim stretched out on the back seat of the old rust-bucket with his head in my lap. We had to hot-wire the car because he was too out of it to tell us where the keys were. Mark jumped on any excuse for fast driving, so he tore up the roads on the way to the clinic. Sharon turned sort of pale, and I think she forgot to breathe once or twice, but she didn't say anything.

Eventually a cop stopped us. Those guys never know when to leave people alone. "Okay, kid, where's the holocaust?"

"There." Mark jerked his thumb toward the back seat.

The cop looked worried. He really did. "Turn on your hazard lights and stay behind me."

"Let's go." Mark flipped on the emergency flashers. "Bet I can beat you to Harding Street."

"I said stay behind me," the cop warned. But we made record time to the clinic anyway, with the siren on the squad car clearing traffic for us.

"Stick with me, guys," Tim moaned through his puffy lips. "Don't leave me, okay?"

"Trust me, pal, we're not riding along for the scenery." I steadied the cardboard splint on the seat as Mark screeched to a halt in front of the clinic. "Now would you quit bleeding?"

The doctor on duty wanted to know right away what had happened, but Tim wouldn't give up any information, and me and Mark weren't talking either. Finally, a nurse made Sharon follow her into an empty exam room. I never did find out if the nurse got Sharon to spill her guts behind the closed door or not, but I didn't figure it would matter much either way. Tim had gotten thumped on for as long as I could remember, and his stepdad had never been in any trouble over it.

The doctor put a bunch of stitches in Tim's forehead and slapped his arm in a plaster cast. Tim cussed blue and green about that because he found out he would have to drag the cast around for at least six weeks. He likely had a concussion, but his skull was in one piece, so the doctor doped him up on painkillers and sent him home.

Me and Mark half dragged and half carried him to the car. Sweat and tears glistened on his face, but he didn't complain. He just spat some more four letter words between his clenched teeth. He was panting hard by the time we got him settled on the back seat again. The pain must have scrambled up his brains because he started singing some really dirty rap tune on the way home, daring me and Mark to join in. I felt my ears burning. Sharon pretended she didn't hear. Somehow we managed to get Tim up to Mark's apartment and onto the couch.

"Man, I ain't feeling good," Tim admitted when the three of us were alone. He didn't have to knock himself out proving he was tough just to Mark and me. We knew he was tough.

"Those pills they gave you ought to numb you out soon." I tucked an afghan around his shoulders and took off his tennis shoes for him.

"I'd do better with a cold one."

"No way. You're already strung out from here to Christmas." Mark put on a scowl that let Tim know there was no point in arguing.

"A smoke then?"

"Well, I guess." Mark braced him up with pillows and stuck a cigarette in his mouth. But Tim dozed off before it was half gone, so we took it from him and settled him on his back again.

I think a starving vampire would have been an easier patient to get along with than Tim was. Grandma and Sharon did everything they could to keep him comfortable. They were both angels, and I wondered what in the world the crew would ever do without them. I should have told them that then, but I've never been too good at opening up to people, so I just waved at them and went to help Mark and Daisy muck out Tim's trashed apartment.

~~~

I was bone tired by the time I fell into bed that night. Between my hangover and the business with Tim, I'd put in one of the longest days of my life. And I already said I'm a sound sleeper. So I sat up, groggy and grouchy, when Bryan shook me for the fourth or fifth time at around three in the morning.

"Come on, Rick!" he urged. "Hurry, wake up! It's Grandma!"

"Huh?" I yawned. "God, it ain't even light yet. What are you raving about?"

He yanked the quilt off me and dragged me to my feet by the back of my sweats. "Get a move on, damn it! She's dead!"

That lit a fire under me. I took off like a torpedo with Bryan hot on my heels. Daisy followed us up the stairs in her nightgown, rubbing her eyes.

The silence was so heavy in Mark's place that I felt like I was pushing through a set of wet drapes as I stepped into the room. Tim was propped up on the couch staring blankly at the ceiling, and Sharon sat beside him but didn't dare touch him. It was a good idea to leave Tim alone when things were stormy.

Stace was slumped in a chair at the kitchen table with his face buried in his arms. Every now and then a little squeak or a sniffle would escape from him and be choked off. Bad breaks didn't get through to that kid too often, but they blew him away when they did. His dad stood behind him with a hand on his shoulder, looking as grim as I'd ever seen him.

I didn't want to glance over at the corner of the room where Grandma slept, but I made myself do it anyway. Mark knelt on the floor by the bed, wearing nothing but a pair of boxers. Grandma lay on her side, facing Mark, and he had both of her wrinkled hands clasped in his. I saw his lips moving, but no sounds came out.

"Did somebody call an ambulance?" I asked with a thick tongue.

"I did, but it's way too late," Ed said. "She must have gone in her sleep quite a while ago. Tim just found Mark like this and roused up the rest of us." He gave me a pleading look. "Nobody can do a thing with Mark."

I sighed and went over to the bed. After a little coaxing, Mark let me take his hands away from Grandma and pull the sheet up over her face. He was trembling violently, trying not to break.

"I s'pose I should pray or something," he murmured numbly. "She wanted me to pray with her like always before she turned in, and I said I'd had a real bad day and she ought to get a grip because God never listens to downtown slobs anyway. And now look what happened."

I shook my head. "Mark, she's been sick, you know that. This didn't happen because you decided not to pray with her."

"The hell it didn't!" Suddenly Mark leaped to his feet like someone had kicked him. He jerked Grandma up, sheet and all, by her bony shoulders and started shaking her savagely. "Damn you, Grandma! What are you trying to do to me? You're leaving me high and dry, just like my mom!"

"Take it easy, buddy." I put a hand on his arm, but he didn't even notice.

He was shouting by then, and his words poured out so fast they got all jumbled together. "I ran off one time and wouldn't come back when you hollered for me, and you said you'd be waiting with a strap when I showed up! And then after I dragged my butt home and you worked me over, you baked me up that batch of sugar cookies, and we ate every single one of them with chocolate milk! I need you, Grandma! For the love of Jesus, don't leave me!"

He had towed her body half off the bed in his fit, and she flopped like a rag doll as he shook her.

"Get hold of yourself, Mark!" I pried his hands off Grandma and let her body drop back onto the mattress. I flipped the sheet quickly over her face again.

Mark took a swing at me, and I hauled off and decked him as hard as I could to stop his hysterics and then shoved him into a chair. He went limp and drooped there, sobbing and whispering in broken bits of Spanish. I stood beside him and kept a hand on his arm, wishing I could think of something else to do. No one spoke as we waited for the ambulance. The only sounds in the room were the ticking clock and Mark's wrenching sobs.

It felt like forever before the paramedics hurried up the stairs and rushed into the apartment. They went to the bed without saying a word to anyone, swept the rumpled sheet aside, and shook their heads.

"She's gone," one of them said quietly.

"Did you go to med school to get so brilliant or are you a natural genius?" Bryan burst out.

Stace chimed in with a few colorful insults of his own, but a gesture from his dad quenched the stream in mid-flow.

"You took your own sweet time getting here! Did someone from Snob Hill have heartburn or a hangnail or something?" Before anybody could react, Mark erupted out of his chair and grabbed one of the paramedics by the throat. "You could have saved her, damn it! You could have! You could have!"

I tried to yank Mark off, and Bryan darted over to give me a hand. But Mark was strong for his size, and right then he was insane. So Ed, the human mountain, twisted his arms behind his back and forced him into a chair. Mark sat there snarling Spanish curses like a mad dog, throwing in an English word now and then to make sure nobody missed his point.

The paramedic stared at Mark and rubbed the reddening welts on his throat. "You know, I could press assault charges."

"Shut up and do your job," Tim snapped.

Ed didn't turn Mark loose till the paramedics had lifted Grandma onto a stretcher and taken her out of the room. Then I made a run to Tim's place for a couple of six-packs, and we poured beer into Mark till he was mellow.

"I think I'm a little splashed," he giggled. "Tell Grandma that no-count Lincoln hasn't showed up to finish the dishes yet."

I cupped his face between my hands and turned it up so I could look straight into his eyes. "Don't start spouting off again. You'll be okay tomorrow, once you get some rest."

"I'll be okay after I rest," Mark mumbled. "I'll be okay tomorrow."

"Yeah, tomorrow." I felt like I was going to choke on my words. I hated to lie to him. Without Grandma, he wouldn't be okay for a long time. Once the shock of losing her wore off, the loneliness would set in and rip him to shreds from the inside out. I knew all about that.

Me and Bryan hoisted him to his feet, and he slung an arm around each of our necks. But he fell on his face before we'd gone ten steps, so Ed picked him up and carried him down the stairs. He was out cold by the time we had him settled on the couch in the twins' place.

He slept like a dead man till late the next day, and he woke up with a killer headache. Tim still wasn't feeling exactly great, either. Sharon and Daisy took turns with the nursing, and me and the twins cleaned out Mark's place and moved his stuff into my apartment. Mark couldn't stand to be in the room where Grandma died, and besides, her pension check had covered the rent.

The county had to bury her. We couldn't scrape up the money for a decent funeral. I guess people like us can't even afford to die. I went to the service with the others, and most of it was in Spanish, so I didn't understand what the priest said. That was probably a blessing.

Chapter 5

Things were pretty bleak at the Barn for the next few weeks. Mark slept off his hangover, but he didn't go back to being the happy-go-lucky Mark we'd always known. He dragged around looking as black as a summer thunderstorm, and we all took care not to cross him because we were apt to get pasted.

Tim's stepdad didn't show up, either, and I could tell Tim missed him a lot, even if he was too proud to say so.

Everything in my life seemed to have turned flat and meaningless. I felt like I was stuck in a bad dream I couldn't wake up from. I'd felt that way for ages after Mom and Dad died, but the crew had pulled me through then, and we wouldn't let Mark and Tim down when they needed us most. Like I said, knowing how to patch each other up came in handy lots of times, not just after fights.

I think everything might have been bearable if it hadn't been for the telephone. Calls started pouring in for Mark from the ambulance service and the doctors he hadn't paid off yet. It got to where no one answered the phone at all, and it rang and rang, echoing in the bare hall. Finally Mark ripped it off the wall and chucked it into a corner, leaving the wires hanging. Nobody even bothered to pick it up off the floor.

Old Man Garner had a fit when he saw it. "If you animals feel the need to tear up the telephone, you're certainly not getting another one!"

"Really?" Mark glared at him. "So if I feel the need to tear up the landlord, maybe we won't get another one of those, either."

Me and Mark went for groceries one evening after work. We were on our way out of the store when he remembered he needed a pack of smokes, so he ran back in to get it. I started checking out a display of rings in the window of the jewelry shop next to the supermarket. There were a lot of them that would have looked real sharp on Daisy's slender fingers, but I knew even the cheapest ones were way out of reach for me unless I was ready to take up a life of crime. I was so dazzled by the rows of shiny baubles that I didn't hear Mark coming up behind me.

He put a hand on my shoulder. "I see those diamonds in your eyes. You're thinking of a certain someone, aren't you?"

"Naw, just eyeballing," I lied. "It's about time you got through dawdling."

I turned away from the window, and we started walking home. Mark didn't say a word for a while. He hadn't been big on extra chatter lately, and I was busy with my own daydreams anyway, so I didn't think anything of his silence.

"You ought to take it slow with Daisy," he blurted out suddenly. "You haven't known her that long."

"What? Are you handing out romantic advice, all for free?"

"I just don't want to see you get hurt. You're awful young to settle down yet."

"And you're a wise old grandpa who has to make sure I know the facts of life." I grinned. "I ain't exactly on the fast track to the altar, but the thought has crossed my mind. There's just something right about me and Daisy. She makes life seem worth living, even with Mom and Dad gone."

"Yeah. I've seen you finally start to mend since she came along. But things have a way of going sour around here. The social workers will track her down sooner or later."

"They better put the ambulance on alert if they plan to take her. I'm a pretty fair hand at busting heads when I need to be."

Mark laughed. "You'll have plenty of backup if it comes to war. I wasn't trying to rain on your parade. But think real hard before you give your heart away for good."

I got the feeling Mark was a little too late with his warning. I chalked his doubts up to his missing Grandma. The future is hardly worth looking at, much less looking forward to, when your world is smashed in a million pieces around your ankles. Mark must have run out of free romantic advice because he let the subject drop. We trudged on home without talking. When we got to the Barn, he handed me a Coke from one of the sacks he was carrying and hauled the rest of the groceries inside.

I'd put in a long day at the candy store and needed a few minutes to myself, so I sat down on the porch steps. I had just popped the top on the Coke can when I saw the fat man in the dented green Jeep cruise slowly past the Barn. He stared straight at me for a second as he went by. Then he parked on the far side of the vacant lot next door and cranked his rear view mirror around so he could get a good look at the building.

I hadn't worried much about the spy in the Jeep lately because of everything else that was going on, but suddenly there he was, so close to home I couldn't ignore him. If the social workers had tracked Daisy to the Barn, it would only be a matter of time till they sent the cops after her, and I really wasn't anxious to deal with the crap her dad could stir up if he was on the prowl.

I thought about reminding Daisy to stay under cover while I was at work, but I didn't want to upset her till I knew for sure if she was in danger. There was no point in freaking her out before I had all the facts. She might decide to leave town or something, especially if she believed her dad was closing in on her. On the other hand, I cared more about her safety than I did about my wish to keep her at my apartment, and maybe it would be smart to find her another hideout. I didn't have the money to take her underground, though, and there was nobody we could go to for help because she was a runaway.

As I sat there mulling over the fix I was in, the future started feeling way too risky for me to face on my own. I got to missing Mom and Dad something fierce, and I had to scrub hard at my teary eyes with my fists. Parents are a pain in the butt lots of times, but things can get kind of tricky when they're gone and you don't have anyone to turn to if you run out of ideas. It didn't seem fair to me that when I wouldn't have minded being told what to do, for once, there was nobody around to give the orders.

I watched from the porch, sipping on my Coke and lighting one cigarette off the end of another, till the man in the Jeep finally got tired of snooping and disappeared up the street. My uneasiness didn't disappear with him, but by the time I'd cursed him and his line of ancestors clear back to the first ape that walked erect, I decided I better not say anything about him till I figured out what to do next.

The Jeep had been gone for quite a while when Daisy came outside to look for me. She settled herself on the steps beside me, and I took her hand protectively into mine. We sat in silence for a long time as the August evening started to cool down around us. I tried to stop the unanswered questions from tumbling around in my mind like clothes in a dryer. But I couldn't keep my eyes from darting up and down the block in search of the Jeep, and when a car door slammed in the parking lot across the street, my whole body stiffened, ready for action.

"What's with you tonight?" Daisy asked. "Something's got you wound up like a clock."

"It's been one of those days," I said, hoping the answer would satisfy her.

"Oh really? What have you been out here stewing over for the last hour?"

"I was thinking about my folks. They used to sit out here a lot, holding hands and watching the sun go down. I always laughed at them because there's nothing to see from this porch but a gravel parking lot and an ugly brick building across the street, and there they'd be, taking in the view like they thought they were in Tahiti or something."

"My mom was that way. She'd describe places to me, ordinary places like a flower shop or an empty field beside the interstate, and they'd sound totally exotic." Daisy fingered the silver cross on her necklace. "I wish you could have met my mom. She would have loved you."

I smiled. "Naw, she'd have said you were way too good for me. Did she give you that necklace?"

"Yeah. The night before she died, when I was with her in the hospice, she took it off and slipped it into my hand. She told me to wear it every day so it would remind me that God is always with me, even if I get scared or lonesome."

I laughed bitterly. "Do you really buy that religion crap?"

"Well, it seems hard to swallow sometimes, God taking my mom away from me and letting my dad keep on living and breathing, loser that he is. But I have to believe that somehow, to somebody, everything that goes on in the world makes sense."

"So God thinks it makes sense to snatch your mom out of your life and let my folks skid off a wet road and die in a ditch on their way home from the city one night? He has a strange way of doing things, I guess." I stood up, shooting another quick glance at the spot where I last saw the Jeep. "I'm starving. I'll fix us some sandwiches, if Mark hasn't wolfed down all the ham by now."

~~~

I didn't see the Jeep on my way home from work the next afternoon, but when Daisy said we ought to practice a little with her braille, I jumped on the excuse to keep her indoors. The braille was too cool.

Her slate, which was small enough to slip in her pocket, was covered with clusters of tiny pits, and the point of her stylus fit into each hole. She'd fasten an index card on the slate and then poke the paper down into some of the holes with the stylus. She worked from right to left, writing each letter backwards. Different letters were made by which holes she poked and which ones she didn't. That way, the back of the paper was dented with pits like the ones on the slate, and when she turned the page over, she could feel the braille dots on the front side.

I'd gotten pretty good at reading letters and picking out words with my eyes, but I couldn't get the hang of writing with the slate and stylus. Daisy was a patient teacher, though. She never laughed at me or made me feel stupid.

"You did a lot better that time." She ran her fingers over my latest muddle.

"Yeah, it looks like I wrote in English instead of Chinese maybe. Did I tell you I got promoted at the diner?"

"No, that's great!"

"I've been bussing tables there for almost a year, and now the manager wants to train me as a cook. She likes me, probably because I don't give her hell about that mustache of hers."

"You lived on hot dogs and frozen pizza before I came along, and soon you'll be cooking? I guess you're moving up in the world."

"Hardly. But I was thinking I might join one of those free study groups at the library and get my high school equivalency. I'd like to have my own restaurant someday."

"Right on. You can name the place after me, and then I'll be famous."

"It's a deal." I was surprised by the hint of excitement that crept into my voice. "You know, I never thought much about the future before, about what to do with my life and everything. But the manager says I have a natural eye for the way food ought to be laid out on a plate. She thinks I should go to chef school, and I kind of like the idea."

"I do too, Rick. Find out about those classes at the library, and I'll study with you if you want." Daisy wrapped her arms around me and gave me a quick kiss on the cheek, and her proud smile had me believing, if only for an instant, that I could do anything I put my mind to.

Then Tim flung the door open and exploded into my apartment, yelling for me. He seemed startled when I stood up right under his nose.

"I ain't deaf, Tim," I said. "What's up?"

"They hauled him in! I just now found out they hauled him in!" His fists were clenched so tight that his knuckles were white, and his eyes blazed.

I reached out and grabbed his shoulder. "Get a grip already. Who hauled who in?"

"The cops! That jackass Garner called the cops on my old man! They got him on child abuse charges!"

"Is he in the cooler?"

"Yep. Garner set the cops on him, and they did some digging around at the clinic where I got patched up." Tim had lowered his voice, but his face had gone as hard as nails. "Nobody sticks his nose in my business and gets away with it."

"What are you gonna do?" I tightened my hold on his shoulder, suddenly worried.

Tim had a mean temper. He smashed a window in a drugstore once just because the clerk accused him of lifting a pack of cigarettes. None of us were above swiping a pack of smokes, but Tim didn't happen to be doing it that time. So he whirled around and put a fist through the window, shredding the knuckles on his left hand and scoring himself a trip to reform school.

Tim pulled away from me and stormed out of the room, bellowing for Mark and the twins. He sprinted out of the Barn with the whole crew on his heels. We stood around watching while he flipped out his switchblade and slashed all four tires on Old Man Garner's van. He didn't even miss the spare above the back bumper.

"Worse happens next time, pal. Jack with me again and that fancy wood panel interior is toothpicks." Then, with a wild war whoop, the redhead snatched up a chunk of concrete that was busted out of the sidewalk and hurled it through the windshield.

Tim moved into my place that evening. He couldn't pay his rent without his stepdad's poker winnings, and the landlord was hounding him for money to fix the hole in the closet door. He couldn't get a job because of his broken arm, and none of us had anything to give him at the moment.

I was trying to keep me and Daisy afloat on a couple of paychecks that had barely stretched far enough when I was by myself. Mark was scrambling to get the doctors off his back, and Ed and Sharon had spent more than they could spare to fix the brakes on their truck.

"The fat's hit the fire now," Mark called as we lugged Tim's stuff down the stairs. "I think Garner's having a heart attack."

I glanced out the open front door. Mr. Garner and his girlfriend had pulled up in her white ragtop Mustang. The landlord was staring at his trashed van with his eyes bugged out. I wanted to go tap him on the shoulder and remind him to breathe. But he remembered on his own after a few seconds and charged up the steps and into the building.

"What in the name of red hot hell happened to my van?" he thundered.

"Who knows? None of us saw a thing." Mark walked calmly past him into my apartment with an armload of couch cushions.

"Those tires were barely a month old … and I just had that windshield put in last spring!"

Tim flipped him a coin from his jacket pocket. "There's a quarter. Call someone who gives a damn."

"You're liable to burst all the veins in your face if you turn any redder," Stace snickered.

The landlord forced himself to take a deep breath. "I've got insurance on my van, and I can't prove you did anything to it, Tim, even if we both know the truth. But I was thinking of giving you a break on your back rent, and there's no way in hell that's going to happen now."

"You had the king of the card table locked up before he got done teaching me his tricks, so I'm in financial meltdown anyway. Don't tell me you didn't know you were taking poker profits all these years." Tim lit a cigarette and blew a perfect smoke ring as if he didn't have a care in the world, but I could see the muscles in his face and neck tensing up.

"I did you a favor by getting your stepdad out of your life. What you do now is your own business. But you better cough up the rent you owe me soon, and the money to put a new door on the closet, or I'll take it up with the police."

Tim shrugged. "Go for it. Just make sure you have your tombstone bought first."

Garner must have known he was playing with dynamite because he let Tim stomp off into my apartment, shooting a few X-rated remarks over his shoulder as he went.

He turned to me instead. "You seem to be running a thriving motel out of your room, Rick. Every time you crowd another person in there, it's cash out of my pocket."

"Cry me a river. You have on that designer suit and all I've got is a Dallas Cowboys T-shirt with one sleeve torn off, and you think I give a damn how much money you lose? That's too much, even from a blowhard like you."

"Too much? If I don't fill those empty apartments soon, the county will shut this place down, and then you'll be on the streets."

"Yeah, and you'll lose your penthouse and your private john, too. See you at the soup kitchen." I left him standing in the hall with his mouth hanging open.

"You're getting to be a regular outlaw, Tim," Stace was saying as I walked into my overcrowded apartment. Tim didn't answer, and Stace jabbed him roughly in the ribs.

It was like teasing a sleeping lion. Tim sprang to his feet. "Back off or you'll be making a quick trip to the morgue!"

"Let's have it out right now then." Stace didn't always use his head.

Mark tried to shoulder the kid out of the way. "You don't wanna swing on him. Plug in your brain while you still got one."

But Stace had to bull on through, as usual, and he pushed past Mark and got right in Tim's face. "Who died and made you God anyway? You're just pouting because your stepdad ain't around to keep the moonshine flowing."

Tim struck too fast for any of us to stop him, and the next thing Stace knew, blood was gushing from his nose.

"Anybody else?" Tim shot a furious glance around the room. "Bryan, are you man enough or dumb enough to stick up for your bleeding brother?"

Bryan just shrugged, and Stace glared at him. "Thanks, old pal. You sure know who your friends are in a pinch."

"If you decide to pick a fight you can't win, don't expect me to join in." Bryan hardly looked up from his sports magazine.

I handed Tim my last can of beer as a peace offering and tossed Stace a paper towel. "Cool off, guys. We've all had it rough lately. It won't do us any good to take it out on each other."

"Rick's right," Mark said. "Let's get out of this dump before we all go crazy. How about cruising the Line?"

The Line is the main boulevard that cuts through the middle of Bertha City, making the border between the bad part of town and the ritzy territory. It's a long strip of fast food joints, convenience stores, and gas stations. It's a neutral zone between the social classes, so you see Cadillacs and clunkers cruising it together. I didn't really want to take Daisy out in the open with the stranger in the green Jeep floating around, but I couldn't think of a good reason to veto the trip without telling her about the spy, and anyway, I was dying for a change of scenery.

~~~

We all piled into Tim's car, and I drove up and down the Line, stopping in one parking lot after another so we could talk to chicks and people we knew. Tim found a bottle of rum stashed under the back seat, and since Mark had just cashed a paycheck from the filling station, he bought Cokes for everybody to chase it with. I cranked up the radio, and we laughed and horsed around, the way we always used to before our lives started falling apart at the seams.

The night was clear and cool—for August, at least. Nobody was in a hurry to go home, so when it got late and the gas tank was almost dry, I parked in front of a movie theater. We loafed in the car for a while, swapping raunchy jokes and smoking. I felt myself beginning to unwind for the first time in days, and I kind of liked the way Daisy had to press up against me in the cramped front seat.

Then, before I knew what was happening, the familiar green Jeep zipped into the parking lot and took the space beside us. The fat man got out from behind the wheel and made a beeline for Tim's car. I guess I should have been scared, but I was sick of playing peek-a-boo with him. If he was finally going to make a move, well, I was ready to see it. From the look of his scruffy beard and his dirty denim jacket, I figured he'd probably been living out of his Jeep lately.

He leaned in the open driver's window of Tim's car, and the whiskey fumes on his breath were so strong they made my eyes water.

"Well, if it isn't my Daisy," he said, smiling wickedly. "Ain't it time you came home, sweetheart?"

"Oh my God!" Daisy's eyes flew wide open, and the color drained out of her face.

"Who is it?" I demanded. "The Mob?"

"My dad!"

"Are you sure?" But I knew that was a dumb question as soon as it popped out of my mouth. I'd learned that Daisy picked up on an awful lot of what went on around her, even without her sight. She could recognize a voice after hearing it only two or three times.

I should have fired up the car right then and made a clean getaway, before the bad situation we were in got worse, and if I'd been born with a lick of common sense I might have done it. But I figured Daisy would jump at the chance to tell her dad once and for all where he stood with her.

Sure enough, she turned to face him, and her spunk was back. "I didn't know they let you loose."

"You do now. Bring your mutt and come on."

She shook her head. "I'll never go home with you. I told you that in the hospital, when the doctors and the cops said you couldn't see me anymore. Remember, the night they had to put a steel pin in my leg because you—"

"Shut up! This ain't about me. Your foster mother is gonna have a nervous breakdown if she doesn't get you back soon."

"How sad for her. I'll have to send her a sympathy card or something."

"I told her not to lose any sleep over you!" Daisy's dad slammed a fist furiously against the side of the car. "All you are is a stupid blind whore, willing to move in with the first punk who takes you in off the street."

"Rick isn't a punk!" Daisy's hand fluttered up to the silver cross on her necklace, and a hint of fear crept into her voice. "He cares about me, which is more than I can say for you. I wish you'd go away and forget you ever knew me."

"That sounds like a damn good plan to me." I started to roll up my window. "Get back in your Jeep and keep driving, jailbird. She's not going anywhere."

He glared at me, his face only inches from mine. "And who the hell are you?"

"Just some punk who loves your daughter more than you do." I felt a wave of anger rushing up inside me, but my voice was calm. "I wasn't around to stick up for Daisy when she lived with you. But she's mine now, and you won't lay your hands on her again, not unless you kill me first."

"Fair enough." His hand shot out to grab the handle on the car door.

I shoved the heavy door open so hard and fast it threw him back against the fender of his Jeep. I was on my feet and in his face before he had a chance to get his balance. He packed a hell of a punch for a fat man, but I remembered how scared Daisy had looked the night she woke me up from my bad dream, and I tore into her dad like I'd never done to anyone before.

The doors of the Jeep flew open, and three more middle-aged losers leaped out. I can get turned on by a good fist fight sometimes, but I hate it when idiots who weren't in it at the start make it into a brawl. Stace was a decent fighter for his age, but Bryan had never gotten much practice at it. So they teamed up on one guy, and Mark took another. Tim was having a rough time because of his broken arm. He could usually handle two at once and have a lot of fun doing it.

Daisy bailed out of the car and hurled herself at Tim's opponent when he scrambled past the open driver's door. She grabbed a fistful of hair and clawed at his eyes, and she didn't let up even when she took a few vicious blows to the face.

Tim cussed her out for having more guts than brains, but when the guy got her in a strangle hold, it only took the redhead an instant to free her. He drew back his cast like a baseball bat and smashed it down on the balding skull of his enemy so hard the plaster split clear in half. The dude with the thinning hair was out cold before he landed with a sickening thud on the asphalt.

Captain picked that moment to vault into the battle. He didn't sink his teeth into anybody, but his booming bark and the hair standing up on his neck stopped the action.

Then, before anyone had time to react, Daisy's dad yanked a pistol from inside his jacket and cracked her across the head with it. She crumpled and lay still in the pool of light from a street lamp.

I went berserk. I felled the fat man with a blow that seemed to surge up from my toes. As he hit the ground, I followed him down, driving both of my knees squarely into his flabby belly.

He grunted as the air rushed out of his lungs, and his grip on the gun loosened.

I grabbed it and checked to see if it was loaded. In that awful instant when I thought Daisy might be

105

dead, I knew I loved her with all my heart, and murder was in me. I jabbed the business end of the pistol into the hollow of her dad's throat while he quivered, gasping for breath, underneath me. My hand was steady. My mind was perfectly clear. My thumb slid up to cock the pistol. This was going to feel real good.

"You damn lunatic! You kill people with those!" Tim lunged at me from out of nowhere and yelled right in my ear, making me jump.

The pistol jerked sharply upward as he wrenched it out of my hand, and the front sight raked the fat man's throat and the underside of his chin, slashing him so that he thrashed around on the asphalt and bellowed in pain.

"I been shot! Jesus, I been shot!" he squalled, clutching at the bloody gash on his neck as I lurched to my feet. I stared down at him in disgust, wishing I'd managed to squeeze the trigger before Tim stopped me.

Tim flung the gun into the bushes at the edge of the parking lot. I turned fiercely on him, still half-crazy with rage. He must have seen the demented look in my eyes because he slammed a dose of reality into the side of my face with his balled fist. The blow sent me reeling, but it cleared my head instantly, so I didn't hold it against him.

Bryan and Mark picked Daisy up, and we bolted for the car, dog and all. I don't know how I ended up at the wheel, deranged as I was. Daisy came to, and Mark took off his shirt and tied it around her head to stop the stream of blood that was matting up her
106

curly hair and trickling down her face. Captain kept thrusting himself between Daisy and anyone who made a move toward her.

I drove like a maniac. Tim may have knocked the idea of murder out of my head, but there was still plenty of anger in me and although I didn't feel it, the rum in my veins probably wasn't doing me any good either. I dodged in and out of traffic, barely missing car after car and getting honked at and flipped off.

There was no trace of the Jeep anywhere, and when I'd gone ten or twelve blocks at top speed, I started to hope against hope that we had outrun the demon who drove it. I decided I better get off the highway.

"He's gonna kill us all!" Bryan shouted as I swerved suddenly into the far right lane with the brakes squealing, kicking up dust. "You're lucky you can't see this, Daisy!"

"Naw, she'd love it." Tim was high off the fight and the fast driving. "Really, lady, I didn't know what Rick saw in you at first, but you're not half bad. You fight like a fury."

"To tell the truth, Tim, I didn't know what Rick saw in you, either, but you're not half bad yourself." Daisy tried hard to sound cheerful, but she was obviously in pain.

I made a sudden right turn onto a side street, then another quick right that put me in a dark alley next to an empty warehouse. If I doubled back, I figured the fat man wouldn't have a chance of picking up my trail. After all, I'd gotten a big head start on him, and he likely had his hands full binding up his bleeding throat.

And then, to my horror, I saw a set of headlights bounce at the far end of the bumpy alley, and the Jeep was hurtling toward me like a rocket. A squad car rushed up behind me with its reds-and-blues flashing. The wail of the siren swelled in my brain. The Jeep raced closer for one terrifying second, getting larger than life before my widened eyes. My hands went white and froze on the wheel. Then there was the roar of impact and Daisy's shrill scream. Something bashed me on the skull, and I blacked out.

Chapter 6

I felt myself being lifted into an ambulance. Someone bent over me, shining a bright light into my eyes, and I looked up into the grim face of a paramedic. My mind slowly cleared as the ambulance sped toward the hospital. I was checked over and eventually released with only cuts and bruises and a killer headache.

As soon as the emergency room nurses turned me loose, a cop approached—with handcuffs. He must have had a good heart somewhere between his salt-and-pepper hair and his big silver belt buckle. When he saw how much it meant to me, he told me we could stick around to get word on Daisy before he took me to the station for questioning. He snapped the cuffs on me without making me put my hands behind my back, and we sat in the waiting room, each lost in our own thoughts. After what felt like at least a hundred years, a doctor appeared.

"It's about time!" I sprang to my feet. "How's Daisy?"

"I'll speak only to a member of her family," the doctor said. "No one else."

"Look, jack, her mom's dead and her dad ain't worth the trouble it would take to kill him," I argued breathlessly. "I'm the only family she's got. Please?"

He shook his head. "I'm sorry, kid."

"Not half as sorry as you'll be if you don't start talking!" I stepped toward the doctor, glaring. The cop was at my elbow in a flash.

The doctor sighed. "All right, I'll level with you then. She has a fractured hip and a shattered femur, and we'll have to wait till the swelling in her spinal cord subsides to find out if she sustained a loss of function in her lower limbs."

I stared blankly at him for a second, trying to make sense of what he was saying. Then the truth hit me like a fist between the eyes.

I gulped for air. "You mean she could be ... maybe ... she might be paralyzed?"

"Precisely." A flash of anger lit up the doctor's hard black eyes for a second and then quickly faded. "And even if she isn't, she's got a long road of recovery ahead of her. And all because of a few moments of sheer recklessness."

"I gotta see her!"

"Absolutely not. No visitors."

"I gotta see her! I'm gonna see her!" I took another step toward the doctor, not sure what I'd do with the cuffs in my way. "Cut the crap already! Where is she?"

The cop took hold of my arm and tried unsuccessfully to steer me toward the door. "Settle down. We're leaving now."

"Like hell we are! Not before I see her!" I yelled.

"Oh, what can it hurt? Poor desperate kid." The doctor motioned for us to follow him. "Ten minutes, not a second longer. Got it?"

Me and the cop hurried after him through the brightly lit trauma center. Hospitals give me the creeps with how solemn they seem underneath all their noise and chaos, and the way they smell like fear and disinfectant soap, and I had to swallow down the urge to cut and run.

"How's the driver of the Jeep, doc?" I asked.

"Dead." He dropped the word on me like an atom bomb, not even looking over his shoulder as he said it.

The spotless white tiles on the floor swam before my eyes. I felt like I was going to pass out again.

"She's in there." The doctor gestured toward a curtain on my left and kept on walking down the hall without breaking stride. "You've got exactly ten minutes."

I pushed through the curtain and found myself in a dim little alcove. The cop slipped in behind me and squeezed around the stretcher into a far corner where he would be out of the way, but he could still see and hear everything. I glared at him, then ignored him. Cops just don't have any decency sometimes. I mean, he could have stayed outside and given us some space, for God's sake.

Daisy was lying on the stretcher with her eyes closed. I gazed down at her for a long moment, too blown away to say a word. She had a blanket draped over her, so I couldn't see anything except her face, but that was bad enough.

A half a dozen bruises from the fight stood out sharply against her pale skin. Her golden curls were tangled on the snowy white pillowcase, and there was a gauze bandage above her left temple where the pistol had hit her. A few flecks of dry blood clung to her hair around the edges of the dressing. She was hooked up to an automatic blood pressure monitor, and some kind of clear liquid was dripping into her arm through the biggest needle I'd ever seen.

I couldn't believe things were turning out this way—because of me. Daisy didn't deserve any of what had happened to her, and it was all my fault. I wished to God that it was me instead of her lying there, bruised and broken. I wished it so hard it just about turned me inside out. But that kind of longing wouldn't change anything.

I'd learned that the terrible night I got the call from the sheriff about my folks. Grandma had rocked me in her arms like a baby that night and sung Spanish lullabies through the endless hours till sunup. I heard my world splintering again over the rhythmic hissing and puffing of the blood pressure machine, but there was nobody around to sing me through till morning this time.

"Daisy?" I finally took her hand, and her eyelids flickered.

"Rick?" She smiled, and I still couldn't get over the way that smile lit up her face.

"Yeah, it's me. I would have told you, but I forgot you couldn't see me."

"That's the best compliment anyone can ever give me, to forget about my blindness and think of me as an ordinary girl."

"You'll never be an ordinary girl to me. Are you hurting?"

"Not really, just drowsy. They've stuck so many needles in me tonight, I could pass for a human pincushion."

I tried to laugh, but the sound came out more like a strangled moan. "Listen. The doctor told me … well, he said …"

"That I might never walk again." Fear blazed up in her voice. "I want to walk! I want to run in the park and feel my heart beat fast, the way it did at the dance when you held me!"

I'm tough. I always have a plan. But that's with an enemy I can see and scare and knock down. I had sworn the night Daisy woke me up from my bad dream that I would keep her safe, but I couldn't do it. I was helpless and half crazy, and a lump rose in my throat. I swallowed it down, feeling like I was about to choke on it. Daisy didn't need to hear me cry, and neither did the cop in the corner. I leaned over and kissed her pale cheek.

"Don't get juiced up, okay?" I said as I drew back. "I gotta tell you. I killed your dad … when we were driving …"

"You didn't kill him. He was drunk, like always."

"Wait. Let me finish. You need to know that I …" But the words wouldn't come. I wasn't man enough to tell her how many times I'd seen the spy in the green Jeep, how many times I'd worried that it might be her dad, how many times I'd decided to keep her in the dark because I couldn't figure out what else to do. I knew I'd hate myself for it as long as I lived, but it would be pointless to dump my guilt in her lap just to make myself feel better.

"I need to know what?" she asked softly.

"That I love you. I never said that to anybody in my whole life, not even my mom and dad, but I wanted to tell you before …" I took a deep breath. "Before I have to go away."

"What are they going to do to you?"

I made myself speak evenly. "I'll probably get nailed for killing your dad, brawling in a public parking lot, drinking under age and breaking every traffic law on the books, and anything else the prosecutors can come up with."

"My God, you'll be locked up forever!"

"Naw, not forever. I don't have much of a police record, and the courts usually go soft on new criminals so they'll get a second chance to learn the art real well." I hoped I sounded more sure of myself than I felt. "Besides, your dad wasn't exactly innocent, either, and maybe I won't have to take the rap for his mistakes."

"Rick, would you do something for me?"

"Name it."

"Let me touch your face. I want to feel it under my hands one more time so I can remember it till you come back to me."

I raised her hand to my face, and her fingers moved gently over it. My nose was all swollen up from the wreck, and I had a nasty shiner on my left eye, but her tender touch didn't hurt me a bit. It felt good. I almost lost myself for a moment in the caress of her fluttering fingers.

Then she gagged violently, and a stream of horrid reddish foam bubbled out of her mouth and trickled down her chin.

"Jesus Christ, she's coughing blood!" I burst out.

I heard the thud of running feet outside the curtain, and in the next second I was surrounded by white coats. Somebody tried to elbow me out of the way. I made a desperate grab at the rail on Daisy's

114

stretcher, but by then the cop was in on the action, and I didn't have a fighting chance with the cuffs on my wrists.

He shoved me through the curtain and herded me steadily back toward the lobby.

I spat a few savage curses at him, but all at once I choked on the words, and they turned into hiccupping sobs. I bit my trembling lower lip so hard I tasted blood and forced myself to quit crying. You just don't spill your guts in front of cops.

"There's not much happening on the streets tonight." He nudged me into a chair when we got to the waiting room and then switched on the TV and sat down across the coffee table from me. "If you can sit still and keep quiet, we'll stay here and see how things turn out."

~~~

The twins came in a little later. Stace joked about how I was seeing double as they stood in front of me, but his chipper act wasn't very convincing.

"How's Daisy?" Bryan didn't even try to put on a good face. I just shrugged and shook my head.

"Rick, we have to tell you—" Stace faltered and trailed off.

"Spit it out!" I snapped.

"We're getting shipped off to Georgia tomorrow to live with our aunt down there. Mom and Dad said we should've gone years ago."

"They said this was the last straw and jabbered on about how growing up in the ghetto isn't good for kids," Bryan chimed in. "They swore we'd thank them someday."

"If we don't kill them first!" Stace smacked a fist fiercely into his other palm and added a few choice words about his parents.

"They're busting up our family?" I stared at the twins in disbelief. "Are you serious?"

Stace nodded. "They said they had to pull us out now, before we got killed or went to jail."

"I hate them! I hate everybody!" I chomped harder on my bloody lip. "Aw, I guess I don't mean that."

"We don't wanna go." Stace stared glumly at the floor. "We're being sentenced to life in a poky little one-horse town. There ain't even a movie theater."

"The cops questioned us." Bryan wouldn't meet my eyes, either. "What are they gonna do to you?"

"I don't know." I looked daggers at the cop, who was sipping coffee from a paper cup. "I don't care."

"We took Captain back to the Barn, so I guess Mom and Dad will figure out what to do with him," Stace said. "They'll meet us in Georgia as soon as they get up the money."

"Dad's waiting for us in the truck. Here's the address, and if you don't write, I'll come back and personally cut your throat." Bryan passed me a scrap of paper. We shook hands, and the twins turned to go.

"You two are the best." I stood up suddenly and gave each of them a quick, hard squeeze on the shoulder. "Bryan, good luck with your tennis. I'll write, I promise, as soon as I find out what's gonna happen to me."

I couldn't watch them walk out the door. I spent a second or two cussing out their folks under my

116

breath, but it didn't make me feel any better. So I pulled myself together and picked up a magazine, then tossed it back on the table. Hospitals never have good mags, not like drugstores.

I thought about all those nights in the drugstore when we flipped through the gossip mags and gave folks a hard time. Things wouldn't be the same without the twins. None of us could clown around like Stace, and Bryan was a great guy even though he was so quiet.

I leaned back in my chair and let my eyes drift closed, with my head pounding. I must have dozed off because I was startled when Mark suddenly appeared beside me.

He laid a hand on my shoulder. "Hey, Rick."

"Hey, Mark. Man, am I glad to see you."

"What's with those?" He pointed at the cuffs.

"New jewelry," I said bitterly. "I'll probably be wearing them for a while."

"How's Daisy?"

"Real bad off. Coughing up blood." I tried to shut out the memory of her pale face on the pillow, the touch of her fingers on my skin, and that horrible froth dribbling between her lips. "She may not pull through, from the look of it."

"And her dad?"

"I killed him, too." My voice had gone so icy I barely recognized it.

Mark shook his head. "Naw, man, you got it wrong. He was totally plowed. We all gave the cops the straight story."

"I'm going down the river, Mark." I could be honest with him. "I'll get a free ride downtown as soon as the doctor comes out with the latest word on Daisy."

He cussed in Spanish, then in English. "Nothing ever works out right in this neighborhood. Not ever. Street kids get it worse than anybody." He chewed on his fingernail, which he always did when something was bugging him. "Look, you're not gonna like what I'm about to say, and I don't wanna argue."

"Now what? I've had all the bad news I can take in one night."

"Tim got me a bus ticket north, and I'm headed to find work on the harvest crews. I've had it with things around here."

"No way! You can't do that!" I grabbed his arm and held on for dear life. "Come on, Mark, you gotta plug in your brain!"

"The bus leaves in half an hour. Grandma, she was all over me to study up on engines, and me and Tim were talking about opening a garage, but I should have known it'd be the onion fields or the pig farms in the end." He pulled his arm away from me and messed up my hair. "I'll never forget you, Rick."

"But wait! You don't have to ..."

He shoved a note at me. "From Tim."

"Damn it, Mark, listen to me!"

He bolted out of the room without looking back.

The note was scrawled on the bottom of a bus schedule. Tim's handwriting would make an unbreakable code for carrying war secrets, and my brain was scrambling around inside my skull like a fly buzzing against a hot windshield, so I had to read it three times in a dazed mumble before the words sank in.

I'm clearing out. I robbed a liquor store after I left the hospital, and I'll hop the next freight to God knows where. Don't let 'em beat you down, buddy. And if they stick you in reform school for this, take it from me, don't eat the eggs.

The last piece of my world crumbled to the ground. I was too floored to say a word. I wadded up the bus schedule and stuffed it in my pocket, figuring I'd get rid of it before the cops laid their grubby little paws on it. With Daisy fading and the crew cracked up, there was nothing to go home to, so I didn't give a damn anymore what they did to me.

An old man wandered into the waiting room and started flipping through the channels on the TV. He finally settled on a corny space movie, but he fell asleep in his chair before he'd seen ten minutes of it. The paramedics rushed past with a noisy drunk who had a wicked gash on his chin. The cop got up and poured himself cup after cup of coffee from the pot in the corner.

I stared at the black hands on the wall clock as they circled its white plastic face. They barely seemed to move while the endless minutes of that night stretched into hours.

It was almost daybreak when a little dark-haired nurse slipped up on me as quiet as a shadow. She perched on the edge of the straight-backed chair next to mine.

"I'm afraid it's all over, kid," she said softly.

I stared numbly at her for a second, hardly feeling the blow after all the others I'd taken. She tried to put an arm around me, but I jerked away.

"We did everything we could to save her. She weathered the first crisis well, and she seemed to be getting stronger. Then she threw a blood clot to the lung and expired in a matter of minutes." The nurse had tears in her eyes. Or maybe they were in mine.

"Expired! Like she was nothing more than an outdated milk carton!" Suddenly, wrung out of protests and pride, I slammed my fist furiously against the sharp edge of the coffee table. I pressed my mangled knuckles to my mouth.

"We tried to reassure her, but somehow I think she knew she wasn't going to make it." The nurse handed me a braille card and slid Daisy's slate and stylus across the table to the cop. "She wrote you a note. It took her a long time, and we lost her very soon after she finished it."

The nurse and the cop watched me curiously as I started sorting out the bumps on the card. I shot them a withering look, and the nurse scooted away like a scared mouse. The cop didn't budge, so I ignored him.

It took me forever to decode the message. I had to pick out the letters one by one and then write each word down, and I kept losing my place because my eyes wouldn't stop misting up. Finally I read the note straight through.

120

The people who love you are sparks that shine through the darkness from the bright side where I'm going, and no one can ever blow them out. You have your life ahead of you. Live it for me and the rest who believed in you, and don't give up, no matter what this world throws at you.

Dad had beaten me once and only once in my life, when I set fire to an abandoned house trailer with Tim just to watch it go up in smoke. I thought I could never hurt worse than I did when he got through with me, but I was wrong. Later he and Mom took me out for pizza and told me how much they loved me.

They said they expected better out of me than acting like a plain old street punk and knew I was going to do great things someday. Their words had made me feel guilty and proud at the same time then, and I could see their faces clearly now as I watched their big plans for me burn to ashes like the torched mobile home.

The first rays of morning sunlight were beaming through the windows of the hospital lobby. I saw something lying on the floor and bent to pick it up. It was a dandelion. I slipped it into the pocket of my T-shirt. Then I followed the cop out into the sunshine.

PART TWO

Chapter 7

That day drifted by in a blur, and it was definitely the longest one I'd ever lived through. The cops treated me real nice while they were locking me up, but I hardly heard a word they said. About mid-morning, they sent some shrink to gab at me. I didn't even bother to look at him, and after a while he gave up and left me alone.

I lay on one of the beds in my jail cell and studied the dandelion I plucked from my shirt pocket. When it started to shrivel up, I crushed it to powder between my fingers. Then I spent the whole afternoon watching the square of sunlight from my tiny cell window as it stole silently across the floor. I didn't eat. I didn't talk. I didn't cry. I was too numb for tears.

They threw this drunk in with me around sundown. He started carrying on right away about how his wife left him and his kids wouldn't talk to him anymore.

I turned my back on him. "Listen, jack, my life's gone to hell, too, and I'd just as soon cave your head in as look at you. I wish you'd shut up and save me the trouble of killing you."

He shut up and fell asleep. He snored and moaned all night long, and I lay awake, throbbing with loneliness. I still had Daisy's note tucked into the waistband of my jeans. I took it out and read it over and over by the sliver of light that crept in under the cell door, but Daisy had flown too far away for me to find any comfort in her words. Grief sprang out of the darkness to slash at me like a knife, and I kept my clenched fist pressed hard against my mouth most of the night to stop myself from howling.

I got hauled up before Judge Mills first thing the next morning. He was a thickset black man with solemn eyes and a lot of gray in his hair, and there was something about his quiet voice that let you know he wasn't a guy to be messed with. Well, neither am I. At least he didn't look at me like I was a weevil he found in his oatmeal, which most white-collar people always do to downtown losers. I had to respect him a little for that.

"Are you Richard Myers?" The judge peered at me over a pair of wire-framed glasses.

"No, I'm Dracula. Who do you think I am?" I had the old familiar feeling of walking around in a bad dream I couldn't shake off, and I wasn't in any mood to jump through hoops.

"Pull up that chair there and sit down."

I dragged the heavy wooden chair over and sat on the edge of it, drumming my fingers impatiently on the desk in front of me. I wished the judge would just start bawling me out and get it over with so I could be charged and put away somewhere.

"It seems you ended up in some trouble the other night. I want to hear your side of the story."

I shrugged. "I reckon the cops wrote it all down."

"I've read the reports. I said I want to hear your side."

"I got nothing to say."

He took off his glasses and looked straight into my eyes. "I'm going to ask you some questions then, Richard, and you're going to answer them. How did you meet Desiree Bettencourt?"

"Nobody calls her Desiree." I returned his stare with the coldest glower I could manage. "Her name is Daisy."

"Okay, Daisy then. How did you meet her?"

"At a baseball game."

"Did you know she was a runaway when she moved in with you?"

"Yeah. We talked a lot."

"Then she was a good friend of yours."

"She was my girl." I felt tears pooling up in my eyes and blinked them back, annoyed. "Look, damn it, cut the crap and tell me what you're going to do to me."

Judge Mills kept his gaze on my face, and the even tone of his voice didn't change. "What I'm going to do to you depends a lot on whether you get a grip on your mouth or not. How did you meet up with her dad?"

"He pulled into the parking lot where we were hanging out."

"And that's when the trouble started?"

I nodded. "He was set on taking Daisy with him, and she didn't want to go. So there was a fight."

"There had been a history of abuse, and he was ordered to stay away from her. Go on."

"He thumped her on the head with a pistol, and I went crazy and would've blown him away and enjoyed it, but a buddy of mine stopped me." The

125

memory of the gun in my hand and the fat man quivering on the asphalt poured over me, shaking me up since the moment had passed, and I felt beads of sweat popping out on my forehead. I hated the judge for that.

"Then what happened?"

"Everything is sort of hazy from there on. We put her in the car and took off. I was trying to keep her safe. Then there was a wreck, and I got her killed instead. Are you satisfied?"

"Where's the pistol?"

"I don't know. My buddy threw it in the bushes."

"You could be up against some pretty serious charges, Rick. I'm sure that's no surprise to you. There was alcohol in your blood when you were tested at the hospital, and you were driving well over the speed limit when the accident occurred."

"So bring on the charges then." The sadness inside me was giving way to smoldering anger, and I was getting real sick of this guy.

"Shut up and let me finish. There were a good many aspects of the situation that were beyond your control, and the man who deserves most of the blame died at the scene of the crash. You don't have much of a past police record, and you've weathered some heavy losses in your life lately. It has only been a few months since your parents passed away. Is that right?"

"It's been six months. And don't waste your time feeling sorry for me."

A spark of exasperation flared in the judge's eyes, but his voice stayed maddeningly cool. "You
126

have no legal guardian, but you need to be supervised for a while. I can't place you in foster care. An unrestricted family setting would be a disaster in the making, with your emotions as raw as they are."

"So what's your point?" I snapped.

The judge went on speaking calmly as if he hadn't heard me. "No formal charges will be filed against you. But because you are orphaned and you now have a track record of risky behavior, including underage drinking and reckless driving, you'll spend the next nine months in the custody of the state at the reformatory in Potter County. Your stay there will end when you turn eighteen in May, and I expect you to earn your high school equivalency and pass a driving safety course by then. I'll be kept advised of your progress."

"You ought to lock me up for good and forget about me. My life ain't worth a damn anymore, and it should've been me instead of Daisy who died. I suppose you can't change that, though, even with that fancy law degree on the wall."

Judge Mills reached across the desk and laid a hand on my shoulder. "I know you feel pretty low right now. But I'm giving you an opportunity to rebuild your life. I don't owe it to you, but I think you have what it takes to make something of yourself. Don't prove me wrong. Second chances don't come along very often, not for you or me or anybody else."

"Skip the pep talk." I brushed his hand away like it was a dead leaf.

"I'm going to end this conversation now, before your attitude makes me regret my decision to give you a break." The judge got up and disappeared through a door behind his desk without another word, and a cop came to take me back to my cell.

~~~

A van from the reform school picked half a dozen of us up at the jail that afternoon. The other guys started cracking jokes and horsing around as soon as we got on the road, but I fended them off with a few nasty looks, and before long they left me alone with my rage. When we had rolled down what seemed like a million miles of dusty highway, a gate swung open, and we turned into a wide gravel driveway under a faded wooden sign that said, "TEXAS STATE REFORMATORY FOR BOYS."

"Well, Mom, ain't you proud of your son today?" I whispered. "So you had big plans for me, did you?"

My roommate ended up being a guy who was in for stealing cars. He'd been around the block before, so he wasn't big on extra chatter, which was the only good part of the whole day. "What'd you get busted for?" he asked.

I didn't answer.

He shrugged it off. In silence, we put sheets and blankets on our beds and hung up our gray reform school uniforms.

Then the two of us trooped around the place with a bunch of other new prisoners, listening to a social worker gush all over herself about the gym and the library like we'd booked suites at a honeymoon resort or something. After that, we all sat in the mess hall while the warden rattled off a long list of rules. I didn't catch a word.

When the sermon was over, the warden stared hard into each of our faces. "We don't play games around here. If you keep your noses clean and try to better yourselves, you'll do well. If you don't, we won't waste our time on you. I won't think twice about sending any of you back to the courts to be gotten rid of, and the next stop is the state prison."

"You've really got me shaking in my shoes," I muttered. The warden glared at me. I heard a few guys snickering, but I ignored all of them.

I would have done okay if everybody had just left me alone. But some scrawny little moron dumped a bowl of boiling hot soup all over my arm in the chow line the first night. I knocked him on his butt without even thinking about it. They yanked my phone privileges.

"So what?" I said. "I got nobody left to call anyway."

The next afternoon, I had to sit through a math class. I slouched in the back of the room and stared at my shoes. I wasn't causing any trouble. Then the teacher fired a question at me. I shrugged and shook my head, but she wouldn't let it drop, so I threw my chair against the wall and stomped out of the room. They yanked my TV privileges.

"So what?" I said. "The reception's crappy out here, and nobody ever wants to watch anything except football and stupid karate movies."

The day after that, I was at the breakfast table. Tim was right about the eggs. They could have knocked a dog off a gut wagon. The same slob who had dumped soup all over me spilled a cup of coffee into my plate.

"Get the hell away from me, you damn klutz!" I yelled. He flipped me off, and I decked him again.

Then two cafeteria workers had me by the arms, and I was dragged off to see the warden one more time. They ought to have had the decency to let me walk on my own. I couldn't care less where I was going anyway, but I've never been one you could get through to by bullying.

The warden scowled at me from behind his big wooden desk. "Sit down."

"Make me."

"So you think you're tough. You've gotten off to a real impressive start around here."

The guy reminded me of my old boss at the candy store with the way his face was all scrunched up like he couldn't get a bad smell out of his nose. There was a heavy crystal paperweight on the desk in front of me. I kept from having to listen to any more of the lecture by imagining it crashing into his perfect white teeth. I pictured the gap in his grin and the blood dripping down his chin.

"I asked you a question!" His sharp tone punched a hole in my fantasy.

"Oh, yeah, whatever."

"I believe, Richard Myers, that you are what is known as a rotten apple. I won't waste another minute talking to you. You'll never be anything but a lowlife."

I didn't think it through. All I know is that red rage clouded my vision for a second, and then the

130

paperweight left my hand. The warden ducked, and it smashed through the window behind his desk. A couple of security guards jumped me from out of nowhere and pinned my arms behind my back.

"You just earned yourself a stretch in isolation!" the warden roared. "If that doesn't clean up your act, the state prison will!"

Solitary confinement was fine with me because I got a dreary little room to myself. There were no pictures on the walls, but I found a stub pencil on the floor under the bed and added my own X-rated scribbles to the collection of graffiti. I didn't see anybody for the first day except the kitchen helpers who brought me my meals, and I thought I was finally going to be left to rot in peace.

Then this pesky youth counselor started bothering me. He made me crawl out of hiding to suffer through a lot of lame therapy groups, but he couldn't make me open my mouth. I figured out that if I sat stone still and kept my eyes glued to a hole in the toe of my left tennis shoe, I could make my mind go totally blank and not be stabbed by thoughts of Daisy and the crew. Anybody who broke my concentration was asking to get his head bitten off.

A few days after I pitched the paperweight, I got herded into the therapy room with ten or twelve other hostages. The counselor told us all to draw pictures of how we felt about our lives. Then we were supposed to sketch in stuff we could do to make our situations better.

After a few sighs and grumbles, the rest of the guys started doodling away, but I didn't even pick up

131

my pencil. The blank piece of notebook paper on the long table in front of me showed how I felt plenty well enough, and there was nothing I could add that would make things look up for me.

The counselor parked his lanky frame in the metal folding chair next to mine. "You won't get a thing out of these therapy sessions if you don't participate."

"I didn't ask to be put through these therapy sessions in the first place."

"I understand how you feel. It's like there's a tape recorder going inside your head, and it keeps repeating the same angry messages over and over. But I can help you start a new tape that plays more positive thoughts instead."

"I don't know what makes you think you have a clue how I feel, pal, but I don't wanna hear about your tape recorders or your positive thoughts, either."

He leaned toward me like he was about to tell me a big secret or something. "Your friend Daisy wouldn't want you to be miserable. She'd be sad to see you like this."

I banged a fist down hard on the table, and a dozen bent heads snapped up around me. "If Daisy was here to see me, I wouldn't be miserable! My world's blown to hell because she's gone, and you can't fix it, so lay off your sissy dribbling and leave me alone!"

The counselor sighed and stood up. "It's pointless for me to talk to you if you aren't ready to listen. You might as well go back to your room till you decide to quit feeling sorry for yourself and start facing the future."

"Thank God! I've never been so glad to get booted out of a place in my life!" I made a mad dash for the door before he got a chance to change his mind.

~~~

I had some company that evening. I guess it was a last ditch effort to get through to me because the warden had pulled my visitation rights when I went into solitary. I'd just sent away my supper tray without touching it when a brawny goon in a security uniform opened the door to my cell.

Ed and Sharon walked in, smiling, as if they thought I'd be glad to see them or something. They both tried to hug me, but I shook my head and backed away, so they sat down together on the bed. I stood against the far wall with my hands jammed in my pockets. The guard leaned in the doorway, blocking my escape.

"We've been thinking about you, Rick," Sharon said gently.

"You should've thought about me before you busted up the crew."

"We had to do what was best for Bryan and Stace. Can't you see that?" Her friendly smile slowly wilted under my smoldering glare.

"Yeah, me and Tim and Mark were bad influences on them. So you had to yank them out of the only home they ever had before we got them arrested or buried. Is that it?"

"They're doing great in Georgia," Ed said, skating around my question. "Bryan's already got a spot on the varsity tennis team down there."

"Well, you must be proud as hell." I shooed them toward the door with a wave of my hand. "Aren't you ready to leave yet?"

Sharon bit her lip, and tears welled up in her eyes. "Honey, I know your life seems pretty bad right now, but it'll get better, I promise. Please don't shut out the folks who care about you."

I tasted hatred like dry dust in my mouth. "I had a family. You sent the twins away, and Tim and Mark split. I hope you can live with yourselves every time you walk into our empty apartment building. If my life turns out, which I doubt it will, it'll be no thanks to you."

Sharon stood up and took a step toward me, crying harder. "Rick, please! Listen to me!"

"Why should I?" I snarled. "When you hear a train whistle in the night, do you lie awake and wonder where Tim ended up? Do you worry about Mark, busting his butt on a harvest crew someplace without a friend in the world?"

Ed pushed to his feet, firing me a dirty look. "Rick, you better straighten up. You've been in way too much trouble around here. There was talk of sending you back to the judge after you tried to assault the warden, but we put in a good word for you."

"Save your breath."

He took his sobbing wife by the arm and handed me an envelope. "You might like to have this. We packed up the stuff from your apartment and rented a storage shed for you. We'll be on our way to Georgia the week after next."

They walked out the door without saying anything else. I paced back and forth across the cell for a long time with the rage inside me boiling hotter than ever. I finally tore open the envelope and found a snapshot of my folks. It had been taken last New Year's Eve at a party we got up in the Barn, and Mom and Dad were wearing matching paper hats and laughing, not knowing they'd be dead in six weeks. I shoved the picture into my pocket with Daisy's note and cussed Ed and Sharon up one side and down the other for rubbing more salt in my wounds.

Then I stretched out on the narrow bed without undressing and tried to shut off my mind, but recollections of Mom and Dad washed over me anyway. I thought of the times Mom took the crew out for ice cream before we got too old to be seen with her and the way the smell of her perfume stayed on the sheets after she did the laundry. I thought of the hours me and Dad spent shooting hoops and the little wooden race car we built when I was a Cub Scout.

I remembered how embarrassed I'd been the day I walked in on my folks while they were kissing and how I'd griped once because we didn't have a yard like some of the other kids at school. Dad brought a foil packet of marigold seeds home from the hardware store where he worked, and Mom helped me plant the seeds in paper cups. I sat by the kitchen window every afternoon for a week waiting to see the first sprouts pop up.

I wasn't sure when the memories turned to dreams in the darkness of my cell, but I woke up in the morning with red eyes and a splitting headache.

I was still sprawled on the bed when I heard a tap at my door, and an old Mexican lady brought me a breakfast tray. I waved the food away without even sitting up.

"Are you sure, *mijo*?" the lady asked. "You've hardly eaten a bite since you came here. There's French toast and bacon this morning."

I opened my mouth to holler at her, but the knot of white hair under her checkered scarf made me think of Grandma, so I just shook my head and stared at the floor.

"I'm going to leave this for you anyway." She set a carton of orange juice on the bedside table. She started to walk out of the room, then turned back and patted my hand with a shy smile. "I'll keep you in my prayers."

"Thanks." I didn't bother to tell her it wouldn't do any good. Her kind face got to me somehow, and I didn't want to hurt her feelings. But she took all the sunshine with her when she went away, and I was more lonesome than ever in the gloomy cell.

A few minutes later, a chick in a business suit opened the door without knocking and bustled into the room like she owned the place. Her blond curls reminded me of Daisy's, but her preppie look put me off right away.

I glared at her. "Didn't anybody ever teach you to knock before you bust into a room?"

She sat down in the chair next to my bed, leaving the door wide open. She wouldn't look me in the eye, and I knew she was scared of me.

"Good morning, Richard," she chirped. "My name is Dr. Kelly, and I'm a psychologist."

"Let's get one thing straight, doc. There were three ladies in the world who could call me Richard. Two are dead and one is on her way to Georgia and likely never to speak to me again, so I guess that makes none of 'em you."

"What would you like to be called?"

"I'd like to be left alone, but if you feel you have to bug me, my name is Rick."

"Rick it is then." She flashed me the cheesy grin you always see on people who are paid to be nice to you. "I came to talk to you because you haven't responded well to group therapy, and I thought you might be more comfortable expressing your feelings in private."

"So you're barging in to invade my privacy."

"There's a lot of anger inside you. I'm here to help you find a way to let it out."

I erupted off the bed. "I don't want your help! There's the door! Go on, hit the bricks!"

She stood up and put a hand on my shoulder. "Take a deep breath and yell as loud as you can for me."

"Clear the hell out!" I drove her to the door and shoved her roughly through it. "Am I yelling loud enough for you?"

"I'm going to recommend that you be sent back to Judge Mills first thing this morning," she snapped, dropping her fake smile.

"Why don't you just have the warden set up a firing squad right there in the hall? I'm sure he'd get a charge out of that!" I slammed the door and flung myself onto the bed.

That little mouse of a shrink had finally pushed me over the edge. I pounded the mattress and sobbed and swore till I ran out of breath. I took out the photo of my parents and Daisy's note and begged God over and over to let my heart stop so I could go to them.

God didn't finish me off. I don't know why I asked Him. He wasn't in the habit of listening to me anyway. I calmed down after a bit and tossed the note and the picture into the wastebasket.

But then I had second thoughts and reached in to get them back, and there among the dust bunnies and scraps of paper, I found a disposable razor. So God had listened after all.

I sat on the dingy linoleum floor for a long while with the note and the picture spread out in front of me and the blade in my hand. I read the note one last time and decided I was ready to see the bright side of darkness if I ended up in heaven. If I went to hell, well, it couldn't be much worse than where I was now.

I gritted my teeth and made a few quick, deep slashes across each wrist before I had a chance to chicken out. Then I leaned back against the Army green bedspread, fixing the image of me and my folks on the Ferris wheel in my mind. I closed my

138

eyes so I wouldn't have to watch the blood soaking my reform school uniform and trickling onto the floor in two widening smears. It felt like a year had dragged by when I started getting cold. Suddenly the room spun out of control, and I plunged headlong into a pit of blackness.

Chapter 8

I wondered groggily whether I was waking up in heaven or hell. Then I figured out that the beams of light passing overhead were the fluorescent bulbs in the trauma center at the Bertha City Memorial Hospital, and I was whizzing along on a stretcher. I was even a failure when it came to killing myself, for Christ's sake.

A white-haired doctor in the emergency room stitched up my wrists, grousing the whole time about how I was way too young to die, especially by my own hand, and how I was lucky because I hadn't lost quite enough blood to need a transfusion. After he finally got done sewing and scolding, he had me planted in the mental ward. I was still pretty doped up on painkillers, but when the heavy metal doors of the nut house slammed behind me, the sound sent shivers down my spine. I knew beyond a doubt that I had hit rock bottom.

I ended up in a little closet with bars on its one tiny window. There was nothing in the cell but a bed and a sink with a stainless steel mirror above it and a trash can on the floor underneath, but it didn't matter. I was getting used to staring at bare walls lately.

The room was right in front of the nursing station. I didn't care at first because I was so out of it, but the racket at the counter started to get on my nerves after a while. So I got up and closed the door. I hadn't made it back to the bed, which was all of four steps away, before the door was snatched open.

I spun around. "Hey! Can't a guy have any privacy? Shut that damn door, and make sure you're on the other side of it!"

"It stays open. That's one of the rules around here."

I glared at the tall, beefy nurse who stood as straight as a soldier in the doorway. "And who made up that lame law?"

She looked me right in the eye. "You tried to take your own life this morning. You've proven that you can't be trusted, so you'll have to be watched."

"Fine. Then will you all shut up out there so you can watch me sleep?" I went back to bed, and nobody shut up. Before long the nurse brought in a lunch tray. I wasn't the least bit hungry, but she said I needed to gain my strength back, and that was the truth. I felt as weak as a baby and kind of light-headed.

My plans for chowing down died quick, though, when I went to slice up the rubber chicken with the plastic knife and fork that came on the tray. I might as well have been trying to saw through the bars on my window.

"Got any decent silverware in this joint?" I held up the handle of the fork, which had snapped off in the chicken. "I'll starve to death if I have to get by with this cheap crap."

"No sharp objects. It's against the rules." The nurse opened my milk carton for me and turned to leave.

"Another one of your lame laws, Straw Boss?"

"I'm sure if you think real hard, you'll understand why we have to keep sharp knives out of your hands."

I flung the chunk of chicken at the trash can. It thumped against the wall, leaving a greasy spot by the sink, and then hit the floor with a splat. Straw Boss grabbed it up and tossed it into the wastebasket. I had to snicker a little at how disgusted she looked.

"You'll be attending a group counseling session in half an hour," she rapped out from the doorway.

"No thanks. I had enough of those mind games in reform school."

She snapped around to face me. "You obviously didn't have enough of them or you wouldn't be a patient of mine. If you plan on getting off this ward any time soon, you'll cooperate."

"How about some real clothes then? This gown thing you've got me decked out in leaves way too much skin free to the breeze."

"No street clothes. It's—"

"Against the rules! Why this time, for God's sake?"

"You're not likely to try breaking out of here in just that costume."

I went to the therapy session in the hospital duds. I refused at first, but Straw Boss flagged down two burly orderlies, and they told me I could either walk or be carried. I hadn't built up enough strength yet to take them both on at once, so I walked.

I spent most of the afternoon huddled in a hard wooden rocking chair, listening to a bunch of losers whining about their sorry lives and wishing I was somewhere else. I had only one thing to say. The counselor told me it was high time I joined in, and then the room got quiet and everybody was staring at me.

I shot a furious look around the circle of faces. "In case you can't guess it from my bandages, I'm in this dungeon for trying to kill myself, and I wish I'd finished the job. Then I wouldn't be stuck here while you people snivel all over the place."

"You won't ever get better unless you start thinking positive," said a sallow old lady with stringy hair. She twisted her bony hands around and around each other in her lap. They made a rustling sound like dry leaves skittering along a sidewalk.

"I don't need a nut like you telling me how to get better," I snarled. The old bat started crying, and all the other crazies glared at me like I'd stabbed my own mother or something.

After that, Straw Boss yanked me out of the rocking chair by one arm and marched me back to my room. "You're going to rot on this ward if you don't straighten out your lousy attitude in a big hurry."

"It's as good as any place else to rot."

I didn't even bother to glance at my supper tray. After a while, things settled down at the nursing station, and I fell asleep. I must have given the nurses a lot to talk about because I woke myself up with nightmares more times than I could count.

It had been bad enough when I had to watch my folks flying off the Ferris wheel and disappearing in the clouds every time my head hit the pillow. Now

143

my dreams kept replaying that last terrifying second in Tim's car when the Jeep rushed up in front of me and Daisy's scream of agony filled my ears.

I shattered the midnight stillness of the hospital when I shot bolt upright, gasping for breath and yelling out Daisy's name as I shook free of another bad dream. There were three nurses clustered around the dimly-lit desk, and they all busted out laughing and pointed at me. I sprang up off the bed and strode across the hall to face them.

I leaned over the counter and poked a clenched fist under each of their noses. "Listen, damn it, I ain't one to hit a woman, but I could lay out all three of you with just this thumper of mine before you ever knew what happened. I don't take it kind to be laughed at."

I turned and stalked back to my room. Straw Boss strutted around the desk and followed me in. She closed the door behind her, not quite slamming it.

"Who invited you in?" I demanded, climbing back onto the bed and reaching for the blanket.

Her starched white uniform swished in the silence as she flounced across the room. She bent down so her face was right up close to mine. I could feel her warm breath on my lips and smell her cinnamon chewing gum.

"You may think you're hot stuff out on the streets, punk, but in here you're nothing." The nurse jabbed me roughly in the chest with a meaty forefinger. "I have my own way of dealing with squeaky little ghetto rats like you."

"If you lay a hand on me, I'll have you hauled up in front of every suit in this hospital before breakfast."

Her lips curled into an ugly sneer. "And who's going to believe you? You're a mental patient, a nut case, a babbling lunatic. You slipped on a wet floor in the bathroom and got banged up, and the idea that I did anything to you is a delusion of your poor confused mind."

I stared at her, dumbstruck. This chick was totally serious. I've been in enough fights to know it's a big mistake to show surprise when you're cornered, but this was coming straight out of left field.

Before I could figure out what to do, the nurse snatched me up by one shoulder and slapped me savagely, laying a streak of fire across my cheek. Her fingernails dug into my shoulder, and between my shock and my weakness after the blood loss, I couldn't move. Again and again she struck, first on one side of my face and then the other, and I couldn't even squeeze out a whimper or a curse between my ragged breaths. After a while I drifted to a place where I heard the sharp crack of the blows from across the room and saw my blond head jerking back and forth like it belonged to somebody else.

When Straw Boss finally had enough of her game, she threw me back onto the hard mattress as if I was nothing more than an old wet newspaper. She washed her hands at the sink.

"Maybe now you won't be so quick to open that smart mouth of yours." She flashed me a nasty little smile and shoved two tiny pills and a paper cup of water in my direction.

I shook my head at the pills, still too numb to talk.

"If you choose not to take the medication by mouth, I'll be happy to give you an injection." Her nursing act was back in full swing, but barbed wire glinted just underneath the honey in her voice.

I've always hated needles something fierce, so I swallowed the pills without thinking to ask what they were. Straw Boss went back to the desk. I heard her say something in a low voice to the other nurses, and then they all guffawed.

I curled up like a caterpillar between my sheets and tried to stop myself from shaking. Both sides of my face smarted and ached like crazy, and my throat did, too, because it was all clogged up with silent sobs. I wasn't even hacked off at the nurse for what she'd done. I was way too broken up inside by then to get mad.

She was right anyway—I was nothing. There was nobody left who would cry for me if I died, and I couldn't even manage to do that. I slipped in and out of sleep for the rest of the night, and none of my bad dreams scared me as much as the cold hard facts of my real life.

It was just past dawn when I woke up for good. Sunbeams slanted through the bars on my window and fell across the floor. The nurse at the desk was lost in a magazine. Straw Boss had been replaced by a chick who must have been older than dirt. The skin on her face reminded me of fish scales, even in the gloom of early morning. I shuddered to think what she might look like in broad daylight.

I dragged myself out of bed and splashed water from my cupped hands onto my face. There were bruised patches on both cheeks, and the cold water brought the fire in my skin back to life. I could hardly believe the guy in the mirror with the dark circles under his sad eyes was really me. As I turned away in disgust, I stubbed my toe on the trash can under the sink and had a sudden flash of inspiration. God had put one razor in the right place at the right time. Maybe He would do it again.

I found two foam cups, a postcard, a bunch of wadded up paper towels, and the petrified chunk of chicken from yesterday's lunch tray. No blade. That figured. Things couldn't go my way twice in a row.

I was still squatting on the floor with the skimpy gown stretched over my knees when I heard footsteps behind me. I told the intruder to get lost without glancing up.

Judge Mills hunkered down next to me. "This isn't exactly what I had in mind when I encouraged you to rebuild your life."

I looked at him with dull eyes. "If I'd done the job right, I wouldn't have a life to rebuild."

"I see that." He turned one of my wrists over and frowned at the neat gauze bandage. "I would have been truly sorry if you'd done yourself in."

"Why?" I pulled my hand away. "I'm what's known as a rotten apple and a waste of time, so I don't need your pity."

"Sometimes you need somebody to give a damn about you when you don't have enough of your soul left intact to care about yourself." He looked from one bruised cheek to the other, and his frown deepened. "What in God's name happened to your face?"

"I fell on a wet floor in the john." I stared him straight in the eye, daring him not to believe me. I didn't want to think about what had happened last night ever again, let alone talk about it.

I could tell the judge didn't buy my story for a second, but he didn't push the issue. He took my snapshot and braille note from his pocket and laid them on the floor in front of me. "Your folks cared about you."

"They can't help me now." I turned the picture face down on the linoleum.

"Daisy cared about you."

"I got her killed."

"Did she teach you braille?"

"Yeah, and a lot of other things." I flicked a tear off my lashes. "Look, pal, don't you have a job to go to or something? Why does everybody have to bug me?"

"It's Saturday, so I don't have to glare across the bench at anybody today. May I read the note?"

That surprised me. Someone had respected my privacy for once. "Go for it. Where'd you get it anyway?"

"It was with the picture at the nursing station. A custodian found them next to you in the reform school."

"I printed the words above the braille so I could read it any time I want to, but I know it by heart."

The judge shifted his glasses a little on his face and read the note aloud. "The people who love you are sparks that shine through the darkness from the bright side where I'm going, and no one can ever blow them out. You have your life ahead of you. Live it for me and the rest who believed in you, and don't give up, no matter what this world throws at you." He laid the braille card back on the floor and added softly, "She's right, you know."

The sound of Daisy's words spoken out loud was like a kick in the stomach. "I should've died, not her! She wanted to live, and they couldn't save her! I wanted to die, and they wouldn't let me!" I tried to choke down the sobs that rushed up in my throat, but they tumbled out anyway. "Why! Why did she have to die? Why!" I started banging my head against the edge of the steel sink, not even feeling any pain. "I loved her, damn it! I loved her! I loved her!" My words blurred together into a crazed animal howl.

Judge Mills dragged me away from the sink and put his arms around me. I took a few swings at him, and he blocked them on one shoulder without saying a word or letting go of me. He was a strong man. I don't know how long we stayed on the floor like that, but I screamed and moaned till I didn't have much of a voice left, and he held me tight and let me rave on and on, blubbering all over his white shirt.

I finally came to my senses, and the judge retied the hospital gown, which had slipped almost all the way off my body. He propped me up with my back

149

against the wall so I could catch my breath. I'd given myself a nosebleed in my tussle with the sink, and he wiped my face gently with a wet paper towel and then dabbed at the stains on his shirt.

Fish Face darted in with a sedative and a paper cup of water. She held them out to me without really bothering to look at me.

The judge waved her away. "A little company will do more for him right now than your magic pills."

"His chart says he has shown a lot of hostility on the ward, Judge Mills. I was only concerned for your safety." The nurse's voice was as old and rusty as her face.

"I think I can handle him in his present condition, thank you. Oh, and close that door on your way out."

When the door had clicked shut behind her, the judge got me a drink of water and sat down beside me. "They tell me you were quite a handful in the reformatory."

"They're all buttheads over there anyway."

He smiled. "I won't argue with that."

My pride kicked in. "Now that I've made a complete idiot of myself, I wish you'd go away."

"Whether you know it or not, that tirade was your first step in starting over."

"I don't want to start over. It would have been better if nobody sewed up my veins at all."

"I'm not going to dignify that statement with an answer. It's true you've lost the people who cared for you, and your life is changed forever. But sooner or later, you'll have to decide what you want to do with the rest of it."

I held up a bandaged wrist. "I decided once already."

"I'd say you don't show much promise as a surgeon. You were about to train as a cook when the trouble hit. You could begin there."

"Me and Daisy talked about opening a diner, but she ain't coming back from the dead."

"There's no reason you can't open one yourself in her memory."

"Yeah, there is. I screw up everything I touch."

"What makes you think that?"

I laughed bitterly. "I washed out in school. Daisy's dead. The crew's busted up. The warden at the reformatory wants my scalp. I'm doomed to rot in the city loony bin, under twenty-four hour watch, no less. Shall I go on?"

"Would you like to know why I came here today?"

I nodded. "You were the last person I expected to see."

"I saw your suicide attempt in the paper when I was glancing through the police reports. I spotted a lot of potential behind your smart mouth when you came through my chambers, and it would have been a terrible shame if you'd bled to death on the floor of an isolation room at a state detention center. You deserve more out of life than that."

"You sound like my folks." I picked up the picture and traced my finger over the smiling faces.

"They told me over pizza once that I was going to do great things someday."

"You can't let them down." The judge read Daisy's note again. "You have your life ahead of you. Live it for me and the rest who believed in you. Daisy was a smart girl."

"Yeah, she was." I glanced around the dreary little room. "I guess she wouldn't be too impressed with how far I've come."

"Are you ready to do something about it?"

I stood up and washed the blood and tears off my face. It looked like whether I wanted it or not, I had a life to live—for the people who had believed in me.

The judge pushed to his feet and strode toward the door. "That's a good start. Now we better find you some real clothes. That outfit you're wearing doesn't leave much to the imagination."

Chapter 9

Judge Mills agreed to suspend my sentence at the reformatory, provided that I lived with him till I turned eighteen in May so he could make sure I finished high school and got counseling. I tried to beg off the counseling part, but he wouldn't give an inch. He rescued me from the funny farm and took me straight home with him. I never thought I'd have an address on the classy side of town.

There we were, though, slowing down in front of a big brick house with a wrought iron fence around it. The lawn was thick and green, and there were a couple of giant trees in the yard that looked like they'd been standing since the beginning of time. There were two wicker rocking chairs on the wide front porch, which had a border of bushes along it that dripped with pink and white flowers.

"My God, Judge Mills, I never saw such a nice place before," I said as we turned into the driveway.

He hit the button on his automatic garage door opener and pulled in next to the sweetest red convertible I'd ever laid eyes on. "When you're not facing me across a bench in a courtroom, you may call me Walter."

"Well, Walter, can I take your hot little Mustang for a spin?" I ran a hand along the gleaming fender of the ragtop. "Tim and Mark would flip over a car like this."

"That car is my wife's pride and joy. You'll have to settle for a bicycle right now. That's it in the corner."

I peeled my eyes off the ragtop and glanced where he pointed. "Cool, that'll work."

"You won't be getting behind the wheel of a car till you pass a driving safety course," he went on. "The city offers one every other weekend, I think."

I sighed. "Oh, yeah. I forgot about that."

"I didn't." Walter offered me a little grin as we climbed the porch steps, but I started to get the feeling that living with him was going to be a lot different than anything I'd been used to in the last few months.

I bet I looked pretty stupid standing in his living room with my mouth hanging open, but I could hardly believe the place was for real, and I was afraid to blink in case it disappeared.

The living room was just about as big as my old apartment. There was a soft brown carpet on the floor and a leather couch that dared you to sink into it and drown. A brick fireplace took up most of one wall, and a portrait of a guy in an Army uniform hung over it. I thought it looked kind of like a younger picture of the judge. The open windows let in the morning sunshine and the summery smell of the flowers by the porch. I felt almost high with freedom after the chokehold the reform school and the psych ward had gotten on me.

The judge's wife came bustling into the room, bubbling over with smiles and greetings. She was nearly as stocky as her husband, except he didn't have an ounce of fat on him, and she was a little on the chubby side. She sort of reminded me of Sharon with her cheery voice and laughing eyes.

She tried to hug me right away, but I put up a hand to stop her. "I ain't much into the hug thing, Mrs. Mills."

"Well, we'll have to see if we can fix that. Call me Alice. Mrs. Mills makes me sound much too old, don't you think? How about a tour of the house and then a big stack of pancakes?"

I would rather have drowned among the comfy-looking cushions on the couch, but I plodded after Alice anyway. The first stop was the judge's library. There was an antique writing desk in the middle of the room, and two walls were lined with shelves of books from floor to ceiling. I didn't know there were so many books in the whole world. I wondered if Walter had read them all and how he could sit still long enough to do it.

Alice pointed at a closed door farther down the hall. "The master bedroom is in there. Don't be afraid to knock if you ever need anything at night. I'm a light sleeper." She waved her hand at another door like a magician with a wand. "And this will be your room."

The double bed was made up with a dark blue comforter and a couple of big fluffy pillows, and the chest of drawers beside it held a lamp and an alarm clock. There was a desk, too, smaller than the one in the library, and I saw a stack of school books on it. The judge and his wife obviously meant business about my education.

"And now for the pancakes," Alice said. "You look a little pale, and it's no wonder after all you've been through, but I'll soon have you fixed up right."

"I'd really rather be left alone for a while." I was starting to feel smothered, and the grand house I'd suddenly landed in made me more homesick for the crew and my old life than ever.

"You may come back and rest as soon as you've eaten, but nobody goes hungry under the same roof with me."

There was no way to shake Alice off without hurting her feelings, so I followed her to the kitchen. The room was warm and homey, with flowered wallpaper and a matching cloth on the table. There was a china pitcher of daisies on the counter by the phone and a potted red geranium on the window sill.

Alice poured a few drops of oil into a heavy iron skillet to heat and got busy mixing up a bowl of pancake batter, and I saw my chance to give her the slip.

I sneaked out the back screen door and would have ducked around the corner of the house and scouted for a place to hide. But the next thing I knew, a German shepherd had landed in the middle of me, all wagging tail and muddy paws. I fought him off, then knelt down and started petting him. He took a few swipes at my face with his sloppy pink tongue and then rested his head against my shoulder. He looked a lot like Captain.

"I knew a dog like you once." I stroked the silky place between his ears. "I bet you're as smart as he was, too."

The dog dodged away and came back with a ratty old tennis ball in his mouth. We had ourselves a tug-of-war till my wrists started hurting and I had to throw him the match. He pushed the ball impatiently into my hand, then dropped it at my feet, panting with excitement. I scooped it up and tossed it for him. He was after it in a flash, weaving around a birdbath and a couple of leafy shade trees.

There was a glass patio at the far end of the yard. When I looked inside, I saw a swimming pool shining in the sun. I blinked. It was still there, as real as you please. Man, if the crew could see this place! The dog ran up with the ball and skidded to a stop on the flagstones of the back porch.

"I think Victor found him a friend," Alice called out through an open kitchen window. "That dog is all play. Come get your breakfast now."

I wasn't really hungry, but I made it through Daisy's famous raspberry pancakes with a killer hangover the morning before Grandma died, and I psyched myself up to put away another plateful while the judge said grace. I'd never heard anybody pray the way he did. He talked to God like he honestly meant what he was saying, like God was an old friend of his or something.

As soon as breakfast was over, I made a beeline for the couch in the living room and switched on the TV. I'd never watched a movie on such a big screen before, and it was pretty cool, but I dozed off after a few minutes and didn't pry my eyes open till the middle of the afternoon.

The judge and his wife were sitting on the front porch in the matching rockers. When Alice noticed I was awake, she asked me to join them for lemonade. I went out and plunked myself down on the steps with my glass. I felt almost human again after my snooze.

We saw the mailman go by, and I walked down to the box at the curb to get the letters. I waved to this shrimpy little rich kid who was flipping through a magazine by his gate.

He gave me a going-over with his eyes and started smirking. "I see the judge brought home another one of his pets. Why don't you slink back to the slums where you belong? You're nothing but an eyesore on this street."

I put a fist right through his snooty smile for an answer. That knocked him off his high horse. He tottered back a step, then lost his balance and landed on his butt in the gutter.

The judge cleared the porch and made it down the sidewalk before I took my next breath. In the same second, a lady wearing high heels and violently pink lipstick busted out of the yard next door, screeching like a fury.

"Walter Mills, you're ruining the neighborhood bringing those hooligans here! Look what he did to my David!"

The judge didn't seem too concerned. "This time maybe David will learn to keep his tongue behind his teeth."

"He's no better than a savage!" The lady jabbed her finger at me like a sword, and the jewels on her hand blazed in the sunshine. "My David could buy and sell his kind all day long!" She put an arm around her son, who had scrambled out of the gutter by then.

She took care to keep his bleeding mouth away from her silk blouse.

"Your David may be able to buy and sell my kind, but he needs his mommy to rescue him when a savage like me starts to kick his scrawny little—"

Walter grabbed my arm and flashed an evil eye that just about froze the marrow in my bones. "Mrs. Graham, there's no reason for you to stand here screaming on the street. I suggest that in the future you discourage your son from being so quick with his insults."

"I suggest you keep your charge on a leash from now on!"

David pulled away from his mom and threw a dirty look in my direction, which he could afford to do, since the judge had a tight hold on me.

I lunged for him with my free fist raised, but Walter dug his fingers into my arm and turned me firmly back toward the house.

"As for you, David," he said over his shoulder, "you need to get it through your thick head that you aren't better than other people because you were born with a silver spoon in your mouth."

The judge didn't let me loose till the gate closed behind the squawking hen and the bleeding peacock. Then we walked together to the porch. I couldn't believe he'd come down on my side in favor of a rich kid. It made me feel good.

But the good feeling didn't last long. When we climbed the porch steps, Alice took the letters from my hand and hurried into the house, and Walter settled himself in his rocker.

He pointed at the other chair. "Sit down."

"I reckon I'll just stand here."

"I said sit down." The judge didn't raise his voice, but he dropped the evil eye from hell on me again. I sat down.

"You're going to have to find another way to express your anger, Rick. That act you just put on won't cut it around here."

"And who the hell do you think you are, my dad or something?"

"I'm the man who pulled your butt out of reform school. You could be back there on assault charges before you ever knew what hit you."

I stood up and bolted for the steps. "So send me back. I guess I ain't good enough to set foot in your neighborhood."

The judge moved to block my getaway. "It's not that easy, kid. I'm not about to let you throw your life away."

He herded me back toward the rocker, inch by inch, and he didn't let up till I was parked in it again.

I spat a string of four letter words at him that would have made Tim proud.

He clapped a hand across my mouth. "We don't talk that way in this house."

When he took his hand away, I started to push to my feet again, pressing my clenched fists down on the arms of the rocker and ignoring the burning pain in my wrists. The judge stood in front of me, as still as an oak tree, and I had nowhere to go. Before I made it halfway through my upward thrust, he put a hand on my shoulder and nudged me easily back into the chair.

"Keep your cheeks glued to the seat, Rick. You're not tough enough to take me on." Walter stayed as calm as ever, but I've been around enough to know when to walk away from a losing battle. I leaned back in the chair.

He took his place in the other rocker and poured us both lemonade like nothing had happened. "No more fist fights. I want your word on that."

I shook my head. "He was asking for it, Walter."

"That's beside the point. While you live under my roof you play by my rules, and that means you won't lay a hand on David Graham, or anybody else, period."

Our eyes locked, and after a second I looked away. "Okay, I'll leave the schmuck alone. But I ain't about to apologize."

"I wouldn't ask you to." Walter's face softened. "There isn't a person in the world who is any better than you are. You can't pop some guy in the mouth for putting you down, but you don't have to buy into his crap."

"What do you know about that anyway, living in this big house? I could show you a whole different universe, and all we'd have to do is cross the highway."

"I know all about that universe. I meet a steady stream of guys from there every day, and I can tell the winners from the losers because I grew up in their shoes."

I stared at him, goggle-eyed. "You mean you came from the projects and ended up in a place like this?"

He nodded. "I did, and you can, too. I sentenced a good many of the guys you were in reform school with, and most of them don't have the gumption to amount to anything. But I saw right off that you have dreams. You just need a chance to make them come true before the world crushes them."

I suddenly thought of Daisy, turning to face me in a dumpy little city park on the bad side of town and telling me I could be anything I wanted to if I put my mind to it.

I stood up. "The world's done a damn good job so far. Can I go to my room now?"

"I have a better idea. Come with me."

I followed Walter around the house and into the glass patio where the pool was. I found out that day where he got his strength and stamina. He set the pace for the next half hour or so of swimming laps, and when I finally heaved myself out of the water, panting for breath, he was barely winded.

He tossed me a towel. "It's okay to be angry, Rick, but when you feel like you want to explode and clobber somebody, this is a better place to put your energy."

"Do you ever feel like you want to explode and clobber somebody?" I asked through the folds of the towel.

"You bet. I get to deal with the worst society has to offer most days, and there are times I have all I can do not to knock some mouthy kid right off his chair."

162

The judge grinned. "As a matter of fact, I had to swim a couple extra laps the day you sat across the desk from me. Now let me see about changing those soaked bandages."

~~~

I helped Alice with the dishes that evening and then hung out on the back porch for a while, watching the sun go down and petting Victor, the German shepherd. It seemed almost impossible that less than two weeks ago I'd been living a different life with the crew and Daisy at the Barn. It felt kind of trippy, like I'd dozed off on one planet and opened my eyes on another, and the only thing that hadn't changed was the look of the sunset in the western sky.

I knew one thing for sure, though. All the sleepless nights I'd put in lately were finally catching up with me. I was bone tired even after snoozing half the day away, so I decided to go to bed as soon as it got dark.

Alice met me in the hall outside my room. "Be sure to set your alarm so we're not late for church in the morning. I'll have breakfast on by eight."

I shook my head. "I don't play the church game."

"It's not a game, Rick. The Mills household attends the Bertha City Church of Christ every Sunday morning."

"We got us a problem then." I felt my mouth drawing down into a stubborn scowl. "I'll pitch in with the dishes and try to keep from slugging your snooty little neighborhood kids. I'll watch my language and step outside to smoke and even put up with a hug once in a while. But the next time somebody hauls me into a church, I'll be in a coffin or a straitjacket."

I walked past Alice into my room, hoping to end the conversation right there, but she slipped in behind me before I got the door closed. She sat down on the bed.

I stood facing her with my hands jammed in my pockets. "I ain't meaning to be rude, but I won't give in this time, even if you get me sent back to reform school."

"I'm not going to get you sent anywhere." She patted the bedspread next to her. "Sit here and we'll talk about it."

"There's nothing to talk about."

"Well, sit here anyway."

I perched reluctantly on the edge of the bed, figuring I owed Alice that much. She'd been awfully nice to me.

"Okay." She folded her hands comfortably in her lap. "You don't want to go to church. That much is pretty clear. Can you tell me why not?"

"Sure." I laughed bitterly. "God snagged my folks last Valentine's Day so they could join some stupid choir in heaven. I didn't appreciate it."

"Who told you that?"

"The preacher at their funeral. And I know for a fact neither one of them could sing a note if you paid them to."

"Sometimes people with kind intentions say ridiculous things." Alice stared solemnly into my eyes. "God didn't take your parents to heaven so they

164

could sing in a choir. The preacher made that up. He tried to draw a pretty picture in your mind, hoping he could ease your sadness a bit, that's all."

"Yeah? What was God after then?" I looked down at my holey tennis shoes. "I needed my folks, you know. My life might still be in one piece if they hadn't died."

"God didn't make them die. Their brakes failed on a wet road. It's that simple."

"While God was off watching the news or something?" I demanded. "And what about Daisy? She wore a necklace with a silver cross on it every single day, and she said her mom told her to remember that God would always be with her. Is that why she drowned in her own blood one night while I prayed for her as hard as I could? I don't pray, but I did then, for all the difference it made."

"Bad things happen to everybody, honey, there's no way around that. God doesn't make them happen. The world is just real unfair now and then." Alice took my hand and held it tight. "What God gives us is a choice, a way to live with hope instead of sorrow."

"Whatever." I shrugged, not really understanding a word she said. "The only thing God ever gave me was the razor to slit my wrists, and even that didn't work out right."

"It worked out perfectly. The custodian found you before you bled to death, and I'm glad she did. You will be too, sooner or later."

"Don't bet on it." I shifted impatiently on the bed. "Anyway, forget the church thing. It's not gonna happen."

"Okay, I won't make you go," Alice said. "But I plan on putting a batch of cinnamon rolls in the oven at sunup. So unless you want Walter to beat you to the feast, you better set your clock for breakfast."

"It'll take more than that little ticker to rouse me up." I offered her a grateful smile. "Give me a yell on your way past my door in the morning, would you?"

I lapsed into a coma the moment my head hit the pillow that night, and the next time I opened my eyes, the window in my room was bright with sunshine. The smell of hot cinnamon rolls filled the air, making my mouth water, but I didn't get up right away. I stretched out under the soft blue comforter for a few minutes, feeling lazy and peaceful, sort of like I used to feel when I woke up and saw my folks sipping coffee on the couch in our old apartment with the Sunday paper spread between them.

Alice waited till she was on her way out the door to ask me if I would tend her pot roast while she was at church.

I shook my head and gave her a pleading look. "I'd like to help, Alice, but I'll screw it up. I've never done anything like that before."

"Oh, it's easy." She opened up the roaster and spooned the pan juices over the meat and vegetables. "That's all you have to do, every twenty minutes or so."

When I was alone in the kitchen, I got bored and started flipping through a cookbook Alice had left open on the table. It had all kinds of cool pictures in it, and I found a page that showed how to make a real fancy salad with radishes cut like roses. Just for

166

kicks, I dug some radishes out of the fridge and tried my hand at making the flowers. The first couple I carved were pretty lopsided, so I ate them and tried again, and in a while I had the whole salad fixed up exactly like the picture. I stood back to check out my work. As I reached to straighten a piece of yellow pepper, Walter and Alice walked in the door.

"Hey, that looks really good." The judge dropped his suit coat on a chair and popped a radish in his mouth.

I felt my ears burning. "I was just messing with something I saw in the cookbook. I guess I should have asked first."

"The food in my kitchen is always free for the taking." Alice lifted the lid off the roasting pan. "You did a good job with the meat, too. I think it's about ready to eat."

Chapter 10

Alice took me to get signed up at the high school on the ritzy side of town the next morning. It was a grand building with vaulted ceilings and tall stone pillars at the doors, and most of the kids there were dressed a lot sharper than I was. School would be a drag whether they held it in a palace or a pool hall, and I felt like a traitor joining up with my lifelong enemies, so the only thing I really liked about the trip with Alice was the ride in her classic '67 Mustang.

I had to take a few extra classes to make up for the ones I failed after Mom and Dad died. I got me a job flipping burgers in the cafeteria, and they set it up so I could skip out of study hall every Tuesday afternoon to see my counselor. I wasn't thrilled about having a counselor, but I found out the guy Walter hooked me up with wasn't into the mushy head trip stuff I'd hated so much in reform school. He talked to me like I was a regular person instead of somebody he got paid to pick apart. I started opening up to him bit by bit, and it actually made me feel a little better to say Daisy's name out loud instead of screaming it all the time inside my head.

"I'd like you to begin keeping a journal," the counselor said one afternoon.

"What's that?"

"You just spend a few minutes every day jotting down your thoughts about the world. It's a place where you can say anything you want without worrying about how it sounds to other people. I'll give you a brand-new notebook to start in."

I tried writing in the notebook, but I felt like some kind of a basket case rambling on to myself, and all I came up with was a bunch of chicken scratch. The counselor said I ought to make up letters to Daisy and the crew, but I put the squash on that idea right away. I couldn't stand the thought of writing letters when there was nobody to send them to. So he gave up the journal scheme and just pumped me with questions about my old life and helped me start to get used to my new one.

I took to swimming laps every evening with the judge once the bandages came off my wrists, and when I got home from school each afternoon, Alice had a snack ready for me. Most days I did my homework at the kitchen table while she puttered around the room and hummed hymns to herself.

She kept real busy in her church and was always baking for one affair or another. Sometimes she asked me to measure or mix something for her, and she taught me how to decorate cakes and cookies with a pastry bag. She had a bunch of different tips to squeeze the frosting through, and each tip made its own particular design because of the way it was shaped. I got pretty good at making fancy patterns out of stars and squiggles.

One day I sat at the table, fighting an uphill battle with a column of fractions. A breeze ruffled the curtains at the kitchen windows, and I was itching to be out in the fresh September air. Fall has always been my favorite time of year, and I get to feeling like the ceiling is coming down on me when I'm shut up indoors, especially in school, for a long stretch in any season.

When I couldn't stand it anymore, I slammed the book shut and lobbed it across the room. "To hell with that steaming pile of—" I clapped a hand over my mouth. "Sorry, Alice."

She picked up the book and glanced at the page I had marked with a paper clip. "I see you're having a hard time."

"Me and math never were on friendly terms. I swear those numbers jump around the page like a pack of grasshoppers every time I look away."

"Well, forget this for a while. Come help me put together a fruit plate for the church luncheon tomorrow."

Slicing up the fruits must have unscrambled my head somehow because after I hacked a couple zillion peaches and pears into wedges, the halves and fourths and eighths seemed to make a little more sense.

It was hot and stuffy in the house that night, so we ate supper at the picnic table in the back yard. The tree branches rustling overhead got me feeling more fidgety than ever.

"There's a new space flick at the dollar theater," I said. "I think I'll catch the late show tonight."

"You've got a big math test tomorrow," Alice reminded me. "The movie will still be playing this weekend."

"Up yours, Alice!" I burst out. "In case you forgot, you're not my damn mom!"

"She's not your mom, but she is my wife, and she won't be spoken to like that in this house." The judge's even tone made me wonder how far he had to be pushed before he lost his cool and yelled loud enough to shatter glass.

"Screw you, too. The last thing I need is another set of parents, so get the hell off my back already."

They both stood up at once and made their way toward the kitchen door with their dishes.

"You're welcome to come in when you decide you can be fit company." Walter shut the door behind him.

I sat there fuming to myself for a long while, glaring at the closed kitchen door. I thought about ducking out the back gate and making tracks for the movie theater, but I lit me up a smoke first, and before I was done with it, Victor came and rested his chin on my knee. I scratched his ears and gave him a few scraps of pork off my plate.

"I don't know what they're breathing down my neck for," I griped out loud to the dog. "So what if there's a big math test in the morning? I never gave a damn about math anyway, and I don't need nobody telling me how to run my life. What do they think, I'm still in diapers or something? It's a drag, staying cooped up in this strange house all the time and—"

I trailed off, suddenly embarrassed, as I heard how stupid and selfish I sounded. The judge and his wife were bending over backwards for me. I couldn't even guess at their reasons for it, but in a way it was nice that they cared so much. I put out my cigarette and stuck the butt in my shirt pocket, then took my plate into the kitchen.

Alice was almost finished loading the dishwasher. She flashed me a friendly smile like I'd never snapped at her.

I rinsed my plate and handed it to her. "Sorry about all that out there. It's just hard to get used to taking orders again."

She measured soap into the machine and fired it up. "Talking to Victor is a good way to clear your mind. I bend his ear a lot when I get in a bother about something."

"He's a cool dog. Where'd you get him?"

"He came from a school out in California. They breed shepherds and retrievers to train as guides for the blind, and the ones who aren't suited for the job are adopted out as pets. Victor would sooner goof off than put in an honest day's work of any kind."

"Daisy had a guide dog from a school in California. The twins' folks sent him back after she died, so I guess he's probably steering somebody else around by now."

The judge called me into his library and drilled me on fractions till I had them down pat. I went to bed that night all psyched up to ace the test.

Alice wished me luck the next morning and waved to me from the front porch as I took off on my bike. I felt sure of myself all the way to school, but when I pulled into the parking lot, I got cold feet. One look at the fancy brick building and the noisy mob of rich kids milling around the entrance was enough to tell me I couldn't drag myself in there to suffer through a math test and then face the mountains of frozen hamburger patties waiting in the

172

kitchen. I got back on the bike and hit the road before anybody saw me.

I rode hard for a long time, not paying much attention to what I zipped by. It felt good to be out on the streets again with the wind in my face and nobody bugging me. I crossed the Line on a pedestrian bridge, and pretty soon I ended up in front of the drugstore where I used to hang out with the crew. I thought about going inside to see if the old man who chased us off with the baseball bat was still breathing fire. But it stabbed at me to remember the good times me and the guys had there, horsing around and flipping through the gossip mags, and I sped away without looking back.

Cruising my old neighborhood ripped the scabs off the wounds inside me. I felt worse and worse as I pedaled up and down the streets. I passed the gas station where Mark used to work and the clinic where we took Tim the day his stepdad beat him up. I buzzed around the park where me and Daisy had talked about dances and dandelions. Once it had been paradise, but now it was just a windswept patch of litter and loneliness.

I rested for a while at the playground where me and Tim rescued the little girl from the kids with rocks. I watched two guys playing tennis on one of the courts across from the pool. Bryan could have clobbered them both with one hand tied behind his back.

Finally I coasted to a stop in front of a liquor store. Maybe I couldn't plug up the empty hole in my heart forever, but at least I knew how to numb out the

173

ache for a while. There was a drunk camped out on the curb.

I tossed him a bill from my jeans pocket. "Go in there and get me a fifth of Jack. The change is yours."

He shuffled out of the store after a minute and handed me a paper sack, mumbling what I took to be a word of thanks. I ducked into a gravel alley and found myself a private spot behind an empty garbage bin, and me and Jack Daniels settled down for another rap session. When my vision got blurry, I closed my eyes and saw Daisy's face on the inside of my eyelids. Her voice floated to me from somewhere far away, and the sound of her laughter started to lull me to sleep.

I guess I stayed dead to the world for quite a while because the next thing I knew, it was almost dark. Big fat drops of rain beat down on me, and my wet clothes stuck to my body. In no time, I was shivering violently. My teeth started chattering so hard I felt like my face might fall off if I didn't keep one hand tucked up under my chin.

I slumped against the garbage can with my bike beside me, cursing the gusty wind and the glowering sky, till I decided facing the music at the Mills house would be better than freezing to death in an empty alley. I hauled myself to my feet, clinging to the trash bin and breathing heavily. When I finally felt steady enough to stamp life back into my numb legs, I got on the ten-speed and started for home.

The gravel in the alley was rutted and slippery, and my shaky balance on the bike didn't help me any as I wobbled toward the wet street. When I got there, the pavement looked like it was swimming under my wheels in rolling waves. I hadn't put the first block behind me before I had to stop and throw up in the gutter. It took me ages to make it back across the highway because I never got far between bouts of retching. Every few minutes, some jerk would wave or honk at me and drench me with a shower of muddy water as he swooped by in his car.

Eventually I piled up the ten-speed during a bad dizzy spell and tore the skin off one side of my face. Everybody knows drunk driving is a dumb idea, but believe me, getting plastered and trying to ride a bike doesn't work out much better.

Anyway, it was real late by the time I got to the judge's house, dragging the wrecked bike along behind me. I paused at the front gate and almost didn't have the guts to go through it. The porch light was on, and I saw shadows moving behind the curtains in the living room. I took a deep breath and pushed my dripping hair back from my face. Then I stumbled up the sidewalk and dropped the bike at the foot of the porch steps. I had to give myself another pep talk before I got up the nerve to open the door.

Walter and Alice were sitting on the couch holding hands. Alice jumped up as soon as she saw me. The strained look in her eyes cleared my head like a clap of thunder.

"Rick, thank God! I was worried sick!" She put her arms around me and held me tight for a second, then stepped back, frowning. "Oh, honey, your face is bleeding. And your breath—you got drunk, didn't you?"

"Yeah, kind of. I'm awful sorry, Alice." And I really was. I'd forgotten how it felt to have someone give a damn if you made it home or not. "And now I got mud all over your housecoat and your carpet, too."

"Never mind the mud. You made it home. That's the main thing." Alice's voice shook a little, and she wiped a few tears off her cheeks with the back of her hand. Then, still eyeing the cut on my cheek, she went and sat beside Walter again. He hadn't moved a muscle since I walked in.

I stood where I was and studied the expression on his face, but I couldn't tell what he was thinking. Finally, I said, "Go on, start in on me."

"I don't need to say a word. You look like you've been through a war."

I didn't have a chance to answer because I had to make a quick exit right then to do some more heaving into Alice's flower beds.

The judge followed me out onto the porch. "How did the math test go?"

"It didn't. I couldn't face it, Walter."

"Then you'll have to face the damage to your grade, which is too bad because you worked hard to get ready for the test."

"No sweat. I've always been good at failing in school."

He bent over the broken bike. "It's high time you set a new standard for yourself. Anybody can fail without even trying, but it takes a whole lot of grit and hard work to make a success of something."

I pressed my throbbing head between my hands. "Those rich kids over there look at me like I'm an alien, and I missed the crew and—"

"I don't want to hear your excuses. You better clean yourself up and hit the sack." The judge picked up the ten-speed and turned toward the garage. "You'll have to get an early start in the morning because you'll be on foot till we put your bike back together. Take off those muddy shoes out here so you don't track up the floor."

Alice cornered me in the bathroom with a bottle of peroxide and a cotton swab. The scrape on my cheek stung like the devil as she cleaned it out. So to keep myself from wincing or swearing, I told her how Grandma always made us guys choke down nasty herb teas when we got skinned up.

Alice grinned. "She probably hoped the bitter taste of her brews would teach you to be more careful."

"I never thought of that. Grandma was a sweetheart, but she was a crafty one. I wouldn't put a sly scheme like that past her." I laughed out loud. "We all must have been pretty dense, though, because it never kept any of us out of trouble."

Alice pressed a bandage onto my cheek. "There. You'll look like a desperate character for a while, but I don't think you'll have a permanent scar."

I peered at myself in the mirror above the sink. "Say, Alice, have you ever pruned hair? I might look a little more civilized if I wasn't so bushy around the face."

Alice trimmed my bangs right then and there, and she took me to buy some decent clothes when I cashed my next paycheck. Nothing else was ever said about what happened that night, but I always made it a point to tell the judge or his wife where I was after that so I wouldn't have to see tears of worry in Alice's eyes again.

Me and Walter fixed the bike in his workshop behind the garage, and I paid him back for the parts we needed out of my burger flipping money. I started getting used to the empty ache that flared up in me whenever I thought about the crew. I wondered at least a hundred times a day how the guys were all doing.

Then right before Thanksgiving, a letter from the twins came to me by way of the reformatory. It was leaning up against my glass of lemonade when I got in from school. I dropped my books on the table and pounced on the envelope. I couldn't get it ripped open fast enough.

Bryan wrote all about how much he liked his new school. He was shooting for a spot on the Honor Roll and had already won gobs of ribbons and trophies for the varsity tennis team. He'd even hooked up with a girl who went as crazy over sports as he did, although she was a swimmer instead of a tennis freak.

Stace wasn't so thrilled with his situation. He hated the town he'd been dragged to, the school he was stuck in, his parents, his aunt and uncle, and everything else he could think of. He said he'd met more hicks in the last few months than he could ever hope to count, and everybody was always harping on

178

him to be like Bryan and make good grades. He missed the crew and wished he could come home.

I scratched off an answer right there at the kitchen table. I told Bryan not to kill himself studying and not to let the mermaids on the swim team take his mind off his tennis game. I said I knew what Stace was going through, trying to fit into a new life and everything. Then I filled up the rest of the page with stuff about the judge and his wife and their big house.

At the end of the note, I asked the twins to tell their folks I felt bad about the way I lit into them when they visited me at the reform school.

I went into Walter's library after supper to put a stamp on my letter. The judge was thumbing through a thick book with his bare feet propped up on his desk.

"It's like a miracle hearing from Bryan and Stace again." I sealed my letter and snagged a peppermint from the jar on the window sill. I can't stand the taste of the glue they use on envelopes. "I've missed the crew something awful, but I came down pretty hard on Ed and Sharon when they dropped by the reform school, so I didn't think they'd let the twins have anything more to do with me."

"It'll do you good to write to them." Walter took a sip of coffee and adjusted his reading glasses. "Put your letter in my briefcase. I'll mail it on my way to work in the morning."

"Thanks." I glanced around the room at the shelves of books. "Have you read all these, Walter? I've never seen so many books in one place."

"I've at least skimmed most of them. You're welcome to browse in here any time."

I shrugged. "I'm not big on reading when I don't absolutely have to."

"Those volumes on the bottom row are ones I've had since I was a kid." The judge slid his feet off the desk and stood up. He pulled a dusty paperback off the shelf. "You might enjoy this one. I bet you'd get a kick out of Mark Twain."

I backed toward the door, wishing I'd never opened my big mouth. *The Adventures of Huckleberry Finn* looked way too fat for my liking.

"How about we read it aloud? I'll read a chapter, then you read one." The judge was beaming like a kid at a carnival, so I knew I wouldn't get away easily.

I sat down in the leather armchair by the window. Walter started reading right away. He was really good at it. I liked the sound of his voice, and Huck Finn wasn't so bad after all. He looked at the world sort of like I do even though he lived before they had cars and airplanes and things, and he didn't talk in that stuffy schoolteacher way characters in most books do.

"It's your turn," the judge said when he got to the end of the first chapter.

"I'd rather listen to you. I'm really not much good at reading out loud."

He tossed me the book. "It's not up to me to do all the work. Give it a shot."

I plunged in, hoping I wouldn't sound completely stupid, and I did okay at first. When I hit a word that looked too hard to figure out, I just skipped it. But

Walter got wise to that when I left three words out of one sentence. He made me stop and sound out the letters. I know about the sounds different letters make—I wasn't always as thick as a brick in school—but I'd never had the patience to pick words apart. I humored the judge so we could get on with the story.

"We better call it quits for tonight." Walter finally yawned and closed the book. "Shall we start again tomorrow?"

"I guess so." I grinned. "You won't have to twist my arm too hard."

Me and the judge got in the habit of reading a few chapters aloud every night when I wasn't drowning in homework. Sometimes I hated to put the book down because I was all hot to see what crazy tangles Huck Finn would weasel out of next.

"You know, I bet books would be as easy as cigarettes to get hooked on," I said when I finished reading the last page. I thought I'd be glad to make it to the end of the story, and I was, but I was kind of sorry it was over, too.

"This is one vice I won't mind you picking up. There's another whole tale about Tom Sawyer and his buddies. You have two full weeks off for Christmas, lucky you, so feel free to read ahead if you get antsy while I'm at work."

~~~

I wasn't looking forward to Christmas much.

Mom and Dad had always made a big deal out of it with a tree and a fancy dinner and everything, and I missed them a lot. I tried to keep the blues to myself, though, because Alice really got into the spirit of the season.

Her kitchen smelled like home cooking from morning till night as the holidays got closer, and I learned how to make fudge and toffee and lots of other sweet things during my vacation from school.

I screwed up a batch of peanut brittle because I didn't let it get hot enough before I spread it on the cookie sheet to harden. The stuff would have made the best glue ever invented, but it wasn't fit for anything else. Alice couldn't even pry it off the pan, so she tossed the whole mess in the trash can before anybody saw it. Whenever folks banged their gums together too much after that, me and Alice joked about how a taste of my peanut brittle would do them a world of good.

I woke up Christmas morning feeling sorry for myself. I stood the picture of my folks up against the lamp on my dresser and told them right out loud how much I missed them. I wondered if it was true like Alice said that my parents were looking down from heaven, waiting to see me again someday. I hoped they knew that I loved them and thought of them all the time.

There was a tap on my door, and Alice called out my name. She'd learned to keep at it because rousing me up in the morning wasn't an easy thing to do, so I knew she wouldn't give up and go away if I didn't answer.

"Have breakfast without me, Alice," I called when I was sure I could trust my voice. "I really don't want any company right now."

She opened the door and stood there, wearing a faded cotton nightgown and a pair of wool socks. "Good, you're dressed. Could you help Walter bring a crate in from the car? I'd do it, but it's half past freezing out, and I got a slow start this morning."

I put on my shoes and trudged to the garage, wondering if I would ever be left in peace again. The judge had his back to me, and when he heard my footsteps, he opened the front door of his car. Captain jumped out and hurtled toward me like a rocket.

"Captain!" I knelt down before the dog had a chance to bowl me over and threw my arms around him. His tongue went into overdrive on my face. "Holster that tongue, you mangy mutt. How did you get him back, Walter?"

"He had to be retired from guide duty because he was pretty traumatized by the car accident. The folks at the school were going to adopt him out anyway, and I told them it would only be right if he came to you."

"Well, old boy, I was pretty traumatized by the accident, too, but I guess me and you will make a hell of a team." I blinked back the tears that had suddenly pooled up in my eyes. "I'll have to do something about that toxic breath of yours, though."

Victor was a little jealous of Captain at first, but they got along all right once he figured out I wasn't deserting him for another hound. I watched through the kitchen window as the dogs tore around the back yard after each other while Alice rolled out biscuits and the judge read the Christmas story aloud from the Bible.

Later on, we went to help the Bertha City Church of Christ serve a holiday dinner for a lot of homeless people and needy families. I spent most of the afternoon dishing up mashed potatoes and gravy, and I started to feel a little better about everything because I saw that there were plenty of folks who were worse off than I was.

When the meal was over, I kept the kids out of trouble till Santa Claus came to my rescue. I did card tricks for them and juggled a couple of red and green Christmas balls I snitched off a wreath above the fireplace. Stace had taught me to juggle after he learned at summer camp a few years back, and I never knew the skill would come in handy, but I held off a riot till the fat man in the red suit finally showed up with his bag of toys. I recognized the judge's dark eyes between the phony white beard and the knitted stocking cap.

Chapter 11

My common sense jumped the track a few days after Christmas. I was still out of school for the holidays, and one morning I slept in late and woke up to an empty house. A note on the refrigerator said Alice had gone with a neighbor to do some cleaning at the church. She had set a pot of stew meat to simmering, and I was about to start cutting up vegetables like she asked when I saw her car keys on the kitchen counter.

I'd been drooling over her sweet little red convertible for months. I decided there wouldn't be any harm in taking it for a quick spin. I wouldn't be stealing it because I'd have it in the garage again way before Alice got done at the church, and nobody would ever be the wiser. I laughed off a pesky poke or two from my conscience. Tim and Mark would never forgive me if I let a chance like this pass me by.

I put the carrots back in the fridge and went for the keys instead. I thought about taking along a bottle of brandy the judge had got from a friend at work, but I left it on the counter in the end. I wasn't looking to get loaded. I was just out for some good clean fun.

The car handled like a dream. It was too nippy out to have the top down, but I opened the windows to let the morning breeze blow in my face. I hadn't been alone at the wheel since the night Daisy died, and it put me on a high, so I kept going and going, jamming to the radio and not thinking about the time.

Then some idiot in a station wagon dodged right in front of me. When I swerved to miss him, I hit a wet spot in the road and slid into the curb. There was a horrendous grinding noise from the front of the car, and it didn't take a rocket scientist to figure out that I wasn't going to make it back to the judge's garage.

Fate had a double whammy in store for me, too. The flashing lights appeared like magic in my rear view mirror before I had a chance to do anything but swear a few times, and then the cop hit his siren to make sure the whole neighborhood knew I was busted. Either that or he just liked to play with the buttons on his dash. I sure as hell wasn't going anywhere.

He strutted up to my open window. "Okay, let's have the license, kid."

I handed it over. "Look, I might as well save you some detective work. The car ain't mine. It belongs to my guardian, Alice Mills, and I was only taking it for a little test drive. That's not the same thing as stealing it because I was planning to have it home again before she knew it was missing."

"We'll see what she has to say about that." The cop wasn't impressed with my logic, and neither was I, to be honest, especially after I got a good look at the mutilated tire on the ragtop while I was trudging over to the squad car.

Alice and her neighbor came to pick me up at the cop shop. Alice had the Mustang towed to a garage so they could straighten the bent axle and replace the mangled wheel. My stupidity was going to cost her a thousand dollars. I couldn't look her in the eye as I climbed into the back seat of the neighbor's car.

The neighbor, a pudgy little lady with red cheeks and frizzy blond hair that showed gray roots, clicked her tongue and shook her finger at me. "This was a fine thing for you to do after the judge and his wife took you in. I suppose it's to be expected from a downtown thug like you."

I just stared at my tennis shoes. There was no point in getting steamed. She was telling the truth.

She kept on telling it, too. "Really, Alice, I don't know why you and your husband insist on setting yourselves up for things like this. You're just asking for trouble, opening your home to these hoodlums."

"Well, Emily, if Walter and I choose to open our home, I guess that makes it our business," Alice said coolly.

"Maybe so, but I feel it's my duty to warn you, since you're so soft-hearted and all. One of these days, something more serious is bound to happen. I heard of a case down in Austin where an orphan burned up his foster parents in their bed."

"And you have warned me many times." Alice's politeness was wearing kind of thin around the edges.

The neighbor went on warning and whining all the way home, and I wished I could turn into a tiny black ant and disappear under one of the rubber floor mats in her shiny silver Volvo.

Alice didn't say a word to me till we were alone in the kitchen. Then she opened a drawer and took out a vegetable knife. "You have some work to do. The stew should have been bubbling for hours by now."

I started slicing carrots. Alice tied on her apron and punched down the bread dough she'd left rising on the counter. The dough gave off a strong yeasty smell that would have been nothing short of heavenly if I wasn't so uptight, but the silence kept getting louder and louder in the room as I watched her kneading.

"Aren't you going to yell at me or anything?" I asked when the suspense got to be too much for me.

Her hands never broke rhythm. "I think you're the one who needs to do the talking."

I didn't know what to say. I felt a hot red blush creeping up the back of my neck and into my face. I popped a piece of carrot in my mouth and chewed it slowly, hoping I'd come up with the right words by the time I swallowed it.

Finally I looked straight at Alice. "It's true what your neighbor said on the way home. It was a lousy thing for me to do after how good you and Walter have been to me."

"Emily needed a big bite of your peanut brittle." A little smile played for a second at the corners of Alice's mouth.

"Aren't you ticked off at me?"

"Disappointed is probably a better word. Why did you do it?"

I shrugged. "I don't know. I just got to thinking about old times and the wild stuff me and the crew used to do, and I felt sort of tied down. I guess that doesn't make much sense, you not having any kids of your own."

"I understand it perfectly. I raised a son, and he did his share of dumb things."

"You have a son? Why didn't he come see you for Christmas?"

"Arthur was a soldier, and he never came home from Vietnam." Alice spoke calmly, but she smashed down a bulge of dough a little harder than she needed to.

"Is that his picture hanging over the fireplace? I always thought it was Walter."

"They looked alike. I put the portrait away in a closet when Arthur died, but after a while I realized I could either let his memory cripple me or inspire me. So I hung his picture where I would see it every day, and thinking about him helps me find joy in the world. Arthur loved his life more than anyone I ever knew."

I dropped the carrots into the Dutch oven and turned to the sink to scrub potatoes. "Why did you take me in, Alice? I was just another loser who drifted through Walter's chambers, and I've been a lot of trouble to you."

"This house seemed like a tomb when Arthur was gone. He had a way of filling up a room when he walked in, and the stillness almost drove us crazy. Then Walter started thinking about how most of the kids he dealt with every day were throwing their futures away because there was no one to teach them how to live. Arthur got killed, but he'd always wanted to join the Army. He made his choices and didn't have to settle for second best." She dabbed at her eyes with a corner of her apron. "One thing followed

189

another, and pretty soon our house was full of life again."

"Then I'm not the first guy you two ever rescued. I must be about the worst one, though, wrecking your car and all."

She laughed outright. "You're not the first, and you're not the worst. You'd have to try real hard to do something Walter and I haven't seen before."

"You must be saints or something, putting up with all this."

"We lost one son, and we'll grieve for him every day as long as we live. But God gave us lots of sons in Arthur's place. You boys do as much for us as we do for you. You keep us young."

"I bet we put most of those gray hairs on your head, too. Should I use this whole onion?"

She nodded. "You've lost someone special in your life, too, Rick. We've cut you some slack around here because we know how it feels to have a person you love torn away from you."

"You talked about memories either crippling or inspiring you. I wish thoughts of Daisy could inspire me, but they just rip me up inside. She's the last thing I think of before I fall asleep, and when I open my eyes in the morning, she's an ache that hasn't gone away. I have a lot of bad dreams about the night I got her killed, too." I was glad the onion gave me a good excuse for blinking back tears.

"I know. I sometimes hear you call her name in your sleep."

"Do I wake you up? I'll be sure I pull my door all the way closed from now on."

"Don't worry, I nap like a cat." Alice rinsed her hands and came to stand next to me. "Time will stop the bleeding inside you. There will always be a scar, but one day you'll forgive yourself for a tragedy you couldn't prevent, and you'll remember Daisy with a smile instead of a silent scream."

"I hope so." I dropped the onion into the kettle and added a few shakes of salt and pepper. "I reckon we'll eat good tonight after all."

"We sure will. Now I think you better make yourself scarce for a while. Walter will be home soon, and he'll be on what was known where I grew up as a rare old tear."

"Where I grew up we called it flat pissed off, and he's got the right." I started to walk out of the kitchen, then turned back and gave Alice a quick hug. "You're a great lady. If you take one more chance on me, I won't let you down again."

I went to my room and closed the door. I tacked the snapshot of my folks and Daisy's note on the wall where I'd see them first thing when I woke up every morning. Then I sat down at the desk and tried to get interested in a magazine, but I kept losing my place as I read because I was listening for the judge to come in.

After a while I heard his car pull into the garage and then his footsteps on the kitchen floor. He and Alice started talking, but I couldn't make out the words, so I sneaked over to the door and eased it open a little.

"I've just about had it this time, Alice. I could have that kid back in reform school so fast his head would spin for a week."

"He's a good kid. He just didn't think. Nobody got hurt."

"He stole your car and wrecked it. I expected better out of him than that."

"The car can be fixed. Here, the bread is fresh from the oven. Put it in your mouth before you say something you'll regret."

There was a short silence.

"That's good eating, honey. There's nothing like a slice of hot buttered bread to take off the chill. We'll get a heavy frost again tonight."

After another lull, Alice said, "Rick knows he blew it today. We talked about it some while he was fixing the stew."

"How many times does somebody have to blow it before he drops his brain in gear? Stealing cars is a big deal, you know."

"How many times did my dad give you the benefit of the doubt? Your life would have turned out a lot different if he'd washed his hands of you after you pulled a stupid stunt or two."

A ticking clock always seems to make more noise than usual when things get tense, and mine sounded like a time bomb for a minute.

Then Walter sighed heavily. "I suppose you're right. I'll speak to Rick later, but I better go have a swim first."

There was a little more muffled conversation, like maybe they were hugging each other, and then the kitchen door closed and the house was quiet. I paced back and forth across my room and cursed myself under my breath for letting the judge down. It wasn't just that I was scared of landing in reform school again, either. I was surprised how much it hurt to hear Walter say he was disappointed in me.

Alice switched on the radio out in the kitchen. She liked to listen to some Bible study program every evening while she got supper on. I never paid much attention to it, but that day I heard the preacher on the radio quote from the book of Luke. "To him who strikes you on the one cheek, offer the other also."

That didn't make a lick of sense to me. I guess God has figured out a thing or two about running the world, but He sure wouldn't come out on top in a fist fight with that way of doing things. I couldn't believe He didn't know that because Alice had told me Jesus grew up in a crummy neighborhood and worked as a carpenter most of his life. I parked myself at the desk and chewed on the idea for a long time, but I didn't see where getting two bruises instead of one would do a guy any good at all.

It felt like forever before I heard a tap on the door, and then the judge pushed it open and stepped into the room. He closed the door behind him and sat on the bed.

I started talking before he had a chance to say anything. "Look, Walter, I wouldn't blame you if you never wanted to see my face again, and if you wanna call the cops on me, I'll dial the phone for you."

He ran his fingers through his damp hair. "I thought seriously about shipping you back to reform

193

school, and if you'd copped an attitude when I came in here I might have done it. But I'm going to give you one more chance to show me your true colors."

"What makes you so sure about my true colors? I acted like a jerk today."

"Yeah, you did. But I was a kid once, too, and I didn't always use my head, either."

"I bet you were the kind of kid who helped old ladies across the street and all that jazz."

He shook his head. "I was fourteen when my dad rode off into the sunset, and I found out real quick that I could walk all over my mom. I was headed down the wrong road with all my skid row buddies."

"What turned you around?"

"Alice and I went to school together, and she looked like the princess out of a fairy tale to me. Her dad believed in me when I didn't even believe in myself. He put me back on the narrow way and made sure I stayed there till I became somebody fit to marry his daughter."

"Did you ever steal a car?"

"No, but I stole a half a dozen piglets from Alice's next door neighbor."

I laughed. "What would you want with those?"

The judge held his mouth in a stern line, but he couldn't keep his eyes from dancing. "Me and a buddy greased them down and let them loose in the school late one night. The principal and a whole crew of teachers spent a couple hours rounding up those little squealers the next morning." The sparkle went out of his eyes, and he looked hard at me. "I'm not giving you any ideas, am I?"

194

"Naw, I'm done with all that. I'll make you proud this time."

"I hope so. Sometimes you have to fall once or twice to learn that you can pick yourself up. On the practical side of making me proud, though, there's the matter of a thousand-dollar repair bill. You'll be signing paychecks over to me for quite a while."

"No problem."

"Let's go get some supper then. Alice claims you make a pretty mean stew." He stood up and put a hand on my shoulder. "I expect you to walk the chalk from now on, kid. You only have a few chances to screw up in this life before you get tagged as a permanent loser."

I took Walter's warning to heart. I went back to school after New Year's and really buckled down for the first time ever. I can't say I enjoyed myself, but I made decent grades that semester, and I was kind of proud of my report card. I tacked it up on my bedroom wall next to the picture of my folks. The judge helped me start filling out financial aid papers. He said I could get money to sign up for a cooking program at the community college after I finished high school.

"Who's going to pay for me to go to college?" I asked, amazed.

"There are grants out there for regular guys like you who don't have a fair shot at an education," Walter explained. "Wealthy people shouldn't get all the breaks in this world."

Chapter 12

The night before Valentine's Day, I sat up late, not anxious to face the thoughts of my folks that were waiting to haunt me when I was alone in the dark. When my eyelids got too heavy to read any more, I gave up on my history book and switched off the light.

But my eyes popped open right away, and I tossed and turned till the sheets on the bed were twisted in hopeless knots. Finally I drifted off to sleep, and sure enough, the nightmares started. I dreamed of my birthday party at the traveling carnival. I dreamed of the New Year's Eve bash where the photo of my parents in their matching holiday hats was taken. Then I dreamed of the night I got the call about their car accident. I relived it all in vivid detail—the ringing phone, the soft-spoken sheriff dropping the bomb on me, my tennis shoes pounding on the pavement as I ran screaming out into the windy darkness. I felt Tim and Mark dragging me back to the Barn and then Grandma's arms around me. I heard her soothing voice as she sang. Then the headlights of the battered green Jeep were bearing down on me, and Daisy's shrill scream ripped through the rhythm of the Spanish lullaby.

I woke up in my room at the Mills house, and at first I didn't know where I was. I lay on my back in the double bed, breathing hard and staring blankly into the darkness. My throat burned like I'd swallowed a handful of hot ashes. I squeezed my eyes shut to hold back my tears, but they trickled out anyway and ran over my cheeks and down into my hair. I curled up in a tight ball under the comforter and buried my face in my pillow to muffle the sobs that suddenly poured out of me, and pretty soon the pillowcase was drenched.

I got up for school like always in the morning, but splashing my face with cold water couldn't wash away the puffy red proof of my hellish night. As soon as she saw me, Alice called the school and pulled me out of my classes for the day. She took me to put flowers on the graves of my loved ones.

"I haven't been to the cemetery since Mom and Dad were buried a year ago," I said.

"I didn't visit Arthur's grave for a long time, but I found out it really does help." Alice stopped the convertible, which had been fixed up like new, to buy roses from a street vendor.

The cemetery was divided in half by a wide gravel path, kind of like the Line split the city in two. The grass on one side of the path was kept trim and green, and there were fancy statues of angels and birds and things on most of the tombstones. I walked through a sagging wooden gate into the other section, which was hidden from view behind a tall, unpainted privacy fence. Scraggly weeds grew up between the markers, and some of the stones were tipped at crazy angles. You couldn't read the names and dates on a lot of them.

I laid flowers on Mom's grave and then Dad's, then stood there in awkward silence, not knowing what to do. Alice backed off a ways, and I plunked myself down on the scruffy grass and started thinking about my folks. I pictured the three of us chatting at the kitchen table in our old apartment like we used to do every night, and for a minute I almost forgot I was sitting by myself in the cemetery.

"Hey, Dad, you'd flip out if you saw my report card. Alice and Walter are taking good care of me, Mom, so don't worry. You know, I wish you could have met Daisy. She was real special to me." I trailed off and closed my eyes, not wanting to let go of the moment. I stood up when the image of my parents started to fade from my mind. "You wait and see. I'm gonna do great things with my life someday, the way you knew I would."

Then me and Alice walked up and down the rows of gravestones, searching for the one with Daisy's name on it.

"I'm not sure she's even here," I said. "I didn't ask the people at the hospital what they were going to do with her."

"There it is." Alice pointed at a tiny statue of a cross. It was almost hidden in a tangle of dead weeds.

I dropped down in front of the marker and started ripping the old brown weeds out by the roots and flinging them furiously away, cussing the whole time between my clenched teeth.

Alice knelt beside me. "Watch how you talk in a cemetery. The departed deserve a little respect."

"She ain't getting any!" I tore out another clump of prickly vines. My fingernails were broken and crusted with dirt, and blood oozed from a stinging scratch on my thumb. "Look at this. It's like they just threw her away, and those stones on the other side are all kept up nice and proper. Grandma's here, too, and Mark ain't around anymore to tend her grave."

Alice patted my shoulder. "I know, honey, it isn't fair."

"Damn right it isn't!" All at once I crumpled over Daisy's pathetic little white cross and started bawling again. This was getting to be a regular thing, much to my disgust. Alice ran a hand tenderly over my hair.

"I love you, Daisy," I whispered after a few minutes, sitting back on my heels. "Oh God, I'll never stop missing you."

I glanced at Alice and blushed, but she didn't seem to mind my blubbering. She just handed me a tissue from her purse and waited while I pulled myself together. I saw her wipe her eyes on her shirt sleeve.

"Tears don't make you weak, Rick, I promise. They make you human," she said quietly. "There's a whole lot of pain deep down inside you, and if you don't let it out, it'll cut your soul to pieces. I know a thing or two about that."

"If Walter will let me borrow his weed trimmer, I'm going to come hack away the jungle around these graves. All these folks ought to have a nice place to rest."

"I'll help you this weekend, and I bet Walter will, too." Alice looked right into my eyes. "But remember that Daisy and your parents aren't really here. Their graves are just places you can visit when you need to feel close to them."

"So they're in heaven or something? What if they weren't ready to go yet?" I asked. "I know Daisy wasn't. The night she died in the hospital, she told me she still wanted to run and dance and do a bunch of things."

"When Walter and I lost our son, we must have asked each other a million times why it had to happen. Arthur was young and good and full of dreams he never got to follow."Alice took my hand and squeezed it hard. "I don't understand why you had to lose Daisy. But eventually, maybe years from now, your life will be better because you knew her, I truly believe that. Remembering her will inspire you and give you courage, and that'll keep her alive in your heart, where it really counts."

"I wish I could buy that." I got up and started picking my way through the maze of tilting stones toward the gate. "My life isn't ever going to be better because of Daisy, though. If she hadn't met me, she might not be dead, but I got her killed. That's the cold hard truth, and there's no getting around it."

For a second, Alice looked at me like she wanted to say something. Then she just sighed and shook her head, and we walked back to the convertible in silence.

We sweated all that Saturday and part of the next one at the cemetery, clearing away the weeds and sprucing up the headstones. Both times other families who had brought flowers for their loved ones decided to pitch in, and it wasn't long before we had the poor section of the graveyard in decent shape.

I started reading the names and dates on the stones as I worked, and there were a lot of young people, some my age and some closer to the age my parents had been. It still stabbed at me to know I'd never see Mom and Dad or Daisy again, but I didn't feel so much like God had cheated me anymore. Most of the folks under these markers had family and friends who were missing them, too, so maybe I hadn't been singled out for a raw deal. Somehow that made me feel a little better.

We were on our way to Alice's car when we'd finished at the graveyard. Suddenly she stopped in her tracks and snapped her fingers. "I got it!"

"Got what?" I almost bumped into her.

"A plan, that's what." Alice turned to me and Walter, beaming. "We've been searching like crazy for ways to get more men active in the church. You can't drag them to an ice cream social or a salad luncheon on the end of a tow chain, but I don't see why they wouldn't chop down weeds and rake leaves at the cemetery three or four times a year."

"I suppose you couldn't offer burgers and beer afterward, but it would give us all a chance to show off our electric yard toys." The judge laughed. "That's a good idea, honey. It's a shame the way those graves have been let go."

Alice nodded. "I can't believe I never noticed it before."

~~~

I took Captain for a long walk later that afternoon so I could have some time to myself. I met up with the snooty rich kid from next door when I got home. I'd seen the puny little creep a lot on my way to and from school, and he always looked at me like I was something he scraped off the bottom of his shoe, but he'd been too chicken to give me any crap after the day I popped him in the mouth.

He must have grown guts or something because he planted himself in front of me on the sidewalk when I paused to pick up the mail. I tried to push past him through the judge's gate, but he wouldn't let me by.

He looked me up and down. "I see you've trimmed your shaggy hair and done something about those rags of yours. I guess you're being domesticated in the Mills household."

I drew back, intending to smash his face like a pumpkin, but I managed to stop myself in mid-swing.

He snickered. "What's the matter, loser, you scared? Take your best shot."

I hitched my thumbs in my belt loops to keep myself from killing him. I'd been watching my step since I wrecked Alice's car, and I wasn't about to blow my clean record on a runt with a big mouth and a death wish.

"You know you'll never be anything but a lowlife even if you sponge off Walter Mills and pretend you're civilized forever."

"Listen, damn you, the only reason you aren't seeing God right now is that I told Walter I'd leave your rancid rack of bones alone! You better run to your mommy before my savage nature kicks in and I wrap your ugly face around that mailbox!"

The little maggot turned to walk away, still smirking, and I reached into the box for the letters. I was too busy fuming under my breath to hear anyone come up behind me, but the rich kid let out a yelp of surprise, and Captain hit the end of his leash so hard it almost jerked my arm off. When I looked around, Walter had the kid by the collar.

"David Graham, what the hell is your problem?" The judge had finally lost his temper, and everybody on the block knew it. "I wouldn't have blamed Rick if he hadn't left a tooth in your head!"

"He doesn't belong in our neighborhood. Let go of me or I'll have you up on charges. And tell that mooch of yours to call off his dog."

"Shut up. I have something to say to you. If you're insecure enough about yourself that you have to walk around flapping your mouth like an idiot, that's no concern of mine. But if you say another word to Rick, I'll have you up on charges. Now go!" Walter shoved the kid toward his gate. "And don't you think for one second I'm not serious!"

When David had scuttled away and I'd got Captain settled down, the judge grinned at me and shook my hand like I'd just won a million dollars.

"I'm proud as hell of you for turning the other cheek," he said.

"It took all I had not to break his nose, but I guess he ain't worth my time." If this was what turning the other cheek was all about, it was a tough order to fill.

I had to swim laps for an hour that day to get the rage out of my blood, but the pride stayed with me. If Walter was so sure I was somebody worth sticking up for, maybe I was. I started holding my head a little higher and even raised my hand now and then in school when I knew the answers. I never would have been caught dead doing that before.

There was this brunette who sat next to me in my math class. She smiled and winked at me a few times when I started speaking up. I didn't pay much attention to her at first. She was usually swept out of the room by a flock of clucking chicks as soon as the bell rang, and there were always plenty of guys buzzing around her, too. I made it a point to steer clear of the social scene at school. But one day in the spring, I picked up a pencil that fell off her desk, and I introduced myself when I handed it to her.

"My name is Trina, but everybody calls me Tree because I'm so tall," she said.

I smiled at her. "You're only two or three inches shorter than me."

"Yeah, and it's the pits. All my dance partners have to reach up to give me a peck on the cheek."

"Well, everybody's talking about that spring ball they're getting up next weekend. I wouldn't have to stretch my neck to plant a kiss on you." The words popped out of my mouth before I had a chance to plug in my brain, but I figured Tree had guys lined up around the block to take her out anyway, so I was probably safe.

Tree's eyebrows shot up in surprise. "Was that an invitation?"

I shrugged. "Yeah, I guess so."

She giggled. "I haven't heard you say this many words in a row all year."

"I'm not big on banging my gums much when I don't have to. I'll pick you up at six next Saturday." I walked away, wondering just what kind of fix I'd landed myself in now.

204

The judge and his wife were tickled to death because I was finally reaching out to the other kids at school. Walter loaned me a dress shirt and a tie for the dance, and Alice took me to pick out a corsage for Tree. She even decided to let me borrow her ragtop for the evening.

"You look very handsome," she said as I was walking out the door. "Be sure you bring back my car in one piece this time."

I laughed nervously. "I promise I'll drive like a little old lady all night."

I climbed into the Mustang, wishing I'd kept my trap shut. School dances weren't usually my cup of tea, and Tree was a total stranger to me. Besides, I felt like I was cheating on Daisy even though I knew she was gone forever.

Tree lived in the biggest house I'd ever seen. She must have been watching out a window for me because she floated down her porch steps in a glittery evening gown and slid into the seat beside me before I had a chance to go ring her doorbell. We drove over to a little barbecue joint I knew to grab a bite, and my palms were sweating on the steering wheel all the way. I thought I saw a flash of disappointment in her eyes as we pulled up at the restaurant, but it was gone so quick I couldn't be sure.

"You've been a tough nut to crack, but I made a bet with a friend of mine that I could get you to ask me out before the school year was up." Tree laughed. "I dropped that pencil off my desk on purpose, you know. Guys fall for that every time."

I couldn't think of anything to say. I wasn't thrilled to be taking a chick out to satisfy a wager, but I was already in up to my neck, so there wasn't anything I could do about it.

I parked the car and went around to open the passenger door. "That's a pretty dress you're wearing, Daisy ... I mean ..."

"Tree," she said frostily. "The two names sound so alike. It must be a real challenge for you to keep all the women in your life sorted out."

"Well, they're both plants," I mumbled in a lame bid for peace. I couldn't look her in the eye as I led her into the restaurant.

I must have really ticked her off because the evening went downhill from there. I ordered steaks for both of us and tried to fill the awkward silence with small talk. I told Tree a few stories about me and the crew, but that was a big mistake. It was clear we lived on two different planets, and she turned into an ice princess as soon as she found out I came from the projects. So I dropped the subject and started asking her questions instead.

She chatted a little about how she'd signed up to go to cheerleading camp in the summer, but after a while she excused herself and made a beeline for the bathroom. She hid out in there for a long time, and our plates were on the table when she came back, so we kept busy eating and let the conversation fizzle out.

We got a lot of curious looks when we walked into the hotel where they were having the ball. Tree knew just about everybody there, and she stopped to gab every few steps. She didn't even bother to introduce me to her friends. I tagged along behind her feeling like a shaggy dog on a leash. Finally we made it onto the floor, and she was a good dancer. I did my best to keep up with her, but the music jangled out of tune in my ears.

I couldn't stop remembering the way my heart had raced when I held Daisy under the spinning colored lights at the Midsummer Madness Dance in the gym of my old high school. It seemed like that had happened years and years ago, in another lifetime, and yet I remembered every detail as if I had just been there yesterday.

"I guess we could sit down," Tree said after a while. I was relieved beyond words.

We scouted out a table, and I went to snag us some sodas. Tree drifted away before I got back, and I spent an eternity sipping root beer while she flitted among her friends in her strapless party dress.

I caught her pointing at me a couple of times, and then a group of girls would huddle up and giggle behind their hands. I was sure she was making me out to be a real oaf, but I didn't care.

I'd never given a damn where I stood with the popular crowd, but I'd always had the crew to hang out with before. I watched the nervous dance of my fingers as I drummed them on the table and wished I'd stayed home and finished my report on the ozone layer for science class.

Tree wandered back to the table in her own sweet time. I was about to offer to take another spin on the floor with her when some guy in a tux came up behind her and started massaging her bare shoulders. He looked like he was enjoying himself a little too much to suit me.

"You best keep your hands to yourself unless you want them sliced off at the wrists, jack," I warned.

Tree glared at me. "Chill out, for God's sake. This isn't a downtown barroom, you know. Keep it up, Jerry. That feels good."

Dad had made me give him my word when I started dating that I would never hit a girl, no matter how riled up she got me. Keeping my promise hadn't been a problem before, but I was hard pressed at that moment not to put a shiner on that snobby little cheerleader right there in front of God and everybody.

I gripped the arms of my chair till I simmered down enough to walk away, then stalked out to the patio for a smoke. I gave serious thought to making a quick getaway while I had the chance, but I wasn't the kind who would stand a chick up on a date, even one who hated me. So I dawdled over my cigarette as long as I could and then went back inside.

Tree had the decency to dance with me off and on during the rest of the night. She held her body as stiff as a board, though, and looked everywhere except at my face.

I offered to take her for pie and coffee after the ball, but I thanked my lucky stars when she tossed out a lame excuse about having to get up for church in the morning.

"It's been fun, Rick," she said as I turned into her driveway.

"Yeah. I guess I'll see you at school." I leaned over and gave her a peck on the cheek, since that was what got us into the whole mess to begin with.

I cruised the dark streets for a long time after I let Tree off. I didn't bawl or anything, but I felt Daisy's memory ripping my heart to shreds. All at once I saw that Tree had left her corsage on the dashboard, and I opened the window and chucked it out into the night. I swore aloud as I yanked off the judge's tie. Then I drove back to the Mills house.

I felt out of place for a minute as I pulled into the garage, but I remembered the way the judge and his wife were always rooting for me, and that helped a little. Tree had made it plain she thought I was something the cat dragged in, but I decided her charm left a lot to be desired. Walter and Alice believed I was good enough to set foot on the classy side of town, and they knew more than some snooty cheerleader anyway.

Alice had left the kitchen light on for me, but the house was quiet. I switched off the light and crept into my room without making a sound. I was glad I didn't have to face any questions that night.

I told Walter about the whole sorry business over oatmeal and coffee the next morning. I hadn't planned to, but he had a way of drawing me out before I knew what he was doing. I suppose that's why he made such a good judge.

"I reckon I'll be a diehard bachelor after this," I sighed when I'd laid out all the gloomy details.

"You're a little young to be talking that way," Walter said quietly. I was thankful he didn't laugh.

209

"You reached out and got slapped back pretty hard last night, but don't take it to heart. A lot of narrow-minded people snub away the true friends in their lives and never even know what they've missed. I honestly feel as sorry for Trina as I do for you."

I shrugged. "Don't lose any sleep over it. Did you and Alice ever go dancing?"

He nodded. "I asked her to marry me between the lilac bushes at her front gate the night of our senior prom. It was one of the sweetest moments in my life."

"Well, I should have known better than to go out with Tree anyway. I'll never meet another girl like Daisy if I live to be a hundred."

"No, you won't. But you're bound to meet someone else who will make you happy in her own way."

I shook my head. "Daisy was counting on me to take care of her, and she got killed because of it. I guess I'd rather keep to myself than be with a girl I can't stick up for when push comes to shove."

The judge took a deep breath and laid a hand on my shoulder. "Rick, you've got to stop blaming yourself for Daisy's death. It was an accident and a terrible shame, but it wasn't your fault."

"I froze up, man. I saw that Jeep coming right at me, and I couldn't move." I tried to pull free from Walter's grasp.

His grip on my shoulder tightened, and he looked straight into my eyes. "You had less than one split second. What do you think you could have done—that fast?" He snapped his fingers.

"I should've swerved or something. Anything but locking up like a gutless wonder."

"Average reflexes don't work that quick, and neither does the steering system in a car. Do you have some kind of superhuman powers I don't know about?"

"Hardly. Give it a rest, for Christ's sake."

Walter let his eyes bore steadily into mine, and his words hammered at me like stinging hailstones. "Do you think I would have gone out of my way to give you a break if I thought you ought to be held responsible? What about the driver of the other car?"

"They planted him, too." I stood up and turned my back on the judge before the pain in my eyes gave way to tears. "You're a square shooter, Walter. I know you believe what you're saying. You've started to show me that I'm worth a damn in a lot of ways. But the bottom line is that I promised to keep Daisy safe, and now she's dead. I ain't fit to be with a girl even if I ever do find one who measures up to her, and that's not likely."

"I can't talk you out of clinging to your rightful sorrow, but guilt and grief are going to offer you mighty cold comfort till you choose to let them go."

I carried my breakfast dishes to the sink and walked out of the kitchen without saying anything else, and Walter must have known better than to bring up the subject again. I switched seats in my math class so I wouldn't have to talk to Tree. She fired me a few prissy looks and whispered about me to her friends a lot, but school was almost out anyway, so I kept my eyes on my homework and tried not to let her uppity act get to me.

~~~

I got my high school diploma in May. Walter and Alice talked me into dressing up and going through the graduation ceremony, and I sort of got a bang out of it, even though I thought I looked like an idiot in the cap and gown I had to wear. Afterward, the three of us went out to celebrate at a fancy restaurant.

"Choose anything on the menu, Rick," Walter said. "And if I catch you sneaking a peek at the prices, I'll put your eyes out with my salad fork."

"What he's trying to say in his own twisted way is that we're proud enough of you to bust." Alice wrapped an arm around me. I was getting used to hugs by then, even in public.

"I can't believe I actually got a diploma. I wish my folks could see it." I scanned the menu for something I recognized. "I guess I'll have the steak and shrimp. I never ate shrimp before, but it looks mouth-watering in the picture."

I stayed with Walter and Alice through most of the summer, but I got to thinking it was about time I found a place of my own. First I had to land a new job. I beat the bushes till I was ready to smack somebody. Job hunting in the blazing Texas heat is the closest thing on earth I can think of to hell. Finally I hired on at a taco bar.

Looking for an apartment in August is a drag, too, especially when you're faced with living alone for the first time in your life. None of the nooks and crannies I poked into felt much like home, but all I needed was a roof to keep the rain off. After a lot of searching, I picked a place on my old side of the highway. I felt more like myself over there, and it was all I could afford anyway. I wanted to be settled before it was time to sign up for cooking school in September.

Alice and Walter helped me move in. We got my furniture out of the storage shed the twins' folks had rented for me, and the judge and his wife bought me an electric skillet and a mess of pots and pans. They gave me a couple of cookbooks, too, and a paperback collection of the works of Mark Twain.

When they were on their way out the door, the judge tossed me a set of keys. "Those belong to that reconditioned Gremlin outside."

I stared at him, flabbergasted. "I can't take that from you!"

"Sure you can. You earned it. I saved all those paychecks you signed over to me after you wrecked the convertible and picked out the car for you when I saw that you were going to fly right. She's not much to look at, but she runs like a top."

Alice hugged me tight, and her eyes were wet. "You call us whenever you need anything, you hear? Anything at all."

Walter shook my hand, then thought better of it and put an arm around me. "You don't have to wait till you need something to call, you know. Don't be a stranger at the Mills house."

Me and Captain went for a spin that afternoon. I'd never owned a car before, and I had the time of my life getting the feel of the Gremlin. I bought a burger and fries at a fast food joint and munched them in the front seat with the German shepherd beside me.

I shared the fries with him. "Daisy would have killed me for this, but I might as well let you live it up a little now that you aren't a working stiff anymore."

Captain eyed the hamburger and panted like he was starving, so I flipped him the last scrap of the bun. "Do you think you're special or what? Well, it's you and me from now on, bud, so maybe you are."

I was about to pull out of the parking lot when I saw Mr. Garner coming out of the restaurant. I hadn't noticed my old landlord's van sitting a few spaces away from me. I hoped he wouldn't recognize me in the strange car.

He did. He walked over and held out his hand. "Hello, Rick. That's a nice set of wheels you've got."

"Thanks." I shook his hand, wondering what he wanted from me.

"I haven't seen you around for a long time."

"I moved on. I guess you have a new set of tenants in the Barn now."

He shook his head. "There was an electrical fire in one of the units, and the county shut the place down. They're going to demolish the building in a week or two."

"Well, it's about due, I suppose. It was good seeing you again, Mr. Garner." I really meant it, too, much to my surprise. I smiled at him. "You know, me and the guys gave you a lot of crap when we were kids. We should probably have taken it easy on you."

"I'll admit there was no love lost between us. But I've thought long and hard about how I demanded respect from you boys and didn't give you any in return. I wasted a lot of years looking down on people I could have been friends with."

My jaw went slack. "What made you see the light?"

"An empty building and a big stack of bills. I eventually landed another job, of course, but things got rocky for a while. Some of us strut around thinking we're snug and secure, but the wolf isn't choosy about whose door he knocks at."

"What are you up to now?"

"Running another housing project, with a little more decency this time. And you?"

"Getting ready to take some cooking courses at the community college. I've got grants to pay for most of the first semester, but I don't know if I'll earn the last hundred dollars by the end of the week. If I miss the deadline, I'll start in January."

Mr. Garner flipped out his checkbook and started writing in it on the hood of my car. He tore out a check for a hundred dollars and handed it to me.

"Thanks, but I can't take money from you." I tried to give it back. "If I can snag an extra shift or two at the taco bar before Friday, I'll be all set."

"Consider it a loan." Mr. Garner wouldn't touch the check. "I never thought you boys would amount to much, and I certainly didn't do anything to encourage you. But you've obviously taken charge of your life, and I'd like to see things work out for you."He turned toward his van. "Good luck. When someone else needs a hand, give it to him. You can repay me that way."

"It's a deal. See you around." I put the check in my pocket and backed out of my parking space. I'm so lucky it spooks me sometimes.

I decided to cruise over for a last look at the Barn. It was in pretty sorry shape. Most of the windows were busted out, the building was plastered with graffiti, and the neon star was gone from the roof. The front door hung open on one creaking hinge.

The sight of that empty building stirred up the old aching sadness in me. I missed the crew so bad it was like a hunger. I was about to speed away and never look back when a tall guy in ragged overalls slouched up behind my driver's window.

"Say, man, could you spare a couple bucks so a guy could get a hot meal?" he asked from under his battered straw hat.

I pulled a five dollar bill out of my jeans pocket. "This is all I've got, but it ought to keep your guts from grumbling for a while."

He gave me a quick nod of thanks and took the money without ever really looking into my face.

As he turned to walk away, I caught a glimpse of the red hair that hung limply down past his dirty shirt collar. "Tim?"

He whirled to face me, and his eyes were hard. Then recognition slowly softened them. "Hey, Rick!"

I leaped out of the car and threw my arms around him, not caring who saw. "Now park yourself in my wagon, and we'll get you that hot meal. Move your butt, Captain, you've been bumped to the back seat."

PART THREE

Chapter 13

Tim glanced around my apartment. "Hey, this is a nice place."

"It ain't bad if you can get past the blaze orange carpet."

"We didn't have carpet in the Barn at all. You're moving up in the world. That's no clunker you're tooling around in, either."

While I put on a pot of coffee and fried up a skillet of ham and eggs, I told Tim about Walter and Alice and how they'd taken me in, but I left out my visit to the psych ward. It isn't something a guy likes to brag about, and I'd done my level best never to think of the joint again after I skipped out of there with the judge.

"You always were a lucky dog anyway. I guess you just fell up the stairs one more time when Walter Mills took a liking to you."

"Yeah, and get a load of this." I held up the check from Mr. Garner. "I saw him in a parking lot today, and he talked to me like I was a real human being. When I said I was saving up to go to cooking school, he made out the check right there on the hood of my car."

Tim's eyes got as big as bicycle tires. "No kidding! So the old fleabag has a decent streak in him after all. I'd still like to shoot him on sight for getting my stepdad locked up, but this is too cool."

"He says they're going to tear down the Barn in a week or two."

"It looks like it might fall down before that."

I topped off our coffee cups. "So tell me where you've been keeping yourself for the last year. I ought to knock your block off for walking out of my life with just a note like that."

"I didn't have much choice. Ed picked us all up at the hospital that night, and he pitched an unholy fit. Me and Mark couldn't talk him out of packing the twins off. Hell, we had all we could do to keep him from going into cardiac arrest."

"I suppose he had to do what he thought was best for his own sons."

"Well, there was nothing left for me and Mark here, so I robbed a liquor store, bought him a bus ticket, and hopped a freight that took me to California. I could go for another slab of ham if you got it."

Tim's face looked thinner than I'd remembered it, and kind of pale, so I cracked a couple more eggs into the skillet, too. I figured he wouldn't turn them down. "Then you've been in the land of movie stars and beach babes all this time? I take it you didn't find much gold there."

"Naw, it's all sewed up in the pockets of the fat cats, like every place else. I saw the back alleys of all the big cities out there, but you don't get to play tourist much when you're on the run."

"So what did you do?"

"Worked when I had to, ate when I could, and came home when I got totally fed up. I figured I

218

might as well starve to death in my own town, but you've put off my funeral for a while."

"Are you planning to have some toast with that jelly?"

Tim grinned. "I've been ready to kill for something sweet lately. Do you hear anything from Mark or the twins?"

"Mark rode a northbound bus right off the map, but I write back and forth with the twins all the time. Bryan's getting real big on the tennis scene back east. He's already got most of the top colleges in the country sweet-talking him."

"And Stace?"

I sighed. "He just can't get used to it out there in Georgia. He's got a chip on his shoulder because everybody wants him to be like Bryan, making good grades and acting like a Boy Scout, so he raises a lot of hell. Ed was thinking about sticking him in military school, but I talked him out of it for now. Maybe with a new term starting up, Stace will get his poop in a group."

"I haven't been this fat and happy since the days of Grandma's taco feeds," Tim said when he finally pushed back from the table. "It's been great seeing you again, and you're making out better than I thought you would. If I can crash on your couch tonight, I'll disappear before daylight."

I glared at him. "You're not just gonna waltz out of my life again, are you?"

"In case you forgot, I'm on the dodge." His voice was suddenly cold.

"You could turn yourself in."

He shook his head. "I ain't going to prison. My stepdad used to tell me horror stories about that."

"When you robbed that liquor store, how did you pull it off?"

"Nothin' fancy. The clerk was all alone in there. I told him to open up his drawer. He wouldn't, so I put a fist in his face and cleaned him out while he was still seeing stars."

"Second degree assault and robbery then. How much money did you get?"

Tim shrugged. "A few hundred dollars maybe."

"Have you hit other places since then?"

"No. I've eaten things the stray cats passed over in the garbage, but I never had the heart to hurt people when there was some other way. What are you, a cop or something?"

"Let me talk to Judge Mills for you. I told you how he spots the good in people. He'd likely go easy on you."

"There's no good in me to spot."

"That's what I said when he took me in, but he showed me different."

Tim stood up. "I better go now."

I planted myself between him and the door. "You won't make it out of here without a fight, and you don't look like you're in any shape to take me on."

"Why are you so hot over what I do with my life?" He tried to stare me down.

Drastic action was called for. I looked Tim dead in the eyes. "I told you Walter pulled me out of reform school. Actually he rescued me from the nut house." I held up a scarred wrist. "Take a good look at this."

There was a long silence while Tim stared at the scars. Then he let out a low whistle. "You opened your vein?"

"Both of 'em." I held out my other hand. "I wasn't fooling around."

Shock and then anger flashed across his face as the truth hit home. "I know you had it rough, but if you'd bled to death, I would have had to look you up in hell just so I could kick the crap out of you!"

"If you walk out that door, you're throwing away your life the same as if you took a blade to your arm. I ain't moving out of your way, so when you're ready, bring it on." I was glad for all those laps I'd swam with the judge. I'd put on a fair amount of muscle in the last year.

I didn't have to use it. Tim hesitated, then sagged into his chair again. He rubbed a hand over the knife scar on his forehead like it was bugging him. "All right, damn it, we'll go see this judge of yours. I'm sick to death of always watching my back, and you're the first friendly company I've kept in a year."

"Anyway, we don't fight much among ourselves." I sat back down at the table. We had a lot of catching up to do.

I found Tim something decent to wear in the morning. The clothes hung on him because he'd got so thin, but when he'd had a shower and a shave, he didn't look half bad. He cussed and complained all the way to the courthouse.

I fired him my best evil eye as I pulled into a parking space. "Don't you even think of spitting the hook while I'm in the building. I swear I'll hunt you down and tear you limb from limb."

"I ain't going anywhere till you see if your buddy will cut me some slack. Hurry up, will you? The suspense is killing me."

The judge was between appointments, so I got to talk to him right away. It was a good thing because the suspense was killing me too.

"Good morning, Rick. You look a lot more respectable than you did when you sat across the desk from me a year ago." Walter stood up and shook my hand. "What can I do for you?"

"I've got this friend, Tim Bennett. He robbed a liquor store for the cash to clear out of here the night Daisy died, and now he wants to turn his life around."

Walter grinned. "Is this friend invisible or small enough to curl up in your pocket?"

"I was kind of wanting to put in a good word for him first. I see as much promise in him as you saw in me."

"Why? What makes him different from any other punk who knocks over a liquor store?" The judge was all business now.

"Well, he's a magician with a set of auto body tools. And he has a big heart in him underneath his tough act. He got clobbered around a lot as a kid, so he ran a little wild. Fighting, you know, drinking and all. I'd like to see him get on track, and he's willing to take the rap for his mistakes, but I think a stretch in prison would kill his kind side. He'd be a hardened criminal after that."

"Go pry him out of hiding and let me talk to him."

Judge Mills worked it out so Tim got six months in jail and an order to pay restitution to the liquor store clerk.

"If you truly plan to clean up your act, Tim, you better do it now," Walter said. "You were under age when you robbed the liquor store, which is the only reason I could go to bat for you. Stay out of the adult courts. You won't find much compassion there for a guy with a rap sheet like yours."

I dropped by the jail every chance I got between school and work, and the twins kept the Post Office hopping when they found out where Tim was.

"Sometimes I wonder if turning myself in was such a bright idea," he griped one afternoon just before Thanksgiving. "The eggs around here are worse than the ones in reform school."

"When you were on the dodge, you'd have said they were a feast for the gods."

"I guess so. I'm going to be the best body man in Texas when I get out of this joint. They've got me studying for my high school equivalency, and I'm getting hands-on training in the shop where they fix up all the county vehicles."

~~~

But when Tim got out in March and launched a job hunt, he was turned down by every garage in the city. No one was ready to take a chance on a guy who was fresh out of jail, especially one who didn't have much work experience. I don't know where they thought he was supposed to get experience if they wouldn't give him a shot.

I let him room with me while he was getting on his feet. He was sort of hard to live with because he's a worse slob than me even, and most of the time he was at least half plastered. But it was so good having him around again that I didn't make a big deal of it. After a few weeks, he got a job at a junkyard.

I had a night class the day Tim started work, so by the time I hit the door, he was drunk on his butt. The TV was blaring, and the floor around his chair was littered with beer cans.

He opened up on me as soon as he saw me. "So I was supposed to turn myself in and rebuild my life? They've got me running like a dog over there, and no body shop will give me the time of day!"

"You have to start somewhere. Do you think maybe you could lay off the brew long enough to get some grub going when you come in before me?"

"You're the chef in this outfit."

"Can't you read? There's a whole stack of cookbooks right there on the counter."

"I can't make heads or tails of those recipes. You have to learn a foreign language to understand all those cooking words. Beat, whip, cream, fold—it sounds like boxing, not baking."

I didn't have the energy to argue, so I let it drop. But I made sure Tim got moving in the morning so he wasn't late for work on his second day.

"Crack the whip a little harder, will you?" he muttered as he chugged his third cup of coffee. "I'm so hung over I can barely stand up."

"Whose fault is that?" I snapped. Then I flashed him a grin. "Don't worry. If those body shops don't want you, it's their loss. You could start buying a set of tools one at a time, and pretty soon you'd be ready to open up your own garage and put them all out of business."

Tim cheered up a little. "Now you're talking. See you tonight."

But when I walked in that night, he was crying in his beer because he'd got himself fired from the junkyard.

"Damn it, Tim!" I slammed the bucket of tacos I'd brought home onto the table. "How did you manage to get the sack already?"

"I reckon telling the boss to get bent had something to do with it." He popped the top on another beer can.

"Yeah, maybe. What the hell did you say that to him for?"

"He accused me of stealing a wrench out of his truck."

"And did you?"

"No, I didn't. He found it in his own jacket pocket."

I shoved the taco box across the table. "Well, enjoy your last decent meal. We'll be on short rations till you land another job. I got the bill for my renter's insurance yesterday, and I have to scrape up the bucks to buy a set of kitchen knives before I start studying fresh fruits and vegetables next month."

I really couldn't blame Tim for blowing up at his boss. You get sick of always being looked at as a thief just because you don't have any money, and he was getting slapped back every time he tried to take a step in the right direction.

I came home to an empty apartment the next afternoon. Captain wasn't even there to greet me at the door. Then I saw the blinking light on my answering machine, and when I pressed the play button, I heard Tim's voice.

"Me and the hound went for a walk, and he split his paw wide open on a piece of busted glass. I hitched a ride to the vet clinic by the mall, so come pick me up."

Tim was still waiting for Captain to be patched up when I rushed into the clinic. He was chatting with a lady who had all she could do to keep a golden retriever puppy from leaping off her lap and taking wing. The puppy had a little green jacket on, and when he stopped wriggling long enough, I saw an emblem on it that said, "Guide Dog In Training."

"Hey, Rick. I was just telling this lady how we used to know a girl who had a guide dog. She heads up a 4-H club where they raise the puppies."

"Cool. How's my partner?"

"They'll be done with him in a few minutes. Anyway, this is Judy, and she says the 4-H kids keep the pups for about a year and teach them to behave in public. Then they get sent back to the school to be trained as guides."

An old man with a cat in a basket opened the door just then, and the puppy broke away from Judy and tried to shoot between my legs to freedom. I nabbed him and put him back in her lap.

"It looks like this guy's got a lot to learn about being cool in public," I laughed.

"I guess the kids take their pups wherever they go, even to school and into stores and everything." Tim was really excited, which surprised me. "You know how Captain never freaks out, no matter what's going on around him? That's because somebody got him used to being in the thick of things, right from when he was six or eight weeks old."

Captain came stumping into the room on three legs just then. One of his front paws was all done up in a gauze bandage. I took his leash from the vet and bent down to greet him before he got so thrilled to see me that he forgot to stay off his lame foot.

Judy stood up to follow the vet into an exam room. "It was nice talking to you, Tim."

"Say, you wouldn't need any help with your club or anything, would you?" he asked a little doubtfully.

She was plainly skeptical. Tim looked more like a street thug than a community volunteer. "Well, I don't know—"

He turned away. "I was just wondering, that's all."

"Wait." She tucked the puppy under one arm and searched in her purse for a business card. "We're having a barbecue at the rec center Saturday to send some dogs off for training and pass out a bunch of new puppies. Can you grill a good hamburger?"

"The best," Tim promised, flashing her a million-dollar grin. He wasn't lying, either. I could vouch for that.

Tim went to lend a hand at the barbecue, and he came away more pumped up about the puppy-raising project than ever.

"You should have seen them, Rick. The ones who got new pups were proud enough to bust, and the ones who had to send theirs back looked like they'd lost their best friends. But they knew they'd been part of something important anyway."

"Having Captain opened a lot of doors for Daisy." I bent down and scratched the dog's ears. "Why are you so turned on by all this, though?"

"I got to thinking. If something had been going on that really mattered to me when I was a kid, I might have kept my nose clean. Judy asked me to help out at the 4-H meetings once a month." Tim knelt beside me and rubbed Captain's belly. "Being laid up this way is gonna flat spoil him."

"I guess I better change his dressing." I got up and dug my first aid kit out of the junk drawer by the kitchen sink. "Now that I think of it, Tim, when you hit the road the night Daisy died, you had one paw in a cast yourself. How did you get rid of it, being on the run and all?"

"I got sick of the damn thing one day and sawed it off myself." Tim held Captain's head while I cleaned his gash with peroxide and bandaged up his foot again. "I hope this lazy varmint heals up fast. There's nothing like walking a dog to attract chicks."

228

I poked him playfully in the ribs. "There's nothing like having a job to keep them interested."

When I got home from school a few days later, I saw Tim and a cute little towheaded kid flying a kite in the field behind the apartment complex. Tim was spending more time chasing the kid out of the street and off the fire escapes than he was keeping the kite in the air. I hung out for close to twenty minutes watching his gentler side shine through.

Then he caught me spying and brought the kid over to my car. "Jake, this is my buddy Rick. Shake his hand."

The blue-eyed ball of energy did better than that. He took a flying leap and landed in my lap, wrapping his arms around my neck. I tickled him till he started squirming and then set him on his feet.

"Are you wanted for kidnapping now?" I asked. "Where did you find this guy?"

"We met at the barbecue the other day. His foster sister got a new puppy to raise." Tim grinned. "I don't know who has more wiggle in him, Jake or the furry little Labrador his sister took home. The girl wasn't thrilled to have Jake tagging along that day, but she said her folks need a break from him sometimes."

"So have you started a baby-sitting service?"

"I got bored this afternoon, so I knocked on his door and told his foster mother I wanted to make friends with him. She thought it was a great idea, either because he needs friends or she needs some peace and quiet. Hey, Jake, that ain't your car. Don't be climbing all over it."

"He sure is a cute kid."

Tim laughed. "He's a tornado. I'm taking him to a fishing derby on Saturday. Wanna come?"

I sighed. "I'd like to, but the taco bar owns me that day."

When I finished slinging tacos on Saturday, I found Tim scrubbing the kitchen floor with the stereo going full blast.

I stepped around him to pour myself a glass of ice water. "Back from fishing already?"

"We couldn't go. Jake got busted for goofing off in school. I told him I'd wet a line with him next weekend, though, if his teacher gives him a star for staying in his seat every day."

Pretty soon Tim landed another junkyard job. He picked up a battered old toolbox at a pawn shop so he could start putting his extra money into auto body gear. Just for kicks, I bought a couple of pistols, and we took to practicing at the firing range every so often. One stormy April night, I found a brand new set of cutlery on the kitchen table.

I tested the heft of a knife in my hand. "These are perfect!"

"Merry Christmas." Tim took a frozen pizza out of the oven. "This is as far as my cooking will ever go, but I thought those knives would suit you."

"You didn't swipe them somewhere, did you?"

He glared at me. "No, I didn't. I went down to that hoity-toity little gourmet store at the mall and laid cold hard cash on the counter. And a lot of it, too."

"Sorry. I forgot you turned over a new leaf."

"I'd hate to set a bad example for Jake and the 4-H kids. Want some iced tea?"

"Yeah. Since when did you drink something so tame?"

"I got to thinking I better back down on the hooch before I end up like my stepdad. His brain was so pickled he couldn't remember anything except how to deal a poker hand." Tim dropped some ice cubes in a glass. "I get a bang out of having Jake around. He's a holy terror more often than not, but he just needs somebody to look up to. That's what I needed, living with the world's greatest drunk."

"I always thought you and your old man were pals."

"We were tight enough I guess. My mom went through husbands like most folks burn up light bulbs. She tossed me off on my stepdad when I got too big to be cute and skipped out to Bermuda with some guy she met at a tanning salon."

"I didn't know that."

"It wasn't something I liked to broadcast. He kept a roof over my head, but he never took me fishing. He never asked to see my report card." Tim flashed a hard, humorless smile. "Remember when your dad let you have it for torching that trailer with me?"

I shuddered, even after all the time that had passed. "How could I forget?"

"My old man just grinned and popped me a beer. We were buddies, but it would've been no great loss to him if I was arrested or burned alive."

"We all used to get madder than blazes to see the way he thumped on you."

Tim ran a hand thoughtfully over the scar on his forehead. "He beat me up when he lost a card game or had a bad night's sleep, and he laughed with me when he was feeling his liquor, but he never bothered to teach me right from wrong. I don't want Jake to learn the way I did. I want him to know someone gives a damn about him whether he climbs the walls or not."

There was a hammering at the door. I got up to answer it, wondering who would be dropping by in the driving rain. Stace stumbled in looking like a drowned rat.

"Hey, look what just blew into town!" I shut the door and threw my arms around him. Alice had kind of warmed me up to the hug thing. "It's been ages, bud. You sprouted yourself some peach fuzz since I saw you last."

Tim rushed over and clapped Stace on the back. "I always knew you were too dumb to come in out of the rain."

"Aw, stuff it." Stace laughed and shrugged off his dripping jacket. "Do you have coffee on?"

"This ain't a diner." Tim grinned and went to make up a pot. "You best get yourself into some dry clothes from that laundry basket before you die of pneumonia right there on the rug."

"What in the world are you doing here?" I asked when we were all sitting at the kitchen table.

"Aren't you glad to see my smiling face?"

"Well, it hasn't turned me to stone yet, but I'm a little surprised. I thought school wasn't out for six more weeks."

232

"I had a terminal case of the backwoods blues, so I bummed a ride with a trucker as far as Dallas and then wore the soles clean off my tennis shoes. This state goes on forever when you're hoofing it."

"Was it really that bad at home?" I topped off his cup and popped another pizza in the oven.

"Yeah. It was pure hell with my dad on my case all the time and the school giving me grief for never showing up." Stace scowled into his mug. "They're all so proud of Bryan they can't see straight. He's going to summer school so he can start at Princeton next January instead of waiting to graduate with the rest of his class."

"He's in at Princeton already? That's great," Tim said.

"You aren't gonna start singing the praises of the star child, too, are you? All I ever hear is how if I tried half as hard as Bryan I might pass my math class, and if I took life serious like Bryan I might make something of myself."

"So what's your plan now?" I probed.

"I'll do whatever it takes to stay out of Mayberry for good. I think God made Georgia just so there'd be a place to stash all the hicks on the planet."

We let Stace camp on the couch that night. I felt bad for not getting hold of his folks to keep them from worrying, but I was sure they'd drag him home within the hour if they found out where he was, and I thought maybe if he had a little break from Georgia, he'd get a better outlook on the situation.

No such luck. I brought up the subject of him phoning home a few times, but I let it drop once and for all when he threatened to hit the road. He hid out in the apartment while me and Tim were at work, and he seemed satisfied to lay low and run the vacuum cleaner, so I decided to let sleeping dogs lie for a while.

Chapter 14

Mark walked into the taco bar while I was manning the cash register one sunny afternoon in May. I didn't recognize him at first. He pulled up in a shiny blue pickup truck with a set of toolboxes in the bed. He had on new jeans and a clean work shirt. But I finally got a good look at his face when I rang up his order.

"Mark Romero!" I burst out. "If this ain't a blast from the past!" I blinked, half expecting him to disappear before my eyes.

He stared blankly at me for a second, then grabbed my hand and just about pumped my arm off. "Hey! I didn't know you with short hair and that retarded sombrero on your ugly head."

"All the poor slobs who work here have to wear them." A couple of high school kids got in line behind Mark, but I ignored them. "Man, it sure is good to see you. What brought you back to town?"

"I got to missing the smell. Between the ranches and the oil refineries, there's nothing like it anywhere else in the world."

"Well, it looks like you've done all right for yourself." I blew off the lady with two little tykes who stepped up behind the teenagers. "Is that your truck parked outside?"

"It will be after twenty-three more payments to my friendly Ford dealer."

The manager hollered at me to quit gabbing and get to work. Mark said something to him in Spanish, and he glared at me from under his sombrero and then broke out into a grin.

"I'm off at three. Stick around for an hour." I handed Mark his change. "What did you say to my boss?"

"I said if he didn't ease up on you, I'd tell all my friends he craps in his beans to make them stretch a little further." Mark carried his tray to a corner booth, and I started waiting on the mob of hungry customers before they got a chance to turn hostile.

I ditched my sombrero at three on the dot and made a beeline for the corner table. The boss was a decent guy at heart, and when he heard me and Mark were joining up after not seeing each other for almost two years, he brought us out a mess of free tacos and a pitcher of lemonade.

"Grandma would roll over in her grave if she knew I was eating this fake Mexican garbage," Mark laughed.

"It ain't bad if you're hungry enough. I've only seen three or four people drop dead from food poisoning this month." I upended a bottle of hot sauce over my tacos. The bottle had a picture of flames on it, but I could drink the stuff like water. "So what happened to you after you lit out of here that last night?"

"I got me a job in the onion fields like I said I would." Mark made a sour face. "Believe me, that was the hardest work I ever did in my life. I had blisters as big as baseballs on my hands for months, and I'm surprised my spine ain't bent in half to this day."

"You didn't get that four-wheeled beauty of yours playing in the dirt."

"I topped onions till the smell of them made me want to retch. I probably would have kept at it till hell froze over, too, if the tractor hadn't broke down one day last fall. We were scrambling to get the crop in while the weather held. I thought the foreman was going to have a heart attack right there in the field."

"I take it he didn't know you can doctor damn near anything with wheels under it."

"I went to look at the tractor, and he threatened to fire me if I didn't get the hell back to work." Mark laughed bitterly. "Those white crew chiefs don't think much of Mexican farm hands. Nobody else does either, as a matter of fact."

"And you decided it was your moral obligation to knock him down a peg or two."

"Damn straight. I spotted a busted tie rod end and said we could try replacing it with a part off an old truck that was rusting away by the river. The boss told me I wasn't getting paid to think, so I asked him if he'd rather let the rig rot there in the field with the onions. He wasn't in much of a spot to look down his nose, which really pissed him off. Anyhow, me and a couple of guys breathed enough life into the tractor to ease her back to the barn."

I refilled our paper cups. "It sounds like you saved the day."

"I reckon so. The foreman started to hog the glory, and I was about to walk away, but the other hands told how the whole thing was my idea. So the farmer asks me to look at this lemon he wants fixed up for his son. He says his regular mechanic never gets around to it because he's either busy giving

237

himself a hangover or sleeping one off most of the time. One thing led to another, and pretty soon I traded my hoe for a wrench and a screwdriver."

"I bet that broke your heart. I guess a sober Mexican mechanic beats a drunk white one."

"Money talks. The farmer started hiring me out to some of his old buddies. Before long, a couple of them put in a good word for me at a shop in town."

"And you started saving up to come home?"

"I started buying tools. The guy who owned the garage was building a car for the race track. So I helped him out after hours. When the car won a few purses, I put money down on a truck and headed south. Those Colorado winters are no fun for a Texas boy like me."

"It sure is good to run into you again, bud. When you bolted out of the hospital that night without looking back, I thought it was the last I'd ever see of you."

"I'm like the bad penny that keeps turning up. What have you done with yourself since then?"

I told him all about how the judge and his wife had helped me get on my feet and into cooking school.

"You're going to be a chef? God help the poor souls who eat in your roach roost."

I blew a straw wrapper at him. "Anyway, Walter and Alice are cool people. Tim turned himself in and got an easy sentence from the judge, and—"

"Tim? Do you know where he is?"

"Sure. He's working at a junkyard, and we've got a place over by the flea market."

"Is he there now?"

I glanced at my watch. "I expect so. Stace, too."

"What the hell are we wasting time in this joint for then?" Mark jumped up and scooped our trash onto the plastic tray.

"I'm driving the little blue hatchback. Follow me."

After Tim and Stace got through squeezing the stuffing out of Mark, he went to talk to the manager of the apartment complex and rented a place a few doors down from mine. We followed him to the thrift store in my car and loaded his truck with furniture.

I sprung for steaks that night and grilled them on my balcony. It felt like old times with all of us together again except that Stace started pouting whenever Bryan's name came up. Tim had Jake with him. The kid bounced in and out the sliding glass door of the apartment like a squirrel on speed.

Mark scooped a bite of ice cream right out of the carton. "I sure missed all the times we used to hang out like this."

"I knew you'd be back." Stace gave him a friendly poke in the ribs. "I told Rick once that if you ever start feeding strays, they never leave."

"Is that why you showed up on my doorstep?" I asked. "Come to think of it, I must be a magnet for strays. Tim just about ate me out of house and home when I found him, too."

"And it was the best skillet of slop I ever put away." Tim flipped through the channels on the TV. "They never show any good blood-and-guts movies anymore. Jake, get down off that railing before you fall and kill yourself!"

We all glanced out and saw the kid perched on the rail of the balcony, swinging his feet, with a big grin on his face. Tim made it to him in two steps and swept him down, then shoved him inside and slammed the sliding door.

"You just took ten years off my life, you little monkey." He made Jake sit down beside him on the couch. "Chill out a minute or you're liable to spontaneously combust."

"I don't know what that is, but I think I'll do it after I grow up."

When we all busted out laughing, Jake blushed and climbed onto Tim's lap.

Tim ruffled the kid's mop of blond hair. "It means burst into flames, so it probably isn't a good career goal for you."

"Hey, porker, are you going to leave some ice cream for the rest of us or is that your own personal slop bucket?" Stace held out his empty bowl.

"You don't look like you're withering away, pal." Mark filled the bowl and then kept on eating out of the box.

Jake hopped up. "Me, too! Me, too!"

"Just give him a taste," Tim said. "He's wired enough without pumping sugar into his system."

Mark popped a spoonful of ice cream into Jake's mouth and then dropped a glob of it down the back of Stace's shirt. Stace let out a startled squawk and chucked a couch cushion at Mark without putting down his dish. In the next second, every pillow I

240

owned was in flight. It's funny how guys can get older but never outgrow a good pillow fight.

Jake launched himself across the room at me like a torpedo, and I caught him and tickled him while he giggled his head off. Tim cut loose with an Indian war screech and tossed a cushion at Stace. It knocked a lamp off the coffee table, and a terrific shattering noise added to the anarchy.

"Cut it out before you trash my whole place!" I yelled, more amused than mad.

And then we heard the knock at the door. I killed the stereo on my way to answer it, figuring it would be somebody griping about the racket.

The sheriff pushed into the room as soon as I got the door open. "What's going on here?"

I smiled sweetly at him. "Just a pillow fight, sir. Do they always call out the sheriff to put down pillow fights?"

He shot me his best "Do you really expect me to believe that?" look. They must teach cops how to raise their eyebrows in just the right way at the police academies because they all have it down to a science.

"Is there a Stacy Thomas here?" the sheriff asked.

"I don't think so." Stace tried to sound innocent, but the panic in his eyes gave him away.

"You'll have to come with me, kid. Your parents have a bulletin out on you."

"I don't know why. Their favorite son is safe at home. Really, they ought to be glad I got out of their hair."

The sheriff shrugged. "Be that as it may, there's a bus ticket for Savannah with your name on it in my pocket."

"You might as well wash your face with it because I ain't going back there." Stace didn't move off the couch.

The sheriff stepped toward him, frowning.

I got between them before Stace could do anything stupid. "Listen, officer, let me call his folks. Maybe I can get them to back off."

He shrugged again. "I doubt it, but it's no skin off my nose, I guess."

Ed answered the phone, and I managed to spit three or four words out before he fried the wires from my apartment all the way to the east coast.

"You tell that kid he best be on a bus back here by morning, Rick, if he knows what's good for him! I ought to charge you with something for harboring him! You two don't have a lick of common sense between you!"

"Put a cork in it. Maybe if you'd give Stace a pat on the back instead of a kick in the butt once in a while, he'd do a little better out there."

"Oh, he'll do better, don't worry! This is the last straw! He'll be in military school before the week is out, unless I kill him first!"

I slammed down the phone. "Sorry, Stace. He's way too hot to handle right now. Maybe his brain will have stopped smoking by the time you make it back to Georgia."

"I wouldn't get on that bus at gunpoint!" Stace pushed past the sheriff and made a mad dash for the door.

Mark grabbed his arm and jerked him to a halt. "Don't be an idiot. You're about to land yourself in a whole lot more trouble than you can weasel out of. You'll have to hack it in Hicksville for one more year and then come back when there's nothing your folks can do about it."

Stace knew he was up against impossible odds, so he gave in and followed the sheriff out of the apartment, cussing up a storm. I bet the lightning in his eyes burned holes in the back of the blue uniform before the two of them parted company. Ed and Sharon hadn't cooled off by the time their son made it back to Georgia. Me and Tim and Mark wrote to him in military school as often as we could, but he never answered our letters.

~~~

Mark hired on at a local auto shop, and Tim finally got work as a body man with a good reference from his boss at the junkyard. The two of them started saving up to open a garage together. Mark met Anita at the meat counter in the supermarket one evening in June, and they hit it off before they made it to the cash register. You couldn't keep those two lovebirds apart after that. Anita was a cute little dark-haired dressmaker, but she was real shy, and her English wasn't too good. She mostly just nodded and smiled when me or Tim said anything to her, but her eyes lit up whenever she looked at Mark, so we liked her well enough.

I took an internship for cooking school with a catering service, so when I wasn't slinging tacos for minimum wage that summer, I was serving miniature sandwiches and fancy dips and things at high-class banquets and lawn parties. I liked the job all right even if I had to wear a white shirt and a tie, but rich folks sure are stingy at their get-togethers. I can't for the life of me figure out what they see in nibbling everything off crackers or toothpicks like fish taking bait from a hook. Grandma never had much money, but if you left one of her taco feeds hungry, well, that was your own fault.

I was walking around the dining room of a swanky hotel with a tray of crab canapés one evening when I met Emily, the neighbor with the frizzy blond perm and the whiny voice who'd brought Alice to pick me up at the cop shop after I wrecked the convertible.

She looked hard at me from behind her bifocals. "Have I seen you somewhere before, young man?"

"Yeah, I lived with Judge Mills for a while."

"Well, I never! You're the little car thief, aren't you? I certainly didn't expect to meet you in a place like this."

I felt curious stares boring into me from all around the table, but I kept my voice as pleasant as I could. "Walter and Alice have a way of bringing out the best in people."

"They've worked miracles in more than one case, though I'm sure I don't know why they put themselves out like they do. There's another hellion staying with them now, and I'm afraid he's a very bad specimen."

I didn't tell her she'd be the perfect model if they ever made an Over-the-Hill Barbie. The words itched to roll off my tongue, but I counted to ten inside my head and flashed her my best smile. "Just think. If the judge and his wife had said I was a bad specimen, your taxes would likely be paying for my cable TV in the state prison now. Would you like another canapé?"

She took one, and I hurried away before my big mouth landed me in trouble. This turning the other cheek thing was getting a little easier.

I got my certificate from the cooking school at the end of August. Tim and Mark came to watch me graduate, and Alice was there, but Walter couldn't make it.

"We've got another boy living with us, and he's a real handful," Alice explained. "He ran away last night. They picked him up in some little town in Oklahoma, and Walter had to go after him today. He told me to be sure and let you know how proud he is, though."

I drove home after the graduation ceremony and tacked my chef certificate on the living room wall. I was feeling pretty pleased with myself as I stood back to admire the fancy lettering on the parchment, but all at once I saw the certificate through a mist of tears.

Daisy should have been sharing the moment with me. She'd been there when my cooking dream first took root. I tried to imagine her smiling down on me from somewhere in heaven, but the picture didn't offer much comfort in the quiet apartment. I suddenly felt like one of those helium balloons that droops after all the gas leaks out. I sank onto the couch and cradled my aching head in my hands.

Captain rescued me from my misery. He wagged up to me and pushed his wet nose into my face. When I ignored him, he started licking the tears off my cheeks.

I had to chuckle. "Okay, Turbo Tongue, that's enough. I'll quit sniffling all over you if you quit slobbering all over me."

He picked up a holey old T-shirt off the floor and gripped it in his teeth. I accepted his challenge, and we had ourselves a tug-of-war that turned into an all-out wrestling match on the carpet. We always made a big show of snapping and snarling at each other, and usually we went till we were both out of wind. But that time we called it a draw when Mark and Anita stopped by on their way out for the evening.

Captain dropped the shirt and strutted up to Anita, ready to be fussed over. She knelt down and started stroking his head and neck. "He is a beautiful dog."

"He knows it, too. He's as much of a heartbreaker as Tim ever was." I laughed. "You'll have to watch out for him, Mark. He's apt to lure Anita away with him one afternoon while you're doing emergency surgery on somebody's Pontiac."

Mark grinned. "Naw, I think I'm safe. Captain's too hairy for her to stay with for life, so the worst she'll do is have a little fling with him on the side."

246

Anita had hidden her face in Captain's neck, and she was blushing so red I wondered if his fur was being singed. It was all I could do not to bust out laughing.

I put a hand on her shoulder instead. "Don't take us too serious. We're always spouting off with stuff like that."

She smiled shyly up at me but didn't say anything. I shot Mark a puzzled glance, then shrugged. Maybe she just needed a little time to open up. Daisy had jumped right in the middle of the crew with both feet, but I reckon it takes all kinds of chicks to make life interesting.

The phone rang. Mark answered it and then tossed the receiver to me. "It's the catering service."

I swore under my breath, figuring I was about to lose my one day off out of the week. But it turned out to be the boss offering me a full-time job.

"Sure! I'll put in my notice at the taco bar tomorrow." I hung up the phone. "I guess God smiles on downtown slobs once in a while. I'm going to break out of the Ptomaine Temple before I'm old and gray after all."

Mark slapped me on the back. "Way to go. You'll have to bring your sombrero home as a memento."

"Only if I get to burn it in the parking lot at midnight."

Anita gave Captain one last caress and stood up. She looked at her wrist watch and said something to Mark in Spanish.

"Late is a four letter word, you know." Mark grinned and took his princess by the hand. I couldn't help but notice the twinkle in his eyes as the two of them walked out of the room. I was tickled for him. I knew there would never be anybody like Daisy to light up my life again, but I was going to get a kick out of watching Mark fall in love.

Chapter 15

The ringing phone jerked me out of a sound sleep late one autumn night. I stumbled into the living room to answer it and whacked my shin on the coffee table as I passed.

"This better be important," I growled into the receiver, bending over to rub the pain out of my throbbing leg.

"Rick? Sorry to wake you." Alice's voice was shaking.

I forgot my aching shin in a flash. "Alice, what's wrong?"

"Can you come to the hospital? It's Walter."

"Is he sick?"

"He's in surgery. The kid we had living with us, he ... he ..."Her voice broke. "Please come sit with me!"

"I'll be there in ten minutes." I hung up the phone, scrawled a quick note to Tim, and raced out the door in the ratty old sweats I always slept in.

The night was clear and cold, and the streets were almost empty. It was a lucky thing I didn't meet any cops on my way across town because I put that old Gremlin of mine to the test.

I barreled into the hospital at a dead run. Alice was huddled miserably on one of the hard plastic chairs in the lobby, wearing a faded cotton housecoat under her winter jacket. When I saw her slumped there with her hair a mess and her eyes all red from crying, memories of the night Daisy died slammed into me like a freight train, and my breath jammed up in my throat. Alice rushed over and put her arms around me. We stood together like that for a long moment. Then she drew back, and I caught sight of a knot as big as a golf ball on one side of her face.

"What happened to your cheek?" I turned her head so I could get a good look at the ugly purple bruise.

She guided me into a chair and sat down next to me. "Promise you'll stay calm."

"I'm calm, damn it!" I snapped. Then I sucked in a deep breath and spoke quietly. "Okay, tell me. What's going on?"

She took my hand and pressed it between hers. "It was Travis, the kid who's been staying with us."

"Did he clobber you?"

She nodded. "I caught him watching an indecent movie in my living room. When I went to shut it off, he hit me with one of those brass candlesticks I have on the mantle."

Hot rage started pouring through my veins. "And Walter?"

"I didn't see him coming, but all at once he lunged between us, and then it happened quick as a wink." She squeezed my hand hard. "I saw the flash of a blade and the splash of blood on his nightshirt, and he went down like a big old oak tree."

"Where's Travis now?"

"I don't know. He ran out of the house while I was calling the ambulance."

I sprang up, trembling with fury. "The little bastard better hope the cops find him before I do

250

because I'm gonna rip his heart out and shove it down his throat while it's still beating!"

Alice grabbed my arm. "You can't touch him, Rick."

"The hell I can't! Just give me a clue what he looks like!"

"Sit down, honey. I need you to stay with me tonight."

It went against every rigid fiber in my being, but I forced myself back into the chair. "What do the doctors say?"

"It's all up in the air right now. They'll know more when they get a look inside him." Suddenly her control splintered. "Rick, I can't lose my Walter! I can't lose him!"

She broke down into a fit of wrenching sobs, and I took her in my arms and held her tight, letting her bury her face in the folds of my sweatshirt. I was afraid she would never stop crying. She settled down eventually, but I didn't let her go.

I ran a hand gently over her graying hair. "Take it easy. Walter always lands on his feet. Don't give up on him yet."

She started murmuring a prayer, asking God to be with her husband in surgery and to keep her strong as she waited for news of him. I didn't figure it would get me anywhere, but I sent up a few silent wishes of my own, just in case. Alice even put in a good word for Travis, but I couldn't bring myself to do anything except plot his murder.

"Does God really listen to you?" I asked when she finally signed off with an amen.

She nodded. "He does. I have no doubt about it."

"So will Walter be okay? I mean, since you prayed for him and everything?"

"I don't know. I hope so, but praying for someone isn't like waving a magic wand. There are no guarantees in it, not for me or anybody else."

"Why do you bother then?" I asked bitterly. "On the worst night I ever lived through, when I knew Daisy was slipping away from me, I begged God over and over not to let her die. I might as well have been talking to my tennis shoes, for all the difference it made."

"I prayed for my son every single day while he was in Vietnam." Alice straightened up so she could look right into my face. "When the Army officer knocked on my door and told me Arthur wouldn't be coming home, I swore I'd never speak to God again. I stood in my living room and screamed out a promise at the top of my lungs, vowing not to offer up another prayer as long as I lived."

"What changed your mind?"

"I eventually figured out that walking away from God only left me alone with my sorrow. It didn't bring Arthur back, and it didn't ease the sadness that was drowning me."

"So you started praying again and going to church and stuff. What did you get out of that?"

"Hope," she said simply, leaning forward and putting a hand on my knee. "Life is a risky business, you know that as well as I do. God never said it would be easy. But every human being on the planet has a choice to live in hope or fear, in victory or

252

despair. Even when tragedy strikes, my faith reminds me that God made the human spirit stronger than grief, stronger than evil, and even stronger than death."

"Will you still believe that if Walter doesn't make it?" There was a hard edge in my voice, and I regretted the question as soon as it popped out of my mouth.

Alice winced and bit her lip, but she didn't look away from me. "Walter Mills is the love of my life. I've known that since I was twelve years old. If he doesn't come out of surgery, I'll want nothing more than to lay down and die. But God will give me a reason to carry on if that's what I have to do."

"What reason is that?"

"He adores me, Rick. He delights in watching me live and grow, the same way I delighted in watching my baby Arthur take his first steps and learn to read."

I glanced at the clock and wondered how the Big Guy felt about watching Alice suffer the way she was now, but I decided it would be better not to ask her that.

"Yeah, well, I bet God will get a bang out of seeing Travis burn in hell," I muttered instead. "I know I would."

Alice shook her head. "He won't. He cares as deeply for Travis as He does for me, and He loves you a million times more than Walter and I or even your folks ever could."

"Really?" The conviction in Alice's voice had been making me curious somehow, much to my surprise. "How do I get to know this God of yours?

He isn't the one most people talk about. When Mom and Dad died, the preacher made it sound like He swooped down and tore my world apart just for kicks or something."

"Nothing could be further from the truth. God doesn't toss blessings and curses around like paper airplanes. But when you decide to live victoriously, the pain you go through doesn't have to drag you down. It can make you kind and brave and determined instead."

"So how do I pull it off then?"

"It's a gradual thing, a decision you make every day, every moment," she explained. "Try talking to God, the same way you've been talking to me."

"Look, Alice, I'm not much of a talker, even to someone I can see. You do it, okay? I'll say something stupid."

Alice smiled. "God is used to hearing people say stupid things. I've said plenty of them myself. I'll start you off, and you can join in when you feel comfortable."

She clasped both of my hands in hers and asked God to make His presence known in my life. I didn't see any lightning bolts or angels or anything, and I didn't get a peaceful feeling inside like Grandma used to say she got when she prayed. I was a little disappointed, but I told the Man Upstairs I guessed I was willing to get acquainted and find out what came of it. It seemed silly chattering away at thin air, but it made Alice happy, so I went along with it, even though I felt my face and ears turning red. I was glad nobody but Alice was around to hear what I was saying.

"If God pulls Walter through, I swear I'll go to church every Sunday as long as I live."

"God doesn't make bargains, honey, and it isn't about going to church. You may want to find a church where you can learn about the Bible and get to know other believers, but the key is what happens in your own heart as God touches you inside. You wait and see." Alice picked up her black leather handbag and fished around in it till she found a sealed envelope. "I have a surprise for you."

When I ripped open the envelope, my heart did a somersault in my chest and then started pounding. "Daisy's necklace! Where in the world did you get this?"

"You mentioned it the first night you lived in my house, remember? When you refused to set foot in a church. I knew Daisy passed without any family, and I wondered what happened to the necklace, so I came to the hospital and did some poking around."

I turned the smooth silver cross over and over in my hands, picturing the way it had sparkled in the hollow of Daisy's throat. "I can't believe you tracked it down."

"Nobody in the emergency room knew who it belonged to. It had been floating around for a couple of weeks when I asked about it, so someone must have lost it about the time Daisy died. I had a feeling it was hers." Alice took the cross from me and fastened it around my neck. "I've been saving it in my purse for years. I knew someday it would mean more to you than a keepsake or a good luck charm."

I felt tears pooling up in my eyes and brushed them away with the back of my hand. "Thanks so much, Alice. Having Daisy's cross makes me feel like she's right here with me."

"I hope it reminds you that God is with you, too, now and always. If you decide to wear it regularly, I'll get you a heavier chain to put it on." Alice fidgeted in her chair and glanced at the clock. "It's after two. Isn't that surgeon ever going to send word?"

I got up and switched on the TV. "There's nothing but sappy old movies showing in the wee hours, but maybe they'll keep your mind off the time for a while."

Me and Alice sat in the lobby through most of the night. Finally, when I was ready to go find the operating room and bust the door down myself in search of news, a doctor came into the room from the hallway. At the same time, a cop rushed in from outside.

Alice looked straight at the doctor. "Tell me!"

"He's going to be fine, Mrs. Mills." The doctor grinned. "His recovery will be slow, but that man is as tough as a Texas range bull and twice as stubborn."

Alice sagged against me, sobbing again. The doctor said a few more words, but neither of us heard him, and after a minute he hurried away.

I turned to the cop. "Did you nab the rotten son of a—" I glanced quickly at Alice and stopped myself. "Did you catch Travis?"

"Yeah, we got him. He'll be charged first thing tomorrow morning, and if we're lucky, he'll be tried as an adult."

Alice blew her nose and dried her eyes. "Thank you, officer. I'll go to my husband now."

I led her by the hand out of the waiting room and down the quiet hallway to an information desk, where I paused to get directions.

"I'll have to ask the surgeon if Judge Mills is receiving visitors." The nurse behind the desk reached for a telephone.

I stopped her hand in mid-air. "He's receiving visitors."

"But I—"

"Don't argue with me, lady." I looked at Alice's drawn face. The night had put years on her. "If you won't tell me where he is, I'll hunt him down myself."

"Turn left at the end of this hall. He's in the second room on your right."

"Thanks. We'll only stay a minute." I steered Alice away from the counter. She followed me like a sleepwalker.

We found Walter in a bare little room that was dark except for the light coming in from the hallway. He had on a hospital gown, open in the front, and a wide bandage covered the upper part of his belly. Zillions of wires crisscrossed his chest and snaked their way along the floor to a machine that hummed and clicked to itself in a corner. All kinds of wavy lines crawled across a flickering screen on the wall. The judge had a needle in his arm, and I wondered if it was morphine or something dripping into him from the bag on a pole beside the bed. His eyes were closed, and his breathing was steady. I thought maybe he was asleep.

I pulled a chair up to the bed, and Alice sat down and took Walter gently by the hand. I stood behind her and massaged her tense shoulders.

The judge opened his eyes and looked straight at Alice. "How are you holding up, honey?"

"Just fine, now I know you're all right." Alice lifted his hand to her cheek and held it there while she fought back a fresh flood of tears. "I was so afraid I'd lose you, Walter."

"I've got a kick or two left in me yet." His words were sort of slurred. "Where's Travis?"

"In custody."

"And who's that handsome escort of yours?"

I stepped up to the bed. "Hey, Walter. It's me, Rick."

He flashed a weary smile. "Good. You take my wife home with you and make sure she gets some rest."

I snapped him a salute. "Yes, sir. You get some rest, too. We'll be back in the morning."

The sky was just starting to turn gray as I guided Alice out of the hospital and tried to remember where I parked my car.

"Oh, there it is. Well, I guess you'll think twice about putting yourselves out for any more wayward kids after this."

She laughed weakly. "Don't bet on it. Arthur's old bedroom never stays empty too long. That's the nature of taking chances. Sometimes things work out, sometimes they don't."

I drove to my apartment and made Alice close the blinds in my room and catch a few winks. I dozed on the couch for a while and then called in sick at the catering service and jumped in the shower. When I came out, Alice was putting on her jacket.

"Where are you off to?" I took the coat from her and pointed at a chair. "Sit there. I'll fix you some coffee."

"I want to go to him."

"The taxi ain't leaving till you've got some food in you. Your bruise is almost black this morning."

Tim dragged himself out of his room just then, rubbing his eyes. "Did I hear something about coffee? I saw your note, Rick. Is everything okay?"

"The latest Mills delinquent stuck a knife in Walter, but he's going to pull through." I filled up all our cups and poured Alice some cereal. "They've got Travis in the cooler."

"I hope he fries," Tim snarled. "I hope he rots in hell."

I nodded. "I wish they'd let me have a crack at him. He'd think he was in hell."

"I feel sad for him," Alice said.

My jaw dropped. "Sad! After all he put you through?"

"Walter will be okay, thank God, but Travis destroyed his own life. We offered him a hand up, and he wouldn't take it."

259

I gulped down my coffee and then paced around the room till Alice finished eating. She and Jesus could bleed for the loser as much as they wanted to. The way I saw it, Travis was the only one who ought to be bleeding. I knew Tim was inclined to agree with me.

When we got back to the hospital, Walter was propped up in bed. He looked pretty drained, but he grinned at us over the morning paper. I guess word gets out fast because he had two vases of flowers and a box of chocolates on his bedside table.

"Well, aren't we popular?" Alice said. "Oh, the roses are from Skip. He must have seen you on the news last night."

"The phone hasn't quit ringing all morning. Michael even called from Canada. He's doing fine in the landscaping business up there." Walter laughed. "He told me he heard about all this from Danny. Our sons must be a bunch of gossips at heart."

"They all care about you, honey." Alice sat down on the edge of the bed. "How do you feel this morning?"

"I've felt a lot better. The bonbons are for you from Jim and Jordan. Those two were in love with you from the moment they laid eyes on you. Munch away. I'll be on hot tea and chicken broth for a while."

Alice offered me the candy. "Rick kept me in one piece last night. I don't know what I would have done without him."

"We're even then. I'd be in the slammer or in my grave if it wasn't for you two." I popped a chocolate into her mouth.

I stopped to see Walter at the hospital every evening when I got off work, and most days I followed Alice home to make sure she ate a decent meal before she hit the sack. I went to church the next Sunday for the first time since my folks died.

Alice's church was too big and fancy for my liking, so I slipped into the back row of an old chapel on the bad side of town. A couple of people shot sideways glances at my faded jeans and scuffed boots, but the preacher had a plain way of talking that made me feel right at home.

Mom had told me a few Bible stories when I was a kid and even packed me off to church camp one summer, much to my despair, but it blew me away to hear that God knew all about me and wanted to see my life turn out right as much as I did. I wasn't really sure it was true, but I'd been lonely deep inside for a long time, so I didn't see the harm in giving religion a try. It seemed to work for Alice.

~~~

When the doctors finally let the judge go home—he threatened to pull off a jail break in his bathrobe and slippers—I started swimming laps with him two or three times a week. He'd lost a lot of strength, but he swore it wouldn't be long till he was giving me a run for my money again. Tim came to the pool with me now and then, and he brought Jake along one day near the end of November. Jake had never learned to swim, and all the way to the judge's house, he was so excited he couldn't sit still.

Finally I had to pull the car over to the side of the road. "The wheels on this wagon don't roll another inch till everybody is belted in."

Jake let Tim buckle him up, but he bounced on the seat as best he could anyway and kept up a steady stream of chatter the rest of the way across town. I doubt if that kid ever had a quiet moment, even in his sleep.

I stopped in the kitchen to chat with Alice for a minute, so by the time I made it to the glass patio, Jake was decked out in the new red swimming trunks Tim had bought him. I froze in my tracks and stared at him in horror. His back and legs were crisscrossed with dozens of ugly white scars.

"God Almighty!" I blurted out before I could stop myself. "What happened to him?"

"It's awful, ain't it," Tim said. "You know he's got a hyperactivity problem. His dad used to keep him peeled off the ceiling with a horsewhip."

"I'd like to get ten minutes alone with that jackass in a dark alley!"

"You and me both. I saw six shades of red when his foster mother told me about it."

I turned away, feeling sick inside. I knew the memory of those hideous scars would stay with me for the rest of my life. Tim led Jake by the hand toward the water, but all at once the kid lost his nerve. He backed away from the pool and hunkered down on the deck with his hands clasped around his knees.

Tim crouched down beside him and patted him on the shoulder. "What's the matter, bud? You've been chomping at the bit all afternoon."

"I don't wanna go in the water," Jake whispered. His blue eyes brimmed with tears.

"You don't have to if you're scared, but I'll be right there with you. Let's just go sit by the edge and dangle our feet in."

Me and Walter started swimming laps. Tim coaxed Jake to the side of the pool after a while and got him to splash his feet in the water. Then he sat on the top step in the shallow end, and Jake climbed onto his lap. The next time I glanced over, the kid was paddling around in the safety of Tim's arms, and both of them were obviously pleased with themselves.

Walter caught up with me, and we watched the fun while we took a breather at the far side of the pool.

"I'm a sea monster!" Jake called out when he saw us spying. He put on a ferocious face and growled at us, then giggled and went back to blowing bubbles and kicking his feet.

Walter grinned. "Isn't that a precious sight? Look how patient Tim is with him."

"Tim likes to think he's tough stuff, but he's always had a soft spot for kids, especially kids who've been hurt."

"I've had a lot of time to reflect on my life while I've been on the mend, and this is where it's at. Alice's dad caught me on my way down. I pulled you back from the brink, and you gave Tim a hand up.

263

Now Tim is reaching out to Jake." The judge ran his fingers through his damp hair. "My friends and neighbors have questioned my sanity for years. They say taking in troubled kids is like dropping ice cubes into hell and hoping to quench the flames, but I believe you can save the world one person at a time."

"It sure beats sitting around griping about the high crime rate and the way teenagers will never amount to anything."

"You have to pick your cases carefully, and I guess I made a big mistake with Travis. But most kids respond well when I let them know I care about them and expect success."

"When my good sense left town and I slit my wrists, it was because I thought there was nobody left in the world who'd give a damn if I lived or died. You and Alice dropped into my life like a pair of angels."

"And now the crew is all accounted for, complete with a mascot. If that youngster grins any wider, he'll split his face in two." Walter pointed to the shallow end of the pool. Tim had Jake riding around on his shoulders, and the kid positively glowed.

"Jake soaks up Tim's attention like sunshine, and no wonder. The sight of those scars was enough to make my stomach turn."

Walter nodded. "I'll never know why brutes like his dad are allowed to raise children."

"Yeah. I was lucky to have a good set of folks even though they died while I still needed them."

By the end of the evening, Jake was splashing all over the pool like he really had turned into a sea monster. He rolled out his lower lip and started putting up a fuss when it came time to get out of the water.

Tim snapped his fingers. "Knock off the whining if you want to come back. You're supposed to be home by seven, and it's already six-thirty."

Jake put a cork in it and clambered out of the pool. While Tim dried his streaming hair, he did his best impression of an overactive jumping bean.

He suddenly darted out from under the towel, laughing, and zipped across the room. "Try and catch me!"

"Stop running before you fall and hurt yourself!" Walter rapped out, a split second too late.

Jake slipped on the wet cement and took a header into the deep part of the pool. He sank under the surface, came up flailing, and sank again.

Tim bounded to the edge and plunged in without thinking twice. He reached the kid in a few powerful strokes, but Jake was so frantic by then that he'd turned into a windmill of kicking feet and clutching fingers. He twined his legs around Tim's knees and got a desperate hold on his neck with one hand. Both of them disappeared under the water.

"Jake, you gotta stop fighting," Tim gasped when their heads broke the surface for a second.

Walter grabbed a metal bar that was leaning against the wall and rushed over to the edge. "Tim, get hold of this!"

I took the pole from him. "The last thing you need to do is rip your stitches out."

The two grappling figures spun around and around in a whirl of thrashing limbs and splashing water. I could hear Tim's ragged breathing as he struggled to get Jake in one arm and pull for the shore with the other. Finally he drew back and slapped the kid as hard as he could across the side of the head. Jake sucked in a huge gulp of air and went limp, and Tim got a good grip on him and latched onto the pole I held out. I hauled them to the side of the pool. Tim heaved Jake onto the deck and then rested a minute, coughing and sputtering, before he dragged himself out of the water.

Jake curled up into a ball, whimpering and choking. I stepped toward him, and he threw one arm in front of his face as if to stop a blow and then scrambled away on the cement. He hadn't calmed down by the time Tim got his wind back. Tim knelt beside him and pulled him close, and Walter spread a towel over both of them.

"Take it easy, kid. You're okay now." Tim wiped Jake's pasty white face with a corner of the towel.

Jake tried to squirm away, and his eyes were wild. "Don't touch me! Don't touch me!"

"Are you scared of me?" Tim asked. "I had to hit you like that to make you quit fighting."

Jake shook his head and pointed at me as I stood there with the heavy bar in my hand.

I stared at him, stunned. "Did you think I was gonna club you or something?"

He nodded, and I dropped the pole and squatted beside him. I put a hand under his chin and tipped his face up so I could look straight into his eyes. "Listen, pal, I never clobbered a guy with a chunk of pipe in my life without a damn good reason, and if I ever do it again, it sure as hell won't be to a kid."

"Promise?" he asked through chattering teeth.

"I promise. Anyway, Tim wouldn't let something like that happen to you."

"Not on a bet. Now let's get you into some dry clothes." Tim stood up and lifted Jake to his feet. "You need to watch yourself around swimming pools from now on so you don't end up getting hurt."

"Can we still come back again?"

"You want to?" Tim glanced at Walter. "What do you say after all this?"

"You're welcome any time as long as Jake remembers not to run in here anymore."

Jake managed a shaky smile. "I'll remember. Tim's going to teach me how to do an underwater somersault."

"Don't ever dive in after somebody, Tim," Walter said. "Even a kid has insane strength when he thinks he's dying, and Jake could have taken you down with him. Always hold a lifeline out to a drowning person from solid ground."

As we were leaving, the judge turned to me. "By the way, Rick, what good reason did you have for busting some guy with a piece of pipe?"

"A couple no-count punks who lived across from the Barn took a notion to jump Grandma for her pension check one day. Me and Tim had to make it damn clear she was no easy target."

Tim laughed. "We have our own way of keeping order on the bad side of town, and it don't involve cops. Me and Rick are better at it than most, but it was a good thing Mark wasn't in on that incident. Somebody would have ended up in a body bag."

~~~

Tim and Jake started spending a few afternoons a week at the pool. I asked Mark's girlfriend to drop by the Mills house with me one evening right before Christmas, figuring Alice might like some female company. Anita was scared to death of strangers, but no one could stay clammed up around Alice for long, so in no time the two of them were all clicking tongues and crazy giggles. Anita helped out with some ironing and cooking that day, and she took to tagging along with me every so often to give Alice a hand. Pretty soon, Alice insisted on paying her.

"It's been a great load off my shoulders to have you take over some of the work so I can tend to Walter." Alice wrote out a check and pressed it into Anita's hand. "I'd love to have you once a week if you want the job."

Anita sparkled like a sunbeam all the way home. "I will be sending money to my family in Mexico every week now."

"I didn't know you had folks down there," I said.

"Yes. My father is very sick, and my mother and sisters do their best, but times are hard in that place."

By the end of January, Anita had landed jobs with two of Alice's neighbors. She rode the bus uptown after she got off at the dress shop and cleaned houses three days a week. Mark always went to pick her up because he didn't want her walking home in the dark by herself. He coddled her like she was a real live china doll. I guess maybe that's how you're supposed

268

to treat a chick when you're in love, but Daisy would never have put up with it.

Walter was on his feet and behind his bench again by the time Travis's court date came around in the spring. The trial had to be moved to some cow town out in the middle of nowhere because Walter and Alice were both well known in Bertha City, especially at the courthouse, and they were highly thought of everywhere they went. I guess the lawyers figured there was no chance of scraping up a fair-minded jury for Travis in his home town. They were probably right. They could have called out a lynch mob in less than five minutes, though.

I took some time off work so I could sit in the courtroom with Alice. I gave more than a passing thought to smuggling my pistol in and sending Travis straight to hell, but the judge and his wife had invested too much in my life for me to throw it away on a stupid move like that.

When I got to the courtroom, I was surprised to see that there weren't many empty chairs. The room was filled with grim-faced men of different ages. I snagged a seat and introduced myself to the guy next to me.

"So you're Rick. Alice wrote me all about you. I'm Mitchell. I was the stray the judge took in right before you." He pointed at a guy in a leather jacket sitting behind him. "Abel there came before me. And before him it was Pablo."

I whistled. "I guess Walter could've got up quite a posse if the cops hadn't tracked Travis down as quick as they did."

"You know it." Mitchell pounded a clenched fist on his knee. "I'd like to have that kid by the throat right now."

"You'd have to fight me for the honor," said a man in a faded work shirt. He looked to be about forty or so. "I was the first hard case the judge got hold of, so first blood is mine."

During the opening arguments, the prosecutor made Walter unbutton his shirt so the jury could see the scar where he'd been slashed and sewed up. But the defense attorney started spinning this sob story about how Travis had a troubled childhood and should be given a break because the world had been so hard on him.

Travis sat up there the whole time looking smug, and once when I saw a little smirk flit across his face, rage drove me half out of my chair. I heard a stirring all around me, and the judge's whole pack of sons was on the move. Then Walter threw down his famous evil eye, and we all put the brakes on.

The trial was short. I really don't even know why they blathered on as long as they did. The only thing that counted in my book was that Travis's fingerprints and Walter's blood were lifted off the same knife. In any case, the jury didn't buy the rotten childhood crap, so Travis went down the river for attempted murder. I got the feeling he was safer in prison than he would have been on the streets anyway. Things got a little tense for a few minutes after the trial because Walter and Alice had every one of their sons, including me, arguing for the right to take them out to eat.

Finally, the judge put up a hand for silence. "All of you quit squabbling and get yourselves over to my house, and that's an order from my wife. We'll have us a Texas barbecue like none of you have ever seen. Rick here has a full-fledged chef certificate, so I guess it's time for him to show us his stuff."

I charred steaks till I was sure we'd wiped out the entire population of beef cattle in the state. Finally I got to snag a hunk of meat for myself and sit down. I saw that the judge had sneaked off to a quiet corner, so I went to join him.

"Hey, Walter, mind if I park here?" I gestured at an empty chair.

"I don't see what's stopping you."

"You look bushed. Are you feeling all right?"

He took off his glasses and turned them over and over in his hands. "I was just thinking about Travis. It's wonderful to have all of you guys here, of course, but his downfall is nothing to celebrate."

"He did it to himself. You must be a saint to have any good thoughts about him at all. I'd just as soon see his hide tacked up over the fireplace."

"Oh, I've had moments when I would have gladly wrung his neck, believe me, but it's still a damn shame."

"The damn shame is what he did to you, and after you and Alice went out of your way for him. The rest of us had it rough as kids, too, but we didn't go around driving blades into people." I saw my white knuckles and gave up the death grip I had on my steak knife.

"I know. You all learned to use your trials as compasses instead of crutches, and I'm proud as hell of you. I could hardly stomach all that drivel the defense lawyer was spewing out. But it's hard to give up on someone I had such high hopes for."

"Was Travis the first kid you couldn't get through to?"

Walter shook his head. "I've had to ship off a few guys over the years who weren't ready to help themselves. That goes with the job. But I always feel like I've failed somehow."

I got up and put an arm around him. "You and Alice ought to be proud of yourselves. There are fifteen guys in your house tonight who'd likely be in jail or dead if you hadn't brought out the best in them, and two more who called you on the phone because they couldn't make it in person. I'd say that's a pretty good way to measure what you've done with your life, but that's just my opinion."

He cheered up a little. "What you're really telling me is that I better quit feeling sorry for myself and get on with it. I think I'll start by rustling me up a cup of coffee."

"I'll bring it to you. You're still supposed to be taking it easy, you know."

The judge was already walking away. "I want to talk to Rocky over there anyway."

Alice stood up to speak at the end of the night. There had been a lot of racket going on, but it got as quiet as a church in her living room when she took the floor.

"I've been doing some thinking, and I've decided it shouldn't take a close call like Walter had to bring us together. I expect to see you all back in this house one year from tonight, and if I haven't had at least two letters or phone calls from each of you before then, I'll set Victor on you."

The German shepherd heard his name and marched right up to Alice. He sat down beside her, and we all laughed and cheered.

Chapter 16

The obnoxious buzzing sound shattered the silence. I did my level best to ignore it, but it wouldn't go away. After a minute, I groped for the snooze button without cracking an eye.

"Don't you even think of lapsing into a coma again," Tim warned. I groaned. He yanked the covers off me and zipped out of my room before I woke up enough to kill him.

I dragged myself out of bed and stumbled into the kitchen. "I'd like to get my hands on the heartless jerk who invented the alarm clock. Stirring at sunup on a Saturday is a sin, you know."

Tim offered me a cup of coffee and a jelly doughnut. "Rise and shine, pal. Mark was probably down at the garage an hour ago."

The coffee started to clear my head. "It's way too early to be so perky, but I guess you got the right. It isn't every day a guy launches his own business."

He grinned. "We'll see how perky I am the first time I don't get a regular paycheck."

We loaded my hatchback with paint and cleaning supplies and drove over to the old building Tim and Mark had rented on the Line to open Brothers Auto Service. The June morning was fairly cool, but there was no breeze, and I knew the day was going to turn into a real scorcher.

We could hear Mark singing in Spanish at the top of his lungs as soon as we got out of the car. He was already perched on a ladder nailing up the wooden sign he and Anita had painted the night before.

He jumped down when he saw us. "It's about time you lazy bums showed up. We better get hopping if we want to finish before we have to pick up the twins at three."

"This ain't a chain gang, Mark," I laughed. "Where's that little sweetie of yours?"

"She has to work this weekend. She says the dress shop is always swamped during the wedding season."

"So is the catering service. The colors on that sign are liable to blind somebody."

"That's what I'm aiming for." Mark stepped back to see if he had his masterpiece hanging straight. "Grandma told me she was sure me and Tim would open our own garage someday. She thought of the name years ago because she said the crew was like a pack of brothers."

"I hope she's smiling down on us from the sky today," Tim said. "Her knack for stretching nickels into dimes would come in handy about now."

"Yeah, but this is a great location. I could throw a rock into the ritzy territory from here, so we're bound to pull in a Cadillac or two along with the crop of clunkers." Mark reached into the back of my car for a keg of paint. "We won't get anywhere just standing here, though."

The three of us kicked it in high gear. When the place was spick-and-span, Tim and Mark started arranging the tools on their workbenches. I left them daydreaming aloud about all the wrecks they were going to bring back from the dead and went to put the office in shape. There was a little apartment above the shop, too, but we didn't have a chance to mess with it much before it was time to meet the twins at the airport.

"You two can go for them in my car, and I'll drive the truck home." I glanced around the garage. "This joint don't look half bad with a fresh coat of paint. Hell, you could eat off the floor in here."

"I'm so hungry I could eat the floor," Mark said. "What's on the menu tonight, Chef Richard?"

"You'll be swallowing your teeth if you call me that again. Bring the twins to my place for a fish fry. Stop and get some onions first." I laughed. "That was a sour face, Mark. You don't have to eat them or anything."

My apartment had been shut up all day, so it was an oven when I got home. I wasn't looking forward to spending an hour in a sweltering kitchen, but the twins were partial to fish and fries. The crew would be all together that night for the first time in nearly three years, and we'd always jumped on any excuse to pig out. I was up to my elbows in grease by the time Tim walked in with a suitcase in each hand.

He dropped the bags on the couch. "Don't step between the twins unless you're ready to be run through with blue lightning."

"Are they having one of their famous Thomas squabbles?" Bryan and Stace were tighter than any two brothers on earth, but they could fight like a couple of rabid dogs when they took the notion.

"I don't know if they plan on making up this time. Got a cold one handy?"

I jerked a thumb toward the fridge. "Three six-packs on the bottom shelf. Iced tea won't do it tonight?"

"Jack Daniels may have to step in before it's over." He popped the top on a beer can. "They both need serious attitude adjustments if you ask me."

Stace and Mark walked in just then, laughing, and Bryan trailed silently behind them. He was all decked out in a dress shirt and a tie. I could see the sweat pouring down his face from across the room.

I waved a greasy hand at them. "Hey, guys, long time no see. You're looking mighty dandy, Bryan. This ain't an executive dinner, you know."

"He thinks he's too good for T-shirts and jeans." Stace snagged a French fry from the platter I was heaping. "I hope he roasts to death. It's hotter than hell out there."

I threatened him with a fillet knife. "Do you want to keep those fingers?"

"Touchy, aren't we?" He filched another fry.

"Make yourself useful and get out some dishes. Mark, where are the onions I asked for?"

"We forgot." Mark took a beer from the fridge and handed one to Bryan. "They'd smell up the whole place anyway."

"No onion rings then. Let's eat."

We all loaded up our plates. Stace bubbled on and on about how great it was to be liberated from military school, but Bryan hardly said a word. The death ray looks that flashed back and forth between them were just about hot enough to cause a nuclear reaction.

"I'm back here for good. I never want to see Georgia or my aunt and uncle again." Stace reached across the table for the ketchup. "I swear, I wouldn't give a damn if the whole east coast fell right off into the ocean."

"Try asking someone to pass you the ketchup next time," Bryan snapped. "You don't have to lean over everybody's plates like a slob."

"Lay off the high and mighty act," Stace snarled back. "You're no better than me even if you do go to some stuffy college."

"At least I know how to eat with a fork."

Stace aimed the ketchup bottle at Bryan and decorated his face and shirt collar. Bryan leaped up, kicked his chair out of the way, and rushed for his brother with both fists swinging. Stace fired off another blast of ketchup before Mark snatched the bottle out of his hand.

"Stace, act your age, for Christ's sake." Mark tossed Bryan a paper towel. "Chill out, bud. It washes off, you know."

Bryan grabbed the napkin and stomped off into the john, cussing under his breath all the way. He stayed in there for a long time, and he came out wearing a fresh shirt with no tie. He went and sat by himself in a corner.

Stace downed a beer and belched, trying to count to ten before he ran out of gas. "I was wondering if I could stay with one of you till I find a job."

"You can park your butt on my couch for a spell if you help me deal with the wreckage of this fish fry," I said. "As long as Tim don't object."

278

Tim shrugged. "Suits me."

"You drive a hard bargain, Rick." Stace carried a stack of dishes to the sink. "I should feel special cleaning up after real live business owners. How long till you all get your first limo?"

"It'll likely be one bomb after another for a while," Tim sighed.

Mark thumped him on the shoulder. "Give it time, buddy. Rich folks wreck their cars, too. They'll be lined up around the block once we build up a name for ourselves."

"We're stuck with Stace from now on. How long will you be walking among us, Bryan?" I asked.

"I'm taking classes this summer, so I catch a flight to New Jersey the day after tomorrow."

"Bummer. It's been way too long since we all hung out like this. Anybody up for chocolate cake?" I started passing out hefty slices without waiting for an answer.

"Cooking school was good for you," Stace said with his mouth full. "Your cakes aren't crunchy around the edges anymore. Did you make the frosting yourself?"

"From scratch."

"That means he scratched his butt before he opened a tub from the store," Tim said.

We sat around that evening watching movies and spinning tall tales about the good old days. I was tickled pink to have the crew reunited, but somehow it didn't feel quite right without Daisy there. I slipped out for a walk when her memory got to be too much for me. I imagined her strolling beside me with her hand in mine, and there was nobody around to see the tears that dripped off my lashes and mixed with the sweat on my face.

It was almost dark when I got home. Tim was sitting on the curb in the parking lot smoking a cigarette. He waved me over.

I hunkered down next to him and rested my chin in my hands. "Did you get kicked out of your own apartment?"

"Those two little brats were driving me crazy with all their yapping back and forth, so I thought I better quit the scene before I flattened both of 'em."

"I've never seen the twins like this. They always had their spats, but it looks like they honestly hate each other now."

"They'll get over it." Tim put a hand on my shoulder. "You were out here missing Daisy, weren't you?"

I nodded. "I've pretty much learned how to live without her, but once in a while her memory gets a strangle hold on me. I sometimes wonder if I'll ever really heal up inside."

"I never fell heart and soul for a chick the way you did for Daisy, but I think I know how it must tear you up to let her go. I've come to love Jake like he's my own son, and it would kill me to lose him."

"I wouldn't worry about him going anywhere. You couldn't chase that kid off with a loaded machine gun." I wiped the sweat from my forehead and stood up. "It's still Africa hot out here. If the twins want to bicker like a couple of kindergartners, they can sit on the sidewalk and fry."

Tim tossed his cigarette butt in the gutter. "Maybe Mark will take one of them off our hands for the night."

~~~

Bryan and Stace made it through the next day with only a half a dozen minor clashes, but war broke out in a big way that evening. Tim and Mark had gone to Brothers to fuss over some last minute details, and I took the twins to scope out the garage when I got off work.

"This is a nice setup you all have here. It'll look even better with a few cars in the bays." Stace flicked his cigarette butt at the ashtray and missed.

Bryan shot him an icy glare. "Mom isn't here to pick up after you. Most people know what ashtrays are for."

"I've had all the etiquette tips I can stand from you, so back the hell off!" Stace flared.

Tim put up a hand for silence. "I swear to God, I'll muzzle both of you if you start in again today."

Tim never made threats he didn't plan to back up, so Bryan plunked himself down on a stool with a sports magazine, and Stace pulled the classifieds out of the Sunday paper.

"That was a waste of time." He tossed the ads aside after a few minutes and started flipping through the funnies instead. "There's never any work around here in the summer."

"I know it ain't much, but we'll probably have an odd job or two you could do from time to time," Mark suggested.

"Thanks for the offer, pal, but I'm looking for a bigger challenge than that."

"You screw up everything you do, so you better start small," Bryan said.

Stace sprang up and knocked him straight backward off his stool for an answer. Bryan started to scramble to his feet, but Stace sent him sprawling again and drew back to put a boot heel through his skull.

Tim shoved Stace into a chair. "Give it up, you made your point." He helped Bryan off the floor, none too gently, and looked right into his eyes. "I should've let him cave your head in for saying that. What the hell is your problem anyway?"

Bryan jerked away from Tim and grabbed the rag Mark held out to him. He wiped the blood off his mouth and nose. "I'm going to make something of myself at Princeton. Stace just wastes his life goofing around and then bitches about how he gets the shaft all the time."

"How long did you think I could hack watching you be everybody's pet while I settled for the table scraps?" Stace asked. "Even before we went to Georgia, you were the darling and I was the dimwit."

"Because you acted like the dimwit. I waited all my life for a chance to break out of the slums, and when the chance finally came, I jumped on it. I thank God every day that Mom and Dad pulled me out of this pit. Now I'm going to play tennis all over the country and fly to places none of the rest of you will ever see, and I'll forget I ever set foot in the ghetto."

The four of us could only gape at him with our mouths open. All those years I thought Bryan was just keeping to himself because he was quiet, but he was really praying for a way out. It hurt to listen to him. It hurt like hell.

"You can't really believe this line you're feeding us," Tim finally said.

"Sure I can. If you all want to be riffraff till you die, that's your concern. I'm going to have more money than you've ever dreamed of. I'll drive big cars and eat at fancy restaurants with pretty girls. You'll see me on TV someday, and your friends won't believe it if you say you knew me way back when."

We watched in stunned silence as Bryan made tracks for the door.

"I'll get me a hotel room for the night and hire a cab to take me to the airport in the morning," he spat over his shoulder. "So long."

Stace leaped to his feet. "You may swagger out of here like God's gift to the world now, but you'll fall flat on your ass someday, and I'm going to laugh while I watch you hit the ground!"

"You just keep watching, loser," Bryan jeered without looking back. "I'm headed straight for the big-time."

"If you ever pull your head out of your butt long enough to get a deep breath of fresh air, come back and see us," Mark said. He added a few thoughts to himself in Spanish as the door slammed.

"I hope he rots in hell!" Stace sounded like he was choking on his words. "I don't give a damn if he ever comes back!"

"He's just been pumped full of the crap they spew out at those snobby colleges." Tim ruffled Stace's long black hair. "He'll wake up and smell the toast burning sooner or later."

"I don't know who he thinks he is anyway!" Stace bounded up the stairs three at a time and disappeared into the apartment above the garage. Me and Tim and Mark just stood there looking at each other for a long moment.

"He'll wake up sooner or later," Tim finally said again.

But we didn't hear another word out of Bryan for ages. He sent postcards to his folks from different parts of the country and even some foreign places, and sometimes there was a clip about him on the news or a blurb in the sports page when he shook up the tennis world. I watched him on TV whenever I could catch a live match, and the boy got on a winning streak that wouldn't quit, but he kept his word and forgot all about where he came from. Stace never said any more about his brother, and he always walked out on a conversation as soon as Bryan's name came up.

In the meantime, me and Tim let him bunk with us for a while. We tried to give him a chance to heal up from the bruises Bryan had left on his ego, but before long we got tired of coming home to find him glued to the couch with the TV blaring and a pile of beer cans on the floor. Most days he didn't even bother to get dressed.

"Damn it, Stace!" I exploded one night when I looked into the empty refrigerator. "Don't you ever do anything but stuff your face and watch soaps?"

He grinned. "I watered your plants today and took Captain for a walk."

I wasn't impressed. "That thing on the table making the ticking noise is an alarm clock. When it sounds off, you're supposed to get up and go on a job hunt, not roll over and reach for a beer."

"There's no jobs around here in the summer, man. It's a real drag being turned away all the time."

"Mark told you there was work at Brothers."

He made a sour face. "I want something more exciting than that."

"Then hoist yourself up off your butt and go after it. I saw a sign in the window at the bowling alley on my way home."

"Dare to dream!"

I glared at him. "This ain't a hotel. You're going to have to start earning your keep from now on."

Stace promised to get on the stick in the morning. But when I dropped in during my lunch hour, he hadn't moved off the couch, and the smell of pot just about knocked me over when I opened the door.

I strode across the room and jerked him up by one shirt sleeve. "Clear the hell out!"

"Keep your hair on, Rick. I was just working up a little nerve before I went to the bowling alley."

"Well, you can work up the nerve somewhere else! This ain't a dope den!" I shoved him toward the door.

"Where am I supposed to go?"

"There's a shelter down by the train depot. Maybe they'll put up with you and your funny cigarettes there."

He wrenched free from my iron grip and whirled to face me. "This is a hell of a way to repay that judge you talk so much about, booting a friend out into the streets when he needs a hand!"

"Judge Mills would be the first to tell me if a guy won't help himself, there's nothing you can do for him. Come back when you get your act together." I slammed the door on his protests.

Stace was gone for more than a month. I was afraid Tim would be hacked off at me for kicking him out, but he agreed that we shouldn't have to carry the kid forever.

~~~

Mark came to my place for a round of heads-up poker one sweltering August evening. I could tell his mind wasn't on the game, though. He could usually clean my clock without half trying, but that night he spent more time staring out the window than he did looking at his cards.

"Are you senile or something?" I razzed when I won the fourth hand in a row. "You'd have lost your shirt by now if we were playing for keeps."

He laid down his cards. "I'm a little off tonight. I've been thinking about Anita."

"She's cute enough to turn a guy's mind away from a poker game. What about her?"

"I love her so much I can't talk myself out of it, and it scares me half to death. It seems like when you give your heart away, the chick slips right out of your hands. Look what happened to you and Daisy."

I nodded. "I still can't believe I got her killed."

Mark scowled at me. "I wish you'd get off the guilt trip already. She died in an accident, and it was mostly her dad's fault. She'd be the first one to call you an idiot for still beating yourself up after all this time."

"She ain't here to call me an idiot. Anyhow, some people do live happily ever after. Walter and Alice are pushing fifty years together, and he still thinks she's an angel straight from heaven."

"Anita's going to move in with me when her lease runs out in October." Mark started shuffling the cards without glancing at them. "I've thought about tying the knot, but I haven't got up the guts to pitch that plan to her yet."

"It's a heavy question for a guy to ask. Just be sure you're ready to hear the answer first."

Tim busted into the apartment, flinging the door open so hard it hit the wall and almost slammed in his face again. He was cussing up a storm, but I could see the tears in his eyes from across the room.

"What's up, Tim?" I asked. "You look like you want to murder somebody."

"I do!" He banged the door shut and then put a dent in it with his balled fist. "They moved Jake to another foster home today!"

Mark slid over so Tim could sit on the couch. "What's wrong with that? They do it all the time."

Tim flopped down and kicked his shoes off. "His new foster parents won't let me see him, that's what's wrong. They say I'm apt to be a bad influence on him with my shady past and everything."

I gaped at him, shocked. "You're the best thing that ever happened to that kid. He was starting to buckle down in school and act like a human being in public just so you'd let him hang out with you."

"I made the rounds this afternoon. I can't apply to be his foster parent because I'm single and poor. I can't be his partner in one of those big brothering programs because I've been in jail. The folks down at the county building told me I better just forget about him because he ain't my concern, damn their hides." Tim's voice cracked, and he trailed off and stared at the floor.

Mark shot me a sideways glance. "See what I mean about losing the people you love?"

I got up and poured us all iced tea, not knowing what else to do. "Those partnering programs pass over way too many good people because Jesus Christ is the only one perfect enough to meet their guidelines. It seems to me troubled kids would relate better to guys who've been through the mill anyway."

"I've screwed up a lot in my life, and I was doing my level best to teach Jake different." Tim emptied his glass with a gulp. "I think I need something stronger tonight. Can I bum a shot or two?"

"Sure, but you've been doing real good at sticking to Coke and tea lately."

He shrugged. "What's the point in going straight when nobody lets you forget where you've been anyway?"

288

I was about to get Tim a bottle, but Stace dragged himself through the door just then, so I went to meet him instead. "Hey, bud, you look like you've had a long hike through hell. Could you use a hamburger?"

He grinned. "I could use a dozen hamburgers. Can I hit your shower first?"

"You know where it is." I looked him dead in the eyes. "If you're back to stay, I'm glad to see you."

"Is that job still open at Brothers?"

"You can start tomorrow morning if you're clean and sober," Mark said.

Stace disappeared into the john, and I started hunting in my cupboards for a bottle of whiskey. I hadn't had the taste for it much lately, so it was buried someplace behind my stash of groceries.

"I guess vinegar won't do the trick. It must be clear up on top with the extra light bulbs and junk."

"Never mind. The mood's off me now," Tim said.

"It's here somewhere. I'll find it."

He shook his head. "It'd only give me the blues, and I got enough of those already. I ain't willing to face the headache in the morning."

I sighed with relief as I put a couple of burgers on for Stace. "Anybody else hungry?"

"Dumb question alert." Mark grinned. "Have we ever turned down a plate of food in our lives?"

Stace hired on at the garage the next morning, and he turned his hand to anything he saw that needed doing, but he wasn't his old smart-off self. He moped around most of the time looking at the floor, not saying a word to anybody, and he spent a lot of hours staring moodily out the window. He guzzled a ton of beer, too, but it only seemed to make him feel more down.

"He probably just misses Bryan," Mark said. "He'll snap out of it pretty soon."

When he still showed no sign of perking up after three weeks, me and Mark kidnapped him and took him to lunch at the taco bar where I used to work.

"What's the occasion?" he asked when we'd eaten in silence for a while.

"We want to know what's bugging you," Mark said. "We figured you'd either tell us willingly or put away enough of this slop to give you botulism and end your misery."

Stace only shrugged and doused a taco in hot sauce.

"Is it Bryan?" I pressed. "He's just being a jackass."

"I don't give a damn about him."

"Is it your job? You could find something different if you don't like it." Mark picked a stray sliver of onion off his food and dropped it on my plate.

"The job's fine. It's the best I'm likely to get anyway."

"It's a start, that's all. What would you rather do?" I probed.

"I don't know how to do anything. You have your cooking, and Tim and Mark are all set with Brothers, and Bryan's making his fortune in tennis. And then there's dumb old Stace, good for a laugh and not much else."

"Judge Mills used to tell me that everybody's got a niche in this world, and it just takes time to find out where it is."

"Yeah, sure. He never had to put up with me."

Mark laid a hand on Stace's shoulder. "You got the grief and Bryan got the glory for a long time, but you don't have to buy into that crap. Did something happen while you were on your own this summer to take all the fun out of you?"

"Nothin' happened. That's the point. I walked a million miles up and down the streets of this town trying to think of what to do with the rest of my life, and I came up with nothin'."

I stood up and cleared our trash off the table. "Don't sweat it, buddy. You'll hit your stride sooner or later. If somebody had told me a few years ago that I'd be cooking today, I wouldn't have believed it for a second, but here I am."

Stace wouldn't be convinced. He moved into the little apartment above the garage, and he didn't show his face much away from the place. Tim tried to get him involved in the 4-H club, and we took him to the firing range to test out our pistols. He was a fairly good shot, but he didn't get any joy out of it. Tim was in a slump, too, because he missed Jake something awful, so the blues hung heavy in the air as summer turned into fall.

Then one morning I stopped by Brothers to pick up a jacket I'd left there, and Stace was all smiles. I hadn't seen him grin in so long I wondered if his face ached.

"Come upstairs a second. I want to show you something."

"Sure, Stace, but I've only got a minute."

I followed him up the narrow staircase.

Sitting on the card table in the tiny kitchen of the apartment was a sculpture of an eagle. It was twisted out of copper wire, and I was blown away at how real it seemed. The wings were stretched out, and the beak and claws looked wicked enough to make you shudder.

My jaw dropped. "Hey, that's cool. Did you make it yourself?"

"Yeah. I found some old junk battery cables when I was mucking out the shop last night. I started curling the wire around in my hands, and then the bird just popped into my head."

"It's perfect. You know, I bet you could sell this."

"Naw, I was just goofing off. Nobody would pay me for it."

"Bet me. Let me take it to a few of the swanky parties I drudge over, and someone will pounce on it."

Stace had his doubts, but I took the bird to work with me anyway. A lot of people gushed over it, but nobody offered to buy it till I sprung for a glass case and a little brass plaque with Stace's name engraved on it. Then some lady snapped it up as a one-of-a-kind birthday present for her husband, and Stace found his calling. He kept his job at Brothers, but in his spare time you'd always see him with a piece of wire and a pair of pliers, twisting away.

Chapter 17

Brothers Auto Service got its first fancy car that fall. I walked into the garage one evening, and Alice's hot red Mustang was sitting there with its front end caved in. I rushed to the phone and dialed the judge's number.

"Hey, Alice, it's Rick. I just saw your car. Is everybody okay?"

"Sure, we're all right. Chris went for an unauthorized joyride this morning and wrapped the convertible around a light pole."

"I take it Chris is your new wild child. He crunched up your car a lot worse than I did that time. Does Walter know?"

"He knows. He's out swimming laps, so I guess the roof won't blow off this house tonight." Alice chuckled. "Can you stop by after a while for pie and coffee?"

"I'd like to, but I'm due back at work in an hour. We're gearing up for a debutante party Saturday, so I'm stuck with loads of overtime this week."

"Well, how about Sunday then? I've got two peach pies here that need to justify their existence."

I laughed. "You'll break my arm if you twist it any harder. I'll drop in after church."

Alice had a scheme up her sleeve. I knew that little twinkle in her voice. I tried to puzzle out what she might be up to all week while I slaved over the buffet for the debutante ball. I could be bribed into going along with just about anything for a hunk of her peach pie.

She got down to business as soon as we were settled on the front porch with our dessert plates. "You always talked about opening your own restaurant someday. Is that still something you want to do?"

I nodded. "It would be great, but I don't exactly have heaps of cash laying around, so it's no better than a daydream right now."

"They'll have more work than they can handle at the catering service during the holiday season, won't they?"

"Yeah. They keep us hopping over there." I was getting a little suspicious. "They'll have to turn down jobs right and left between Thanksgiving and the end of the year."

"What's to stop you from planning a few parties on the side to start a cafe fund?"

"Hit the brakes, Alice. You mean put on the whole show myself?"

"I knew you could fix a nice platter from the first Sunday morning you lived here, when you skipped church and made that lovely salad with radishes cut like roses."

"I've built millions of relish trays since then, but it sounds kind of complicated, bringing off a whole party on my own."

"No, you can do it. You just give the guests a lot of choices about what to nibble on, they'll be happy."

The judge stirred sugar into his coffee. "Once you prove yourself at a soiree or two, folks spread the word. The trick is to charge enough for your time and effort above the cost of the food. People will pay well

294

so they don't have to lift a finger. Then they'll beam at their friends like they did everything down to growing the vegetables, and you can laugh all the way to the bank."

I grinned. "You let your wife do the slick talking and then threw in your two bits when I was almost hooked."

"I'm no dummy. She's the one handing out the pie and ice cream."

Walter and Alice helped me work out a flight plan that afternoon, and it wasn't long before I had my first customer. Tim took over as the leader of the 4-H club, and I put on a spread in his honor. I hosted a retirement party when Judge Mills walked away from the bench after Christmas. Then I landed a housewarming brunch and two wedding receptions.

I didn't get much of a thrill out of the catering gigs, to tell the truth, because the folks I fit in with were more into laughing loud and dropping quarters in the jukebox than bragging about their sons at Harvard and their latest business deals. But the balance in my savings account inched a little higher each month, so I didn't complain too often.

~~~

I was slogging through a swamp of bank statements and grocery receipts early one morning in February when the phone rang. I picked up the receiver. "Lucky's Love Lounge. What's your pleasure?"

"Is Tim there? I need Tim!" The small voice sounded so sad and scared I could have bawled.

I pounded on the bathroom door. "Hey, bud, it's your long-lost sidekick. I think he's in a jam or something."

Tim exploded out of the john, wrapped in a towel, and snatched the phone from my hand. "Jake? What's wrong?" There was a long pause. "Where are you?" Another pause. "You gotta chill out and quit crying so I can help you. Look around and tell me what you see." He scooped a bundle of clothes out of the laundry basket. "Stay right where you are till I get there. Promise?" He waited for an answer. "Jake, I mean it. Don't you run off on me. I'll come as quick as I can."

He hung up and ducked into his room with the clothes. Less than a minute later, he rushed out in a mismatched pair of sweats and reached for my keys. "I'll be right back. I swear I won't wreck your car."

I was halfway into my jacket. "You won't wreck it because I'm driving. What's the deal?"

"He went AWOL on his way to school and tried to make it to Brothers, but he got lost." Tim sprinted down the stairs with me on his heels. "He said he thought I forgot about him."

"Where is he?"

"At the old water tower."

"Clear over there? He couldn't have ended up farther from the garage if he tried to."

"I know. I'm glad he had enough sense to find a pay phone and call me."

I burned rubber on the way across town while Tim kept an eye peeled for cops and ran a comb through his wet hair.

"It's awful windy for him to be out and about," I said.

"If they'd let me see him once in a while, it wouldn't have come to this. They can't just expect him to pretend he never met me. Step on it, for God's sake, you're driving like a granny."

"Take it easy. The Mob ain't after him or anything."

"I'd like to drop him off at school before the bell rings. He might as well not add cutting class to his list of other crimes over there."

We pulled up at the water tower, and Tim hit the pavement on the run almost before I got the car stopped. Jake shot out from behind the building and into his arms. Tim held him tight for a long moment and then slid back into the seat beside me without letting go.

All at once he set the kid off from him. "What's that in your pocket?"

"Nothin'." Jake tried to wriggle away.

Tim got a good grip on his red windbreaker and pulled half a pack of cigarettes and the label off a wine cooler bottle from the pocket. "Aren't you a little young for this stuff?"

Jake pouted up like he was about to cry. Then, when Tim wasn't impressed by that, he switched gears and put on his best tough guy face. "I wanted to be like you."

That hit Tim between the eyes. He started to swear, then changed his mind. "You don't wanna be like me, bud. All drinking ever gets you is a headache or a wrecked car, and cigarettes make you cough your lungs out every morning when you wake up."

"But you look cool with a smoke in your mouth."

"How much money did you give for that pack?"

"I took it from my teacher's desk yesterday."

"Great," Tim groaned. "Have you smoked any yet?"

"No. I'm not supposed to play with lighters or matches. A real fireman told me that when my class went on a field trip last year." Jake's grin blazed up suddenly. "My teacher picked me to sit in the engine and turn on the siren and everything because I stayed quiet the whole time the firemen were talking."

Tim ignored that. He lit a cigarette and stuck it in Jake's mouth. The kid started gagging right away, but Tim didn't take the cancer stick from him till he was good and green.

Then he flicked it into the ashtray. "Was that worth stealing for?"

Jake shook his head and kept on coughing. The way his face was all scrunched up with disgust was priceless, and I had to bite my lip to keep from laughing out loud.

But Tim stayed dead serious. "If you'd bought those smokes, you would have spent one dollar and three quarters. How long do you think it would take to blow all the money you've saved for your new bike?"

Tears pooled up in Jake's blue eyes. "Are you mad at me?"

"I'm not real happy. Did you drink the wine cooler?"

The kid perked up a little. "Yeah. It tasted good. And it isn't stealing if you get it from your own fridge, right?"

"Well, let's see. Did you take it while your folks were around, or did you wait till nobody was looking?"

Jake hung his head. "I waited till nobody was looking."

"That sounds like stealing to me. How did your guts feel after you drank it?"

"Sort of yucky."

"Stick to lemonade. And keep your hands off stuff that ain't yours, okay?"

"Okay." Jake squirmed around so he could look into Tim's face. "Are we still buddies?"

"Sure we are." Tim settled the kid on his lap and turned to me. "What are we waiting here for? The school's on Grover Street. Make a left at the next light."

"No way!" Jake sat bolt upright and busted out crying. "I don't wanna go to school! I wanna go home with you!"

"You gotta go to school. It's like your job, remember? The same way I work at Brothers."

"How come you never take me places anymore? I miss you."

"I miss you, too. I think about you all the time. But you have other friends to hang out with now, don't you?"

"I'd rather be with you! You did forget about me, I know you did!" Jake pushed away from Tim and started kicking my dashboard as hard as he could, cussing violently between his sobs and sniffles. He had a pretty advanced vocabulary for a third grader.

"Take a chill pill. You'll break your toes or crack that console, and either way, it won't solve anything." Tim leaned forward and grabbed hold of Jake's tennis shoes. He didn't let go till they quit moving. "I'll never forget about you. Not ever. But it's better if I leave you alone for a while."

"Who says it's better? I don't think it is!"

"Damn it, kid, I can't explain it. You'll understand when you get a little older." Tim cuddled the kid in the curve of his arm and fired a helpless look at me. "Sometimes things don't turn out the way you want them to, and there's nothing you can do about it, even if it makes you really sad."

Jake cried all the way to the school, and Tim rubbed his back and stroked his mop of blond hair. He kept his eyes closed tight, but when the light caught him just right, I saw the glistening wet line along his lashes. He got out of the car at the school and led Jake over to the playground.

I had to swallow hard once or twice myself while I watched him coax the kid onto a swing and then push it as high as it would go and walk away without looking back. We'd pulled out of the parking lot by the time Jake got the swing stopped, and he didn't come after us, but he waved till we rounded the corner.

Tim tried to drown his hurt in a stream of four letter words, but the tears got the best of him in the end. "How can they do this to him, Rick? It don't matter if it breaks my heart, but he thinks I'm letting him down. They're making me into one more jerk he can't trust."

"They're trying to protect him. They're screwing up, but they want the best for him, the same as you do."

Tim sighed. "I guess so. A pack of smokes and a wine cooler, for Christ's sake, and he ain't even ten. Maybe I did steer him wrong."

"Naw, all kids try that. You could keep him out of a lot of trouble because he looks at you like a hero. You ought to go see if you can talk some sense into his foster parents."

He shook his head. "They were dead set against him having anything more to do with me. I bet that chick had her house fumigated after I left."

"Why didn't you tell Jake that?"

"What good would it do to make him hate them? I reckon they've got more to offer him than I do."

"I don't know about that. Anyway, I hope they keep their liquor cabinet locked up tight if they drink anything stronger than wine coolers."

Tim dried his eyes on his shirt sleeve. "That boy sniffs out devilment like a bloodhound."

I laughed. "Remind you of anybody? You had your first run-in with the cops when you were nine or ten, if I remember right."

He managed a halfhearted smile. "Yeah. I chugged one beer too many in the back of a movie theater."

We rode the rest of the way home in silence. Tim's mouth was set in the hard line that used to mean he was about to deck somebody. But he'd

301

finally come up against a problem in his life he couldn't solve with his fists.

I was afraid he was going to slide back into his old drinking habits. It seemed to me Jake was the main reason he'd put his life on the right track and kept it there. But his hands were so full at Brothers that he didn't have time to pray to the porcelain gods.

Business had picked up a lot since he and Mark snapped some pictures of Alice's restored convertible to hang in the window. I put in a plug for the shop whenever I heard people moaning and groaning about their car troubles at the dances and dinner parties I helped stage. Stace claimed Brothers was on a roll because there was a starving artist in the attic to bring luck. And who knows, maybe he was right.

~~~

I dropped by the garage one warm spring evening so Mark could put new plugs and wires on my car. Anita walked in while he was still poking around under the hood of the trusty old hatchback.

"Hey, Anita, I've been meaning to talk to you," I said.

She smiled shyly at me and then ducked her head and stared at her shoes. "What about?"

"Don't worry, I'm not going to ask you to run away with me or anything, at least not when Mark is around. I was wondering if you'd like to hire on to help me with some of my catering jobs. I'm starting to get more work than I can handle by myself."

"I would be glad to if Mark doesn't mind."

"It's okay by me," Mark said from under the hood. "Rick ain't much of a romeo, so I'll trust him with you."

I pitched an oily shop rag at him, and it hit him on the side of the head. "I never knew you to sow many wild oats yourself, old pal, so I wouldn't be talking a lot about romance if I were you."

Mark laughed and chucked the rag back at me without looking up, and then Stace joined the attack with the hose he'd been using to wash down the floor. He never could pass up a chance to clown around. I bolted out of harm's way, and the full force of the flood hit Anita square in the face. Water poured down her cheeks and soaked her dark hair and her white blouse. She squealed and scrambled for the door with her arms folded across her breasts. I couldn't tell if she was crying or not because her face was streaming with water, but she was obviously humiliated.

Mark straightened up and turned fiercely on Stace. "I swear you're about to get the world's greatest enema with that hose! Aren't you old enough to know how to treat a lady?"

"Keep your shirt on. I wasn't aiming for her, and she ain't gonna melt. She needs to learn to stick up for herself anyway."

"You need to learn to be civilized!"

"Mark, please," Anita broke in from the doorway. "You don't have to fight about it."

Mark draped his jacket over her shoulders and walked her out to his truck, still fuming under his breath. Stace rolled his eyes at me and went back to spraying down the floor.

"I can't figure out what Mark sees in that chick," he muttered. "She's way too spineless for my liking."

I nodded. "Daisy would have wrapped that hose around your neck and shoved the nozzle down your throat. But Mark gets off on playing the hero. Remember the way he stuck up for his cat when we were kids?"

Stace laughed. "Yeah, he used to get pretty riled when anybody messed with Scrappy. We'll need to teach Anita how to bust a guy in the chops, though, if she's ever going to hold her own with the crew."

"She might surprise you. I bet there's a she-devil inside her somewhere."

"In your dreams. She's a jellyfish if I ever met one," Stace scoffed. "Now that little barmaid I've been seeing, she's another story. We're going to scope out the mud volleyball games this weekend. You ought to rustle up a date so we can double."

I shook my head. "I'm a professional bachelor, remember?"

"You're too young to live like a priest, Rick. You'll have to let Daisy go sooner or later and find yourself another dance partner."

"Mind your own business, will you?"

He shrugged. "Whatever. Anyway, you're missing out on a lot of fun. And I ain't talking about all that sappy hearts-and-flowers crap Mark goes nuts over. I like my women ready for action."

"Yeah, and we all know what kind of action. Watch it, though. Too much fun always costs you."

304

Mark came back in and bent over to take a last look at my engine. "Sorry I blew up at you, Stace. Anita doesn't have a sense of humor sometimes, and she's been sort of weepy lately for some reason."

Stace let the incident drop with his usual lighthearted grin. "She just likes to be rescued by her knight in shining armor."

Chapter 18

I set the heavy topper on the cake and then swore under my breath as it slid downhill on a river of frosting. The kitchen in the banquet hall was hotter than the boiler room of hell. It's beyond me why so many idiots feel they have to get hitched in June when the icing on their cakes runs like molten lava and their flowers die by the dozen in the heat.

Anita came to the rescue. "I'll hold the topper while you brace it up with toothpicks."

"Folks ought to pass out Popsicles at their weddings and be done with it." I jabbed in the toothpicks and then hid them under a ring of sugar flowers. "There. That should put off the avalanche for a while."

"I hope nobody bites into those skewers." Anita stood back to admire the cake. "You do beautiful work."

"I'm glad you were here to help me. I couldn't have managed without an extra pair of hands that time."

She flashed me her timid smile. "I'm happy to have the job. I got a peek at the bride a while ago, and she looks like a princess with a wreath of roses in her hair."

"She is a princess. Her dad is blowing more money on her today than I make in a year. I can't see the sense in it, but I know enough to take his cash and keep my mouth shut."

"There's no sense to see in it. It's—how do you say—romantic." Anita took a sip of ice water and fanned herself with a paper plate. "I wonder if Mark ever thinks about weddings."

"I bet he'd sooner seal his fate in a courthouse than stuff himself in a tux and show off in front of a church."

"Most girls dream of the long white dress and the fancy party all their lives. But if you settle down with the right man, I guess the rest doesn't matter much."

"I never met a guy who gave two hoots for all the frills. Let's see if we can get this cake into the place of honor without another landslide."

Anita laughed. "It's been fussed over more than the bride has. I don't have any family around to see me married anyway, so I'll just have to enjoy other people's fairy tales."

"Or horror stories," I muttered as I watched the topper start to slip again.

The cake stayed intact long enough to get devoured, and I landed another catering gig while I was making the rounds with a coffeepot at the reception.

"Did you design this lovely cake, young man?" asked a lady in a sequined evening gown.

I nodded and then plucked a toothpick out of the frosting on her slice while she wasn't looking.

"My husband bought an airplane last week." She shot a quick glance around to see if anyone at the table was impressed by that bit of news. "Could you serve refreshments at the christening next Saturday?"

"Sure thing." I wrote down my name and number for her. "Would you like some more coffee?"

~~~

I was making out the shopping list for the christening at my kitchen table a few nights later when Mark put in an appearance. He'd been working long hours and trying to find time to spend with Anita, so I hadn't seen him much lately.

He took the chair across from me and lit up a smoke. "I came by to ask you a favor."

I laid aside my pencil and paper. "Ask away."

"It's Anita's birthday the day after tomorrow. I was wondering if you'd fix her a cake."

"Okay, I guess, but you can bake as good as anybody."

Mark shook his head. "I don't mean just a regular cake. I want a real pretty one with roses on it like you always make for those classy weddings."

"You're going all out. What's the occasion?"

He leaned forward in his chair, and his sunny smile lit up his whole face. "I've decided to pop the question."

"No kidding! You finally gathered up the guts." I reached across the table to shake his hand. "Her birthday lands on my day off this week. We can have the party here so it'll be a surprise."

"I doubt if I'll sleep any between now and then. I'm all on pins and needles."

"I'm real happy for you, bud."

He laughed. "Don't be happy yet. She hasn't given me an answer, you know."

"I don't think you have a lot to worry about. She's put up with you for two years, hasn't she?"

"She's so nice to me I can hardly believe she's for real."

308

"She's been sort of tricky for the rest of us to get to know, but her English has gotten a lot better. She still looks at me sometimes like I'm going to sprout fangs and chew her up, but we got to shoot the breeze a little at that wedding last weekend."

Mark stood up to go. "I can't sit still another second. Toss me that grocery list. I'll run to the store for you." He was whistling to himself as he walked out the door.

But he sure wasn't whistling on the afternoon of the party. He stormed into my apartment and flopped down on the couch without saying a word. I'd just put the finishing touches on the birthday cake, so I poured us both lemonade and sat next to him.

"You look fit to be tied today. Are you having trouble with another insurance company at Brothers?"

He shook his head. "It's Anita."

"What about her? You better not be getting cold feet after all the work I put in on that cake."

"No. She just told me she's four months pregnant."

"Really? Congratulations!"

"Shut up talking that way." Mark closed his eyes and kneaded his temples like he had a splitting headache. "She's had a queasy stomach off and on all spring, but she said she thought it was her ulcer acting up again. I can't believe she did this."

I grinned. "I'm no doctor, pal, but I think you had something to do with it."

He scowled back at me. "Yeah, and I'm hitting the road."

"Hold on a minute. I know you're shocked and everything, but you can't run out on her."

"Like hell I can't. I know all about women. They always leave you high and dry in the end."

I put a hand on his shoulder. "Who made you an expert?"

"My mom dumped me off in a grocery store. Grandma went and died right when I needed her most. I met a little gal in Colorado and started saving to get her a ring, and she lit out to California with the farmer's son in the car I fixed up for him. Hell, even my cat disappeared on me. I ain't letting it happen again."

"But Anita's a real sweetheart. She smiles at you like you're the next best thing to Jesus Christ. I don't think she's going anywhere."

"You ought to know what I'm talking about. You haven't so much as looked at a chick since I blew into town two years ago."

"That's different. I've kept to myself all along. You and Anita have been on the brink of marriage for ages, and now there's a kid to think of." I glanced at the triple-decker cake on the table. "Take a deep breath and pop the question, and things will work out okay. That cake is the best one I ever made."

"Damn the cake. Anita's bound to go hog wild over that baby pretty soon and forget all about me."

"That was a selfish statement if I ever heard one. Anyway, it's your baby, too. The three of you will be a family."

"Nope, it's not gonna happen. I already placed an ad in the paper for a mechanic to take over at Brothers, and I came to say goodbye."

"Have another glass of lemonade with me and give your brain a chance to stop sizzling. You're reasoning like a lunatic."

Mark got up and started for the door. "Keep an eye on her for a while, would you, Rick? I ain't cut out for the dad thing."

I strode across the room after him. "You should've thought of that before you jumped in the sack. If you walk away now, you'll be doing the same thing to your kid that your mom did to you."

"Skip the preaching, damn it. I love Anita too much to let her break my heart. I might as well split now, clean and quick, before she has a chance to flake out on me."

"You're being a jackass, Mark! Don't throw away the only true love you may ever have in your whole life so you can end up lonely like me!"

Mark fired off a volley of Spanish curses as he pushed past me and bolted out of my apartment. But the swearwords didn't cut any ice with me because I saw the tears in his eyes before the door slammed.

Anita rushed in like a whirlwind a little while later. She was way too frantic to worry about speaking English, so she just squeezed out a few jumbled scraps of Spanish between her sobs and then gave up talking altogether. It was sort of scary to see a quiet chick like her going off the deep end. I guided her into a chair and calmed her down with a cup of coffee and a piece of cake while I tried to figure out

311

what else to do. I wondered why the crisis always had to land in my lap.

"That's a beautiful cake. You shouldn't have cut it just for me." She finally smiled at me through her tears.

"The guy who ordered it called off his party, so we might as well not let it go to waste." I didn't have the heart to tell her I'd made the cake for her. "By the way, happy birthday."

That was the wrong thing to say. Anita started sobbing again. "How could Mark leave me on my birthday, and at a time like this, too? I don't know what to tell my family, expecting a baby without a ring on my hand. I will be a disgrace to them."

"Don't say anything yet. Mark's just freaked out right now. He'll be back when he comes to his senses."

"No, he won't. He paid next month's rent on our apartment for me and then loaded up his truck and left." She pushed her cake away and buried her face in her folded arms on the table.

I felt my brain reaching the boiling point inside my skull. Anita was going to pieces, and there wasn't anything I could say or do that would make a lick of difference. I tried to think what I would have told Daisy if she had been sitting there, but I drew a blank because Daisy wouldn't have dawdled around crying her eyes out in my kitchen. She would have chased Mark halfway across Texas and dragged him home by the ear.

I stood behind Anita and massaged her tense shoulders. "Try to settle down a little, okay? It won't be good for your baby if you stay all worked up."

Tim and Stace walked in the door just then. I was never so glad to see a pair of ugly mugs in my life. They hacked off giant slabs of cake for themselves and sat down at the table. The three of us looked at each other in silence for a minute over Anita's bent head.

Then Tim reached out and shook her by the shoulder. "Anita, you need to get a grip. We can't do a thing with you carrying on this way." Diplomacy never had been real high on his list of strong points.

She shrank back from him like a scared rabbit. "*Lo siento* … I'm sorry!"

"Take it easy. His bark is worse than his bite." I handed her a tissue and glared at Tim. "Give her a break already. She's got the right to be upset."

Anita blew her nose and wiped her eyes. "I didn't mean to make a scene, but I've been left alone now, and I don't know what to do."

"What are we, chopped liver?" Stace picked a pink sugar rose off his piece of cake and popped it in his mouth. "We'll look out for you till Mark comes back."

"I don't want to be a burden to all of you. It will be better for you to go on with your lives and forget about me."

Tim leveled a scowl at her that just about sent her into orbit again. "Lay off that line of bull before it goes any further. We've covered for each other in the crew since we were kids, so we wouldn't do anything less for Mark now."

We came up with a game plan right there at the kitchen table. Tim and Stace bought Anita a bunch of groceries before they went back to work, and I made her lay down for an hour and then took her to sign up for Food Stamps. But I couldn't stand the way the clerk looked at her like she was a glob of pond scum, so I told him to shove his papers where they would do the most good and marched her out the door.

"You don't need their handouts anyway. Me and Tim and Stace will fill in the gap till Mark gets his act together," I promised. "I might just hunt him down and pound some sense into him myself."

Tim was all for getting up a lynch mob, too, when he came home from Brothers that evening. "It may take me weeks to find another mechanic as good as Mark, and the work's already stacked up to my eyeballs. He better be ready for war when he shows up."

~~~

The summer sweltered on, and before long Anita couldn't squeeze into her jeans. I took her to the charity clinic on Harding Street for a checkup one Saturday after work. The nurse pressed the stethoscope against her swelling belly and let me listen to the baby's heartbeat. It was an awesome thing to hear that sound and know that pretty soon a kid would pop out of Anita and start knocking around the world, and I cursed Mark silently for missing the moment. Then I got to thinking about Daisy, and all

314

the way home I pretended it was her instead of Anita sitting beside me in the car.

"Mark better drag his butt home before his kid decides to burst upon the scene," Tim grumbled to me the next morning from behind the Sunday paper. "Nothing in the world drives me up the wall quicker than a squalling baby."

"I expected him to come crawling back long before now. I figured he just had a case of the jitters, but maybe he really is gone for good."

"He damn well better not be. A kid needs a dad, and I ain't about to get roped into that job." Tim tossed me the sports page. "It says there Bryan's quitting college and going pro. He's due to star on a TV commercial for some twigs-and-nuts breakfast cereal in the fall, too."

The phone rang before I got a chance to look at the paper. I picked up the receiver, thinking Stace probably wanted a lift to the supermarket or something. "Rick's Road Kill Cafe. You run it down, we fry it up."

"Is Tim Bennett in? This is Officer Valdez from the Bertha City Police Department."

"Yeah, hold on." I handed the receiver to Tim. "It's the cops. What'd you do this time?"

"Whatever it is, I'm innocent," Tim said, half to me and half to the cop on the phone. Then he listened for a long moment and let out an exasperated sigh. "Okay, I'm on my way." He hung up and started for the door.

"Where's the fire?" I stood up to follow him.

"I'll be right back. They've got Jake at the station."

I sat down at the table again and reached for the newspaper. I'd dealt with all the emergencies I could handle lately, and this one, thank God, wasn't my problem.

Tim was back in fifteen minutes with Jake in tow. The kid's eyebrows and blond bangs were singed pretty bad, and his cheery grin was missing, but he sulked with as much enthusiasm as he had always smiled.

Tim jerked his thumb toward a chair in the corner. "Sit there till I figure out what to do with you."

Jake started to argue, but he must have decided that wasn't a wise move because he trailed off and trudged over to the chair, scuffing his tennis shoes on the carpet as he went.

Tim plunked himself down at the table and gazed glumly across at me. "How come you aren't on your way to church?"

"I wanted to find out what the deal was. So what is it?"

"That little demon over there got himself hauled in for torching some lady's prize-winning rosebushes. His foster parents left him with a sitter, but he gave her the slip and woke up the neighborhood with a box of matches and a gas can."

I whistled. "So he's a budding arsonist. I bet not too many nine-year-olds can claim that."

"His foster parents won't be home till around sundown, and the sitter wouldn't take him back. He

316

was driving everybody crazy over at the station, so the cops called me. I'm listed as an emergency contact in his old foster records."

Jake dropped his pout and strutted up to Tim with his arms held out for a hug. "I've missed you a whole bunch. Can we go to the pool today?"

"We aren't going anywhere today," Tim growled. "You screwed up in a big way this time. You know matches are off limits."

"I wanted to try out my new fire engine. It has a real siren on it and everything."

"If that gardener hadn't passed by when he did, you'd have sizzled like a sausage. You're supposed to be parked over there."

Jake stood his ground for a second, but Tim could glare hard enough to set a charging grizzly bear on its haunches. So I wasn't surprised when the kid hung his head and shuffled toward the corner again. He stopped to pet Captain on his way across the room, then glanced quickly at Tim and gave up that idea. There were tears in his eyes by the time he made it back to his chair, but his pride kept him from crying out loud.

Tim ran a hand wearily over the scar on his forehead. "What the hell do I do now?"

I shrugged. "How would I know?"

"What would your dad have done? My old man would've blown the whole thing off as a big joke."

"You know how funny my dad thought it was when we burned that trailer down. He probably would have made me pay for the roses out of my allowance or something."

Tim's mouth creased into a thoughtful frown. All at once he stood up and strode toward the door.

"Hold it right there," I said. "You're not dumping this problem off on me."

"Keep your shirt on. I ain't going far." Tim hurried out of the room. He came back in a few minutes, looking a lot more sure of himself. "Come on, kid. We got a job to do."

Jake hopped up. "What job?"

"I checked the bulletin board in the manager's office, and some old lady downstairs needs her living room painted."

"So why do we have to do it?" The bounce went out of Jake in an instant. "I don't know how to paint. I'd rather go fishing."

"So would I, but you're about to learn how to paint. You can't bring back those rosebushes, but if you're going to be a juvenile delinquent, you might as well get used to community service. That's part of the deal."

"Will I get paid real money?" The kid perked up a little with that thought.

"Not a dime. Are you in, Rick?"

"I'll meet you there as soon as I change my shirt."

"Number 37. It's way at the other end of the building, next to the laundry room." Tim took Jake by the arm. "We're burning daylight. Let's go."

"No! You can't make me!" Jake tried to wiggle away. "I don't have to do what you say!"

"Is that a fact?" Tim started walking out of the apartment, keeping a good grip on the kid. "Do us both a big favor, for Christ's sake, don't make a battle out of this."

By the time I found the right apartment and introduced myself to Mrs. Hammond, the retired schoolteacher who lived there, Tim had Jake taping baseboards. He didn't cut the kid any slack all morning, either. He had to run out for more paint at lunchtime, and Mrs. Hammond fixed a batch of grilled cheese sandwiches while he was gone. Jake had been in a royal huff since we started working, but his eyes lit up when he saw the food. He was halfway through a pile of homemade ginger cookies and a glass of milk when Tim came in.

Tim rained on his parade right away, though. "I asked you to have all the brushes clean by the time I got back."

"I'm tired of painting already," Jake said with his mouth full. "I wanna go home."

Tim picked up the plate of cookies and put it away on the sideboard. "Wipe that milk off your face and hop to it."

"Leave me alone!" Jake let go of his pride and started bawling. "You're no fun to hang out with anymore! You're a smelly old butthead, that's all!"

"Would you like to look me in the eye and call me that again?" Tim asked in a dangerously even tone that had backed down more than a few street punks over the years.

Jake shook his head and stared at the floor, scrunching an inch or two lower in his chair.

"I didn't think so. It won't do you any good to pitch a fit, so forget the pity party and get moving."

Mrs. Hammond glanced from Jake's teary face to Tim's hard one. "Can't you see how sad he is? You ought to give him a break. You've been a slave driver since you got here."

"He's in boot camp today," Tim said. "It won't kill him to sweat a little."

She raised her eyebrows. "I suppose you know best, but you look awfully young to be his father."

"I'm only a friend of his."

"Some friend," she muttered as she left the room with the lunch dishes.

I followed her into the kitchen. "Just for the record, ma'am, Tim is probably the best friend that kid ever had."

She shrugged her bony shoulders and set the dishes in the sink. "It's none of my business. I'd like to send the rest of those ginger cookies home with you, though, to thank you for your help."

I smiled. "You won't hear any argument from me."

It was late afternoon when we finally got done painting and went back to my apartment. Tim asked me to watch Jake while he hit the shower, and I could tell by the strain in his face that he was ready for a break. So I had the kid give me a hand cooking supper, and after we ate, Tim made him call the lady with the rosebushes to tell her he was sorry for burning up her garden.

Jake managed to get three or four words out, and then the chick on the phone went ballistic. I could hear her squawking loud and clear from across the room. Jake looked puzzled at first. Then his lip started trembling, and finally he burst into tears. Tim took the phone from him and hung it up without a word. He settled the kid in his lap on the couch.

Jake tried to squirm away. "You don't like me anymore! Let go of me!"

"Chill out. I think the world of you. That's why I went to pick you up at the cop shop this morning."

"You've been mean to me all day! I hate you! Let me go!" Jake lit into Tim with both fists. He kicked his feet and flailed his body around like a fish in a wet sack, crying and cussing. Tim held him tight and let him wear himself out, and I hid my amazement behind the newspaper.

When Jake finally ran out of steam and sat still, Tim cupped his face in both hands and looked right into his eyes. "Tell me something. Did you ever burn yourself on a hot stove?"

"Yeah, when I was making cookies at school. I got a great big blister on my finger, and it hurt real bad. I had to go see the nurse and everything."

"If those flames had gotten on you this morning, it would have hurt like that all over."

"I wanted to try out my new engine, and the dumb old babysitter wouldn't quit talking to her friends on the phone. I didn't mean to set the bushes on fire."

"I know, but your neighbor worked hard to grow those roses, and now she'll have to wait till next spring and plant new ones. How did you feel when you got hauled off in the squad car?"

"I was scared they'd lock me up, but I knew you'd come get me." Jake snuggled down against Tim's shoulder.

"It's best if you don't tangle with the cops. I stayed on you today so you'd remember not to play with matches."

"I'll remember. Can we still be buddies?"

"We'll always be buddies no matter what you do, but it'll be a lot more fun if you stay out of trouble."

There was a knock on the door. Jake was clinging to Tim with all his might by then, so I got up to answer it. A classy-looking lady in a satin party dress rustled into the apartment.

"Hey, Mrs. Maxwell," Tim said. "Jake had kind of a busy morning, but he got away with just some singed hair and a warning from the cops."

"So I've heard." Mrs. Maxwell let her eyes dart around the room, taking in everything at once. "Thank you for picking him up at the station. I got here as soon as I could."

Jake beamed at her without giving up the death grip he had on Tim's neck. "Guess what, Mom? Tim made me paint all day so I'd remember not to play with matches."

"He made you paint all day?"

"Yeah, to make up for wrecking somebody else's stuff."

Mrs. Maxwell offered Tim a nervous little smile. "Jake seems to relate to you better than he does to anybody else. He hasn't stopped talking about you for a year."

"We were pretty tight for a long time."

322

"I'm beginning to think I read you wrong when you dropped by last summer to introduce yourself."

"Most people do." Tim's face had gone as hard as nails, and I knew he was bracing himself for another goodbye. "You better get your jacket on, bud."

Jake shook his head. "When are you gonna come see me?"

"Well, I think about you every day. The picture I took of you with your fishing derby ribbon is still in my wallet." Tim reached for Jake's windbreaker, which had been thrown over one arm of the couch. "Come on. I bet your mom is dying to get home and ditch those high heels of hers."

"No! Not till you say you'll visit me!"

"Jake, I wish I could, but—"

"Mrs. Maxwell—" I started in.

Tim cut me off with a gesture and a death ray glare. I knew he didn't want Jake to find out his foster mother wouldn't let the two of them hang out, but I also knew Tim could be a stubborn fool when it came to his pride. I wished he would ask her to reconsider, just one more time.

He pried Jake gently but firmly off his neck and held out the windbreaker. "You gotta go now."

"No!" Jake tossed the jacket on the floor and scowled at Tim. "Promise you'll come visit me!"

"You may visit him as often as you want to," Mrs. Maxwell broke in as Tim threw up his hands. "It's obvious how much you two care for each other, and I appreciate you giving up your whole Sunday for him."

Tim stared blankly at the woman for a second as if she had been speaking Chinese. Then the corners of his mouth started to twitch, and in the next moment his face lit up with a million-dollar grin.

"Okay, bud, I'll call next Friday. If you keep your nose clean between now and then, we'll go out for ice cream." Tim picked up the windbreaker and held it out to Jake again. He was fighting like mad to get a grip on his smile, but he couldn't keep the joy from shining in his eyes. "You did a good job today."

Mrs. Maxwell opened her black suede handbag and took out a twenty dollar bill. "I made a terrible mistake last summer when I judged you by your past record and your appearance, and I'm truly sorry."

Tim waved the money away, looking disgusted. "We both want what's best for Jake. That's all that matters."

"Don't forget about ice cream!" the kid called as he gave Captain a quick hug and followed his foster mother out the door.

"Not a chance," Tim promised.

"You came down awful hard on him, didn't you?" I asked when the door had closed behind them.

"He needed to learn something. His life will be a whole lot easier if he doesn't let his wild streak get out of hand."

"I wouldn't say he's on the fast track to hell just yet. He's only a kid."

"I'll lose a lot less sleep if he stays out of the back of squad cars from now on. The year I spent on the dodge was a fair taste of hell." Tim snagged a cookie off the plate Mrs. Hammond had sent home with us. "This must be a fair taste of heaven, though."

"I've hardly heard you say a word about California or your outlaw days since that first night I found you."

"I try not to think about that stretch of my life at all. This world's a damn lonely place when you're being hunted." Tim switched on the TV and sank onto the couch. "Thank God this day is over. Remind me never to have a kid. It's killer hard work."

"I sure hope Mark gets over his panic attack in time to do right by Anita. Any kid of his is bound to be a holy terror to raise."

"If he does come back, we'll have to hold him down and put a ring in his nose so she can keep him in line."

"Yeah." I laughed. "I wonder if the lady with the rosebushes has figured out that you hung up on her yet."

"Probably not." Tim snickered, then turned serious. "Oh, one other thing. I wouldn't answer the phone with that line about the Road Kill Cafe if I were you. You'll scare off your catering customers."

"You got a point, and it ain't even on the top of your head. Did I ever tell you it's great having a pal like you around?"

"To know me is to love me." He thumped me on the shoulder. "You're not a bad specimen yourself."

Chapter 19

"Trick or treat!" I sang out as I walked into Brothers on the day of horrors.

Stace glanced up from the coil of wire he was fiddling with. "Is that a mask you're wearing or does your face always give people waking nightmares?"

"Have you seen yourself in the mirror lately? You make Dracula look like a cherub." I sat down next to Anita by the cash register. "That's a pretty blanket you're knitting. How are you feeling today, champ?"

She sighed and brushed her dark hair back from her face. "I feel like a beached whale, but that's nothing new."

"You look spent. Do you want me to drive you home?"

She shook her head. "It's too lonely there. You all have taken good care of me, but I miss Mark when I'm by myself in my apartment. The silence breaks my heart."

I laughed. "Enjoy it while you can. You'll be wishing for a little peace and quiet once that kid of yours pops out and starts squalling."

Tim stepped out of the paint booth at the back of the garage, peeled off his smock and face mask, and switched on the six o'clock news. He flopped into a lawn chair with his jug of iced tea. Bryan flashed on the tube and rattled off a spiel about how some hefty breakfast cereal or other put the zing in his swing.

Stace cussed peevishly and hurled his pliers at the TV screen. "I swear to God, if I have to suffer through that commercial one more time, I'll murder somebody!"

326

"Wreck my TV and I'll murder you," Tim said calmly. "Bryan looks like an idiot flexing his muscles that way, don't he?"

Stace set aside his wire sculpture and hooked up the water hose so he could start spraying down the service bays.

Tim leaned back in his chair and lit up a smoke. Suddenly, he leaped to his feet like he'd been kicked. "Stace, shut off the tap!"

"What's your problem? I do this every day, you know."

"Shut it off, now!" Tim bounded over and cranked up the TV.

As the sound of running water died away, the smooth voice of the sportscaster filled the garage. "Tragedy struck the tennis world today. Bryan Thomas, the bright young star out of Princeton, rolled his rented automobile this morning on a busy Seattle expressway. He was trapped in the wreckage for almost two hours, and surgeons were unable to save his right arm, which was crushed beyond repair. Police say his blood alcohol level was nearly twice the legal limit, and a small amount of cocaine was found at the scene of the accident. It appears that substance abuse has derailed another promising athletic career. Now, on a happier note, the Cowboys are expected to—"

Tim killed the tube. We all stared at each other in stunned silence as a long moment ticked by.

Then Stace picked up the hose again. "So the king fell off the mountain, did he?"

"It's your brother, for Christ's sake!" I burst out.

327

Stace only shrugged as he reached for the water faucet.

I itched to knock the self-satisfied smirk right off his face. I hurried to the phone instead, and dialed up the twins' folks in Georgia. "Hey, Sharon, it's Rick. We just saw Bryan on the news. Do you know what hospital they planted him in?"

Sharon started sobbing as soon as she heard my voice, and all I could get out of her was a bunch of gibberish. She'd always managed to keep her head when one of us in the crew landed himself in trouble, but I guess Bryan had finally pushed her over the edge. I eventually got her to put Ed on the line.

He gave me the name and number of a Seattle hospital. "Me and Sharon are getting ready to fly up there now. We'll keep you posted."

I tried to get hold of Bryan right away, but the charge nurse on his floor said he wouldn't take my phone call. "I'm afraid he has already plunged into a deep depression, which is to be expected, of course."

I sighed, feeling helpless and hating it. "Well, tell him the crew is thinking about him. We'll bug him again in a day or two."

We had no better luck the next time we phoned or the time after that.

Then Ed called from Seattle before I left for work on Tuesday morning to tell me Bryan had checked himself out of the hospital, against the advice of his doctors. He'd slipped past the vultures who were laying for him with their microphones and TV cameras and vanished in the middle of the night. "You boys were always as tight as brothers, Rick.

328

here."

"What makes you think we'd do any better than you and the cops? They know the city. We don't."

"The cops won't step in till an adult has been missing for at least twenty-four hours, and I need all the help I can get. The charge nurse told me Bryan was threatening to kill himself when he walked out the door." Ed's voice was dripping with desperation. "Please, Rick? Sharon's about to have a nervous breakdown on me. I don't dare leave her alone long enough to beat the streets myself."

"I'll see what I can do. The folks at the hospital will know how to get in touch with you, right? Okay, you'll hear from me soon." I hung up the phone wondering how in Samuel J. Hell Ed thought I was going to come up with the money for a last minute trip across the country.

"I'm not going anywhere," Stace said flatly when I rushed into Brothers with the news of Bryan's disappearance. "Let the boy wonder fend for himself now."

"Would you grow the hell up?" I snapped. "He's wandering around a strange city all alone with a death wish. Doesn't that mean anything to you?"

"Sure, I'd love to join you." Stace took a long drag on his cigarette and smiled smugly to himself. "But there's this totally knockout waitress down at Bernie's Barbecue I've had my eye on, and she's free tonight."

"We wouldn't have you along on a bet!" Tim snatched a heavy auto body hammer off his workbench. "Get the hell out of my sight before I bust your skull wide open!"

I eased the hammer out of his hand as Stace made a break for the stairs. "Take a deep breath or two before you do something stupid. We've got a rescue mission to pull off."

I went to the foot of the staircase and yelled for Stace till he came sulkily out onto the upper landing.

"What do you want, Rick? If you feel the need to drop everything so you can chase Bryan from here to Egypt and back just because my dad jerks your chain, go for it. But spare me the particulars. I ain't interested."

"Shut your mouth and listen up. I couldn't care less right now what you think about your brother. Me and Tim are counting on you to watch the garage and stick close to home in case Anita pops. I ain't asking you a favor, either, it's an order. Got it?"

"Fair enough." Stace stalked back into his attic apartment and slammed the door.

~~~

I hadn't made a single withdrawal from my cafe fund since the day I set up the savings account, and I would rather not have done it at all, but I couldn't think of any other legal way to get a wad of quick cash. I plunked down the money for the last two cheap seats on a mid-day flight to Seattle, and me and Tim were airborne by noon. I got a bang out of watching the trees and cars and buildings getting smaller and smaller as we lifted off, but I was really disappointed with the box lunch they passed out during the plane ride.

"That was a nice snack, I suppose, but when's the real food coming?" I asked.

The flight attendant laughed. "This must be your first trip on a commercial airline. Next time, you'll know it pays to eat before you board."

"Don't mind Rick. He's a human garbage disposal." Tim flashed her his best smile. "You know, you're kind of cute. I was always a sucker for a chick in a uniform."

The flight attendant, who was old enough to be Tim's mother, rolled her eyes and walked away, but she came back a while later with two more lunch bags. "I'd hate to see a couple of growing boys like you starve to death before we land."

Tim grinned at me as he unwrapped his turkey sandwich. "A little sweet talk works every time."

I'd never set foot out of Texas in my life, so I was pretty excited when we touched down in Seattle. But the nasty weather put the squash on my enthusiasm right away.

I gazed glumly at the freezing rain that pelted against the windows of the airport. "What do we do now?"

"Find the slums. What else?" Tim snagged a city map off a rack at the baggage counter.

"I doubt if they feature the ghetto on the list of tourist attractions."

We flagged down a cab and asked the driver, a guy in his forties who was fighting off middle age with a gold earring and a tie-dyed T-shirt, where the poor section of town was. He looked at us for a second like we'd requested directions to Mars.

Then he pointed out a couple of areas on the map. "There are other places, but those are the worst ones."

"Well, Tim, you're the man with all the ideas," I said. "Where should we go?"

"Hell if I know. I'll hold up the map, and you can close your eyes and point at it. It's way beyond hopeless, shooting in the dark like this. We shouldn't have come up here at all."

"You two obviously aren't businessmen, and you don't have enough luggage to be on vacation." The cabbie was still eyeballing us as if he thought we were space aliens. "I've been driving these soggy city streets for seventeen years, and this is the first time I've seen a pair of out-of-towners stand in the rain trying to decide which piece of the ghetto they ought to visit. So what are you after?"

"Maybe you've heard of the tennis player out of Princeton who lost his arm? They had him in one of the big city hospitals up here, but he skipped out on them last night," Tim explained. "We're friends of his from way back, and we came to hunt him down."

"Bryan Thomas? I might be able to narrow your search a little. One of our graveyard drivers was bragging to everybody at the gas pumps this morning about how she took him on a hell of a binge last night. I blew her off because she's always spinning some story about carting celebrities around. She may be blowing smoke, but I could give her a call and find out where she claims they went."

"We might as well start there," I said, climbing into the back of the taxi and brushing my damp hair away from my face.

The cabbie had definitely picked the wrong career for himself. He could have made a fortune on the race track. Even Mark would have been impressed by the way he swerved around corners at twice the speed of light. I swear I didn't see the guy hit the brakes once between the time he came back from calling the night driver and the time he screeched to a halt on a street lined with raunchy nightclubs and fleabag motels. I scanned the scene and sighed, wishing I had my pistol with me, but then I shrugged off that thought. Me and Tim had always made a good team in a scuffle.

"Try the motels first. He's got to have found a place to crash and burn by now." The driver shook our hands as we got out of his cab. "Good luck to you."

"Yeah. Thanks for the tip," Tim said.

"No problem. I've got a couple more, too." The cabbie shuddered. "Don't use the toilets around here, and watch out for the roaches. Most of them are eating size."

He wasn't lying. We ducked into one run-down building after another, and between places we dashed through the driving rain.

"I hope the little punk appreciates this," I groused, pulling my jacket tighter around me. "He might not even be in the area at all."

Tim muttered his agreement as he disappeared into another dump. I was about to follow him when I heard the thud of running footsteps on the pavement behind me. In the next second, my breath was cut off by a meaty hand that clamped around my throat. I tried to pull away, but the fingers dug viciously into my windpipe.

"Fork it over. Money, jewelry, car keys," the mugger snarled.

I fumbled to empty my pockets while my lungs screamed for air. I couldn't move fast enough to satisfy the goon. His fist crashed into the side of my face, and my mind swam in a blur of pain and terror. It took all the strength I could muster to keep my knees from buckling.

Then I heard the unmistakable zip and snap of a switchblade, and Tim's chilling tone raised the hairs on the back of my neck. "Which side of your chest would you like slashed first, jack, right or left?"

The thug let go of me and took off down the street before I sucked in my first whooping breath. I leaned against the wall of the seedy motel, choking and gasping, and blinked my eyes to clear away the stars that danced in my vision.

"You okay, buddy?" Tim asked. "I don't see any blood, but you'll likely have a pretty gnarly bruise where he tagged you."

"I'll be fine once I get some oxygen in me," I answered shakily. "Thank God you had that knife with you."

"I don't guess God had a lot to do with it. He probably doesn't think much of guys who carry switchblades."

"How did you get it through the metal detector at the airport?"

Tim laughed. "Good question. Maybe God had a hand in it after all."

"You amaze me, Tim. You can be sweet as the day is long when it suits you and then offer to slice up a mugger on a crummy street in a strange city and joke about it afterward like it was nothing."

"I got an angel and a devil playing tug-of-war for my soul." He opened the door. "If you're all right, we best not stand here gabbing. We could have stayed in Texas and crawled into holes like these without slogging through the damn sleet."

We'd all but given up hope when we finally struck oil after eons of searching. Tim spotted Bryan's name in an open guest ledger at a motel where no self-respecting sewer rat would stay. We explained our situation to the witch behind the desk, but she wouldn't hand over the key to his room.

"Ever heard of a thing called privacy?" she sneered. She was missing one front tooth.

Tim reached over the counter and jerked her roughly out of her chair by one shoulder. "I ain't in a mood to argue. Cough up the keys."

She spat in his face like an angry alley cat. "I'll call the cops!"

"Don't jack with me, lady." He shook his fist under her nose. "I'll mess up your day real bad before they get here."

She flung a key across the desk at me, and I snatched it up before she got a chance to change her mind.

"I thought you'd see it my way." Tim let her drop back into the chair and wiped the spittle off his face with his shirt sleeve. "If I didn't have better things to do, I'd rip your tongue out for slobbering all over me."

We sprinted down the unswept hallway and unlocked the last room on our left. The smell of stale booze just about knocked us over when we opened the door. Tim switched on the light, and I shivered as a roach skittered past the toe of my tennis shoe.

Bryan was sprawled on the cold linoleum floor in his underwear with an empty whiskey bottle in his hand. His face was pasty in the glare of the bare light bulb, and at first I thought he was dead. Then he stirred a little and muttered something I couldn't understand.

Me and Tim lifted him onto the bed. His right arm had been sawed off just below the elbow, and the dirty gauze dressing on the stump was crusted with dry blood. I saw a broken piece of mirror and a drinking straw lying on the floor next to a couple of crumpled plastic bags. I left them lay, not anxious to know whether they belonged to Bryan or some other poor loser.

Bryan opened his dull eyes and stared at us for a second, then closed them again. "Clear the hell out."

"It's good to see you, too, pal." Tim sat on the bed beside him. "We'll get you back to the hospital."

"To hell with the hospital." Bryan raised the empty bottle to his lips. "I'm going straight to the big-time. Ain't you proud of me?"

Tim took the bottle from him and tossed it away in a corner. "You look like you could use a little first aid."

"I could use a little drink."

336

"That ain't working, buddy." I picked up the phone by the bed and dialed up the operator. "I've got Bryan Thomas here, and I need an ambulance."

"Who? The tennis star? Yeah, right."

"I'm an old friend of his, and I don't have time to make you believe me. Send out the medics on the double."

"Where are you?"

"Some cheap motel on a sleazy street that probably leads straight to hell. I guess I should've paid attention to the address."

"Stay on the line while I trace the number. What condition is Mr. Thomas in?"

"About the same as the motel. Drunk, most likely high, but alive and kicking."

I had to drop the receiver at that moment because Bryan was definitely kicking. He started thrashing around like his shorts were on fire, trying to shove Tim off the bed.

"I ain't getting in an ambulance at gunpoint!" he bellowed. "I wanna die! Take your damn hands off me and let me die!"

"You hold his legs, I'll get the top half," I said. "God Almighty, he's strong as an ox."

We did everything we could to keep Bryan still, but there was no reasoning with him. He kicked Tim in the face and split my lip with his good fist. The wound on his stump broke open as he bucked and writhed on the bed, and one spurt of blood after another soaked through the filthy bandage till there was nothing left of the gauze and adhesive tape.

"Don't take this personal, man. I can't let you hurt yourself." Tim thumped him on the chin and laid him out cold. Bryan was a lot easier to handle after that.

I grabbed a spare pillowcase off the bedside table and pressed it against his stump till the bleeding slowed to a trickle and stopped. Tim dug a pair of sweats out of my overnight bag. We managed to get Bryan dressed before the paramedics barreled into the room and slid him onto a stretcher.

Me and Tim bummed a ride to the hospital in the ambulance. The paramedics cleaned up Bryan's arm and gave him something to keep him zoned out for a while. One of them started fussing over the bruises on my throat and face, but I told him to back off.

"From the looks of those marks on your neck, somebody got you in a chokehold," he said. "Did Mr. Thomas do that?"

I shook my head. "We ran into some trouble on the streets of your fine city. We just blew into town this afternoon, and I ain't impressed so far."

"You picked a lousy neighborhood to get acquainted with," the paramedic pointed out. "Most newcomers like to check out the Pike Place Market or the Space Needle. The views are better from there."

Tim jerked his thumb toward Bryan on the stretcher. "That little butthead made our travel plans."

Ed and Sharon met up with us at the medical center. Sharon got all weepy as soon as she laid eyes on us. She must have hugged us and thanked us at least a hundred times before she finally ran out of steam.

"Where's Stace?" Ed asked when the four of us were sitting in Bryan's hospital room, waiting for him to come back from outer space.

"Someone had to stay behind in case Anita went into labor," I said. "Besides, paying for two last minute plane tickets was a stretch. I didn't see any reason to get a third one."

"What you really mean is he wouldn't come?" Sharon shook her head sadly and tugged at a button on her blouse. "I thought he'd be big enough to put his own feelings aside when his brother needed him, but I guess I was wrong about that."

"I can't believe we're even in this mess," Ed grumbled. "I might have looked for something like this out of Stace, but Bryan always had a good head on his shoulders."

Tim sighed and rubbed a hand tiredly over the scar on his forehead. "Maybe the twins would quit feuding if you two kept stupid remarks like those to yourselves. I bet Bryan would be thrilled to death if you let him ditch his halo once in a while, and I know for a fact Stace don't get half the credit he deserves from you—as an artist and a damn good guy, too."

"Oh, yeah, he sure is showing what a good guy he is now," Ed retorted. "He left his brother for the buzzards."

Tim shrugged. "And where the hell has Bryan been lately? He walked away a long time ago, in case you forgot."

I put up a hand for silence. "Knock it off. There's blame enough for everybody. It won't do us any good to pitch it back and forth at each other."

Bryan opened his eyes just then. He glanced groggily around the room and swore under his breath. "So I'm still alive."

"In spite of your best efforts," Sharon said.

"You sure know how to pick scummy hideouts, pal." Tim rubbed his hands together like he was brushing off dirt. "I hope I didn't discover a new disease tracking you down."

"Nobody asked you to butt in at all," Bryan groused.

"Tim and Rick saved you from God knows what fate, and you ought to be thankful for it. I'm sending you back to Texas with them on Saturday, unless they object." Ed looked from his son in the hospital bed to me and Tim, and there was a naked plea in his eyes. "I'm afraid if we haul him down to Georgia with us now, we'll mollycoddle him too much, and he'll spend the rest of his life hanging around the gym or pumping gas at some all-night service station."

"Suits us," I said. "We'll take him home and make a winner out of him, the first ever in the crew."

Bryan scowled at me and pulled his blanket tighter around his chin. "Forget it, Rick. I'm not interested."

"Would you rather come back to Georgia with us then, honey?" Sharon was surprised. "Like your dad says, there ain't much waiting for you down there."

"I'm not going anywhere with you, either."

"Just what do you plan on doing then?" Ed asked, not even trying to keep the exasperation out of his voice.

340

"I plan on laying right here to rot."

"On whose dime?" Ed snapped. "It's costing a couple hundred bucks a day to keep your butt in that bed."

"So tell the nurses to slip me a few extra happy pills, and then all you'll have to spring for is a coffin."

Ed rolled his eyes and turned to me. "I'll put his plane ticket on my charge card this afternoon. I guess the crew can do more to help him now than we can. You boys always had a knack for patching each other up."

"We'll give him an attitude adjustment. Nobody can pout for long around Mark and Stace." I wondered if I'd ever learn to plug in my brain before I opened my mouth. Mark was missing in action, and Bryan and Stace couldn't stand each other.

Bryan tried to prop himself up in the bed, then dropped back onto his pillow with a grunt of pain. "If you buy that ticket, Dad, you better be ready to roll a real expensive joint with it. I damn sure don't want it."

"You'll take wing with us, either in a seat or stuffed in a suitcase in the cargo hold." Tim sounded even more cranky than usual, and I knew he was running out of patience real fast. So was I, to tell the truth.

Bryan shot Tim an icy glare. "Have it your way then. I don't have two fists to defend myself with now, so I guess I won't stand a chance against you in a fight."

341

"Aw hell, Bryan, call off the pity party." A quick spark of anger flashed in Tim's eyes, but he managed to work up a fairly convincing grin before he finished speaking. "Wait till they strap one of those metal hook things on the end of your arm. You'll have what it takes to back down the whole crew at once then."

I got up and strode toward the door, motioning for the redhead to follow me. "Come on, Tim, it's been a long day. Let's hunt up a hot meal and a place to sack out."

Ed bought Bryan's plane ticket and gave it to me for safekeeping, and he and Sharon caught a flight back to Georgia late the next afternoon.

"This cold northern air is hard on old bones like ours, and we still have to work for a living." Sharon gave me and Tim each another quick hug when we saw them off at the airport. "Thanks again for everything. Bryan treated you like dirt for a long time, but I knew you'd come through for him when it counted."

"Don't design us any medals yet," I said. "The crew is just meant to stick together, that's all."

Sharon dabbed at her eyes with her shirt sleeve. "You take care of my son, you hear? I hope he goes back to college pretty soon."

"We'll have his nose shoved in a book again before he forgets how to read." Tim turned away. "I've had my fill of mushy scenes lately. Don't stress your curly head over Bryan. He's in good hands."

"We know he is." Ed took his wife by the arm and led her toward the waiting plane.

Chapter 20

Me and Tim checked Bryan out of the hospital after breakfast on Saturday morning. We decked him out in a big jacket and pulled a baseball cap low over his face to keep people from gawking at him, then marched him between us onto the plane. He'd gotten pretty famous outside the tennis world lately because of the stupid cereal commercial on TV, so we had to fend off a lot of rubberneckers with nasty looks. I breathed a sigh of relief when the passengers around us finally settled down and buried themselves in their magazines and private conversations.

The flight attendant recognized Bryan right away. She just about dropped her basket of pretzels and soda crackers. "Are you Bryan—?"

"Shut up," I hissed, grabbing a handful of snacks out of the basket. "He isn't anybody you'd know."

"He's the tennis—"

"Beat it, lady, and keep your tongue behind your teeth." Tim shooed her away with a wave of his hand. "He ain't ready to be blubbered over."

When she was gone, Bryan took a bag of pretzels from me and tried to rip it open with his teeth. He gave up in disgust after a minute and lobbed the bag across the cabin. It hit a white-haired old man on the back of the head.

I unwrapped some crackers and gave them to him. "Chill out, Bryan. You can't be firing missiles like that."

"Forget the etiquette lesson, will you? If you'd left me the hell alone, I'd be at the morgue by now and glad of it."

"Yeah, and we'd all be feeling real grand about that." Tim turned to stare out the window, and we suffered through the rest of the trip in silence.

Just before we landed, the flight attendant came around with glasses of wine left over from the brunch in the first-class section. I snagged one for Bryan, and he tossed it down in one gulp. I guess a swig of wine was the last thing he needed because he was already strung out on painkillers, so hoisting him out of his seat was like trying to get a bag of water to stand up. The airplane staff wanted to call the paramedics, but after a little arguing, they brought a wheelchair instead. We rolled Bryan out to my car.

Tim climbed into the driver's seat. "Where to, boss? Is it straight to the hospital or would you rather take your chances with our nursing?"

Bryan didn't answer, and Tim muttered something lewd and drove to Brothers. The oil light on my dashboard was blinking, so he popped the hood while I carried our bags inside.

Anita sat in a corner clipping coupons, and Stace was twisting the wing of a dragon into shape. Both of his hands were twined in the sculpture, and he had to slump over his work because there was a piece of wire clamped between his teeth, too.

I dropped the luggage by the door and turned down the blaring TV. "Hey, Stace, that's a cool critter."

"Thanks," he mumbled around the wire in his mouth. "I'm having a hell of a time getting the tail to look right, though."

"Aren't you going to ask me about your brother?"

He shrugged and shook his head, and it took everything I had in me not to knock him off his stool, sculpture and all.

"Where is he?" Anita glanced up from the coupons.

"He's in the car. Me and Tim are going to bring him in, and Stace, if you say anything cute about his missing arm, I swear I'll rip your lips off."

"And I'll feed them to you." The familiar voice came from somewhere above me, and I looked up to see Mark making his way down the stairs with a jug of milk and a plate of doughnuts.

"Don't you be throwing around too many threats, jack. I'm not that thrilled with you right now, either." I couldn't quite decide whether I wanted to hug him or hit him, so I went to shake his hand instead. "What brought you out of hiding after all this time?"

"I saw Bryan on the news and figured you all might need some help with him, so I knocked on Anita's door last night and told her I was ready to come home, where I should have been from the start." Mark stared sheepishly at the floor for a second and then grinned. "She sure has grown around the middle."

Anita giggled. "I think the little one is training to be a prize fighter. My liver is doubling as a speed bag."

"I never expected to hear a crack like that out of her." Mark looked at me and raised his eyebrows. "What have you guys done to her?"

"Corrupted her innocent soul. It's about time you showed up to take care of her yourself." I figured I'd said enough and hurried out to give Tim a hand with Bryan.

"He's sound asleep," Tim said. "Maybe we ought to leave him be for a while."

"We better not. He'd roast like a turkey after just blowing down from the frozen north." I shook Bryan awake. "Get a move on, buddy. This is where the taxi stops."

Bryan opened his eyes and looked groggily at me, then swung his legs out of the car. Me and Tim lifted him to his feet and kept him steady as he shuffled inside. We planted him in one of the nice chairs from the office. He scowled at the floor without speaking to anybody.

Some corny sheriff in a cowboy movie carried the conversation for what felt like a year or two while we all stared at each other, not knowing what to say. Mark rustled up a pair of scissors and sat down to work on the coupons with Anita. They started talking in Spanish, and I don't know why they felt the need to whisper with their heads so close together because none of us could understand a word they said anyway. Maybe it was so they could kiss like crazy and think we didn't notice.

The rest of us were watching a dandruff shampoo commercial like it was the most riveting thing we'd ever seen when Stace finally saved the day. He got up and walked over to Bryan with his wire sculpture, which shocked the heck out of me.

"Check this out." Stace tried a little too hard to sound casual.

Bryan glanced at the dragon, then sat up straight and gave it a closer look. "Cool. Who taught you to make these?"

Stace shrugged and turned away. "You aren't the only one in the family with a natural talent."

"No, you are. My natural talent is in the toilet now." Bryan went back to glowering at the floor.

"You should see all the sculptures he has up in the loft," Tim said, not wanting the conversation to fizzle out. "Stace, why don't you go grab a few of them?"

"Tim, you've just been drafted." The early news was about to come on, and I wasn't anxious for Bryan to catch a glimpse of himself in a sports clip. "Let's try to get him upstairs so he can scope out the artwork."

"It'd be easier for me to bring it down," Stace argued. "Those steps are pretty steep, and Bryan looked sort of wobbly on his feet when you brought him in."

"Yeah, but you have a regular gallery up there with all those nice display cases and stuff. He needs the full effect." I heard the newscaster start jabbering and herded everybody toward the stairs. "Head 'em up and move 'em out."

Stace couldn't hold back to save his life when it came to his sculptures, so he'd already started talking a million miles a minute before Bryan was settled in a recliner in the tiny attic apartment. Me and Tim skipped out when the twins weren't looking. We got downstairs just in time to see Mark and Anita disappearing out the door, laughing.

"Well, I hope they have fun on their honeymoon." Tim grinned. "Get a load of that Cadillac I'm touching up." He pointed at the car in the paint booth. "Ain't she sweet?"

We heard a burst of shouting from the attic, then a long silence and another wave of words. A few moments later, there was a terrific crash and a slamming door.

"Shall we go keep them from killing each other?" I asked.

Tim rubbed his hand tiredly over the scar on his forehead. "I'm sick to death of playing hero. They'll have to hash it out for themselves." Suddenly the old sly gleam came into his eyes. "I know exactly what they need." He grabbed a chunk of scrap wood from the junk pile by his workbench and turned toward the stairs.

"Hey, if you're passing out clubs, you better keep it fair."

"I'm going to wedge this under the door so they can't walk out on the battle." Tim dashed up the steps, then back down a second later. "They'll either make peace or fight to the death, but they won't open that door till they get outside help."

I picked up my car keys. "Let's sneak out and catch that new Army flick at the drive-in then. I don't want to listen to them go at it. This is bound to be worse than you and your stepdad ever were."

~~~

We didn't set the twins free till early the next morning. Stace exploded through the door the second

Tim kicked the wood block out of the way. Bryan was hot on his heels.

"What the hell were you thinking locking us in there? That was worse than a night in jail," Stace burst out, rubbing a fresh bruise below his right eye and then running his fingers through his black hair, which didn't look any neater when he finished than it had before.

"There's nothing to eat in that pigsty except stale doughnuts and something green and slimy in the fridge," Bryan griped at the same time. He tried unsuccessfully to straighten out his collar and smooth his rumpled dress shirt with his left hand.

"It's good to see you two agreeing about something for a change." I thumped each of them on the shoulder and grinned. "You look like you haven't slept all week. We'll go to my place and pork out on pancakes."

I had to stop at the grocery store for butter and syrup, and Stace walked in with me. Tim and Bryan kicked back in the car with the Sunday paper.

"I'm real worried about Bryan," Stace blurted out before we made it halfway across the parking lot. "He's got a royal attitude problem."

"Give him a break. He's been through the wringer. He'll be okay."

"I don't think so. He wants to kill himself. We better not leave him alone for a while."

"We'll keep an eye on him. I guess I'll get some ham, too. You all are probably starving."

I started right in flipping pancakes when we got to my place, and Stace spread the funnies on the kitchen table. I didn't pay attention to Tim and Bryan in the living room at first, so I didn't know they were arguing till I heard Tim's raised voice.

"What the hell makes you say you'd be better off dead? Don't you think the rest of us have been through hard times?"

"The rest of you have all your limbs. In case you haven't noticed, I'm not a whole man anymore."

"Because of your missing arm or your missing brain?"

"I was a tennis player. I just went pro. Money, women, travels, stuff you all have never dreamed of. Now I can't even button my shirt by myself, for Christ's sake."

"And I suppose somebody else got you all jacked up and poured the booze down your throat before you took the wheel?" Tim slammed his fist down hard on the coffee table. "Damn it, Bryan, you haven't even been back in town for twenty-four hours, and your whining is getting old already."

"Thanks for the sympathy. You have no idea what it's like to wake up in the middle of the night and see the stump that used to be your arm laying there on the sheet like a broken tree limb. You have no idea what it's like to look in the mirror every morning and face the fact that things will never go back to the way they were. You have no idea—"

"Fine, I have no idea! But you can't change what happened, and you can't grow another arm, so you might as well gather up your guts and go on with your life. You were getting an education, right?"

"I was working on a business degree, but it was just so I could play tennis. I didn't study or anything. They cut athletes a lot of slack at those classy colleges because they bring in a ton of money and publicity."

"Well, maybe you got lazy, but so what? You always wanted to go to college. You don't need two arms for that."

Bryan laughed bitterly. "I'd rather kill myself and be done with it. And I will, too, once you old biddies stop breathing down my neck. And don't bother bringing up the scars on Rick's wrists. I heard all the gory details from Stace last night. I only have one wrist to slice, so opening my veins will be a problem like everything else is because I can't work a blade with an imaginary hand."

Tim leaped up off the couch, yanked open the closet door, and grabbed his pistol. He plunked it down on the coffee table in front of Bryan.

"Go for it." He jerked his thumb toward the gun. "If you want to take the sissy way out, that'll make it quick and easy. But step out on the balcony first, if you don't mind, so we can just hose off the mess instead of replacing the rug."

Bryan's eyes got as big as dinner plates, and he sat stone still and stared at the pistol, then at Tim, then at the pistol again. You could have heard a pin drop on the blaze orange carpet.

After a few agonizing seconds, Tim got right in Bryan's face. "Well, go on, quitter. What are you waiting for?"

Bryan shrank back. "I'll have to think on it some."

Tim shook his head. "It's either end it right this second or get a life. If you don't blow your brains out now, I better not hear another word about it."

He picked up the gun and tried to jam it into Bryan's hand. When Bryan wouldn't take it, he shoved it back in the closet and slammed the door. He stepped into the kitchen, mopping the beads of sweat off his forehead with his shirt sleeve.

"Are you out of your mind?" I hissed.

"It wasn't loaded." He mouthed the words at me, then said aloud, "I wouldn't make much of a shrink, would I? Are we ever going to eat?"

"I don't see what's stopping you." I set a platter of ham beside the mountain of pancakes on the table. "Bryan, shall I fix you a plate?"

Bryan ignored me and stomped onto the balcony to sulk, and at the same time, Mark and Anita walked in the door. I hadn't seen Anita smile much in months, but she looked like everything was finally peachy in her world.

"We smelled ham cooking all the way down the hall," Mark said. "It's a crime to serve ham any place I'm not invited, you know."

"Grab a plate. Stace, leave some syrup for the rest of us, would you?" I cut up a slab of meat for Bryan to gnaw on after he got done pouting.

Mark poured himself a cup of coffee. "I was wondering if we could get a couple of you to stand up with us at the courthouse tomorrow morning."

"We'll have the shotgun ready," Tim laughed. "I'll even paint it white so you can have a formal wedding."

352

~~~

Mark and Anita tied the knot as soon as the courthouse opened Monday morning. Tim and Stace signed the papers as their witnesses, and I served up a brunch at my place afterward. Anita may have had to settle for getting hitched in a big red maternity dress, but I came as close as I could to giving her the fancy party she'd always dreamed about. A wedding cake with a crown of sugar flowers isn't so hard to pull off in the fall when it's something less than three hundred degrees out. Stace got a little tipsy and tried to kiss the bride, and she dropped an ice cube down his pants.

"Damn!" He jumped back from her. "That's a dirty trick to pull on a guy, but I'm glad you're finally learning to stick up for yourself."

"She has to. She's one of the crew now." Tim filled his glass from the punch bowl. "Hey, Anita, did I ever tell you about the time Mark threw up on his date at the junior prom?"

"This apartment is three floors up," Mark said. "How many times do you suppose a guy would bounce if he got shoved off that balcony?"

I carried a plate of food to Bryan on the couch. "Are you going to quit moping long enough to eat? I cut everything up for you."

He snatched the plate out of my hand. "You don't have to baby me. I could go for another nip of gin."

"You've been nipping too much already. Try this citrus punch instead. It's one of my best catering secrets."

Bryan ignored the glass I held out. I sighed and put it on the coffee table in front of him, then walked away before I said something that would set him off and ruin the party.

Anita had picked almost all of the pecans out of the bowl of mixed nuts when her water broke. She made a little surprised sound in her throat and then started crying as she clutched at her swollen belly.

Mark dropped his drink. "What the hell do we do now?"

"You mop up my carpet as best you can and then go park your butt in the back seat of my car while me and Tim help your wife down the stairs." I tossed him a roll of paper towels. "Stace, you stay with Bryan to make sure he doesn't do anything stupid, and there better be something left for us to eat when we get home."

Me and Tim marched Anita out to the parking lot and settled her in the front seat of my wagon. Tim climbed in the back with a very keyed up Mark, and I took off toward the hospital.

"Come on, man, I thought you could drive." Mark leaned forward to get a peek at the speedometer. "What's this sixty crap? Punch it already."

"You're the speed demon, not me," I told him. "That baby isn't going to pop out in the next ten minutes, so keep your shirt on."

Mark started to argue, but Tim pushed him back in his seat. He growled something in Spanish that made Anita turn around and glare at him. She flashed a pretty mean scowl for being such a sweet-tempered chick, so Mark sat still and shut up.

354

"Well, Tim, I guess we won't have to put a ring in his nose after all," I said. "She's learning to keep him in line."

Mark laughed. "She looks gentle enough, but it's all an act. She opened up on me with both barrels the other night for leaving her in the lurch all these months."

"Good for you, champ." I patted Anita on the shoulder. "I always knew there was a she-devil inside you somewhere."

Anita blushed. Then she groaned and clenched the sides of her bucket seat till her knuckles were white, and I stepped a little harder on the gas pedal.

"Squeeze your legs together, lady," Tim said shakily. "I've patched up a lot of battle wounds in my time, but I don't do babies."

"Would you listen to him?" I grinned at Mark in the rear view mirror. "He'd go toe to toe with the devil just for something to do on a dull afternoon, but the thought of catching a little bitty baby has him shaking in his shoes."

"Shut up and drive," Tim snapped. But he was laughing along with the rest of us, so I knew he wasn't too put out with me.

We pulled up at the hospital, and I dumped the others off by the door and went to park the car. Anita sagged between Tim and Mark as they hustled her into the building. I hurried in after them and found Tim roosting on one of the hard plastic chairs in the lobby.

I took the seat next to him and picked up a magazine, then tossed it back on the coffee table.

"You'd think with as much time as a guy spends in this place, they'd come up with some good mags or at least some decent chairs."

Tim nodded and grinned. "Mark looked like he was getting hauled off to the gas chamber when the nurses led those two away."

"I'm sure glad he showed up in time for the big event. Anita's been stewing ever since he left last summer because having a baby without a husband would have put a black mark on her family name."

Tim rolled his eyes. "Yeah, talk about worrying over nothing. Hell, I told her you and the twins were practically the only kids in our neighborhood who grew up with two parents."

"It must be nice in that Mexican village where she comes from. I mean, since most of the families there stay together and all."

"Maybe, but we have running water and electricity here. That's a big plus in my book."

"True, and they can give Anita a morphine shot or something when the pain sends her through the roof."

"If she gets a grip on Mark like she had on me when we dragged her in here, he'll need a morphine shot. Maybe it'll teach him to keep his zipper up from now on." Tim laughed. "Better him than me, that's all I can say."

I turned and stared out the window at the ragged line of dark clouds that was building above the rooftops of the city.

Tim laid a hand on my knee. "You're thinking about Daisy, aren't you?"

"Yeah. I never told her, but just in the few weeks I knew her, I was already kind of dreaming about what it would be like to settle down with her and raise kids and all."

"Are you ever going to break down and date somebody else? There are plenty of other girls out there, you know."

"When I got Daisy killed, I was sure she took my heart to the grave with her, and sometimes it still feels like she did. But since we started watching out for Anita and everything, I've been thinking I don't want to be alone for the rest of my life. The trouble is, I've never met anybody who could hold a light to Daisy, and even if I did, I'd be afraid I couldn't protect her when the chips were down, like last time."

"They say you never forget your first love, but I hope you don't let her memory and your conscience keep you from seeing the right one when she comes along."

"You should write your own advice column for the papers." I jabbed him playfully in the ribs. "Your problem is you can't get past the third or fourth date with a chick before you come across another one you like better."

"I'm on a quest for perfection, I guess." Tim chuckled, then turned thoughtful. "Seriously, forever ain't in my vocabulary. I'm too set in my ways to make room in my life for anybody long-term."

"You? The greatest womanizer of all time? I bet you ten bucks you're wearing a wedding ring in three years or less."

"You're on." He reached out and shook my hand to sew up the deal. "Make it ten bucks and a beer."

We lapsed into a friendly silence, and after a while Tim leaned back in his chair and dozed off. I watched him snoozing for a long time. It's cool the way a guy's defenses drop when he falls asleep. Tim hardly ever lost the stubborn set of his jaw during his waking hours, but his face softened into a smile as he dreamed, and he looked like a little boy in an oversized denim jacket.

A heavyset nurse walked into the lounge late in the afternoon and dropped some change into the soda machine. She punched a button, and a can clattered into the tray and made Tim jerk awake in the chair next to me.

As the nurse turned away from the machine, I got a look at her straight on. It was Straw Boss, the hag who'd slapped me around years ago in the psych ward. For a split second a wave of panic swept over me, and then my guts knotted up with anger. But I made myself take a few deep breaths. That had been ages ago, and she was nothing to me now.

She studied me for a minute. "Have I seen you somewhere before?"

I shook my head and turned to gaze out the window, hoping to end the conversation right there.

But she wouldn't give it up. "Your face looks real familiar. Are you sure we haven't met?"

"Yeah, I'm sure." I pretended the banks of clouds in the sky were the most fascinating things I'd ever seen. They'd been darkening all afternoon, and now the sun was nearly gone behind them.

358

Straw Boss hesitated a moment longer, then walked out of the room with another glance over her shoulder. I wiped my sweaty palms on my jeans and hoped my heart wasn't pounding loud enough for Tim to hear it.

"Did you ever meet that chick?" he asked.

"Naw, she probably had me mixed up with somebody else."

"She seemed pretty sure she knew you, and you looked flat pissed off for a second when you saw her. Anyway, she's built like a refrigerator. I feel sorry for the guy who shares her bed."

I snickered. "The sight of her face first thing in the morning would do him in if he wasn't crushed to death during the night."

Mark burst into the room just then, practically skipping. His grin was so wide I thought it wasn't going to fit through the doorway. "Hey! You're looking at a real live daddy!"

Tim jumped up. "Way to go, man! Boy or girl?"

"A little girl. Anita Raquel, after the two best ladies in my life."

I pumped Mark's hand till his arm just about popped off. "Congratulations! I hardly ever thought of Grandma as Raquel, though. We always just called her Grandma."

"Yeah, well, he couldn't exactly name her that, bonehead," Tim said. "She'd get teased something awful in school."

"Wanna come see her?" Mark took off down the hall without waiting for an answer, and me and Tim jogged after him. He hit the button on the elevator but couldn't wait for the door to open, so we sprinted up the stairs instead and skidded to a halt in front of the nursery window.

"There's my angel!" Mark pointed to a bassinet. All I could see was a pink blanket with a tiny face peeking out of it, but Mark's grin got even wider, if that was possible. "Ain't she the sweetest thing you ever saw?"

Tim peered through the glass. "If I remember right, you said that about your cat, too, way back when."

"I think this kitten is cuter than Scrappy was." I turned away from the window and gave Mark a hard hug. "Is Anita okay?"

"She came through with flying colors. She clamped onto my hand so tight I thought she was going to crush it, and she prayed to saints I never heard of before, but she's a real jewel." Tears pooled up in Mark's eyes. "I don't know what made me run out on her like I did. I'll never forgive myself, and I'm surprised she took me back. I can't thank you all enough for sticking by her."

"No debts. Crew policy, you know," Tim said. "Can we see her now?"

"They gave her something to help her rest. I better go sit with her for a while. Will one of you come back and pick me up about eight-thirty or so?"

"Sure. We'll take you out for a night on the town," I offered.

Mark shook his head. "My wild days are over. I told you Anita laid down the law the other night.

Besides, becoming a husband and a dad in one day is enough excitement for me."

Chapter 21

"Jesus Christ!" Tim leaped out of my car before the wheels stopped turning and sprinted toward the milling crowd in the field behind the apartment complex. I swerved into the nearest parking space, yanked the keys out of the ignition, and bounded after him.

When I glanced where everybody was looking, I saw the hellish glow of flames behind the sliding glass door of my apartment. Captain scrambled crazily back and forth across the balcony like he was already getting roasted. He and the twins were clearly in a world of danger.

Stace had wrapped a coil of rope between Bryan's legs and over his hips to make a sort of sling, then looped it behind his own back. But Bryan clung to the railing with every ounce of strength he had, and his brother could get nowhere in the struggle to pry his hand off the slats.

I watched in horror as the two figures grappled on the balcony while the inferno raged in the living room behind them. The frantic crowd hollered orders and encouragement up to them, but most of their words just blurred together into the awful sound of panic.

"Break his arm if you have to, Stace!" Tim bellowed above the din. "That glass is about to blow!"

I knew Stace couldn't hear me anyway, so I whispered a desperate prayer to God. I'd gotten in the habit of bending His ear now and again, but I hoped He could figure out that if there ever was a time I needed His full attention, this was it. Without thinking about what I was doing, I let my trembling fingers trace and retrace Daisy's silver cross, which I always wore under my shirt. I felt more and more helpless with each unbearable second that ticked by.

Suddenly Stace drew back and slammed a fist into the side of his brother's face. Before Bryan got done reeling, Stace had heaved him over the railing and started easing him toward the ground hand over hand on the coil of rope.

Just as Bryan touched down and Stace knotted his end of the rope around the bar on the top of the railing, the glass door blew out with a deafening bang, and we heard the terrible roar of the flames as they shot up into the evening sky. Stace scooped Captain up in one arm as if he weighed no more than a puppy and latched onto the rope with his free hand. He bailed off the balcony while we were untying Bryan on the ground. The two of them dropped toward the earth in a shower of sparks and glass shards.

"Hang on, bud!" I yelled. "Don't let go of that rope!"

Stace let go when he was still ten or twelve feet above the ground and landed with a sickening thud. For a horrible moment, he lay motionless. Then a fit of agony swept over him. He thrashed wildly on the grass, sobbing and gasping for breath. His nylon jacket had melted across his shoulders, and he was a mess of blood and singed hair. Someone had hooked up a garden hose in the midst of the mayhem. As the crowd surged forward and the flood hit Stace full force, his tormented scream rose and mixed with the wail of the approaching sirens.

And then, in one shattering instant, the sound put me in Tim's old jalopy, with the green Jeep bearing down on me. I started to run—from the horrific scene at the apartment complex and the one searing my brain from the inside out. It was worse than any nightmare I ever had because there was no way I could wake up. I bolted around the corner of the building, fighting for air. All at once my guts balled up in me, and the citrus punch and wedding cake I'd put away that morning came rushing back.

When I finally got through retching, I dropped to my knees and held my pounding head in my hands till the earth stopped swimming. Then I forced myself to stand up and walk back to the field.

I elbowed my way through the mob and knelt beside Stace on the ground. His swollen fingers clawed at the grass like he was still on fire as he moaned and panted. Tim was wiping the blood and sweat from his face with a wet bandana, and Bryan slumped a little way off with a blank look in his eyes.

"Are you okay, Rick?" Tim asked. "You're ghost white."

I nodded and then pulled Captain into my arms and just sat there rocking him and making myself take slow, even breaths. I barely noticed the paramedics who pushed past me and lifted Stace onto a stretcher. The shouting cops and firemen could have been racing back and forth on another planet.

As soon as the twins were hauled away in the ambulance, me and Tim put Captain in my car and sped back across town, too numb to speak. Tim drove, and I held Captain on my lap and tried to stop him from shaking. He'd gotten away with a few scorched spots on his back and neck and a deep gash across one side of his head. I took off my shirt and pressed it against the wound while I talked to him in a low voice. Nobody can ever tell me dogs don't have feelings. The terror I saw in his eyes will be imprinted on my memory as long as I live.

"I can't leave him in the car," I said. "He's bleeding like a stuck pig."

"Bring him in. It's an emergency room, ain't it? They can damn well sew up his cuts, too." Tim pulled into the parking lot at the hospital and said sarcastically, "It's been ages since I was in this place."

We barreled into the trauma center as the twins were being rushed in on stretchers. Bryan looked more freaked out than anything, but Stace was a sight to give you chills. He lay face down on the gurney, and the sheet underneath him was soaked with smears of blood. He didn't even try to smother his tortured groans, and his legs and arms twisted and trembled mightily under the straps that held them in place.

"Look at him! Can't you give him something for the pain?" Tim barked at the paramedics as they hurried past. They ignored him and wheeled Stace away. We could hear him moaning till the elevator door closed behind the stretcher.

"He's going to have a bad time of it," Tim sighed. "They'll have to scrape that jacket off his back with a wire brush."

Mark dashed into the room a minute later, looking like he was about to faint. "God Almighty, I just saw … What the hell happened to Stace?"

I told him what had gone down at the apartment complex and then said, "You know about as much as we do now. We'll have to wait till Bryan gets patched up to find out the particulars."

Bryan was treated for smoke inhalation and released. He came and sat with us to wait for word on Stace. An official from the fire department dropped by to question him.

"I'd been drinking like a fish all afternoon, and eventually I dug out Tim's pistol," Bryan said bleakly. "Stace wrestled it away from me and turned to put it back in the closet, and I pitched a bottle of whiskey at him. It smashed against the front door. He bent down to scoop up the glass. He'd just lit up a smoke, and that old Zippo lighter of his was in his hand."

Bryan's voice started shaking. "I chucked another bottle, and it clipped his hand and made him drop the lighter on the carpet. We were busy yelling at each other, so we didn't notice the open flame till it touched off the alcohol and everything went up in a flash."

"There was a lot of wrapping paper left around from the wedding gifts," I said.

Bryan nodded. "And Stace had been stripping the insulation off some old battery cables to start another sculpture, so that caught fire, too, and there was a pile of smocks and things from the garage that must have been covered with paint thinner or gasoline or something. The whole place blew up like a volcano."

"I guess we'll be camping in the attic above Brothers for a while." Tim sighed. "It sounds like our apartment is history."

"You could bunk in with me and Anita," Mark suggested.

Tim grinned. "We wouldn't want to bust up your honeymoon. Besides, I'd rather be packed into the loft over the garage like sardines than listen to that kid of yours fuss all night."

"The unit was completely engulfed. There was smoke damage to a few neighboring apartments, nothing major." The fire official smiled at Bryan. "You're lucky to have a brother who knows how to use his head in a crisis. His courage and quick thinking undoubtedly saved your life today."

Bryan stared at the floor. "He should've looked out for himself and left me alone. Everybody would be better off then."

Tim went ballistic. He erupted out of his chair, grabbed Bryan by the shirt front, and jerked him to his feet.

"Damn you, shut the hell up! I can't believe you just said that after your brother put his ass on the line for you!" His rage got the best of him, and he belted Bryan in the mouth so hard it should have knocked every single one of his teeth out through the back of his head.

Me and Mark got between them as Tim was winding up for another swing. It took both of us to force the infuriated redhead back into his chair.

"Give it up already," Mark snapped. "He had the first one coming maybe, but you've never been the kind to keep at a guy who can't fight back."

"Your patience with kids is incredible," I added. "But you've got no knack for dealing with adults at all."

"Kids do stupid stuff because they don't know better, but adults have no excuse," Tim snarled.

The fire official glanced at Bryan, whose lips were already swelling up like a couple of purple grapes. "Do you want to press charges against him for striking you?"

Bryan shook his head and sat down heavily. "We don't operate that way in the crew. Besides, I reckon he had a point."

A nurse led Captain over to me at that moment, and the dog wagged his tail a time or two and laid his head wearily on my knee. There was a neat line of stitches along one side of his face, and somebody had written his name on one of those flimsy plastic hospital bracelets and fastened it to his collar.

"He was a very stoic patient." The nurse smiled. "He didn't say a word against us, even when we brought out the sutures."

"Captain's always been a brave beast." The dog heard me say his name and licked my hand, then lay down and sighed into sleep right away. "Can we see Stace?"

"I think all four of you would be too much for him," the nurse said. "He may have two visitors, but only for a few minutes."

"Me and Mark will watch the hound while you go with Bryan." Tim took the leash from my hand. "I'm too tired to hoist my butt out of this chair. I swear, I feel like I've aged fifty years since this time last week."

The nurse led me and Bryan up to the second floor and stopped outside a closed door. "He's been given a sedative, so he won't be up for a long conversation."

We walked into the quiet, dimly lit hospital room. Stace lay stretched out on his belly in the bed with the blankets turned down so that only his feet and ankles were covered. His long black hair had been shaved off, probably so all of the cinders and glass shards could be plucked out of his scalp.

I figured he was going to be boiling mad about his bald head once he had a chance to notice it. He'd sworn up and down after he got out of military school that he'd never cut his hair again as long as he lived. Bandages swathed his body from neck to waist, and little cuts and blisters dotted his bare arms and legs. His red, puffy right hand had been badly burned by the rope when he slid down from the balcony. His fingers had ballooned up to the size of roasted hot dogs.

Bryan froze in his tracks when he saw his twin. I heard his breath catch in his throat. The color drained slowly out of his face.

"Are you okay, bud?" I whispered. "We can come back later if you need to."

Bryan shook his head and crossed the room to his brother. He knelt on the floor, leaning against the bed, and reached out to touch Stace gently on one shoulder. "Hey, bro. My God, you look like hell."

Stace stirred a little, muttering, and then his eyelids flickered and his lips curled into a faint smile. "Bryan? Did you make out all right?"

"A lot better than you did. How come you bothered to get me down, man? You should have saved your own hide."

"We brothers have to stick together."

"Yeah, I've been doing a real fine job of that lately, haven't I?" Bryan scrubbed hard at his eyes with the back of his hand. "I can hardly remember the last time I had a civil word to say to you."

"Don't worry about it," Stace mumbled sleepily. "The past is in the past. Leave it there."

"Stace, I'm not even a whole man anymore. You should have looked out for yourself and let me burn."

"It's a good thing one of us has a working brain." Stace tried to prop himself up on one elbow, then dropped back onto the mattress with a gasp. "I reckon I never stopped loving you. It'd be a damn shame if you were cremated before your time."

"But it was all my fault!" Bryan cried out, his voice thick with pain. "How will I ever make it up to you?"

"Buy me a beer when I get back on my feet. We'll call it even." Stace managed a quick grin before he let his eyes drift closed.

Bryan bit down fiercely on his swollen lower lip, but it was no use. The dam broke anyway, and he pressed his face against the mattress beside his brother and started sobbing hysterically.

"Don't go to pieces on me, buddy." I tugged him to his feet and turned him toward the door. "We'll be back in the morning, Stace. Oh, by the way, Mark and Anita have a little girl."

"Cool. I'll be her favorite uncle someday," Stace murmured without opening his eyes.

"He could have died!" Bryan blurted out as soon as we made it to the hallway. "If I hadn't freaked out up there, he would have got down off the balcony before the glass blew."

"Don't *if* yourself to death." I urged him into the elevator. "Anybody might have locked up that way, and he didn't die."

"Not yet maybe, but it could still happen. Burns like that, they ooze and seep forever and get infected, and—"

"Stop it!" I dug my fingers into his arm, hard, till he winced and turned to look at me. "Don't borrow trouble. You'll send yourself right off the deep end if you start worrying about that kind of stuff before you have to."

Bryan drew a deep breath and tried to pull himself together, but there were still tears in his eyes when I led him into the cafeteria. I settled him at a corner table with a cup of coffee. Tim and Mark came in with Captain. Pretty soon, a couple of newspaper reporters sniffed us out and started asking Bryan questions.

"Everybody should be lucky enough to have a brother like mine," Bryan said. "Stace gave me my life back, and now I've just got to figure out what I want to do with it."

I took Captain's leash from Mark. "I've had all the drama I can stand for one day. I better take my partner outside before his bladder busts."

I sat on the curb in the parking lot and lit up a cigarette while Captain snuffled around in the bushes and grass behind me. Since the crisis had passed and I didn't have to put on a good face for anybody, I started feeling wrung out and kind of dizzy. The energy poured out of me till I could hardly hold my head up. I decided it wouldn't hurt to close my eyes for a quick second

I was startled when I felt Captain tugging excitedly on his leash, and then I heard footsteps coming toward me on the sidewalk.

Walter hunkered down next to me and gave the dog a scratch behind the ears. "You look played out. I guess you've had a pretty long day."

"You ain't lying. I'm tired enough to die, and I don't even have a bed to go home to."

"I saw the twins on the news. Will they be okay?"

"Bryan's more shook up than anything, but Stace got toasted real bad. I'll be surprised if he gets his feet under him before Christmas."

"And how are you holding up?"

"Oh, peachy as hell," I snapped. "Mark tied the knot this morning and became a dad this afternoon, and Stace got damn near barbecued at sundown, and everything I own went up in smoke to top it all off. I've never been better."

"Did you keep insurance on your apartment?"

"Sure. I've paid premiums ever since I moved in there like you suggested, but I don't suppose they'll cough up any cash on this deal. The twins caused the fire even if it was an accident. I wiped out most of my savings account on a rescue mission to Seattle last week, so me and Tim will have to roost in the attic above Brothers till we scrape up the bucks to get another place."

"You'd better file a claim anyway. Once the investigators rule out arson, you shouldn't have any trouble, and your policy ought to cover Stace's medical bills."

"And then I start building up my cafe fund from scratch again." I sighed and picked at a weed that was growing up through a crack in the sidewalk. "I reckon it could be worse."

Walter laid a hand on my knee. "You won't get anywhere putting your nickels in a jar that way. Have you ever thought about taking out a small business loan?"

I laughed out loud. "They don't give guys like me money."

He studied me from behind his thick glasses. "What do you mean, guys like you?"

"Slobs from the wrong side of the highway, slobs with no business experience and no collateral."

"As a matter of fact, they do give guys like you money. I picked up a brochure at my bank the other day about a program that encourages everyday people to launch new businesses in depressed parts of the county."

I sat up straighter on the curb. "Really? So how would I tap into this program?"

"If you're free tomorrow afternoon, I'll go to the bank with you and help you fill out the papers."

I stood up. "It's a deal. Right now I'm going to round up anybody who wants a seat in my car so I can find a place to bed down and not stir for the next twelve hours."

"It'll do you good." Walter pushed to his feet. "Meet me at the bank across from the courthouse at two o'clock, and don't even think of sleeping through the appointment."

"I wouldn't dare." I reached out to shake his hand. "So you're telling me to quit moping and get on with my life, the same way you did the morning you found me going through the wastebasket in the nut house."

"What were you looking for that day anyway?"

"Another blade. I was begging God for a way out of my misery, and I got an answer, just not the one I had in mind. He sent you along to give me a swift kick in the butt instead."

"Sometimes that's what it takes." The judge grinned and dug his car keys out of his shirt pocket. "See you tomorrow."

~~~

When I walked into the bank with Walter the next day, it brought back memories of the first time I stood in his living room, hardly daring to blink. The vaulted ceilings and polished marble floors made me feel about an inch tall. I hoped I didn't look as goggle-eyed as I felt.

I followed the judge into an office where there was a big wooden desk, and we sat down in some leather armchairs. The guy behind the desk had on a designer suit that reminded me of the one Mr. Garner always wore.

"So you want to open a cafe, Richard Myers," he said, eyeing me skeptically. "Have you had any business experience?"

"No sir, not much. But I've had a lot of experience with food, and that's what folks want when they go to a cafe."

He almost cracked a smile. "That's true. But this bank doesn't simply pass out money. If we accept you into our loan program, you'll have to complete an intensive training course at the community college. You'll write up a business plan and learn to keep good records and make wise financial decisions. Then a panel of local restaurant owners will help you choose a location and get set up."

"Sounds cool to me."

Me and the judge spent a long time that afternoon filling out a thick stack of forms, and Daisy's Cafe and Catering Service was born right there in that fancy bank lobby. I signed up for the training course at the community college. The thought of sitting through a bunch of classes and doing loads of homework didn't make me too happy, but I figured eventually the sweat would pay off.

Me and Tim moved into the attic above Brothers. It wasn't too crowded at first because Bryan spent every waking moment at the hospital with Stace. I don't know if Bryan was being driven by brotherly love or a guilty conscience, but Stace couldn't have wanted for a better nurse. He never had to ask for anything twice, and we could hardly pry Bryan away from his bedside to eat or sleep, let alone go see a movie or get a breath of fresh air for himself.

I hurried into the loft one evening a few weeks after the fire to grab a bite before I had to go to class. I found Tim standing at the kitchen counter, staring at a piece of paper in his hand, with a stunned look on his face.

"What the devil has you gaping like that?" I went to peer over his shoulder.

"They must've made some kind of mistake." Tim held the paper out to me. "There's too many zeros."

It was a check from the insurance company for thirty thousand dollars. My brain did a somersault inside my skull. I felt all the blood rushing away from my head.

I sank onto a folding chair at the card table. "No, I guess this is right. Walter talked me into getting replacement cost insurance when I first rented the apartment."

"Replacement cost insurance?"

"Yeah. Instead of paying you what your stuff is worth when something happens to it, they pay you the amount it will cost you to replace it. There were lots of times I thought about dropping the policy because the premiums were killing me, but I sure am glad now I kept it up."

Tim sat down in the chair across from me. "But all we had was a bunch of worn out furniture and junk."

"So we raid the secondhand store for more and the rest of the money is ours to play with. The truth is, Tim, we made out like a couple of fat rats on this deal."

He shook his head in amazement, looking from me to the check and back again. "What will you do with your share?"

"The little diner across the street from here just went up for sale again. I can't believe this is really happening, but maybe I'll see about making a down payment while I finish my business course. The bank might be willing to finance me if I have a good chunk of cash to start with."

Tim nodded. "The guy who owns this building wants me and Mark to buy it off him. He says he'll cut us a hell of a deal just so he can unload the place. I wouldn't even think about it while Mark was missing in action, but we've been tossing the idea back and forth since he came home."

"So what are your plans now that you're a rich man?"

"It's about time I get me a decent set of wheels instead of running the hell out of your Gremlin forever."

I stood up. "I'm late for class, as usual. There's an apartment above the cafe across the street, too, so if you get tired of hanging out in this hole by the time the deal goes through, you can bunk in with me over there."

"Why not? It's worked up till now."

Stace got out of the hospital the week before Christmas. The fire department put on a banquet in his honor, and the mayor presented him with a medal for his heroism. Ed and Sharon, who had been out from Georgia three times during his recovery, couldn't afford to make another trip to Bertha City for the ceremony, but they saw a blurb about the affair on the national news and called to congratulate him afterward.

"My mom's getting to be a regular crybaby in her old age," Stace laughed after he hung up the phone. "Dad was finally proud of me, too, for once in my life."

"He should've been proud a long time ago," Tim said. "I always knew there was more to you than met the eye. What made you so brave in the middle of the flames anyway?"

"I didn't have time to think about it." Stace grinned, then turned serious. "You know, I always thought of myself as a hopeless screwball. Everybody did. But I found out that day that when push comes to shove, I've got a little sand in me after all."

~~~

One evening in January, I sat in the loft above Brothers with Tim and the twins. We were watching a horror movie on the tube, and Stace was fiddling with a coil of wire, as usual. Me and Bryan were parked at the table as I fought my way through a chapter in my accounting book. Finally, when I couldn't hack it anymore, I slammed the book shut and shoved it across the table.

"Damn that stuff anyway." I stood up and reached for my jacket. "I'm going for a drive. I reckon I always knew I couldn't pass that business class."

Bryan picked up the book. He thumbed through it for a second and then slid his chair around to my side of the table.

"Sit down. This is simple." He turned my paper, which was a jumble of scribbles and eraser smudges, so he could study it.

I sat down, more to be nice than because I thought he could teach me anything. "Simple, huh? Let me in on the secret."

"I slept through a lot of my college business classes, but this looks pretty basic. You ought to start by lining all the numbers up so the decimal points are right underneath each other."

In fifteen minutes, Bryan had helped me sort out my homework and explained it so I actually knew what was going on. Tim gave up on the horror flick and came to look over my shoulder.

"Hey, man, could you work that kind of magic with the books here at the garage?" he asked. "Me and Mark are going gray way before our time trying to keep the figures straight. We'll pay you, of course, anything you want."

"That's an offer you might regret." Bryan laughed. "I guess I could take a look. Stace, are you ready for another glass of tea or something?"

"Naw, I'm fine. How many times are you going to ask me that tonight?"

"Just checking."

Stace put down his wire sculpture and joined us at the table. "You know, Bryan, I don't need to be waited on hand and foot anymore. It's high time you find something else to do with your life."

"You should come to class with me tomorrow night," I suggested. "They're always hiring tutors over at the college, and most of them can't explain stuff half as good as you."

Bryan looked doubtful. "Stace isn't ready to be left alone yet."

"Who says?" Stace asked. "I'm healthy as a horse. I'm going to start work around the shop any day now before I get too fat and lazy for my own good. You ought to go scope out the school."

Bryan shook his head. "Somebody might recognize me from my tennis days."

"So what if they do?" I said. "You can't spend your life holed up in this cave. You'll have to get your rear in gear sooner or later."

"All my plans went straight to hell on that Seattle expressway. I don't really know what to do now."

"Well, you have to do something. I wished I could curl up and die when I got Daisy killed, but I found out there was still life in me, whether I wanted it or not, and after a while I decided I better use it."

"And I suppose that's where God comes in?" Bryan rolled his eyes, and I wondered why. He had seen me getting ready for church most Sundays, but I hadn't ever bugged him to go with me or anything.

"God was helping me get back on my feet before I ever knew it, but that's beside the point. The college gives tutors a break on tuition."

380

"I suppose maybe I could look into transferring my credits from Princeton." Bryan still sounded kind of hesitant, but I knew he was hooked.

"I'll stop for you after work. And don't even think of changing your mind because me and Stace will truss you up and throw you in the back of my car if we get any lip."

~~~

Bryan went with me to the college and hired on as a tutor. He signed up for an economics course and a painting class.

"I didn't know you could paint," I said as we pulled into the parking lot of a pizza joint.

"I took a few private lessons while I was at Princeton, just for something to do between tennis matches." Bryan peeled off his jacket and got out of the car in only a T-shirt, which I hadn't seen him do since he lost his arm. "I'm probably rusty as hell by now, but I'm getting pretty good with my left hand, and I'm finally going to let my doctor fit me for a hook at the hospital next week. My creative bug might as well come back to life with the rest of me. I hope you're buying. I'm flat broke."

"I'll buy. It looks like artistic genes run in the Thomas family."

"It'll never be like tennis, but I'll have to settle for a brush instead of a racket till I get my left arm in shape for a decent serve." Bryan turned to look straight at me. "Thanks for dragging me out of hiding. I guess I'm glad I didn't croak in that crummy old motel room in Seattle or fry to a crisp on your balcony."

"Any time. I know how it is, bud. You wish over and over that your heart would just quit beating, but one day you wake up and figure out this old world ain't about to stop and let you off."

A shy little waitress with big dark eyes came to take our order. I told her we'd each have a combo meal that came with pizza and a trip to the salad bar.

Bryan kicked me under the table. "I don't do real well with salad bars."

The waitress fixed a surprised glance on him when he said that, and she must have suddenly noticed that he was missing his arm. She jerked back with a gasp and dumped her pitcher of ice water all over the table. Bryan turned beet red and flattened the right side of his body against the wall, looking like he'd give anything for a chance to disappear.

"Get a grip already!" I snapped. "He's lost an arm, but that's no reason for you to lose your mind!"

The waitress ran to grab a towel and mopped up the puddle, gushing apologies all the while, and when she finally shut up and scurried away, I walked over to the salad bar. Bryan shuffled along behind me with his head hanging.

"I should've left my jacket on," he fumed. "I'm sick of everybody gawking at me like I'm a freak or something."

"Daisy used to get tired of it, too. Hold your plate still and I'll load it up."

He snatched the dish away. "I can fix my own salad."

"Come off it, Bryan. You got nothing to prove to me." I piled lettuce on the plates. "Daisy told me she learned pretty quick that it was easier to swallow your pride sometimes and ask for a hand. Want cucumbers?"

"I'll have everything. Daisy was sharp as a tack, though. There wasn't much she needed help with."

"You'll get good at doing things when they fit you with your hook." I finished looting the salad bar and carried the plates back to the table. "It probably just takes practice."

"You still think about Daisy a lot, don't you?"

I nodded. "I miss her every day. It was four years ago last August when she died, and I only knew her a few weeks, but I still can't believe I got her killed. She was way too young to go into the ground."

"You didn't get her killed." When I started to speak, Bryan cut me off with a gesture. "Rick, when her dad raced down that alley and rammed us with his Jeep, the angle was just right for me to see the look on his face. He knew exactly what he was doing."

I put down my fork. "Really?"

"Really. It was no accident. He headed straight for us like a Kamikaze pilot."

"But he died in the wreck, too."

Bryan shrugged. "I don't know if he planned on that, but he was gunning for us, no doubt about it. You couldn't have done a thing to stop it. There was no fear in his eyes."

"I sure as hell could have done something!" Bryan's words jarred a confession out of me that I'd never made to anyone, and I had a hard time talking because of the lump that rose up in my throat. "I'd seen that Jeep drifting around three or four different times while Daisy was living with me, and it was starting to make me real uneasy. If I'd told her about it instead of leaving her in the dark so she wouldn't worry, I bet she would have known it was her dad. She would have kept out of sight till she could make a break for it."

"A break to where? She was safer with us than she would have been knocking around by herself with him on her trail, and she would have had enough sense to figure that out." Bryan leaned forward in his chair and let his eyes drill right into mine. "That man was a psychopath, Rick. He did his level best to take out the whole bunch of us without even flinching. You had no way of knowing what you were up against."

I sat motionless and dumbstruck for a long minute as the truth sank in, and somewhere inside, I felt the hard knot of guilt that had jabbed at me for so long begin to loosen a little.

Bryan was still talking. "That's why I hated this place so much. I didn't tell a soul what I'd seen because I was so revolted, but the memory of that face in the windshield never let me rest too long. I wanted to get somewhere far away from here, where I'd never meet up with another sleazeball who would plow into a carload of kids for no reason. I thought it happened because we were poor and living on the trashy side of town."

"There's creeps all over."

He nodded. "I found that out on the tennis circuit. Oh, it was great at first. I had lots of money and lots

384

of friends, and we ate at nice restaurants and drank expensive wine. But those friends were the kind who'd laugh with you when you were up and kick the blocks out from under you as soon as they got the chance. They'd take you out on the town the night before you had a big match, bottles and needles and all, just to see if they could trip you up."

"They didn't wreck your career. I'm not much into tennis, but I watched you on TV every chance I got. You knocked 'em all dead."

"Yeah, maybe. But I'd go back to my hotel room and miss the crew and the old times so bad I thought I'd burst. So I'd order me a bottle of champagne, sometimes a girl to go with it, and I'd end up with nothing but a headache in the morning."

I reached across the table and laid a hand on his shoulder. "We didn't know it was like that. Shoot, we would've hauled your butt home a long time ago."

"That's just it. I figured none of you would even stop to spit on me if you saw me on fire after the way I cut you down, and then my classy friends ran out when I hit bottom, and you and Tim dropped everything and flew across the country to save me from myself. I was running from the slime buckets in this neighborhood, but I forgot about my brothers."

"I hope the crew will always be around for each other. When Daisy died and I thought you all were gone forever—"I trailed off and traced a finger over one of the faint scars on my wrist. "But then Walter and Alice Mills patched me up, so I guess the balance in your bank account doesn't really have a whole lot to do with the way you decide to treat other people."

Chapter 22

Mark poked his head into the attic above Brothers one evening just after Valentine's Day. "Hey, Rick, I stopped by to ask you a favor."

"When have I heard those words from you before?" I tossed aside the business plan I was working on and turned down the radio.

He grinned sheepishly. "I was wondering if you'd fix another cake for me."

"I don't know. The cake idea didn't work out real well last summer."

"Tell me about it. But me and Anita have decided to put money down on a house over in the neighborhood where all the streets have tree names, and we want to have a party there when we move in at the end of the month."

"Cool. I guess you old married folks are getting too classy for the rest of us."

Mark laughed. "It's only a little bungalow with a patch of grass out front. Not much to look at, really. They call it a starter home, which means it needs a lot of fixing up. The foundation's sound, though, and the wiring and plumbing are good, so everything else can be taken care of over time."

"How about we make the crew sweat for a few hours then? I'll put on a spread if you'll buy paint and stuff so we can at least touch up the joint before you get settled there."

We all showed up at Mark's place bright and early on the first Saturday in March. I got a pot of chili going while the others set to work with paint and cleaning supplies.

"Those beans will smell good all day," Anita said. "And that cake is the prettiest thing I ever saw."

"You're the prettiest thing I ever saw." Mark slipped up behind his wife and planted a big kiss on the back of her neck. She let out a startled squawk and then turned her face to him, laughing.

"I'll leave you two lovers alone." I took off my apron and ducked into the living room to join the painters.

"I know how to paint already," Jake told me proudly. He was almost lost in a big denim smock from Brothers. "Tim teaches me everything."

"You better stick to washing windows with me for now, bud. You'd get more paint on yourself than you ever put on the wall." Tim wadded up a paper towel and tossed it at Bryan. It hit him on the side of the head. "Aren't you done with that trim yet? Kick it in gear, slowpoke."

Bryan spun around and waved his hook under Tim's nose. "I've been looking for a reason to try my hand at body piercing. You don't want to mess with me, pal."

"I guess not. That's a deadly weapon you got there." Tim pretended to leap away in terror and almost fell over Captain, who was sprawled out on the carpet, dead to the world. He bent down and rubbed the dog's belly. "You picked kind of a bad place to snooze, muttface. But hell, I wish I could sack out and start snoring whenever I felt like it, you lucky thing."

"Hey, Bryan, you ought to do a mural along this whole wall," Stace suggested as he finished rolling on the first coat of white paint. "It could feature me in ten different looks. I'd even pose naked."

"Not!" Mark said from the doorway. He picked up the paper towel and chucked it at Stace. "Don't strain your brain coming up with any more bright ideas."

Anita came in behind Mark with a plate of cookies and a pitcher of lemonade. "You all gossip like a bunch of old hens. I could have finished painting the room and washed the windows with my own hands by now."

"We better get hopping," I said. "We know who the boss is in this outfit."

Jake marched up to Anita and snitched a cookie off her tray. "Cool, peanut butter, my favorite. I wanna marry you when I get big so you can make cookies for me all the time, okay?"

"Oh, where were you when Mark ran away with my heart?" Anita set the tray down and gave the kid a peck on the cheek.

Jake made a sour face and wiped off the kiss with a corner of his smock. "Yuck! What'd you do that for?"

"Uh oh. Girl germs." Tim laughed and reached for the bottle of window cleaner. "Don't worry, kid. You may not like kisses now, but you'll get a taste for them someday."

"Nuh uh, I will not. That's gross." Jake snagged another cookie and started helping Tim wash windows. He pouted a little because the rest of us were cracking up, but fortunately, it didn't take him too long to get over it.

The baby set up a howl from her cradle in the corner. Stace put down his paint roller and picked her up, bouncing her on one arm. He started making funny faces at her, and she quit crying and tried to grab a fistful of his hair.

"Let me tell you this real dirty joke I know." He stopped her from putting a finger in his eye. "There was this guy who ran a porn shop, and—"

Anita shoved a cookie in his mouth. "I hope you choke on that. I'll go get a bottle for her. Try not to warp her mind before I get back."

"You're taking your chances leaving her with me." Stace sat down on the floor with the baby in his lap and beamed at the rest of us as we worked. "I've got an announcement to make."

"What? Have you finally joined the human race?" Tim laughed.

"I'll let you know what it's like if I do. Anyway, me and Bryan are going on a trip when he gets out of college for Spring Break the first week in April."

"Where to?" I asked.

"I'll never make any money in this town on my wire sculptures. We're gonna haul a bunch of them to Santa Fe, maybe even San Francisco, if I can lay my hands on a cheap set of wheels that'll get us there and back."

"I may have a painting or two to peddle by then," Bryan put in. "Besides, somebody needs to go along to make sure Stace rakes in more money than he spends."

Stace ignored his brother and went on talking. "I've been scared to take the plunge for a long time. I

390

never thought any scheme I cooked up would work. But after I almost roasted to death in that fire, I got to thinking I better do my living while I have the chance."

"I always figured you twins would smoke the rest of us." Mark poured himself a glass of lemonade. "Best of luck to you."

Jake gave up on washing windows and sat down beside Stace to fuss over the baby. He ran his hand gently across the thickened skin on Stace's bare shoulders, then traced one of the ridges on his own back through his T-shirt. "You got hurt bad once, didn't you, just like me."

Stace tousled the kid's blond hair. "Yeah, but scars are good things. They tell you when you've healed up from something."

"I have more exciting news," I said. "You twins will get the loft over Brothers to yourselves in a few weeks. Me and Tim are moving into the apartment above the diner across the street from there."

Bryan grinned at me. "We got treated like the dregs of Bertha City for years, but it's getting to be our own personal Monopoly board lately with all the real estate we're snapping up. Doesn't it say something in that Bible of yours about the first and last changing places?"

"Yeah, and it also says to see that you don't get too cocky for your own good."

~~~

Later on that month, a panel of local restaurant owners signed off on my business plan for the bank. One of them was the guy who ran the taco bar where

I used to work. I set up shop in the building across the street from Brothers.

It was a tiny place, with just enough room for half a dozen tables and a row of barstools at the counter. But the kitchen was nice and big, which was a plus because along with drawing the truckers and out-of-town traffic off the Line for breakfast and lunch, I planned to cater banquets and dinner parties at other locations in the evenings.

The apartment above the diner had two small bedrooms and a little balcony that faced the street. Me and Tim were glad to finally move into some living quarters where there was enough space for both of us to breathe at once.

I placed an ad in the paper for a part-time waitress and hired the first chick who walked through the door. Amy was a cute girl with long auburn hair and laughing eyes, and she had a warmth about her that put me at ease right away. She was in her first year of classes over at the community college, and she needed a job with flexible hours so she could take time off when she had a lot of tests to study for. I figured that would work out all right for both of us.

Early on the first morning in April, I nailed up my sign. Bryan had designed a logo for me of a daisy with a smiling face and a chef's hat.

"Well, Daisy, I did it. You finally get to be famous," I said aloud as I climbed down the ladder. I couldn't see if the sign was hanging straight because my eyes kept misting up, but I knew she would have been proud enough to bust.

I had just kicked on the lights in the cafe when Bryan burst in, grinning for all he was worth. He handed me a brightly wrapped gift, which surprised me.

"Thanks, Bryan, but you didn't have to get me anything," I said.

"Well, are you gonna open it or what?" He was so excited he practically hopped from one foot to the other as I was ripping the paper off. He had painted a picture of Daisy that was so lifelike it was almost creepy.

"My God, she looks so real. You got her smile exactly right." I couldn't believe what I was seeing. I closed my eyes to blink away the tears, but a few of them squeezed out and trickled down my cheeks anyway.

"I'm sorry if it makes you sad," Bryan said awkwardly.

"No, it's great. The way you brought her to life is incredible." I hung the painting on a nail above the cash register. Then, just because it seemed like the right thing to do, I took her braille note and the snapshot of my folks in their matching party hats out of my wallet and stuck them into the frame behind the canvas where only I would know about them.

My stomach was full of butterflies as I tied on my apron and fired up the coffeepot. It would have been a good omen if the sun was out, but it was a cloudy gray morning. A light rain dripped off and on in little streams down the windows.

Mark and Anita were my first customers. They came in with the baby and sat down at the counter.

They ordered coffee and plates of Daisy's famous raspberry pancakes. I was about to start cooking when Tim and Stace appeared. Tim had Jake with him.

"Make it pancakes all around," Stace said. He took the stool next to Mark and reached out to tickle the baby under the chin.

Mark grabbed a straw from the dispenser on the counter and blew it at Tim, for no particular reason I could figure out. Tim took up the challenge, of course, and in a few seconds the floor was littered with paper wrappers.

"Who's going to clean all those up?" I asked. "I had to pay for those straws, you know."

"What a way to talk to your first customers." Mark handed the baby to Stace and bent down to pick up the papers.

The baby started to pitch a fit, and Stace bounced her on his knee. "You know, you're kind of cute for being so short. But don't worry, you'll have plenty of uncles to chase off all the rats who want to take you out someday."

The waitress served up the pancakes and poured coffee for everybody except Jake, who got orange juice. "Would you like anything else?"

"How about a date?" Stace gave her a wink and a smile. "What's a pretty thing like you doing stuck in a dive like this?"

"Beating back bums like you." She laughed and pretended to push him off his stool.

"Way to go, Amy. You'll do well around here." Tim took the baby from Stace and poked a little piece

394

of pancake into her mouth. Most of it oozed out and dribbled down her chin. He wiped it off with a napkin and tried to feed her another bite.

"Don't give her any more of that." Anita picked up the can of whipped cream off the counter and threatened to decorate Tim's face with it. "That's pure sugar."

"It's good for her."

Anita started to push the button on the can. "Is this good for you?"

"Okay, okay. But someday when it comes out in psychoanalysis that she was traumatized by missing out on pancakes in her babyhood, it'll be all your fault."

Jake started drumming his feet on the counter in front of his seat. "Got any tunes in this place?"

I flipped him a quarter from my apron pocket. "That'll get you a couple songs on the jukebox."

"Hey, this kid's sprung a leak!" Tim groaned. "Look at my shirt. When are you going to teach her to use the john?"

"Stace, did you give her the curse of the holey diapers again?" Mark asked.

Stace grinned. "It's the greatest plague ever to fall upon unsuspecting parents."

Mark stood up and took the baby from Tim. He grabbed Stace by the arm and dragged him over to a corner table.

"If you think it's cute to pick holes in the plastic of her diapers so she sprays all over everywhere like a water fountain, you can learn to change her." Mark laid out the supplies Stace would need from the baby's tote bag.

"No way. She's not my brat. I can't hack this." Stace made a sour face and jammed his hands in his pockets.

"Quit whining and hop to it. The pajamas come unsnapped, see, right there along the legs." Mark coached Stace as he undressed the baby and put her in a clean diaper and a dry set of clothes, and Stace kept up a steady stream of complaints, but he lived. He was almost done when the kid started howling.

Anita jumped up. "You all are a bunch of savages. What did you do to her?"

"It's a rare talent I have. I can make chicks cry without even meaning to." Stace passed the baby gratefully to her mama, then ducked away and went back to his pancakes.

"Anybody got more quarters?" Jake demanded. When no one paid attention, he made a gun out of his finger and pointed it at me behind the counter. "This is a stick-up. Hand over your loose change."

"Knock it off, kid," Tim said. "That ain't funny, even as a joke. You better eat those pancakes I bought you."

I laughed. "The rule is you have to finish the whole plate. The morning Daisy first fixed them for me, I was so sick with a hangover I wanted to die, but I put away every bite."

An old man walked in tapping a white cane. Tiny droplets of rain glistened on his mustache and eyelashes. Amy showed him to a table and offered him a braille menu.

"This is wonderful." The guy beamed like he'd just been given a winning lottery ticket. "I really enjoy it when I can read the menu by myself in a place."

"A group of volunteers at the library printed it up for us," Amy said. "Would you like to start with a cup of coffee?"

"Yes, please, and a sweet roll." The guy laid his cane down on the floor and peeled off his wet jacket. Amy poured coffee for him and showed him where the cream and sugar was.

When she walked away, Jake darted over and snatched up the cane. He started swinging it around above his head and snickering because the old man didn't even know it was missing.

"That stick better be back on the floor before I make it over there," Tim warned. "You wouldn't like it if that guy took something of yours when you couldn't see what he was doing, would you?"

Jake laid down the cane. "Sorry, mister. I was just goofing off. I wasn't trying to be mean or anything."

The old man asked him to sit down and check out the braille menu. The kid went nuts over the braille just like we all had when Daisy first showed it to us. You'd have thought with the way he bounced on the chair and rubbed his hands together that he'd just made up a whole new language all by himself.

"I'm gonna tell my friends at school about this," he announced. "It'll make a secret code the teachers will never crack."

Mark put on his raincoat and bundled up the baby. "I better hurry up and get the garage open. I've got work running out my ears over there, as usual. Good luck, Rick."

"Bryan, Stace, drive careful." Anita followed him to the door, turning back to give me a smile as she stepped out into the drizzly morning.

"We've got to hit the road, too. Your foster mother will have my hide if you're late for school." Tim tossed Jake his windbreaker and turned to me. "Say, Rick, there's going to be a dance at the rec center Saturday night, and I'm taking the assistant leader of the 4-H club. She's got a friend she wants to set you up with."

I shook my head. "Blind dates always landed me in a heap of trouble."

Tim sighed and picked up his car keys. "Oh well, I had to ask."

I smiled at the waitress. "I'll double if Amy wants to go."

I'm not sure who looked more surprised, Tim or Amy. Or maybe me. For a second, the only sound in the diner was the soft puffing of the coffeepot behind the counter.

"Hey, why not?" Amy decided. "It sounds like fun."

"Right on!" Tim gave me a thumbs-up sign and herded Jake toward the door. "Try not to poison anybody today. See you later."

"We ought to blow this pop stand, too, Bryan." Stace swallowed the last of his coffee and reached for his jacket. "I'd planned to be halfway to New Mexico by now."

I gave each of the twins a quick hug. "Good luck. You all better drag your butts back here soon, though. I'd hate to see you ride off into the distance and disappear."

"You won't be that lucky," Bryan laughed. "I've been in all fifty states at least once and a few other countries, too, and there's no place like home."

"We'll be back in a week or so," Stace agreed. "We'll have the trunk of my old lemon loaded down with hundred dollar bills."

"Just be sure your head doesn't get too big to fit through the door." I waved the twins out and started helping Amy clear away the mess on the counter.

The phone rang. The sound was loud in the empty diner, and it startled me. The thought of answering it didn't cross my mind till Amy gave me a nudge and a funny look.

I picked up the receiver. "Daisy's Cafe and Catering Service."

"Good morning, Rick. Walter Mills here."

"Hey, Walter, what's up?"

"I've been thinking. This kid Chris we've had living with us is finally ready to strike out on his own. He needs a job, and I know for a fact he flips a mean omelet."

I laughed. "Can he sling eggs better than he can drive? I saw what Alice's snazzy red Mustang looked like when it got towed into Brothers a while back."

"You did quite a number on it yourself in your wild old days," Walter reminded me.

"Yeah, I remember. Bring the kid down for breakfast. I'll talk to him. He'll have to start out

399

bussing tables part time, but you never know where that might lead."

"We'll be there in ten minutes. I'll have biscuits and gravy, if you've got it, and Chris says he wants ham and eggs."

I hung up the phone and paused for a long moment by the cash register to study Daisy's portrait. The clouds outside the windows parted so that a shaft of sunlight fell across her face, and the thought of her made me smile.

Made in the USA
Middletown, DE
20 July 2015